I0651440

Edward A. Lever

Central America

The land of the Quiches and Chontales

Edward A. Lever

Central America
The land of the Quiches and Chontales

ISBN/EAN: 9783337089214

Printed in Europe, USA, Canada, Australia, Japan

Cover: Foto ©Andreas Hilbeck / pixelio.de

More available books at **www.hansebooks.com**

CENTRAL AMERICA;

OR,.

The Land of the Quiches

—AND—

CHONTALES.

—BY—

COL. E. A. LEVER,

FOREIGN EDITOR, TIMES-DEMOCRAT,

Author of "Yzabelita, or a Trip to the Land of the Maya."

(COPYRIGHT SECURED.)

NEW ORLEANS:
E. A. BRANDAO & CO., PUBLISHERS, 34 MAGAZINE STREET.
1885.

TO THE SURVIVING FOLLOWERS OF THE

IMMORTAL MOROZAN,

AND THEIR POLITICAL DISCIPLES,

the sincere Unionists of Central America, this volume is cordially inscribed by

THE AUTHOR.

PREFACE.

A generation has passed away since Stephens informed the scientific world that, in the hidden depths of the primeval forests of Central America, he had discovered the ruins of numerous aboriginal cities, whose crumbling temple walls and fallen towers imparted the sad story of their decline and fall. More than thirty years ago Squiers published an interesting work which advocated the building by Americans of an inter-oceanic railroad across the Republic of Honduras, from Puerto Cortez to Amapala. About the same time an American mineralogist, named Wells, gave to the public a detailed account of the mineral resources of the famous Honduranean departments of Olancho and Yoro.

Since the above mentioned writers published their works on Central America no other American author has occupied his pen with this important subject. Meanwhile a momentous revolution in Guatemala placed the reins of power in the hands of the Liberals, and that republic has entered upon an era of regeneration, of political freedom, and of material progress.

The Liberals of Guatemala were no sooner triumphant than they lent a helping hand to their struggling brethern of Honduras and San Salvador. Thus those governments also enjoy an enlightened and liberal form of government. The people of Nicaragua and of Costa Rica have unassisted worked out their political and material reform. In the former, the enlightened statesmen, Quadra, Zavala and Cardenas, led the progressive movement, while Costa Rica's regeneration was accomplished by two patriotic citizens, Guadia and Fernandez.

At present the five Central American republics are prosperous and happy. The era of revolutions, of anarchy and of bloodshed has passed away, and an industrious, intelligent and contented people have earnestly bent their energies to the prosecution of the different branches of industry. Public schools are found in every village, mining and agriculture have been revived, while the iron horse has become a familiar sight to the descendants of those aborigines who so bravely but vainly defended their native land against the mail-clad Spanish conquistadores.

The foreign traffic of this naturally rich country has for many years attracted the serious attention of the principal commercial nations of Europe. France, England and Germany have earnestly competed for its acquisition. Within the past decade New York city has striven to possess it, and in conjunction with the commercial metropolis of the Pacific coast, has succeeded in wresting no small portion of this trade from the transatlantic competitors.

Nor have the merchants of the Crescent City looked on supinely while their northern and European rivals were struggling for this promising traffic. The Macheca Bros., Oteri, C. A. Fish & Co., and Miller & Henderson, have captured the greater portion of the tropic fruit trade, while Schmidt & Zeigler, Smith Bro. & Co., H. Dudley Coleman, Rice, Born & Co., Woodward, Wight & Co., John Adams, and others, have acquired a fair share of the provision, coffee, hardware and lumber traffic.

But if the merchants of New Orleans have accomplished a great deal in this direction, they should not rest until the greater portion of Central American traffic is in their hands. This city is advantageously situated for the requirements of this trade; thus, if it does not eventually flow hither, the blame can only rest upon our Crescent City merchants.

The intention of the writer of this work is to furnish the people and merchants of this section with a brief description of the forest, agricultural and mineral resources of the land of the Quiches and the Chontales, together with a short historical account of these erstwhile Spanish colonial possessions from the epoch of the conquest down to the present day.

The author has several times visited each of the Central American republics. Last year he crossed Guatemala, Honduras, Nicaragua and Costa Rica, from ocean to ocean, and traveled through San Salvador. He writes, therefore, from personal experience and observation. He has likewise made the history and geography of Central America a special study.

Conscious of its many imperfections, it is with serious misgivings the writer submits this unpretentious work to the public. If, however, the information it imparts should in any way influence the movement of southern capital and southern enterprise into the localities it treats of, his object will be attained and his earnest hopes realized.

NEW ORLEANS, March 8, 1885.

BRITISH HONDURAS.

CHAPTER I.

Works relating to the Colony. Mr. Wilson's Admirable Almanac. Progress of the country under the Barlee administration. Death of that Statesman. Discovery of the Spanish main by Columbus. Settlement of the colony by the pirate, Wallice.

Within the past two decades several English tourists have visited the unique and to them almost hitherto unknown British Colony of Belize, Central America. Upon their return to the mother country, they published narratives of their tour. These works are both interesting and valuable, notwithstanding the writers occasionally permitted themselves to be swayed by the insular and clannish prejudices for which the English are so celebrated. Mr. A. R. Gibbs, in 1883, published in London, a fair sized volume, entitled "British Honduras, an historical and descriptive account of the Colony from its settlement, in 1670." This work is quite popular in England, but is almost unknown in the United States. A Mr. Morris, not long since, devoted several months' time to visiting the different localities of the province. His book "The Colony of British Honduras, its Resources and Prospects," is probably the best work of the kind that has, as yet, issued from the English press. The local government purchased a number of volumes which are retailed to tourists at a price less than cost.

During the Barlee regime, the private secretary of that functionary, Mr. Wm. Grey Wilson, published a so-styled Almanac, which contains more statistical and other information than all the rest of the works on British Honduras published by English authors. But, being an office holder, Mr. Wilson's work was deemed, by the sturdy colonists, to favor the Crown's interests overmuch; for that reason the Almanac has never been popular in the country it treats of.

Notwithstanding the amount of matter printed regarding this out-of-the-way British possession, the statesmen and officials of England, until very lately, knew more of the interior of Africa than they did of their Central American province. One of them, in a public document, speaks of " British Honduras and other islands," while it would doubtless puzzle the great premier himself, to furnish, on the spur of the moment, a fair estimate of the actual importance and value of the Colony.

A southern journal, the *Times-Democrat*, was the first American periodical which published to the world a plain and unvarnished statement of facts regarding this colonial possession of the British crown. Major E. A. Burke, the enterprising and indefatigable owner and editor of that paper, three years ago perceived the importance of attracting the traffic of the Colony to New Orleans. This undertaking could only be carried out by making the merchants of both places better acquainted with each other and with their mutual traffic possibilities and facilities. New York and Europe had hitherto enjoyed a monopoly of the Colony's trade. He determined to wrest a portion of it at least, from the commercial rivals of New Orleans. The means he employed to accomplish this *desideratum*, was to educate the merchants of this section regarding the value and importance of the growing traffic of the Colony. To that end a member of the editorial staff of the *Times-Democrat* was sent to British Honduras, with instructions to examine thoroughly into its trade resources and possibilities.

The results of this mission, which were made known to the world through a series of letters published in the above mentioned journal, proved highly satisfactory. The merchants, and residents of the Colony were gratified by the attention bestowed upon their province, by the great newspaper of the Southwest, while the business men of New Orleans had their attention drawn to this hitherto neglected locality, by these authentic accounts of its traffic resources. The letters were extensively reproduced by English periodicals. The result of this latter action proved very favorable, and gave an impetus to the material progress of the Colony. Capital began to seek investment in that hitherto ignored locality. Emigration flowed thither, and in three years, British Honduras has, if we may believe the assertions of local statisticians, nearly doubled its foreign trade, while the fruit planting industry has augmented in value and importance more than twenty fold.

Notwithstanding that newspaper enterprise, in this case, proved so influential and beneficial to the material advancement of the Colony, there was another factor which exerted a paramount influence toward bringing about its regeneration. A wise and honest man, the Hon. F. P. Barlee, was appointed by the British government to rule the province. During an entire decade, the commerce of Belize had dwindled to almost absolute insignificance. A few logs of mahogany, a limited quantity of log wood, and some bundles of skins and hides, constituted its entire export traffic. Its import trade consisted of small annual cargoes of general merchandise from New York, and the mother country, and limited shipments of western produce from New Orleans, in schooners, which also carried on a fair fruit traffic with the Spanish American settlements to the south.

An American writer has observed, that: "if a colony of Anglo Saxons should suddenly, while clogged with all their human attributes, be transported to heaven, they would soon find fault with, and protest against the celestial system of government." It is needless to say that many of the sturdy British colonists of Belize soon became dissatisfied with Gov. Barlee's administration. He was denounced as a despot. His acts were stigmatized as arbitrary, and it was not long before the well-intentioned functionary became extremely unpopular.

But Governor Barlee was neither arbitrary nor despotic. He had the welfare of the Colony near at heart, and determined to bring about its regeneration, despite the murmurs of the discontented and reckless opposition faction which constantly strove to thwart his measures. The Home Government, which entertained the highest opinion of his ability and patriotism, resolutely sustained him, and in the end, he succeeded in carrying out his numerous measures of reform.

After a thorough examination of the situation he concluded that the future welfare of the Colony depended upon its close commercial connection with this country. To bring about this *disideratum*, he established a line of steamers between Belize and New Orleans, and granted the enterprise a heavy-mail subsidy. This measure, which at the time was very unpopular, proved the salvation of the Colony. Through it, the fruit planting industry was promoted and fostered; commercial intercourse between the province and New Orleans was established, traffic revived and the little colony entered upon a new era of commercial and material progress.

The passage of time and the course of events have vindicated the policy pursued during Governor Barlee's administration. Not long since this good and wise man died at the island of Trinidad, to which government he had been promoted. The news of his demise proved a shock to Belize society. Even his old political enemies, while deploring this sad event, have been heard to acknowledge that he was entitled to be styled the savior of the Colony.

The English residents of British Honduras who number perhaps but 450, in a population of 30,000, are a fair type of the Anglo Saxon race. As merchants and traders, they are active, intelligent, and energetic. Politically, the highest title they aspire to, is to be recognized as British subjects, and they demand the same status they would hold in their native country. The Crown colonial system of government which obtains in the province, and in which an American, at least, can see but little to recommend, is very unpopular with the people. In their colonial ignorance and simplicity, they cannot imagine why men, who leave their country, their homes, and their friends; who spend the better part of their lives in assisting to build up England's commercial prosperity and supremancy abroad; who, through the medium of their energy, business spirit, and natural courage, after braving innumerable dangers and risks, have wrested from the tropic wilds of Central America a rich jewel for the British crown, should be disfranchised, as it were, by a system of government which reduces them almost to the level of a conquered people; a system of government in which the crown officials have the preponderance, and which levies taxes without adequate representation of the people.

Under the administration of an executive of arbitrary disposition, the crown government system degenerates into pure absolutism. The people of British Honduras, as also their fellow countrymen of Jamaica, deprecate the form of government under which they live, and will never rest contented until they recover all the rights and privileges to which they are entitled as free born, true blue British subjects.

The present Governor of Belize, Mr. Goldworthy, is deservedly very popular with the people. He seems to possess many of the same characteristics as his illustrious predecessor, Mr. Barlee, and appears desirous of leaving behind him, when he retires from the scene of his present labors, the same universal opinion that the material progress of the province was the unwearied object of his administrative aim.

The territory of British Honduras, so its residents claim, was discovered by the immortal Cristoval Colon (Columbus) on his third voyage to the west.

Tradition hath it that he landed on the little island that faces the present city of Belize in the year 1502.

The Colony is at present known as British Honduras; the name of Belize being confined to the pretty tropic city, which is the captial of the British possessions on the main land. Together with the numerous cays that nestle lovingly close to the coast, British Honduras comprises about 6400 square miles, or 4,096,000 acres of land, English measurement.

According to tradition, the Colony received its name from a celebrated Scotch buccaneer named " Wallice." As there is no " W " in the Spanish alphabet, the name of the famous pirate chief was pronounced "Baliz" by his Spanish enemies. In the course of time it was corrupted into " Belize." Thus a buccaneer chieftain gave his name to one of the fairest and most valuable colonial possessions of the British crown.

As near as can be ascertained, the pirate Wallice, in the beginning of the seventeenth century, established his headquarters on the site now occupied by the city of Belize. From

here he sallied on his buccaneering expeditions to the Spanish
main ; nor was it long before he became a terror to the whole
coast, from the port of Vera Cruz, in Mexico, southward along
the Mexican gulf, and the Caribbean sea, to the isthmus of
Darien.

From the year 1630, nothing more is heard of him. Whether
he died a natural death and was buried on the Spanish main
or at his little settlement in Belize, or was killed on one of his
piratical incursions into Spanish America, is unknown, but
about the date given above his headquarters at Belize were
abandoned and the territory was claimed by the Spanish crown.

The first purely English settlement founded at Belize was
composed of a few seamen who were wrecked on the coast
in the year 1638. By the year 1670 the Colony was in a
prosperous condition, much more so, in fact, than any other
of the British possessions in America. Its enterprising citizens exported log wood and mahogany to the mother country,

But Spain never relinquished her assumed rights to the territory for more than two centuries, although from the year
1798, the British government " exercised both territorial and
imperial rights openly and unrestrictedly."

On the ninth of September, 1798, a Spanish fleet, composed
of fifteen sail, was utterly defeated by a small British force,
assisted by the gallant colonists at St. George's Cay. From
the date of that event the British have held undisputed sway
over this possession on the main, as well as over about 100
square miles of cays that lie along the coast.

In the year 1861, by consequence of a memorial signed by
the greater part of the inhabitants of the city of Belize, the
Territory of British Honduras was raised to the dignity of a
crown colony, the Spanish claims to the country were quietly
ignored by consequence of the defeat of their fleet at St. George's
Cay and in 1798, it was declared an English conquest, and a
governor was appointed to rule the settlement, in the name of
the British sovereign, by the home government.

The absorption of this strip of Central American territory,
that was so hotly contested by Spain, and whose own right to
which was so often tacitly relinquished by the British govern-

ment, was simply a preliminary step looking toward the conquest of the entire Caribbean coast, from the mouth of the
Hondo river, southwest, to the confines of Costa Rica. In the
chapters of this work devoted to Nicaragua the writer will
enter more at length into the discussion of this subject, will
endeavor to point out the steps taken by the British government toward the acquirement of this vast territory, and will
explain how, when the success of the movement seemed certain, it suddenly and unexpectedly failed of accomplishment.

The people of the go-ahead and prosperous little Latin
American republic of Guatemala as yet regard British Honduras with wistful eyes, and would, doubtless, if the opportunity presented itself, endeavor to annex the coveted territory
to their own country.

Hitherto British Honduras had been a dependency of the
Colony of Jamaica, and its executive ranked only as Lieutenant Governor. Two months since, the happy colonists received
the pleasant news that their adopted country had been created
an independent government by Her Gracious Majesty, Queen
Victoria, and its executive elevated to the rank of full Governor and Commander-in-chief of the Colony. The joy of the
gratified colonists was intense, and, notwithstanding the fact
that their Governor already received more salary than the
chief Magistrate of the great State of New York; they at
once voted him a large increase of annual pay to enable him
to sustain, with dignity, the honors of his new rank.

CHAPTER II.

Description of British Honduras. Its present population. The import and export traffic. Approach to the City of Belize from the north; view from the harbor. The cleanest and neatest city on the Continent.

The writer has gleaned the following interesting facts, concerning the Colony from the Almanac published by Mr. Grey Wilson :

"For the most part British Honduras is flat, with vast swamp and lagoons, having a depth of about three feet. It is to be remarked that nearly all these latter run parallel with the coast, indicating a probable old sea coast of which the present one formed the outer reef.

"The principal ones are : New River (twenty miles long), Crab Catchers, Revenge, Northern, Southern and Mexico. Apart from mahogany and log wood.the forests of the Colony display a great wealth of tropical vegetation, including the cedar, rosewood, bullet tree, fustic, lignum vitæ, sapodilla, Santa Maria, iron wood, red and white pine and india rubber trees, and the sarsaparilla, cochineal cactus, agave, pita, silk grass, istle, Yucatan hemp, indigo, and numerous other useful plants and shrubs, many of which possess medicinal properties. The cocoanut abounds, as does the cahoon palm and the groundnut, locally known by the name of pindas (carachis hypogæa), so extensively grown in and exported from Western Africa, which produces an oil equal to olive oil for domestic purposes, and is also excellent for fodder for horses and cattle.

"The only mountains are the 'Coxcomb' range, with an extreme elevation above the level of the sea of 4000 feet ; behind which there lay an unknown country until last year, when this portion of the Colony was, more or less, explored by Mr. Fowler—the colonial secretary—two Europeans and ten Indians. Starting from Garbutt's Falls, on the Old River, a southeast course was struck to the seacoast at Deep river.

The country crossed was a series of hills and valleys at an elevation of from 1200 to 3000 feet. The westerly portion was slightly undulating prairie, affording a magnificent pasture. No inhabitants were met, but several stone ruins, evidently of great antiquity, were discovered. The soil was as a rule rich, but interspersed with barren and rugged spots.

"A serviceable and direct road is now opened between Belize and the Gautemala frontier, leading to Paten.

"Traveling is almost all done by water in light-draft boats, or dorys; the rivers are tortuous in their course, and in the dry season are almost unserviceable. The Houdo, the northern boundary dividing Honduras from Yucatan, is navigable for about sixty miles; the New river, sixty miles; the Belize or Old river, which rises in Guatemala, for about 120 miles; the Sibnn, the former southern limit of the Colony, thirty miles; the Manitee, sixteen miles; Mullino and Sittee, sixteen miles; North Sturm creek, eighteen miles; the Monkey, Deep, Hope creek and Golden Stream, Maho, and the Tomash, are all navigable for a few miles. The Sarstoon, forming the southern boundary, is a wide and deep stream, navigable by tolerable-sized vessels for ten miles from its mouth.

"The country along the banks of all these rivers is fertile, and affords good pasture land.

"A sea breeze is prevalent during eight or nine months of the year, rendering the climate, which is damp and enervating, fairly healthy. Epidemics are of rare occurrence."

The population of British Honduras, in 1871, in round numbers, was 25,000, but on account of the extreme difficulty of taking the census this number cannot be relied on. The population in 1880, according to the figures given by the late Capt. George Marriner, chief of police, is about 28,000.

In 1870, the statement of the public receipts and expenditures was:

Revenue, $133,617; Expenditures, $131,613; Public debt, $147,950; Imports, $921,685; Exports, $859,885

The same for 1880 was:

Revenue, $216,173; Expenditures, $189,613; Public debt, January 1, 1880, $8,204; Imports, $945,380; Exports, $873,785.

From the year 1871 to 1876, inclusive, the imports and exports aggregated about $1,900,000, but in 1877 they fell off—why, it is impossible to ascertain—to about $1,450,000.

There is no export duty on the produce of the province, while the import duty is, with very few exceptions, but ten per cent *ad valorem*.

Her Majesty's Colony of British Honduras is protected by a volunteer force composed of some twenty officers and about 350 non-commissioned officers and privates.

The commerce of the settlement has within the last six years gradually increased. In 1880 the number of its registered vessels—which averaged twenty-five tons each—was sixty-five; the number of unregistered vessels was. fifteen, making a total of eighty vessels then belonging to the Colony.

Taxation, in all different phases and tints, will amount to about $5 per head upon a population of 30,000.

The land tax on the annual valuation of property in the towns is three per cent. If unoccupied or unused, one-and-a half per cent. Mahogany and log wood works, at the rate of $24 per mile base.

A plantation under ten acres, $100; lands on cays, per square mile, $100; house on cays whether used or not, three per cent, all other lands, per square mile, $200; spirits manufactured in the Colony, per proof gallon 75c; a still license, $500.

Other taxation, wheels of carts, carriage in Belize, each, $200; horses and mules used in Belize, Corozal or Orange Walk, $500; dogs in Belize, Corozal or Orange Walk, $200.

Although there are many other taxable articles, etc., from which the colonial government derives its support, the above mentioned are the principal sources from which the revenue is obtained:"

As the steamer from New Orleans approaches Belize from the north, it passes between a large cay named Nanger island, and the main land. This islet is thirty-six nautical miles distant from the town of Belize. From this point to the port, on the left hand, as the vessel steams onward it passes a succession of cays and islets, covered with cocoanut and mango groves.

They are under the dominion of the British crown and belong to the colony of Belize. They are private property, most of them being possessed by the Belize Estate and Produce Company, whose agents gather from the thousands of trees many myriads of cocoanuts annually, which are generally shipped to the United States per the Macheca steamers and American schooners. On one or two of these little islets small vegetable gardens have been established.

If the steamer approaches in the night, the lights of the little seaport gradually begins to dawn on the western horizon. They grow brighter and brighter, until the city appears in sight, and soon afterwards the anchor drops off the cay fronting the city, where in years gone by a small fort, armed with several cannons and manned by the sturdy English colonists, protected the settlement from sack and destruction at the hands of the buccaneers who then infested the coasts and made their headquarters in the numerous islands that are bosomed on the blue Caribbean sea.

The harbor of Belize is very spacious, and is remarkably well protected. It is almost entirely land-locked by the numerous islets which in reality form it. Large ships entering steer a generally northwest course to the middle buoy, but are compelled to anchor at least a mile and a half or even two miles off the city front. From this buoy the water gradually shoals. To the left of Fort Island, the mud brought down by the Belize river forms a bar which seldom carries more than three and a half to four feet of water. Inside this bar the soundings average ten feet up to the landing place fronting the customhouse.

The charming little city of Belize, the capital of British Honduras, presents a very picturesque view from the anchorage, directly opposite the deserted islet which fronts the mouth of the river.

Far off to the right, situated on a low point, are several long buildings, which are the barracks of the volunteer forces. In their immediate front is a wide level parade, while to the left various neat and comely looking houses comprise the quarters of the officers. Cocoanut trees, laden with their precious burden of both meat and drink, rear their tall heads high above the houses, while along the barracks to the Point a row of young mango trees, many of them bearing fruit, thrive luxuriantly, in this climate so congenial to their production, a climate of perennial spring and of perpetual vegetation.

From the entrance of the military reservation the sea runs a few hundred feet into the land, which soon again stretches outward and forms a little cape called Cox's point. At its extremity is an old schooner, which lies high and dry, having been stranded for some time back. From Cox's point the land along the city front curves inward, its greatest concavity being at that point where the signal station is situated. Then the curve gradually lessens until, at the governor's residence, it flushes with Cox's point.

The whole city front, from the extreme end of the military reservation to a little beyond the governor's residence is about one and a half miles.

A few hundred yards from Cox's point is situated a beautiful residence, deeply embowered in fruit trees and shadowed over by tall cocoanut trees, the nearest of which lean gracefully over the roof of the house. This edifice is owned by a Mr. J. H. Phillips, a rich merchant of the place. This gentleman is one of the colonial commissioners to the New Orleans Exposition.

A small space further to the left is the mouth of the Belize river. This latter discharges its waters into the harbor immediately opposite the inner edge of Fort island, and is navigable for small boats for 120 miles. It is the longest river in British Honduras, and has its source in the interior of Guatemala. It possesses a second mouth about four miles to the north of the one above-mentioned.

The cay which lies a few hundred feet from the mouth of the river has long been deserted.

Between this islet and the shore the water is very shoal, while much of the space is filled by a luxuriant growth of mangroves. Many of them attain the height of at least ten feet. Beneath their branches, which spread downward into the water, shoals of different kinds of fish seek the cool shade and sport among their roots, which, in some cases, curve upwards and protrude above the water and then again strike downward into the muddy bottom.

Still further to the left a tall flag-staff, painted white, stands fronting the wharf. This is the signal station, upon which are hoisted the flags that apprise the colonists of the approach of a vessel, of her class and of her nationality.

In the vicinity of this station are situated the court-house, the police barracks, the council chamber and several other public offices. Immediately over the office of the chief of police, stands the Belize light-house. A few yards more to the left is the Presbyterian church, while near it is the Wesleyan church, which is one of the largest in the city. The rectory, occupied by the pastor of the Church of England, is a pretty but modest and unassuming building. Again, further to the left is the residence of the colonial secretary. This is one of the finest buildings in the Colony. It is surrounded by numerous cocoanut trees, some of which are very tall, while all bend under their load of fruit. At the end of the curve, or arc, as seen from the entrance, of the harbor, stands the house of his excellency the governor of the Colony. It is a very fine building, is airy and well ventilated, and also is shaded by a number of fine cocoanut trees. From this point the shore again seems to recede and curve inward to the left. A few hundred yards from the governor's residence stands a lone, solitary house, which may be considered as the last or most suburban building of the city.

Belize, the capital of British Honduras, is one of the cleanest cities, if not the very cleanest, on God's foot-stool. The writer certainly has never seen in any other Latin American country a town so clean and spruce, and one that presents such a neat appearance. Its streets are level and are kept in admirable order, the centre of them, for about twelve or fifteen feet, being macadamized with calcareous rock, which is broken fine by the long term convicts, who are not permitted to leave the prison yard. These streets are cleaned and kept in repair by the convicts of the common jail, several gangs of whom may be seen, at any time during the day, working in the different quarters of the city. They are well fed and not over-worked, while they are never ill-treated or abused. One policeman is enough to watch a gang of six or eight of these unfortunates.

The convicts of Belize are almost all negroes—miscalled Caribs. There are some few half-castes or descendants of Spaniards and Indians among them, though a very few.

The author never saw a white convict on the streets, nor when he visited the jail. This certainly argues well for the morality of the white colonists, particularly when the circumstance of Belize being a seaport town is taken into consideration.

The buildings of the capital are mostly constructed of wood, and are light and airy. Many of them are roofed with thin corrugated galvanized iron, and some with tiles.

Almost every private residence in Belize has its yard attached, which is adorned by flower gardens, and cocoanut trees. The population of the city is about 7000, according to the last census, which was taken by the late energetic chief of police, Capt. George Mariner. A large portion of the inhabitants is composed of the descendants of Jamaica negroes, and blacks from other localities, who are miscalled Caribs, for they resemble the genuine Carib Indians about as much as an Anglo Saxon does a full-blooded Esquimaux. In fact, but few of the descendants of the brave but ferocious Caribs, who so gallantly defended their native country against the Spanish invaders, now remain. Some of the gentlemen of Belize do not hesitate to assert that the race is extinct.

Quite a number of half-castes live in Belize, but they do not possess that proud and independent mien which so essentially distinguishes their Mexican "costeño" brethern. The number of European inhabitants, or those of pure European descent, is very small when compared to the negroes and half-castes.

CHAPTER III.

For such a small city Belize will compare favorably with Brooklyn, even, in number of her churches, for she boasts of no less than fifteen, two of which are Episcopalian, five are Roman Catholic, six are Wesleyan, one is Baptist and one is a Scotch Kirk. The number of members and communicants belonging to each denomination is difficult to ascertain, but when the absence of white convicts is taken into consideration, an impartial observer can scarcely help from assuming that about all of the white colonists must be church members.

Nor do the pious city guardians of Belize care less for the educational wants than they do for the spiritual necessities of their people, for, if the former head-quarters of the piratical Wallice boasts fifteen churches, it none the less possesses numerous schools, which receive goverment aid to the tune of nearly $10,000 annually, including inspector's salary and prizes for the scholars. Each pupil costs the Colony $5 62½, therefore, more than one-sixth of the entire population of Belize consists of children actually at school. This curious fact may account for the scarcity of jail-birds in Belize, as well as for the still more singular fact that, of the present convicts now serving out their time in jail, less than one-half of them are natives of the Colony, while but very few belong to the city.

As the capital is the commercial centre of British Honduras, most of the principal business firms are established there. They are:

Wm. Guild & Co., B. Cramer & Co., P. Leckie & Co., Belize Estate Co., P. Lefebrre, John Gentle & Co., Chas. Pahmeyer, Henry Gansy, A. E. Morlan, Brodie & Cuthbert, Beattie & McDonald, V. H. McDonald, C. T. Hunter, Dr. A.

Hunter, F. H. Bowen, Henry Lind & Co., C. Metzgen, John Harley, Steven Bros. & Co., Panting & Co., A. H. Brinston, A. A. Richard, Phillips & Co., J. Lainfiesta, John McDonald A. Williamson, Chas. Peters.

The Belize Estate and Produce Company is a huge corporation which owns at least one-quarter of the entire Colony. It is managed by Mr. A. S. Kindred, and is said to swing a very large capital.

Beside the above mentioned firms there is a syndicate known as the British Honduras Fruit Company. It comprises 300 shares of £10 each. These shares are not to be bought, excepting an a large premium.

A savings bank has been lately established under the system invented by the present postmaster general of the British Empire. It is said to have already accomplished very beneficial results.

It is safe to assume that the greater part of the banking business of the city and the Colony is in the hands of the Belize Estate and Produce Company, and that the profits from it add greatly to the annual revenue of the association.

There is a fine opening for an American bank with American capital in Belize, at least so the leading merchants of the place assert.

Belize contains a jail, one poor house and one lunatic asylum. In each of these institutions are separate appartments for females, which are under charge of experienced matrons. There are but comparatively few paupers in the poor house and fewer still who receive out-door relief.

Ten foreign consuls reside in Belize, most of whom are merchants doing business in the Colony. The American Consul the Hon. A E. Morlan, unlike many of his colleagues of the Caribbean coast, is a merchant of standing and consideration. He is courteous and polite to tourists and maintains the dignity of his office. His house is open to all visitors of respectability, and his beautiful and accomplished lady dispenses the hospitalities of the consulate in a most graceful and charming manner.

The entire length of the coast of British Honduras, from the Hondo river on the north to the Sarstoon river which is the southern boundary of the Colony, is 160 miles. The average width of the strip of land which forms the province is about forty miles, while the whole area is estimated at 6400 square miles.

The capital and seaport, Belize, is situated nearly an equal distance from either boundary line. Several flourishing little ports have been opened to domestic commerce and a number of settlements are established at different points along the coast.

The town of Corozal is situated about ninety miles north of Belize. It contains 5000 inhabitants and enjoys considerable traffic. Numerous small coasting vessels, dorys, sloops and little schooners, ply up and down the coast and connect the town with Belize and the other settlements. Corozal is probably the most picturesquely situated town in Honduras. It presents a cleanly and neat appearance, although most of its buildings are thatched with palm leaves. It is the centre of a flourishing and progressive agricultural district. Sugar is the principal staple crop.

In this happily situated locality, the climate is equable, and considering the latitude, is singularly cool, pleasant and healthy. Epidemic fevers never occur, while diptheria, and in fact all bronchial and pulmonary diseases are unknown. Unlike the centres of population in the West Indies of the same latitude, British Honduras is never afflicted with the yellow fever; not even a sporadic case has occurred within the memory of the oldest inhabitant.

In the Corozal district the sugar cane attains a size and yield truly marvelous. There exist plantations that have not been replanted for many years, yet the ratoon cane readily yields an average of 3000 pounds of crude sugar to the acre. Cane five or six years planted will often return as high as 6000 pounds to the acre.

Lack of capital and a corresponding want of modern sugar making machinery prevents the planters of Corozal from deriving the full benefit from their energy and industry. Yet

2

they manage to make a good profit upon their investments, and the crude sugar and rum they manufacture finds a ready sale and fair price at Belize and the markets of this country and Europe. The names of the principal merchants are Jones & Young, Brodie & Cuthbert, and Mrs. Hinkes.

Orange Walk, as its name indicates, was once at least, famous for its yield of a most delicious fruit. The settlement is situated forty miles inland on the bank of the New River, a tortuous narrow little stream, which is, however, navigable for dorys for many miles from its mouth. It is the military headquarters of the northern district, and in days past, when the Indians of Yucatan were troublesome, was an important station. The population is rather mixed, but few inhabitants save those of the military profession are white. Escalante & Co. is the principal business firm of the locality.

San Pedro, a little town containing some 1200 inhabitants, is situated on Ambergris cay. The town engages in quite a prosperous traffic with the main land, which is carried on by small sailing vessels and dorys.

South of Belize several prosperous settlements have, within the past few years, been established. One or two of them however are almost contemporary with Belize. The principal industry is fruit planting.

Mullin's River is a small settlement, situated at the mouth of the river of the same name. It contains a mixed population of about 500 inhabitants. At this place the fruit planting industry has made great progress. The Belize Fruit Company possesses a valuable property with many acres of bananas under cultivation, whose annual yield may be estimated at 50,000 bunches of the standard size. The Excelsior Fruit Company is also a prosperous corporation, but as its establishment is of more recent date than that of the former, it yields but about 12,000 bunches per annum.

Stann Creek, at the mouth of the creek of the same name, is quite an important place. It contains some 2000 inhabitants, most of whom are Caribs. These singular people are remarkably industrious. The men are laborers and mahogany cutters, and the women are the planters of the locality. A fuller description of this race will be given in another place.

All Pines, which is situated somewhat to the south of Settee River, is a settlement that contains a mixed population of 500 inhabitants. This locality, or rather Settee river, boasts several flourising banana walks. The Ross plantation yields annually 12,000 bunches; the Smith plantation 15,000 bunches; The Cramer plantation 10,000. Punta Gorda, situated on the coast, contains a half-caste and Carib population, numbering 1700 inhabitants. It is quite an important place and carries on a flourishing traffic with Belize.

About ten miles back of Punta Gorda, at a locality called Toledo, is a new settlement established by Americans. This Colony contains but about 700 inhabitants in all. The Americans are principally engaged in sugar planting. Several of them own valuable plantations. The yield of sugar to the acre is even greater than at Corozal. The planters at present send the bulk of their harvest to New York.

At Monkey River, certain enterprising gentlemen have lately established banana plantations at favorable localities. The Waliz Company exports 17,000 bunches annually and the Coleman plantation 8,000 bunches . Other parties have also invested in this industry but have not as yet begun to export fruit.

If the late Governor Barlee, by his wise measures, established the commerce of British Honduras on a prosperous basis, the energetic and go-ahead British colonists have taken equally wise steps to keep what they have acquired. The present import traffic of the Colony, which consists of general merchandise from this country will reach to nearly $1,500,000 annually. The export traffic consisting of mahogany and other precious woods, sarsaparilla, skins, hides, etc., and bananas, cocoanuts and other tropic fruits, amounts to almost $2,000,000, annually and is constantly augmenting.

S. Oteri, one of the most prosperous business men of New Orleans, is the pioneer fruit dealer who first opened the fruit trade between the ports of the Caribbean coast and the Crescent City. He began with one schooner, and carried on a small traffic with Belize and the ports to the south. His vessel brought back cocoanuts, plantains, bananas and pine apples. From this small beginning Mr. Oteri has built up a very large and prosperous business. He has three steamers in the trade, several sailing vessels, and also receives and disposes of the fruit brought thither by other dealers.

But of late years Mr. Oteri has practically abandoned the British Honduras fruit traffic and has directed his attention principally to the development of the fruit planting interests of the Bay Islands and the Spanish main, at and contiguous to Truxillo.

The development and the present prosperous condition of the fruit planting industry of British Honduras is principally due to the influence exerted by the establishment of the Macheca line of steamers. In 1880, Capt. James Leitch, who had traded along the Caribbean coast for many years, in various schooners, obtained from Governor Barlee a valuable mail subsidy. He entered into an arrangement with the Macheca Bros., who put staunch little steamers on the route between the Crescent City and the ports of British Honduras, Guatemala, and Honduras as far east as Tela. At that period the Macheca Bros. had several schooners running on the same route.

When the colonists became satisfied that the Macheca line was a permanent institution, numerous of the most enterprising devoted their attention to fruit planting. Many plantations were started and a fair amount of capital was invested in the industry. It would be safe to assume the yield of the various plantations, large and small, at 200,000 commerciable bunches annually. This crop at fifty cents, the average price per bunch, gives an annual amount of $100,000 derived from the yield of bananas and plantains alone.

At different localities along the coast are situated flourishing cocoanut groves. Numerous cays which lie on the bosom of the sea, near the coast, are also planted with this fruit. It is impossible to ascertain the annual yield of the groves, but the value of the nuts must be great, as an important and constautly increasing traffic in this product is carried on with England, and with our own country.

The plan of this work will not permit the author to enter into a minute and detailed account of the various spontaneous and cultivated products of British Honduras. Mr. Morris, in his admirable little book, has not only mentioned the principal of them but has described the method employed in the cultivation of the most important.

Foreigners who propose establishing fruit plantations in Central America, might study Mr. Morris's book to their advantage.

Before the development of fruit planting, mahogany and log wood cutting was the principal industry of the Colony. In fact the prosperity of the inhabitants was gauged by the price of precious woods in the European markets.

For many decades, even after the price of dye woods declined in Europe, this industry continued in a flourishing condition. But in the course of time the trees, most accessible to the streams, were cut, and the expense attendant upon road making to the cuttings, and hauling the logs to the river, has reached the maximum point. Thus the old industry of British Honduras cannot be considered profitable unless the price of wood rules high in foreign markets.

But Mr. Henry Fowler, the present colonial secretary, during his long and hazardous exploring expedition into the interior, discovered many localities where grand mahogany, cedar and dye forests are flourishing. When railroad enterprise develops these regions, wood cutting will again become a profitable industry, but not until then.

An attempt is being made to bring about the construction of a railroad from the port of Belize, to the eastern frontier of Guatemala, by Mr. Walter Regan, and several other gentlemen of this city. Mr. Regan has several times assured the author that his ultimate prospects of success are very promising.

Altogether British Honduras is a prosperous and flourishing Colony. Its few white inhabitants are fully aware of the value of the territory they control, and are endowed with the business courage, energy and perseverance requisite to bring about the speedy development of the vast natural resources of their new country. But they must learn that the future prosperity of their Colony does not depend upon their European connections, but solely upon the interest manifested in them and their commerce by the capitalists of this country. They must cast forever aside their clannish and insular prejudices and sincerely welcome the enterprise of the American merchant, capitalist and emigrant.

REPUBLIC OF GUATEMALA.

CHAPTER I.

Geographical situation. Area and population. Revenues. Import and Export traffic. Telegraph lines. Free schools and educational system employed. Advance of the Republic under the wise administration of Gen. Barrios. The principal departments.

The Republic of Guatemala is situated immediately south of the Mexican State of Chiapas and south and west of the peninsula of Yucatan. It is the third in size of the Central American republics, Honduras and Nicaragua both containing a greater area of territory. It possesses but a small line of coast on the eastern side, which is washed by the deep blue waters of the placid Caribbean sea. On the western or Pacific side the coast line is much more extended and is blessed by two very fine harbors. One of these ports, San Jose de Guatemala, is spacious, fairly protected and carries deep water almost to the beach.

The Republic contains an area of 44,800 square miles, or 28,672,000 acres of land. The climate on either coast line, from the beach to the foot hills, an average distance of thirty-five miles, is warm and enervating, while during the rainy season malarial fever and chills and fever are somewhat prevalent.

The "vomito" or yellow fever, is unknown on the Caribbean coast; while, if at rare intervals exceptional cases have appeared on the Pacific side, it has never become epidemic. By consequence the sanitary condition of the Caribbean coast of Guatemala will compare with the interior of the United States, along the great river courses, from Cairo south to the Gulf coast.

But in the interior of the Republic, along the tall ridges and the foot hills, and amid the beautiful and fertile valleys that break the continuity of the gigantic mountain ranges, the atmosphere is pure and bracing, and during the entire year inflates the lungs of the Guatemaltecan with a constant supply of healthy and invigorating air.

The population of Guatemala may be safely estimated at 1,500,-000 people, of whom, perhaps, at least 950,000 are full blooded Indians, and the other 550,000 are creoles and foreign whites.

The annual revenue of the Republic was in 1883 ,$4,800,000 one-third of which was derived from duties on imports. The expenditures of the government were a little less than its rev-enue. The public debt, which in 1875 nearly reached $4,000,000 is now reduced to about $3,000,000. The greater part of this debt was contracted during a war with the Republic of San Salvador, the Dictator, Gen. Barrios, having carried into effect his system of paying for the provisions consumed by his army instead of living on the enemy's country, a system never before heard of in Spanish-American warfare.

In the year 1883, the imports of the Republic reached the sum of, in round numbers, $3,500,000 annually, while the exports amounted to at least $4,500,000. This year it is esti-mated that the imports will reach $4,000,000, and the exports about $5,000,000 ; for the foreign commerce of the Republic is constantly increasing, while the cutting of mahogany and dye-woods and the exportation of hides, skins, sarsaparilla and fruits during the last four years has wonderfully augmented.

By consequence of the comparatively recent opening of the little port of Livingston to free foreign commerce, the cultiva-tion of coffee at Alta Paz, this side of the mountain range has received a most astonishing impetus. In 1879, the receipts of coffee at the town of Panzos could not have been more than 1,500,000 pounds. The planters of that section estimate their crop for 1884, at 3,000,000 pounds, notwithstanding the coffee trees of Alta Paz received injuries, estimated at $5,000,000, during the unprecedented cold weather four winters ago. For some days the thermometer ranged many degrees lower than it had been known to fall since the epoch of the conquest, or for over 300 years. Many of the planters, to save their youngest trees, cut them to within a few inches of the ground. This precaution has proven a most wise one, for the plants thus treated have sprung up afresh and are reported as healthy and vigorous, while those neglected invariably withered and died.

Guatemala boasts of but two active railroads. One from San Jose to the capital. The Champerico road runs from the port of that name to Retalhulen, a distance of twenty-eight miles from the coast. Since opening both have paid running expenses, as well as interest on the capital stock, while their freight and passenger traffic is constantly increasing.

In March, 1881, the number of miles of telegraph wires that crossed the country was announced to aggregate to 2150 miles. Along these lines a message may be sent to their utmost limits for twenty-five cents per ten words.

These telegraph lines are all, excepting that which belongs to the railroad, owned by the government, and are under its control.

For many years since the era of its independence, Guatemala languished under a retrograde system of government, but, in 1871, the Liberals arose *en masse* and overthrew the Conservatives. Since that period, under the rule of the Liberal chieftain, Barrios, the Republic has made great strides forward in the path of material progress

Every month—nay, every week—witnesses the inauguration of some new reforms.

Before the revolution two or three parochial schools provided for the education of more than half a million of children. To-day over 1000 free schools are in full operation. Education is compulsory, and every adult male in the Republic is taxed to support the new school system.

With political emancipation came commercial regeneration, and at present Guatemala is one of the happiest, and probably the most prosperous, of the many little republics that lie to the far South of us. Agriculture and commerce are both flourishing, and telegraph wires bring the most distant limits of the Republic in constant communication with the capital and with each other.

Guatemala is washed by two oceans, and possesses a most fertile soil. It has three fine ports on the Pacific side, and on the Caribbean—Port Livingston, and Puerto Barrios. Coffee constitutes its most valuable staple, and it exports about 3,500,000 pounds annually. The greater part of the crop goes to California and Europe. The Macheca steamers often bring coffee to this port for reshipment to New York or Europe.

The only cause that can be assigned for this avoidance of our market is self-evident. The merchants of the Crescent City have made no effort to secure any of this traffic, while it might be said that they have been equally as indifferent in the introduction of their goods in Central American markets.

Meanwhile, English, French and German commercial agents are actively canvassing Latin American countries, and, although the greater part of the goods they sell are inferior to American articles of a similar class, they make larger sales and almost glut these markets with their textile manufactures.

The acquisition of this city's small share of Central American trade can be attributed to the fruit merchants of this section. The Macheca Brothers and the Oteri Brothers have built up the traffic by their enterprise and through the risk of their capital. They began first with small vessels in fruit importing. Then they took orders for goods until their schooners had to be replaced by steamers, and the traffic swelled into its present magnitude. They have thus succeeded in wrestling no small portion of Central American trade from the grasp of their Eastern rivals, while, as a natural consequence, they have begun the introduction of American textile goods into these consuming centres.

The Republic is divided into twenty-two departments, each of which has its military commander and corresponding civil officials. Several of these political divisions merit special mention, that of Yzabal being most accessible to this country.

The department of the Yzabal is bounded on the north by the gulf of Amatique and the Bay of Honduras, and on the south by the Motagua River. It is one of the richest provinces in natural resources in the Republic of Gautemala, and contains a population of 5420 souls, composed of Ladinos, Indians and Caribs, with an area of 4500 square miles.

The climate is delightful, a perpetual spring. The thermometer ranges between 80 and 95 degrees for the year round. During the dry season, which lasts from the first of February to the middle of June, the trade winds set in about two o'clock in the evening and last until eight or nine at night. They are followed by a land wind, which makes the nights cool and pleasant.

The sanitary condition of the department is good. The only sickness is chills and fever, which yields very readily to proper treatment. Yellow fever, Chagres fever, cholera and epidemic diseases are unknown.

The forests abound in mahogany, cedar, rosewood, ebony, vera, amarrillo, logwood, fustic, oak, laurel and other valuable timber, as also in india-rubber trees, sarsaparilla, wild cacao and the precious vanilla vine.

The lands on the Motagua and Dulce rivers and on Lake Yzabal are rich alluvial deposits, well adapted to the cultivation of sugar-cane, coffee, cacao, bananas, plantains, rice, corn, cocoanuts, oranges, limes, mangoes, guavas, pineapples and all classes of the tropical fruits.

The remaining lands are very suitable for grazing purposes, and a large traffic in cattle is carried on with the markets of Belize and Guatemala City.

The President of the Republic, Gen. J. Rufino Barrios, with the laudable intention of encouraging agriculture in the department, has, in company with Don Cayetano Rascon and Don Felipe Marquez, established a large cattle ranch, called the "Hacienda del Pilar," some fifteen miles east of Yzabal. The hacienda contains about 36,000 acres of land, and at present is stocked with 4000 head of cattle. The pasturage is abundant and of good quality. It may be safely said that the enterprise is a success, for the proprietors are constantly adding to the number of their cattle.

The President, in company with Col. Henry Toriello, has established a large sugar plantation, on the north side of Lake Yzabal. The land is good, and the work of clearing and planting is being pushed forward with energy. Col. Toriello is also largely engaged in banana culture, near Livingston. At present he is cutting about 500 bunches per month.

The extensive cocoanut plantation of Point Manibique has been leased by Capt. James Leitch and Michael Norrich. This grove contains about 10,000 bearing trees, and will, no doubt, prove a good investment for these enterprising gentlemen.

There are quite a number of cocoanut, cacao, banana and pineapple plantations in the neighborhood of Livingston, all of which are being cultivated with profitable results. Cocoanuts sell readily for $18 per thousand; bananas, fifty cents per bunch; plantains, seventy-five cents per hundred; pineapples, seventy-five cents per dozen; corn, seventy-five cents per fanega (400 ears); rice four cents per pound.

The free port of Livingston is situated on a bluff sixty feet above the level of the sea, at the mouth of the Rio Dulce, and is fast becoming a place of importance. It is connected with New Orleans by the Macheca, Black and National lines of steamers, and with England and the Continental ports by the vessels of the London Line. The river steamers Muncy and Panzos, owned by Messrs. Anderson and Owen, make regular trips between Panzos, touching at Yzabal and San Felipe, and connecting with the Macheca Line every week.

The imports from the United States are flour, pork, cotton goods, canned goods, kerosene and lumber. The exports are mahogany, coffee, india-rubber, sarsaparilla, hides, cocoanuts, bananas, plantains, pine-apples and other tropical fruits.

Gen. Barrios, President of the Republic, is very much interested in the progress and development of this department, and cordially invites emigration. He particularly desires American emigrants to come and make their homes here, and assist in developing the vast agricultural and mineral wealth of the country.

A gentleman who has lived in this department for the past fourteen years, told the author that he has never been molested in any way, and that life and property are as secure at Yzabal as in any other part of the world.

The department of Sacatepéquez, of which old Guatemala city is the capital, is one of the finest agricultural regions of the Republic. Its principal products are corn, indigo, sugar-cane, coffee, croton oil plant and precious woods, honey etc. Some mines were worked in the Magdalena district during the

Spanish regime. The department possesses an area of 250 square miles and a population of 50,000.

The department of Chimaltenango, is also a grand agricultural region. It contains 800 square miles of territory and produces anatto, yams, beans, coffee, corn, sugar-cane, cotton, and in the higher altitudes excellent wheat. The mountain slopes, foot-hill sides and grand semi-tropic valleys of this department contain vast forests of furniture and building timber. When railroads are introduced into this region, these forests will become very valuable. Several beautiful streams and watercourses, containing perennial supplies of this precious fluid reticulate the department in all directions and render irrigation remarkably easy.

The department of Suchitepequez is one of the most extensive political divisions of the Republic. It contains an area of 2510 square miles and 75,000 inhabitants. It is watered by numerous perennial rivers. Its principal agricultural products are coffee, cacao, (chocolate) corn, yams and sugar-cane. The annual export of cacao alone from this district amounts to more than 1,000,000 pounds. The department boasts a large aboriginal population, which still retain many of their ancient customs and habits, particularly their mode of dressing.

The department of Quetzaltenango is also noted for its valuable agricultural products, among which may be mentioned an annual yield of 6,000,000 pounds of Indian corn, 2,000,000 pounds of coffee, 2,400,000 pounds of wheat and 20,000 pounds of wool. It is one of the finest stock raising localities in the Republic, while the capital possesses a few profitable textile factories. Several fine streams of water flow through its wide savannas.

The department of Retalhuleu is not only celebrated for its agricultural activity but also for its vast forests of furniture and building timber. It boasts many valuable coffee and sugar estates whose products are exported from the port of Champerico.

The department of San Márcos contains 750 square miles of territory and 75,000 population. Its agricultural products are sugar-cane, coffee, cacao, corn, wheat and other cereals. The following graphic description of the country contiguous to the volcanoes of Tacaná and Tajumulco is taken from the interesting work of Don Antonio Batres, entitled "A Sketch of Guatemala."

" The volcano of Tacaná forms a regular cone, while that of Tajumulco is capricious in its configuration. They are the chief features of the district, which is traversed by the same Cordillera that extends through Central America. Between slopes of the last named volcano, the Cabus river has its source and then runs a considerable distance through wide woodlands, fertile and arable fields, and sandy deserts. Two suspension bridges span this stream, while another very handsome one has been thrown across the Cotzutchimá river. The Naranjo, Tilapa and Pacaya rivers form the Ocós bar. Hydrographically, San Márcos is traversed by other water courses and brooks irrigate its fertile territory and carry vegetable life into that opulent zone, joining their waters finally with those of the Soconusco. The topographical aspect it unfolds is something superb; as far as the eye can reach, snow-capped eminences; precipices and ravines, the latter the offspring of cataclysms, of which history has no record; fertile highlands diversified by broad acres of waving cereals, and clustering farm houses; the virgin forest with its giants overrun by creepers and intertwining lianas; the fragrant coffee blossoms perfuming the boundless uplands; emerald horizons made up of cane and wheat fields which are surrounded by tall and erect mountain ranges, on whose declivities flocks of sheep find abundant nourishment, while the huts of herdsmen keep watch over them."

The extensive department of Huehuetenango is corrugated by tall mountain ranges which enclose numerous fertile valleys where the temperate climate prevents the production of tropical plants and fruits. It contains 141 villages and thirty-six considerable towns, many of whose inhabitants are engaged in the manufacture of coarse woolen goods. On the border of the river of the same name, are found the remains of the aboriginal fort Tzac—uleu, where the justly famous Indian king, Caibil Calan, for a long time heroically defended this last strip of his ancient patrimony against the repeated assaults of the impetuous Governor Don Pedro de Alvarado. The suspicious death of the great chieftain dispirited his followers, and in the final assault the Spaniards captured the fort. The locality is noted for its abundant yield of all the cereals and fruits of the temperate zone, and also for its deposits of gold, silver, iron, lead and salt.

The department of Quiche is famous as the locality where the aboriginal kings of the country founded their great capital Utatlan. Its last monarch mustered an army of 75,000 men to oppose the march of the famous Alvarado. Its products are Indian corn, wheat, sarsaparilla, hemp, vanilla, textile fibre made from the Agave, white copal, wild incense, India rubber, almonds, copalchi, anatto, aniseed, tea, coffee.

. The department of Chiquimula covers an area of nearly 2200 square miles, and contains 55,000 inhabitants, the majority of whom are engaged in agriculture. According to the report of Mr. Batres, its products are wheat, Indian corn, rice and other sorts of grain; beans, tamarinds, divi-divi and vegetables; coffee and India rubber; tobacco, sarsaparilla; almonds, yuca, storax gum, sesamum orientale, cotton, liquid amber, sugar, indigo, lignum vitæ, fustic, aripin, mahogany and cedar wood, silver, antimony, copper, lead, and iron ores. The celebrated Olotepeque mines are still being worked. The general aspect presented by the department is of the most varied kind, picturesque and overflowing with resources.

'The city of Chiquimula is the capital. It contains 11,000 inhabitants and is situated at an altitude of 990 yards above the level of the sea, with a warm yet salubrious climate.

The above is a brief mention of the most productive and populous departments into which the republic is divided. Alta and Vera Paz will be more generally treated in another chapter devoted to Guatemalean industries.

CHAPTER II.

The ancient people of Guatemala. The Popal Vuh. The founders of Palenque and Copan. First aboriginal kings. Curious traditions. Human sacrifice. Advance stage of civilization, etc., etc.

Four decades ago Messrs. Squires, Stephens and Wells, announced to the wondering savant of the scientific world the discovery of ruins of numerous ancient cities in Chiapas and Central America. Some time previous Yucatecan antiquarians had published descriptions of the grand ruins of Uxmal, of Chicken-Itza, Kabak, Nohpot, Labuoh, Ake, and other aboriginal cities, but the servile insurrection which soon afterward occurred, put a termination to further archæological discoveries in Yucatan. The victorious savages reconquered their ancient patrimony; the creoles were driven to the country contiguous to the coast, and the localities where these vast ruins are situated were, for the time being, occupied by the revolted peons.

But in Guatemala no less interesting remains of the past eras of civilization were discovered at different points. Those of Quirigua, in particular, excited great interest by consequence of their extent and their contiguity to the coast. In the department of Copan, in Honduras, are the ruins of a city which, in its apogee of prosperity, must have contained at least 600,000 inhabitants. It is known to the scientific world as Copan, and was first visited and described by the celebrated American traveler, John L. Stephens.

The ruins of Palenque, in the Mexican State of Chiapas, were also visited by Stephens, who published a graphic and interesting account of the remains of that ancient capital. It takes its name from an insignificant little village situated near it, but we now know that it was called by the aborigines "Nachan."

In 1870, the author of this work, in company with several Mexican archæologists, explored the ruins of Uxmal, Kabak Chicken Itza, in Yucatan, and Palenque, in Chiapas. In 1871, accompanied by two young gentlemen of Philadelphia, he visited the extensive ruins of Papantla, in the State of Vera Cruz, Mexico. It is very probable that he and his two companions were the first persons of Anglo-Saxon descent who ever saw the ruined temples, palaces and vast edifices of this ancient capital.

During the past year the columns of the *Times-Democrat* have contained numerous articles descriptive of Central America, particularly of the republics of Honduras and Guatemala. These publications have attracted the attention not only of merchants and business men in general, but of scientists and archæologists as well. Again the question has been agitated, who were the founders of these large ruined cities, and what degree of civilization did they attain.

As yet this problem has not been solved. The hieroglyphics that cover the temple walls, the monuments and obelisks of Central American ruins, have only been more than partially deciphered; thus their historical records are almost a sealed book to the scientific world.

All we know is that, at a remote period, races of highly enlightened people inhabited the southern portion of Mexico, and almost the entire area of Central America.

In a recent tour through the republics of Honduras and Guatemala the author was presented by Gen. Luis Bogran, now president of Honduras, with a copy of the unfinished history of Central America, written by Don José Milla, a famous Guatemaltican scientist. This accomplished scholar died shortly after he had finished the second tome of his work. The first volume is prefaced by an essay upon the aboriginal inhabitants of Central America. This interesting historical sketch has never, we believe, been published in the English tongue. Believing that a knowledge of these legends, and the traditions relating to the former inhabitants of Central America would be pleasing to the readers of this book, the writer has translated the principal and most interesting portions of Mr. Milla's sketch of the aborigines of his country.

That vast territory which is situated between the Isthmus of Tehuantepec and that of Panama, and the Atlantic and

Pacific Oceans, and which for three centuries was subject to the Spanish crown, has, since the era of independence, received the political denomination of Central America, on account of its geographical position.

The old mines found in different localities of Central America attest not only a most remote antiquity, but likewise an advanced stage of civilization. Neither the mysterious construction of Quirigua, of Palanque, of Copan, and of Tikal, nor the remains of the edifices and temples of Quiche and Tecpan, Guatemala; nor the many other ruins of ancient cities that strew Central America reveal the least insight into the origin, the customs or the habits of the people who raised such monuments. The annals of those great nations are entirely lost, or cannot be deciphered. The inscriptions that cover the walls of the ruined temples, or the huge obelisks and columns that have been found in the tropic forests, have not as yet revealed to the eye of the observer their hidden meaning. The origin of the inhabitants of these countries is a problem which history has not been able to solve, notwithstanding the advance that has been made in the study of American archæology, ethnology and linguistics, during late years. We may hope, however, that the interest that has been awakened in the scientific world by the monuments that cover our soil, will augment day by day, particularly as many scientists are now convinced that this country was the cradle of the former civilization of this continent, if not of the world.

Few, unfortunately, are the remaining historical documents relating to ancient Central America. Some data have reached us, furnished by Indians whom the Spaniards taught to write in Latin characters. It is doubtful what degree of confidence should be placed in the truth of these narrations, in which events are frequently expressed by symbols or hieroglyphics, whose true sense is very often difficult to understand.

One of these historical fountains is the Popal Vuh, or national book of the Quiches, of which there are two versions; the Spanish of the historian Ximenez, and the French of the Abbot Brasseur de Bourbourg. Without differing very materially these two authors interpret differently the legendary and mythological portion of this curious historical document. The translation of the Spaniard has in its favor the authority of an author who was a profound scholar and who for thirty years had studied the Indian languages. On the other hand, the French translation reveals the vast knowledge possessed by its author of the languages and the antiquities of the indigenes. The narration of Quiche appears adorned with thoughts that it is very possible were never the real sentiments of the Indian editor of the Popal Vuh.

In the interpretation of various passages, Ximenez pays tribute to the ideas of his epoch, a fault the Abbot Brasseur should have avoided, writing as he did, in a more enlightened century. Besides the Abbot, in a posterior work, established a new theory concerning the history of ancient America, that contradicted his former interpretation of the Popal Vuh, and other ancient texts.

Another historical document, almost as interesting as the above mentioned, is a Cakchiquel manuscript, of which there is no other version than that possessed by the Abbot Brasseur. He frequently cites it as authority in his writings by the name of the Memorial of Tecpan Atitlan.

He has also made frequent use of the "Titulas Territoriales" of certain Indian peoples to procure information of events anterior to the conquest and also of the military operations of the Spaniards. We have no knowledge of any other than the Casa de Ixcuin Nihaib, although Brasseur mentions others, and refers often to them in the notes of his translation of the Popal Vuh. He carried away with him the original, and no copies remain.

The historian Fuentes cites some Indian manuscripts, from which he asserts he has taken facts relative to the history of these countries anterior to the arrival of the Spaniards. We do not doubt the existence of these documents, but cannot say as much with respect to the fidelity of the translations. Their substance differs notably on various points to all the others we have seen, and as there are many errors in the work of Fuentes, and even falsehoods which appear intentional, the faithful historian finds himself obliged to doubt these data. But unfor-

tunately these errors or misstatements have been widely circulated, and have formed until now the basis of the history of
the epoch anterior to the conquest, for they have been adopted
and popularized by Don Domingo Juarros in his history of the
city of Guatemala, which latter in great part is a copy of the
chronicle of Fuentes.

As we before stated it is very difficult, if not impossible, to
say who were the true indigenes of the country. Going back
to the most ancient traditions we find mention of the coming
of Votan, who found the Territory of Tabasco, where it is supposed he disembarked, peopled by savage tribes, to whom that
chieftian and those who accompanied him, were compelled to
submit before he was able to civilize them. To him is attributed
the foundation of the great city, whose ruins are now known
under the name of Palenque, but whose original name was
Nachan or Na—chan. This city became the capital of a vast
and powerful empire, which Votan and his successors extended
until it embraced certain provinces of Mexico and a portion of
Central America. This empire is designated by Indian his-
torians under the name of Xibalba or Xibalbay.

The Bishop of Chiapas Nunez de la Vega, and two other
writers, Ordonez and Cabrera, have furnished many circum
stances relating to that personage (Votan), who they assure
us, left a written memorial, in which he refers to his great
deeds and his long and dangerous journeys, and also gives a
minute account of the dynasty of the "Votanides." Yet there
are many who even doubt that this hero ever existed, considering him as merely the personification of one of the most
ancient epochs of Central American civilization.

According to the authors who sustain this opinion, the
legend of Votan is of Asiatic origin, and presents certain affin-
ities to others of the old continent.

Afterwards came the Nahuas, or Nahoas, generally known
by the name of Tultecs. They founded the city of Tula, (whose
ruins are near Ocosingo), to the southwest of Palenque, in the
modern Mexican State of Chiapas. The chief of this people,
whose mechanical skill and advanced civilization merited the
eulogies of ancient writers, was Quetzalchutl, whom the Mexi-

caus worshipped as a god, and the Guatemaltecan traditions designated by the name of Gucumatz.

The capital of the Tultecs became, in time, more powerful than the Empire of Xibalba, and wrested from the latter the supremacy of the country. The Xibalbaides were obliged to emigrate, and were scattered in different directions. Some of them founded to the north of the present City of Mexico another capital, to which they gave the name of Tula, and established a new kingdom, which, according to certain writers, existed four centuries. The historian Clavigero says this monarchy was established in the seventh century, and was destroyed in the eleventh by a famine occasioned by the scarcity of rain and the plague that followed in the train of the famine. Other writers assert that the last Tultec king of Mexico, who was named Topiltz Acxitl, emigrated with the remnant of his people to Honduras, where he established the kingdom of Hueytlato and fixed his residence at Copautl.

There are likewise traditions of other emigrations, as for instance, that of certain tribes from the north, who came under the command of two families named Tamub and Hocab. They took possession of the country and completed the destruction of Tula and Nachan. This race was afterward known under the name of Mam, since corrupted to Mem, which signifies stutterers. This appellation was applied to that people on account of the difficulty they encountered in pronouncing certain letters of the Cakchiquel alphabet.

Remnants of the Tultecs, who were formerly established on Mexican territory, were those tribes, which, in this country, took the name of Quiches, as well as others also who came with them. They conquered the people they encountered and took possession of the greater part of the country. There likewise came from Mexican Territory other immigrants who, some time before, had spread along the southern coast as far as the locality, which, at present, marks the boundary line between the Republics of Honduras and Nicaragua. These tribes bore the name of Chorotegas, or Chorotecas, from which came that of Choluteca, a city they founded near the point which terminated their progress to the south.

The editor of the Popal Vuh confuses these different emigrations and refers to the arrival of his nation in this country, accompanying the narrative of the event with mythological and allegorical circumstances, amid which it is necessary to search for those historical facts which the writer seems to have done his utmost to disfigure, if not conceal.

He says: "that having departed from a region in the east," which he does not particularize, " the tribes of the Quiche, of Tamub of Rabinal, the Cakchiqueles, those of Tziquinaha, by Balam-Quitzi, Balam-Agab, Muhncutah and Iq-Balam, they came to a place named Tulanzu, according to the Spanish translator, or Tulan-Zuiva, according to the French translator. It is designated also by the name of the Seven Caves and the Seven Barrancos, but it is no other than the city of Tula, founded, as we have before said, by the Nahuas, in the State of Chiapas.

He adds : "that at this place the languages of the tribes became so altered and diversified that they could no longer understand each other." Here they separated; each nation taking a separate route. They were compelled to cross the sea, which they did in a miraculous manner, for the water divided, and they journeyed over several long straight lines of stones.

The Quiches settled in the wooded foot hills of Hacavitz, in Verapaz, to the north of Rabinal, and did little else, for a long time, save commit acts of vandalism upon the neighboring people, the Mames, who, on their part, vainly exerted themselves to destroy these adventurers by force or by stratagem.

The object of these raids of the Quiches was to capture human beings, for the purpose of offering them, as victims, on the altars of Tohil, a sanguinary deity, who with Abilitz and Hacavitz formed the Trinity of the religious system of these people.

The tribes which inhabited the immediate vicinity of this Quiche colony were compelled to submit to the yoke of the latter, who were led by four fortunate captains. When they had accomplished their mission these chieftains disappeared in a mysterious manner, leaving the government to their three sons, Qocaib (son of Balam-Quitze), Qoacutee (son of Balam-Agab) and Qoahau (son of Manucutah). The fourth chieftain, Iq-Balam, left no successor.

In conformity with the advice given by their fathers, before they disappeared, the three new chieftains made a long journey to the East. They crossed the sea with facility, and presented themselves before a great monarch named Nacgic, who invested them with the supreme command and also with the symbols of sovereignty, and instructed them in the principles of government. On their return they were received with joy by all the tribes, who immediately separated and colonized different localities, for the population had increased to such an extent that the limits of Hacavitz could no longer contain it.

One of the localities they populated was named Chi-Quix-Che, or simply Quix Che, from which doubtless is derived Quiche. This latter afterward became the name of the nation. They built a city which they called Izmachi, in whose construction they used stone and lime, more solid materials than they hitherto utilized in building their miserable habitations.

CHAPTER III.

Fall of the First Invaders and Rise of the Quiches—They Rapidly Consolidate Their Power—The Sanguinary Wars of the Latter, in which they are Invariably Victorious—Their Form of Government—They Arrive at the Apogee of Power.

The occupation of a great part of Guatemaltecan territory by the Quiches, according to the French translator of the Popol Vuh, took place between the fifth and sixth centuries of our era. They established four monarchies, under as many different branches of the royal family; named of Cavek, of Nihiab, of Ahau Quiche and of Ilocab. The principal of these, and that which presents the most historical interest, is the Cavek, which exercised a certain degree of supremacy over the rest. At the epoch of which we treat, their settlements extended from the country of the Lacandones to the Pacific Ocean, with the exception of the eastern districts near Lake Ysabal and the maritime provinces of Escuintla.

In establishing—although with some feeling of doubt—the position of the numerous tribes who occupied the territory which is now the Republic of Guatemala, we place in the centre the tribe of Tamub, whose capital was situated near Santa Cruz Quiche. That of Ilocab peopled the territory which extended to the south and west of the country of the Tamub. These two nations, in conjunction with another whose name is lost, constituted, in conformity with the Tultec system, a confederation which was the head of a grand empire, and which ruled over other sovereignties of less importance.

The Pokomanes, who formed a part of the "Thirteen tribes of Tecpan," settled Verapaz and the lands south of the Motagua river. The Mames extended to the frontier of Chiapas. One of the various branches of this powerful nation took for its capital Qulaha, which became an important city. It was situated at the foot of the volcano of Santa Maria, or Excanul, and was also called Nima—Amang—the grand city. When conquered by the Quiches it received the name of Xelaluon, or Xelahun—Quich (i. e., under the ten deers). After the conquest it was called Quezaltenango.

The Quiche nation played an important part in the history of Central America before the Spanish conquest. The Popal Vuh furnishes a list of fourteen kings from Balan-Quitze to Don Juan de Rojar and Don Juan Cortes, the last sovereigus, who exercised a merely nominal sovereignty under the yoke of the conquerors. The latter judged it prudent to preserve, for a time, the shadow of the Indian monarchy. Other authors give the Quiche nation twenty-four kings. Of course it is impossible to decide which list is correct.

According to the Popal Vuh, Balan-Quitze was the founder of the Quiche monarchy, and the first of its sovereigns. This king has left no other record than that of having brought his people to this country, and his acts of vandalism and robbery of human beings for sacrifice. The most memorable act performed by his son Qocabib was his journey to the East, of which we have made mention. The translation of the Quiche nation from Hacavitz to Chi-qui-che, and the founding of the city of Izmachi, which the Popal Vuh attributes to Qocabib, according to the Spanish translator, are events which the French author supposes to have occurred during the reign of the third king, Balan-Conache. The truth is, the Indian manuscript is somewhat obscure on this point, for in another place it states that the arrival at Chi qui-che, and the founding of capital, took place in the fourth generation, or during the reign of the fourth of the Quiche monarchs.

The version of Ximinez designates this last king by the names of Cotuha-Zttayub, but the French translation derives two distinct personages from this name. Cotuha exercised the functions of Ahau-Ahpop, or sovereign, and Zttaynb, or Iztayul, those of Ahpop-Camha, or associate in command, according to the laws and customs of the Tultecs. The Popal Vuh speaks sometimes of Cotuha-Iztayul as of one person, and then again mentions the King Cotuha and the King Iztayul. It is probable they were two different personages, who governed the nation in conjunction.

The kingdom of Quiche possessed three great families at that epoch: That of Cabiquib, commonly called the Cavek; that of Nihaibab, and that of Ahau-Quiche. All lived in their new establishments tranquil and pacific. But the envy of the kindred tribe, ruled by the family of Ilocab, according to some, or the alarm occasioned by the ambitious projects of Cotuha and Iztayul, according to others, occasioned a sanguinary war. The Ilocab entered with a large army into the territory of the first Quiche nation. Cotuha and Iztayul were not taken by surprise. They gathered their numerous hosts, attacked the invaders and defeated them with great loss. Some of the conquered were reduced to slavery and others were immolated at the altar of the sanguinary god, Tohil.

The Popal Vuh adds that this victory gave rise to the Quiche custom of human sacrifices, forgetting that it had attributed this horrible invention to the first King Balan-Quitze.

Their first enemies subjugated, the Quiches continued to grow more and more powerful. They fortified their city, and established the custom of celebrating the weddings of their daughters with grand feasts. These feasts were paid for from the presents received on the occasion. They might be regarded as semi-religious ceremonies, and were considered a thanksgiving for the augmentation of the population.

At that epoch the nation was divided into seven *capules*, which may be designated as seven judicial districts.

In the translation of Ximinez, Gucumatz-Cotuha figured as fifth king. He was known as "the first of the marvelous or prodigious," a name given him by consequence of the supernatural deeds attributed to him by the entire nation. It is said that the king went to heaven for seven days, and he also passed seven days in hell. Afterward he transformed himself into a serpent for a similar length of time, and immediately after changed into a tiger, which form he also retained for seven days. Another time he took the figure of an eagle for a week, and for another seven days appeared as congealed blood, "and indeed," adds the credulous Quiche annalist, "great was the respect paid him for these marvelous transformations, which were effected before all the lords and all the people of his kingdom."

Grave quarrels between the principal families, who were raised far above all other classes of society, occurred during the government of Gucumatz. The version of Ximenez, of the Popal Vuh, throws but feeble light on the cause of these quarrels. It says: "There were conflicts regarding the invitations extended at the weddings of their daughters, for not offering liquor to the judges of the wards." The French translation is still more confused on this point, and simply says: "Their quarrels assumed a serious aspect, and they threw at each other the bones of the dead."

Whatever may have been the origin of these disputes, they gave rise to occurrences of transcendant importance. The first was the removal of the capital from Izmachi to Utatlan, an ancient and venerable city which was in a ruinous condition. It received the name of Gumarcha, which signifies old or rotten cabins. The second important occurrence was the subdivision of the three great families into twenty-four noble houses, obliging the chief of each to build a palace in the new capital.

The French translator of the Popal Vuh conceives that the object of Gucumatz in subdividing the three great families, and creating new dignitaries, was to satisfy the ambition of the inferior nobility, and to diminish the power of the high aristocracy. He opines, also, that the removal of the capital was a wise measure that effectually contributed toward terminating all discord, by employing many people and a great amount of treasure in the construction of the grand temple, of the numerous palaces, and of the other edifices erected in Utatlan.

The kingdom gained a great access of power and majesty under the firm and prudent reign of Gucumatz, without having recourse to arms to force the neighboring people to respect the orders of that sovereign. His wise policy, which the Quiche annalist is always anxious to attribute to his supernatural powers, obtained the respect of his own people and the obedience and fear of the other tribes who inhabited the country.

The son and successor of this monarch was Tepepul, the sixth sovereign, who reigned in conjunction with another prince of the name of Iztayul. They left behind no record of any memorable action.

The seventh monarch was Caquicab, or Cabiquicab, who reigned with Cavizimah and extended the Quiche domination by means of conquest. Chuvila, near the mountains of Vera-paz, inhabited by the Rabinals, Cobkeb, Zacahaba, Zaculen, Chuvi-Megena, Xelahu, Chuva Tzak and other numerous towns of the Cakchiquels and of the Mames fell under the iron yoke of the Quiches, who passed through the country with fire and sword, reducing to slavery those of their enemies " they did not tie to trees and cruelly shoot to death with arrows."

The Indian annalists eulogize the courage and strength of Quicab, and compare him to the lightning. He cut to pieces with his sword the rocky mountains of the localities he con-quered. To prove this assertion the Indian historian mentions a certain cut rock, in the ancient city of Colche, and another on the coast called Petayab, and which is still in plain sight of all passers-by.

He built a wall around the city, to which labor all his vassals were called upon to assist. Fearing doubtless for the security of his dominions, which were gained in great part by conquest, he established watch towers along the frontier, where sentinels noted the movements of his enemies. He jealously fortified many towers and heights which served as an outer wall to his kingdom.

That these prudent measures were not uncalled for, and that the numerous precautions taken were insufficient to prevent a catastrophe, is succinctly related in the Cakchiquel manu-script, although the Popal Vuh passes in silence over the dis-asters which befell the Quiche nation during the reign of Quicab.

The first was the civil war. The plebe demanded to be ex-empted from the taxes and tributes to which they were sub-ject as vassels. Six of the principal agitators demanded of the king and his assistant sovereign the redress of these grievances. They were refused a hearing and immediately hung. This violent measure was adopted by the advice of the nobility, and was productive of the most disastrous consequences. A formidable sedition broke out; but strange to say, this rebellion was headed by the sons and two grandsons of Quicab. They were not inspired by a sentiment of justice toward the inferior class, but by the culpable desire to despoil their old father of the power and riches he possessed.

The palaces of the nobles were invaded and sacked by the rebels, many of the aristocracy were assassinated, and the king himself was reduced to prison. Quicab was compelled to accede to the demands of the people, several of whom were soon elevated to the principal offices of the monarchy. By means of these concessions the old king was permitted to exercise the executive power, but his authority was really gone. The victorious popular classes were turbulent and ungovernable, and, as is generally the case in such situations, a puerile and insignificant cause served as a pretext for a serious and disastrous sedition.

From the epoch to which we have arrived in our narration, the history of the Quiches is intimately connected with the Cakchiquel monarchy. The latter was a feudatory and ally of the former, but had preserved its political entity. It had proved a faithful ally of Quicab in the wars he waged against the other tribes of the country. Established in the mountains of Chiavar and Tzupitayah, and thus near neighbors to the great nation, frequent and daily intercourse took place between the peoples. At the close of the fourteenth century, or the beginning of the fifteenth, according to the calculations of the French translator of the Popal Vuh, Huntoh and Vukubatz held the scepter of the Cakchiquel monarchy. In conformity with the Tultec custom, the sovereign power was exercised by a king and his associate (joined in power) which custom also obtained among the Quiches.

These two princes enjoyed the affection and protection of the old Quicab, their feudal lord, and visited him frequently at the capital. One day a Cakchiquel woman went to the city to sell tortillas, a common food of the people in those days as

also in the present." One of the soldiers of the plebeian guard
of Quicab attempted to rob the woman of her stock. She
defended herself and ended by beating the would-be robber
with a stick. The law relating to robbery being extremely
severe, the Quiche authorities sentenced the soldier to be hung;
but the people rebelled, and not only prevented the man's
punishment, but demanded the woman's death. The kings of
the Cakchiquel interfered and released the woman from the
fury of the crowd. Then the popular ire turned against them
and the matter assumed serious proportions. Some wished
to avenge themselves on the two kings personally, but others,
more prudent, limited the matter to a demand upon their own
king to procure redress for the alleged wrong done the Quiches.

A meeting of the council of the nation was immediately
called. The violent petition against the kings of the Cakchiquels, demanding their heads, was heard. The petitioners
plainly evinced their jealousy against these, the only princes
in the country, who continued reigning in splendor amid the
ruin of the nations which had fallen under the exterminating
yoke of the Quiches. They demanded the persons of the
monarch and his associate, and menaced Quicab with death
if he refused to accede.

But the king sternly refused and managed to evade the
difficulty, which success the Cakchiquel chronicler attributed
to his wisdom, his magic powers, and his knowledge of the
mysterious science of the Tultecs, of which he was a consummate master. The truth is that Quicab perfectly understood
the situation, and foreseeing the tempest that menaced both
him and his protegé, called them secretly to him, and indicated the only means of avoiding it.

"This war, my sons, is not directed against me alone, but
against you also. Do not think that it has concluded. It has
but just commenced. You have seen what the people have
done to me. They have destroyed my family, and robbed me
of my slaves and riches. They wish to do the same to you.
Come, then, to a firm and decisive resolution. Go, dear friends;
abandon this vile city, filled with a villainous and rebellious
population, who neither respect nor listen to you. Go to

Iximche, upon the Ratzamut; erect there your palaces, and a city where your people will be enabled to live in peace, for it is certain you can no longer remain in Chiavar."

This discourse, which concluded with an imprecation against the plebeians, made a lasting impression upon the Cakchiquel princes, and they hastened to put in execution the prudent advice given by Quicab. They heard the opinion of the old men of their nation, and then abandoned the cities of Chiavar and Txupitayah, followed by their people, who displayed their animosity against the Quiches by burning all the villages on the road. Arriving at Iximche, also called Tecpan-Quauhtemalan, they took up their abode in that famous city, which, from that date, became the capital of the Cakchiquel monarchy. It is very probable that it was also the capital of the first kings of the Tultecs, judging from the title given it by the Indians of the Oher Tinamot or old capital.

They immediately began to fortify the city and make preparations for defense, for they plainly saw that before long the horrors of war would be upon them. The seven factions—or parties—into which the nation was divided, unanimously, and with enthusiasm, approved the action of the king and his associate, and sent ambassadors to congratulate and commend them on their resolution to preserve their independence. They bestowed upon the sovereign the title of Ahpozotzil or Rey De Los Murcielagos, (i. e., king of the bats), which was an ancient nickname of his family, and upon his associate that of Ahpoxahil.

The struggle soon commenced. The Quiche had garrisons in Chakilya and Xivanul, frontier towns near the territory of the Cakchiquels, which after the Spanish conquest took the names of San Gregorio and Santo Tomas. The Cakchiquels, on their part, had not neglected to place forces in the towns near the garrison of their enemies. It was not long before fighting took place. The Quiches were the aggressors, for they attacked the fortified posts of the Cakchiquels. They were not only defeated and their general slain, but they lost the towns Chakilaya and Xivanul, which so demoralized them that for the time being they desisted from further hostilities.

The Cakchiquel kings, relieved from all anxiety on this score, bestowed their attention to certain interior regulations. They distributed their subjects among the chiefs of the tribes, embellished their city, and proclaimed for their nation complete independence.

Some years after these occurrences Huntoh died, and was succeeded by his son Lahunah, or Lahuh-Ah. Upon the death of Huntoh's associate, Vakubatz, his son Oxluhuhtzi succeeded him. The Cakchiquel chronicler eulogizes the wisdom and heroism of these princes, which rendered them terrible to their enemies. He speaks of the campaigns they conducted, but does not mention against what enemies. Upon the death of Lahuh-Ah, his son Cablahuh-Tihax mounted the throne and reigned jointly with Oxlahuhtzi, "and whose majesty commenced to shine after the death of Quicab, the enchanter king of the Quiches."

The history of the two nations, so intimately connected during the reign of this monarch, was even more so in the reign of Tepepul II, the ninth king of the Quiches, who had for associate in the government, Iztayul III.

The hatred entertained by the chiefs of the Quiche army and people against the Cakchiquels, restrained by the respect they still retained for Quicab, was openly manifested as soon as that monarch's eyes were closed in death. Jealous of the greatness of the city of Quahtemalan—ancient Iximche—which evinced signs of great progress since it became the capital of the Cakchiquels, they awaited with "malignant envy" an opportune occasion to discharge their ire upon that centre of population. An unfortunate circumstance occurred which afforded the Quiches the long sought for opportunity. In consequence of an excessively cold spell, which destroyed the cereal crop, a famine wrought sad havoc among the poorer classes of the city. Upon information of this event, the chiefs of the Quiches took counsel together and resolved to make war upon their unfortunate neighbors. They armed the entire fighting population of their nation, and taking with them, on a platform borne on the shoulders of porters, their god, Tohil, they began their march. Their principal captains "ostentatiously adorned their heads with beautiful feathers and their persons with golden ornaments and precious stones."

The Cakchiquels, although prepared for war, by no means appreciated the extent of the danger that menaced them. A Quiche deserter presented himself before the kings, Oxlahuhtzi and Cablahuh-Tihax, and informed them of the approach of the enemy. "They are coming," he said, "not in legions of 8000 and 10,000 and 6000 men, but in multitudes. Day after to-morrow they will be here, and their irruption will be terrible, for they will level the city to the ground and put its inhabitants to the sword."

4

CHAPTER IV.

Fall of the Quiche Nation—Foundation of the Cakchiquel Empire. Wars with Other Nations—Their Civil Wars—Arrival of the Spaniards and Destruction of the Aboriginal Nations.

The kings of the Cakchiquels were not intimidated by the approach of the Quiche lords; and far from fearing the result of a battle, were desirous of deciding the quarrel in the field by the force of arms. They rapidly concentrated their arms and took position at the place where their enemy was likely to appear. The first combat proved favorable to them; thus animated by these partial triumphs, they prepared to receive near their capital the main body of the Quiche army. The description given by the Indian annalist of the battle fought in the vicinity of Quahtemalan is animated and picturesque.

"From the moment the first rays of the rising sun commenced to tint the tall summits of the neighboring hills and mountains with a flood of golden glory, the war shouts of the hosts sounded across the wide valley; the battle flags were spread to the wind; the drums and shells sounded, and in the midst of the confusion the Quiches, whose files moved with menacing velocity, were seen descending the mountains in all directions. When they arrived on the bank of the river that courses near the city, they occupied the houses and formed in line of battle under the command of their kings, Tepepul, Iztapul."

"The meeting of the rival forces was terrible. The war cries and the sound of the military musical instruments frenzied the combatants, while the heroes of either army utilized all their powers of enchantment. Nevertheless, in a short while the files of the Quiche were broken and confusion entered their ranks.

"The greater part of their army fled without striking a blow, and the carnage was terrible. Among those who fled were the kings, Tepepul and Iztayul, who were afterwards captured with their god Tohil, the Galel-Achi, the Ahpop-

Achi, the grandfather and the son of the keeper of the jewels, the sculptor, the treasurer and the secretary (dignitaries of the Quiche court), and a vast number of the plebeians, all were put to the sword. Our old men say, my sons, that it was impossible to count the Quiches who fell by the hands of the Cakchiquels on that memorable day. Such were the heroic deeds by which the kings Oxlahuhtzi and Cablahuh-Tihax, as also the heroes Roimox and Rokelbatzin, rendered forever famous the mountains of Iximche."

This memorable battle established the power of the Cakchiquels on a firm basis and secured them the principal position among the Central American kingdoms, which before had been held by their conquered rivals, the Quiches.

From that date history makes but little more mention of the latter nation than give a list of its seven later kings, including the two shadows who reigned for a while after the conquest of the country by the Spaniards.

The battle of the Quahtemalan did not extend to the other nations the blessings of peace. The Cakchiquels, filled with pride, gave way to ambitious designs; openly aspired to the domination of the whole country, and soon began to develop their plan of conquest. The first country on which they cast ambitious eyes was the territory of the Akahales, a branch of their own people, who occupied a large portion of what is now the Republic of Guatemala, from the volcano of Pacaya to the vicinity of the Golfo Dulce.

These people were vassals of the monarchs of Quahtemalan, and their capital, Holom, rivaled that city. The prince Ychal-Amoyac was guilty of a serious crime, in the eyes of the courtiers of Oxlahulitzi; his great riches, of which they decided to despoil him. Resolved on his ruin, they had him called to the capital, and although he had a presentment of his fate, he obeyed the summons and presented himself, accompanied only by a few of his counsellors. As he entered the saloon of the palace, the courtiers fell upon him and his five companions and cruelly assassinated him in the very presence of the kings. Immediately after the occurrence of this villainous action, the towns and villages of the Akahales

were occupied, and soon afterwards were incorporated with
the dominions of the Cakchiquels.

These events alarmed the neighboring States. A confederation was formed by a great number of nations who were
resolved to defend their independence which was so seriously
menaced by the ambitious princes of Quahtemalan. The
chiefs of this confederation were Wookaok, king of the Atzi-
quinibayi, who occupied the banks of the lake Atitlan, and
Belche-Gih, whose principality was situated in the mountains
near the Quiche nation.

Wookaok erected in his capital, Paraxtennya, a castle or
fortress, surrounded by entrenchments and deep barrancos.
Confiding in these defenses he calmly awaited the Cakchiquel
attack. The kings of the latter nation, proud of their victories,
delayed but a short time, before marching against this enemy,
and besieged the fortress. The strugle was deadly, after
fifteen days of continuous combats, the besiegers mounted to
the assault. They entered the place and beheaded all the
surviving defenders. The unfortunate Wookaok paid with
his life the crime of having dared to resist the unjust enemies
of his country.

The powers of the sovereigns of Quahtemalan had reached
its apogee. The nation possessed the same supremacy that,
years before, had belonged to the Quiches, whose kingdom,
under the reign of the great Quicob was the most powerful of
all the Central American nations. Such was the situation of
these countries, when, during the last years of the fifteenth
century, Cristobal Colon landed on the shores of the New
World.

The copy of the Cakchiquel manuscript, from this epoch,
proceeds in a detailed chronological order, furnishing dates
for each of the events to which it refers. In the year 1497 a
serious insurrection broke out in the capital, which placed in
great peril the authority of the kings whose influence appeared
to have been firmly established by the triumphs they had
secured and the supremancy they had acquired over their
rivals.

The inhabitants of Quahtemalan divided into two factions;
the Zotziles and the Tukuches, and although both chiefs be-

. longed to the royal family, and were vassals of the same sovereign, they occupied different quarters of the city; the first held that portion surrounding the royal palace and was under the immediate rule of the sovereign. The second, recognized as chief, one of the individuals of the minor branch of the royal family, who exercised at court the functions of Atzih-Winak. (He who gives and he who makes the presents.)

This position was filled by Cay-Hunahpu, an ambitious prince, who, in consequence of his great riches and numerous vassals, exercised vast influence in the country. By paying court to the aristocracy, he succeeded in placing himself at the head of a large party. He secretly aspired to the throne and simply awaited an opportunity to carry out his designs. It was not long before one presented itself.

The Tukuches, vassals and clients of the haughty lord, quarreled with Akahales, who since their confederation with the Cakchiquels had remained tranquil. The quarrel had its origin in a violent act committed by the Tukuches who attempted to destroy a field of grain belonging to the Akahales, the latter defended their property and repulsed the aggressors. The dispute between the two factions assumed a grave character, and the king and his associate went to the locality to decide the question. Cay-Hunahpu improved the occasion to carry out his design. He demanded the lives of the Akahals, a bold and unjust demand, as the latter were clearly in the right for they had been attacked by the Tukuches. The kings refused to acceed. Then the insurrection broke out in full force openly headed by the evil minded prince Hunahpu.

The movement assumed alarming proportions. The terrified kings endeavored to come to an understanding with the insurgents. But their efforts proved fruitless, none of their conciliatory measures sufficed to placate the anger of the chief of the Tukuches. Then the monarch and his associate were weak enough to accede to that act of injustice they had so energetically refused to commit before. The Akahales were delivered up and were sacrificed, but this concession did not improve the situation. Cay-Hunahpu was reconciled to the king. The conciliatory policy of his rivals, far from inclining him to peaceful settlements, stimulated his pride and caused him to judge the enterprise in which he was engaged as easy of accomplishment, nevertheless, subsequent events showed the error into which the ambitious chieftain had fallen.

Publicly and without the least attempt at concealment, he continued taking steps to carry out his plans. He appointed a day upon which his armed vassals were to attack the capital, for which purpose he marched them out to a position near the river, which flanked the city. He organized his forces and had begun to make dispositions for the attack, when the faction of the kings perceiving that a conflict was inevitable, decided to seek the enemy and give him battle outside the city.

" What a terrible spectacle it was" says the Cakchiquel annalist " that was presented of the innumerable hosts of the Tukuches, whose divisions were not counted by 8,000 10,000 or 6,000 men." Their chieftains' feather head-dresses were placed over crowns of gold and precious stones. At the sound of the drums and trumpets the combat commenced.

Among the partisans of the kings were four women, accompanied by as many warriors, who used their bows with such skill and displayed so much strength that their arrows reached as far as the litter of Chacuibatzin, one of the most fiery and gallant chiefs of the Tukuches. At length these heroines suddenly disappeared; then one of the divisions of the defenders of the city furiously charged a position held by the enemy. The latter could not resist the shock but fled, and abandoned the position they had occupied. This circumstance decided the battle; the Cakchiquels gallantly charged along the whole line and completely defeated the Tukuches. The prisoners, men, women and children, were put to the sword. Cay-Hunahpu and the other princes of his party paid with their lives their crime of rebellion, while the remains of that immense army which had menaced the capital with destruction dispersed and sought refuge in the neighboring towns and villages.

But the victory of the kings was far from pacifying the monarchy. The chronicle of the Cakchiquels records an uninterrupted series of civil insurrections and foreign wars with the other nations of the country. Among the latter the king of Zacatepequez took up arms against the Cakchiquels and struggled to free his country from this heavy yoke. He finally succeeded, and was hailed by his gratified people by the title of Achi-Calel, and established his capital in the kingdom of Yampuk. This monarch built forts in various places to defend his dominions from the attacks of the Cakchiquels, and was always jealous of their movements.

Once, when a number of Pokomane emigrants, who came from Cuscottan, begged him to receive them, he did so, but placed them in a situation as remote as possible from the Cakchiquels frontier. This monarchy of Yampuk had but two or three kings up to the time of the conquest.

Thirteen years afterwards (1510) Oxlhuhtzi died, and in the following year his associate, Cablahuh-Tihax. They were succeeded by their sons, Hunig and Lahuh-Noh, the dignities of Ahpozatzel (king) and Alpoxahil (associate or assistant king). In the first year of their reign an event happened that left an indelible mark in the history of those people. A Mexican embassy arrived at the Cakchiquel capital. Much has been written about this embassy, but little concerning it is actually known, nor of the object the Emperor of Mexico had in view. The Cakchiquels annalist simply says that "Mexican embassadors arrived and that they were numerous."

Fuentes and the writers who have followed him mention this famous embassy. They do not attribute it to Montezuma but to Ahuitzotl, the eighth king of the Mexicans. They add that its object or pretext was to propose an alliance between the Quiches, the Cakchiquels and the Tzutohilo, and refer to the result of the mission. The embassadors first presented themselves at the court of the King of Quiche at Utatlan, who sent them away without listening to their message, under the singular pretext that he did not understand their language. They next went to Quahtemalan, where, it seems, they were better received, but nothing is said as to the success of their mission. They next proceeded to Atitlan, but the ferocious princes of that monarchy drove them away with a volley of arrows. They returned to Utatlan, but the Quiche king ordered them to leave the capital the same day and the kingdom within twenty-four days. Fuentes says "the Guatemaltecan people believed they came for the purpose of learning the condition and number of the forces, of studying the roads and of selecting the best points of attack.

If this event took place at the epoch mentioned in the Cakchiquel's manuscript, it is not probable that the Mexican emperor had the object in view, attributed to him by Fuentes. In the year 1512, the Spaniards had already established settlements on the eastern shores of the Continent. As it is likely that Montezuma had been informed of this (to him) extraordinary event, it is very likely that he desired to get more accurate information, and probably, also, to form alliances to defend the country from the danger that menaced it.

If such was the object of this embassy it failed completely, by consequence of the terror inspired by the Mexican emperor, and also by the want of forethought on the part of those to whom it was directed. The Mexican empire was invaded before the monarchies of Central America were, but far from assisting the Mexicans, one of these kingdoms solicited the protection of the foreign invaders.

In this place it might be well to examine the assertions of certain authors who assert that at one time Guatemala was subjected to the empire of Mexico. We cannot find records among the Indian documents, of any notice of such a transcendent occurrence. In fact, neither the Popal-Vuh, the Cakchiquel manuscripts, nor any of the ancient historical documents of the country (with the single exception of one called Titulo de la Casa de Ixcuin Nehiab,) make mention of any foreign conquest of Guatemala. It seems certain, however, that Ahuitzotl, a warlike Mexican monarch, led his army to Nicaragua along the Pacific coasts, but there is no record of his having penetrated into the interior of the country.

The American author, Mr. Prescott, speaking of the limits of the Aztic empire, observes that: "at the period of the Spanish invasion the monarchy of the Montezuemas," did not include any portion whatever of Guatemala.

War between the Cakchiquels and the Quiches broke out again in the year 1513. The generals of the former entered the Quiche country, and according to their custom, celebrated their triumphs by the sacrifice of human victims.

But if the fortunes of war still clung to the banners of the Cakchiquels, they were singularly unfortunate in other particulars. In the year 1515, a terrible invasion of locusts, which were preceded by numerous flocks of pigeons, devastated their fields. The same year the greater portion of their capital was destroyed by fire. Yet the Cakchiquel's manuscript refers to the successful termination of several wars during this epoch. But, nevertheless, misfortunes crowded thick and fast upon the nation. A plague broke out in Quahtemalan. It attacked the high and the low. The king Hunig and his oldest son, Ahpop-Achi-Balam, the associate king, Lahuh Noh, and forty great lords, among them some princes of the royal family, succumbed in a few days. The death rate among the people was so great, that the living were unable to bury the dead. The effluvia from decaying corpses assisted the spread of the plague which almost depopulated the city. The remains of many of those who fled to the mountains served to fatten the thousands of Zopolotes—buzzards—that infested the locality.

Upon the death of the king, Hunig, and his eldest son, Achi-Balam, as his other princes were yet very young, his younger brother, Balam-Qat, was elevated to the dignity of Ahpozatzil, and Cahi-Imox, son of Luhuh-Noh, became Ahpoxahil. This latter prince died before the plague ceased.

These princes, upon learning of the occupation of Mexico by Cortes, and the irresistible power of the Spaniards, determined to send an embassy to the stranger chief and solicit assistance and protection against their enemies. This incident, which certain authors either never mention or appear to doubt, is clearly proved by a letter from Cortes to the Emperor Charles V., dated Mexico, October 15, 1824. The authors referred to never heard of this letter.

The period that transpired from the sending of the above

mentioned embassy until the arrival of Pedro de Alvarado in
the country was marked by continued wars between the vari·
ous kingdoms of Guatemala. A revolution having broken out
in Atitlan, the kings of that country were obliged to take
refuge in Quahtemalan. They solicited the assistance of the
Cakchiquels, who acceded to their requests and marched
against the rebels. They took twelve cities from the insurrec·
tionists, which they set fire to after having thoroughly sacked
them. The remaining rebels took refuge in a strong fortress,
to which the Cakchiquels laid siege. It at length surrendered,
and the fugitive monarchs were replaced on the throne.

The rivalry between the different nations gave rise to fresh
discords and more disastrous wars, when at length a foreign
invader crossed the Quiche border. In a series of sanguin·
ary battles nation after nation was subdued, and in a short
time the lately powerful and flourishing Indian kingdoms of
Guatemala were destroyed, and the unfortunate people were
forced to submit to the heavy yoke of Spain.

With the advent of the Spaniards in Central America ter·
minates the historical part of Mr. Jose Milla's essay on the
aboriginal people of Guatemala. The remainder of this ad·
mirable article is devoted to the legends, the traditions, the
habits, the customs, the laws and the religion of these singu·
lar people, who had established flourishing kingdoms, reared
grand palaces and temples, and built cities whose ruins to-day
attest the high degree of civilization, enlightenment and me·
chanical skill to which they had attained.

But neither Mr. Milla nor any other Central American au·
thor attempt to sustain the opinion advanced by the American
writer, John L. Stephens, Esq., that the numerous ruins which
are scattered over the surface of Central America were the
work of the people found by the Spaniards at their arrival in
the country.

The principal of the ruined cities of Yucatan, Chiapas,,
Guatemala and Honduras undoubtedly belong to an epoch far
anterior to the advent of the people mentioned in that portion
of Mr. Milla's essay which we have already translated. Late

explorers have no hesitancy in asserting that Copan, in Honduras, and Chichen-Itzi, Yucatan, were built thousands of years ago, while the opinion is daily gaining ground that the grand city of Papantla, whose remains are found near Tuspam, Mexico, was in ruins long before the builders of Thebes or Karnac laid the foundations of their famous capitals.

CHAPTER V.

The destruction of the Central American republic—Reign of terror under Carrera—Defeat of the reactionary party—Accession of Barrios to power—Rumors regarding that statesman—Pacification and regeneration of Guatemala.

Upon the death of Gen. Morazan and the disintegration of the republic of Central America, Guatemala, in sad company with her four unfortunate sister States, was long the prey of contending political factions. The defeated Liberal party fought the triumphant Serviles until its chiefs were either dead or in exile, and then, in despair desisted from further efforts.

But although flushed with triumph, the Serviles, led by the clergy of Guatemala, were doomed to meet with a crushing disappointment. In their struggle they had made use of a terrible instrument who wrested the reins of power from the united Serviles, nobles and clergy, and held them with a firm hand for nearly thirty years.

During the latter part of the civil war a half-breed—ladino—named Carrera, had placed himself at the head of a horde of Indians, and on several stubbornly contested battlefields succeeded in wresting victory from the gallant Liberals.

This person was a fair type of that class of men who in civil wars rise to the political surface, turn passing events in their favor, grasp control of power and burden history with dark deeds and tales of license and uncontrolled brutality. He could read and write a little, but was otherwise totally uneducated. In early life he had been an humble servant in a patrician family. Soon afterward he was a swine-herd, and while roving the hillsides and valleys in search of food for his employer's herds, became acquainted with certain disaffected Indian chieftains, and with them concerted a plan of insurrection against the government of the creoles, a part of which plan was the total extermination of the entire race, and the elevation of the aboriginal tribes to the position they held at the epoch of the conquest.

The rebellion of the Serviles against the laws of reform and the Liberal party furnished him the long-sought-for opportunity; but he waited until several battles had been fought, and both parties were nearly exhausted before he issued from his mountain fastnesses at the head of his sanguinary hordes and joined the Serviles. He soon crushed the despairing Liberals.

His next step was to capture the city of Guatemala, which he succeeded in accomplishing. Then was inaugurated a veritable Reign of Terror. The principal leaders of the Liberal party were summarily executed without any form of trial, upon the mere identification of their persons. Others, of less importance in the political arena, were exiled, their property was confiscated, and their families were persecuted and separated.

In the first flush of success he restored to the church a portion of the power she had once used and abused. The clergy were regranted many of their most onerous privileges, while even the so-called nobles, descendants of the conquerors, or first settlers, were amused and partially contented with vain titles and specious privileges. But when the clergy and the nobles meddled with politics and endeavored to obtain a share of power he sternly repressed them. He reminded the prelates that their mission on earth was one of peace and had for its object the propagation and preservation of the one universal religion, while the patricians were coldly advised to cultivate and improve their estates, but to leave politics alone, that *he was the State*, and would govern the republic to suit himself.

The high-spirited leaders of the Servile party, who were deeply chagrined that their humble instrument had become their master, rebelled. The cowardly tyrant fled to an estate, he had appropriated. But his brother, at the head of a small but determined band of adherents, retook the capital, trod out the embers of the insurrection and conducted the dictator in triumph to the palace. His return was marked by many sanguinary executions, and the Reign of Terror was revived. His faithful Indian allies sent deputations to congratulate him on the failure of the insurrection and to place thousands of armed aborigines at his disposal.

Then the tyrant showed himself in his true colors, and if
his days were spent in govermental duties, his nights were
passed in lust and debauchery. Woe to the matron or maid
that pleased his brutal. fancy, nor were there wanting instances where patrician ladies sacrifices themselved to save
the life of a brother, a son or a father.

Although rough and uneducated, the man certainly possessed great natural talents and an aptitude for governing.
Had he had the advantages of an education, his career might
have been the brightest of his country's history, instead of
the darkest, every page of which is written in blood. Notwithstanding the numerous insurrections that were inaugurated against his government, and the various plots that were
formed to assassinate or poison him, he died peacefully in his
bed, in the plenitude of power, surrounded by the humble
instruments who, although occupying high positions, trembled
in his presence and servilely obeyed his orders.

Such was the terrible reputation of the tryant and such the
impression his administration had left on the minds of his
countrymen, that for some time his successors governed
through the influence of his name and memory. But the
three decades of servile rule had bred a new generation of
Liberals. The names of Morozan, Cabaños, Soto and other
Republican martyrs were repeated with respect and venera-
tion by thousands of young. men who burned to follow their
example and free their country from the galling and oppres-
sive yoke that weighed so heavily upon it.

At length the flames of civil war broke out. After years
of cruel strife, after seas of blood had been shed on numerous
battlefields, the Liberals were eventually successful, and Gen.
Granados, surrounded by many of the most gallant young
Liberal chieftains of Central America, entered the city of Guatemala in triumph. In his cortege were two young men who
were destined to make a lasting impression on the history of
Central America. One was Gen. Rufino Barrios, actual president of Guatemala, and the other was Marco. A. Soto, the
reformer of Honduras and its ruler during seven years.

The three decades of servile rule had almost entirely corrupted the morals, the intelligence and the politics of the country; thus, notwithstanding his acknowledged talents, his unswerving patriotism, his strong liberal principles and the purity of his intention, Gen. Miguel Granados confessed he was not capable of working out the reformation of his country and he cast his eyes over the Liberal leaders in search of a man able to perform the task he was about to give up in despair. The choice of the Liberals fell upon Gen. Rufino Barrios, and, with a brave heart and a determination to succeed, this chieftain accepted the trust.

His first measure was the reorganization of the army. He dismissed all lukewarm officers and named for chiefs of battalions men whom he could trust. He then humbled the clergy—took from them the education of the young and expelled the Jesuits. He sternly repressed the patricians, and inculcated that dogma of freedom, that all men are born free and equal, and that notwithstanding the accidents of hereditary wealth and social position, all men are equal in the eyes of the law. He reformed the laws and ordained that they should govern the rich as well as the poor. The costly rite of church marriage was declared illegal, and that only the civil marriage was binding on the contracting parties. Couples marrying by the civil law might afterwards, if they chose, have their union blessed by the church, but when the latter ceremony alone occurred, children born to such an union were illegitimate; and the parents' brothers, sisters, and even the most remote relatives of parties married solely by the church, could, in case of their demise, inherit their property to the total exclusion of their children. Notwithstanding the stringency of this decree it was often evaded by the clergy.

Then a law was enacted making it a criminal act for a priest to marry a couple according to the ceremonies of the church until the certificate of their previous marriage by the civil magistrate was produced. The penalty attached to such action was a heavy fine together with imprisonment for a long period. *This law proved effective.*

The commerce of the country was at a complete standstill. The roads were ruined and were almost impassable, while petty chieftains ruled each department and municipality. Agriculture was limited to the simple production of a few cereals that supplied wants of the laboring classes.

Barrios then turned his attention to the public highways. Each municipality was ordered to repair the roads in its immediate vicinity. Those villages too poor to accomplish much were assisted from the federal treasury. In a short time the old roads were repaired and new ones together with bridle paths were cut in different localities. Several of the most onerous taxes that burdened commerce were abolished and honest and efficient revenue officers were appointed at the various ports. Instruction was made public, obligatory and gratis, and no priests or ministers of any sect whatever were permitted to control institutes of public instruction. The municipal and departmental governments were reformed or, perhaps, it might be better to say remodeled. Agriculture was taken under the protection of the government. Land was granted on easy terms to planters and farmers, and bounties paid from the federal treasury encouraged the cultivation of sugar, cacao, coffee and bananas.

The final separation of church and state was the grandest undertaking accomplished by this great reformer. Hitherto the church had overshadowed the state and the clergy comprised a caste whose privileges rendered them independent of the laws. They claimed as inalienable rights all the numerous and onerous taxes hitherto granted their hierarchy, and to make good those claims more than once plunged their country into civil war. Barrios felt that to succeed in curtailing their power and political influence he must first take away their privileges. This he did. For a long period this formidable caste bitterly hostilized him. But the passage of time has proved his greatest auxiliary. The rising generation of Guatemaltecans is essentially liberal. Although many young men from traditional reasons may detest his person and even his political course, at the same time they cheerfully acquiesce in his war against the ancient church regime and cordially sustain his acts in this direction.

An impartial student of Central American history must acknowledge that the pacificator and regenerator of Guatemala, Don Rufino Barrios, is one of the most wonderful personages treated of in its pages. While finely educated, he owes more to his natural abilities than to his scholastic attainments. As a soldier, he certainly ranks peer with any officer developed during the interminable civil wars that have heretofore devastated his native land. In statecraft, he bears comparison with such Latin American diplomats as Juarez, Lerdo and Diaz, and is naturally cool and deliberate.

His dearest hope and greatest ambition is to bring about the speedy reunion of the disintegrated fragments of the once powerful Republic of Central America. If any man can, in the present political situation, accomplish this grand work, he certainly will. His influence in Central American politics is felt even in the distant Republic of Costa Rica, while the Presidents of San Salvador and Honduras are closely bound to him by the ties of both gratitude and interest. His strong arm sustains the unpopular Zaldiva in Salvador, while his potent influence restrains the factious chieftains of the Soto party in Honduras from attempting any revolutionary movement in either of the three northern republics.

The enemies of this truly remarkable man have published the most whimsical and absurd stories regarding him. They have depicted him as an inhuman monster, and as the incarnation of all that is terrible and criminal. He is said to have beaten monks and nuns to death with his own hands, and to have dragged shrieking women about the streets by the hair. Blood-curdling tales have been promulgated regarding the innumerable victims he has sacrificed at his political shrine, while he has been compared to Tiberius and Nero, to Caracala and Caligula.

The fact of the case is that General Barrios, in order to bring about the social and political reforms he meditated, was compelled to resort to extraordinary means. During the brief period of his dictatorship he unhesitatingly swept from his path the factious and lawless spirits who constantly endeavored to thwart his measures. Yet but few, even of the most criminal of his and his country's enemies, were executed. Imprisonment and exile were the punishments he resorted to;

5

and if he shot three or four irreclaimable revolutionists, he simply banished many desperate characters who either meditated or attempted his assassination.

To his unswerving patriotism and great military and diplomatic talents the Republic of Guatemala owes its political regeneration. He is emphatically the Juarez of Central America, and like that hero has been vituperated and villified. He is a fond and indulgent father and an exemplary husband. If his is dictatorial and never brooks open contradiction, he is open to conviction and readily yields to the opinions of others, when convinced that he is in error. His friends esteem and love him, but his enemies fear and respect him. During the last two years he has gradually softened the rigor of his rule and has become popular even with his old enemies, the clergy.

General Barrios wields a facile and powerful pen. His sentences are terse and brief, and his language simple and unconstrained. His famous letter to Soto, which annihilated that gentleman's pretensions to patriotic abnegation, was a masterpiece irony and invective. His state papers are remarkable for their clearness and conciseness, to prove which assertion the following, one of his late passages, is reproduced *verbatim*, but the reader must not forget that in a translation the purity and elegance of the original language is often marred :

" I hail with the utmost satisfaction the arrival of the day upon which you resume the ordinary reunions of the Legislative Power, in the fourth year of the first Constitutional period.

" Brief and simple is the report I have to present you, regarding the situation of the country and the labors that have occupied the attention of the government ; but nevertheless, the cordial welcome I extend you is none the less sincere in this solemn moment of the opening of your session.

" Peace has continued showering its blessing upon the Republic. Under these favorable circumstances the government has earnestly endeavored to improve the condition of the country.

"Our actual relations with all America and the various powers of Europe, are frank and friendly, and the fraternal embrace of Guatemala is happily extended, to-day, to all the Republics of Central America. In accord with the President of San Salvador, I accredited a commissioner, who, in union with another appointed by him, was sent to propose to the other republics the reconstruction of a national Union. If this measure can be carried out, in the pacific and friendly manner with which it has been proposed, it will prove of immense significance to the future of Central America. The commissioners have neither returned nor rendered an official account of their mission.

"The serious questions that were pending during your last ordinary reunion have since been completely and happily settled. Military discipline is improving every day. Public instruction has been continued, although certain points have been suppressed which were considered superfluous. Especial attention has been given to the preservation of the interior order, and the independent and the regular march of justice, while constant protection and impulse has been extended to all classes of useful enterprise.

"Work has begun on the railroad lines from Escuintla and Champerico to the capital. The work on the latter has considerably advanced; the construction company has brought to our coast, the rails and all other indispensable materials; while, if the enterprise is not further advanced, it may be attributed to the scarcity of workmen; for there has not been wanting persons who endeavored to prevent the laboring classes from engaging in these enterprises. I propose, however, to dictate effective measures to place at the disposition of the company all the laborers necessary, which is all that is required to rapidly conclude this important line. The heads of the department, in their respective reports, will give a detailed enumeration of the dispositions taken to obtain those interesting results that in all these different branches has occupied the attention of the administration.

"The fall in the price of coffee has exerted a prejudicial influence on the public and private wealth of all the countries

that produce this precious staple, creating a crisis more or
less serious and prolonged. It has also, naturally, affected
our national revenues and prevented a healthy condition of
the public treasury, notwithstanding the prudent economy
that has been introduced in the public service. The diminu-
tion of the price of our most valuable article of export will
not, in my conception, continue much longer. More favorable
notices have arrived to strengthen the faith of our agriculturists and merchants, and by the suppression of all unnecessary
expenses in cultivation and production, and also by means of
the excellent mode of preparation that is gradually being
perfected among us, coffee production will continue furnishing
profit to the planters, and will also insure the equilibrium of
the national revenues. The low price of the article, at the
same time, will prove an excellent reason to the planters to
develop those other classes of agricultural riches with which
prodigal nature has blessed our priviledged country.

The Minister of this Republic to the government of the
Queen of England has arranged with the bondholders of the
Exterior Debt for its gradual extinction. The government is
at present occupied in the examination of this arrangement
and will soon take, with respect to it, such resolutions as the
true interests of the country require, and will submit these
resolutions, if necessary, to your examination.

" Referring you for information on other points to the heads
of the departments, I entertain sincere hopes that your deliberations will be fruitful in happy results for the country,
and that the most complete success will crown your efforts."

CHAPTER VI.

San Jose de Guatemala—Establishment of the Port—Its Former Importance—Fleets Built by the Conquerors—Port Livingston—Picturesque Towns—Its Increasing Commerce—The Curious Carib Residents.

Immediately after the conquest of the principal Indian kingdoms of Guatemala, by the chivalrous and impetuous Pedro de Alvarado, measures were taken to open communication with Panama, and the port of San Jose de Guatemala was established in the southwestern portion of the new province, on the Pacific coast.

At this locality the coast is low and unprotected from the winds, which, during the entire year blow from the south and the west. The sea is constantly more or less agitated, and the breakers dash high on the shallow sandbars that guard the shore.

Early in the morning and in the evening it is almost impossible to land on the beach with a small boat. The surf is at least six feet high, and the breakers come rolling in toward the shore with an increasing and monotonous regularity, while their sullen thud is heard for miles in the interior.

Within twenty years after the conquest the port of San Jose became a place of great importance. Timber was carried from the pine forests of the interior, on the backs of thousands of Indian tamanies, or porters.

Ironwork, sails, rigging, etc., were transported to the coast in the same manner, and numerous vessels were built at the little port, which carried on a profitable traffic with Acapulco, to the north, and Panama and Callao in South America.

It is true that each plank, each spar and each anchor used to construct and equip those vessels was moistened with the bloody sweat of the poor Indian *peones*, of whom thousands fell dead on the highway, on their weary journey from the forests to the port, beside the heavy loads they were forced to bear.

There has been no correct list of the number of vessels con-structed by the Spanish under such difficult circumstances during the first century of the occupation of the country. We know, however, that the conquerors and their immediate descendants built several formidable fleets at this locality, and equipped them for long voyages of discovery. Some of these squadrons crossed the wide Pacific and trafficked with the East Indies; others coasted the extended shores of North America as far as Vancouver's Island, while others regularly traded with Chili, Peru and Panama.

The interior of Guatemala is extremely broken and moun-tainous. From the capital to Port Livingston and Santo To-mas, on the Caribbean sea, the roads are bad and need con-stant attention to keep them in condition. Although during the Spanish regime vast quantities of bullion and other freight were transported on muleback over these mountain paths to the Atlantic, the bulk of the country's commerce passed through the port of San Jose.

Guatemala City is situated about sixty miles, by the road, from San Jose. The highway has always been kept in a fair condition. Thus the productions of the indigo, cochineal and cacao plantations were collected at San Jose, and transported from thence to Spain via the expensive and difficult route across the Isthmus of Panama. Articles bought for the con-sumption of the province, in the markets of Spain, by the time they reached Guatemala City via the Isthmian route, often cost five times their original value in freight charges alone. Olives, wines, cloths, linen, arms, munitions of war, ironware, tinware, etc., were all imported from the mother country. The exports were silver and gold bullion, cacao, cochineal, sugar, indigo, hides, sarsaparilla and other tropic products.

In less than a century from the epoch of the conquest the formidable buccaneers made their appearance in the North Atlantic and harried the commerce of the loyal provinces. A bold pirate captured Tigre Island, in the Bay of Fonseca, and from this point sallied forth on the Spanish vessels which trafficked along the coasts. In a few years the western commerce of Guatemala was almost destroyed. That of Panama, Chili and Peru was greatly distressed, and the pirates, seeing there was no more plunder for them in this locality, boldly steered their crafts across the wide Pacific and attacked the Spanish fleets and settlements in the East.

From this epoch until the era of independence the port of San Jose was almost deserted. About once a year two or three vessels from Peru and Panama stole slowly along the coast, their crews keeping a good watchout for the dreaded pirates, and landed precious cargoes of much needed supplies of various kinds, at the little port. A portion of the commerce of Guatemala passed over the expensive and difficult route to the Caribbean, but this freight consisted principally of silver and gold bullion.

Meanwhile the agricultural industry was almost destroyed by the unwise policy of Spain. The government, fearing the colonies would become self-supporting, prohibited the cultivation of vines, olives and other products throughout their American possessions. These unjust decrees reduced the colonies to the utmost distress. The planters produced but a small quantity of indigo, cochineal and cereals, the latter entirely for their own use. The principal industry was mining. But the high cost of breadstuffs and the exactions of the crown soon paralyzed this industry also, and in the beginning of the nineteenth century the once flourishing commerce of Guatemala had almost ceased to exist.

The separation of the province from the yoke of Spain imparted a new and vigorous impulse to industry. Coffee plantations were established, the cultivation of cacao, indigo and cochineal was revived, and in a few years the little port of San Jose presented a bustling and lively appearance. During the numerous civil wars that have since convulsed the country, both commerce and agriculture were greatly distressed, but if these industries languished they were never entirely destroyed.

The town of San Jose is built on a sandy ridge running parallel with the coast. It possesses a few wooden buildings which are surrounded by Indian cottages built after the fashion of the country. During the rainy season this ridge is separated from the rest of the town by a bayou. The latter is empty during the dry months.

The port is visited by English, French and German steamers, and is connected with Mexico and California, and with Panama and South America by the Central American branch of the Pacific Mail Steamship Line. In April last six foreign sail vessels, from England, France, Germany and the States, were anchored off the port. Its commerce is carried mostly by sail vessels, which bring their cargoes via Cape Horn; yet its traffic with Panama and San Francisco is very considerable. The village of San Jose contains, perhpaps, 1000 inhabitants.

An English company has built a long iron wharf out into the harbor. It is at least 200 feet long and cost $400,000. The traveler, at first, may be inclined to grumble at being compelled to pay $1 from the steamer to the wharf, $1 more for the privilege of landing and seventy-five cents per 100 pounds on his baggage. But when he casts his eyes on the high, white line of breakers that sullenly dash against the beach he is reconciled to the expense and inwardly confesses he would pay five times as much more for the certainty of escaping the ducking that he would experience if he attempted to land in a small boat.

A narrow gauge railroad, in good condition, connects San Jose with the city of Guatemala, some sixty miles inland, in a straight line from the coast. This road was lately finished by the Huntington syndicate, and forms part of their Central American system.

Livingston, the principal seaport of Eastern Guatemala, on the Caribbean, is situated on a high bluff that overlooks the Bay of Honduras on its eastern side, and the mouth of the Rio Dulce on the southern. It contains 500 houses and about 3000 inhabitants.

Until October, 1879, the town of Yzabal, situated on the lake of the same name, was the eastern port of Guatemala, but at that date the government of the republic decreed the village of Livingston a port of entry, and the custom-house and other government buildings were erected at the foot of the bluff, on the southern or river side of the town.

President Barrios two years ago declared Livingston and the country for eight leagues on all sides of it a free port and zone. So the custom-house has been removed again to Yzabal, and the latter town is now the port of entry for Eastern Guatemala. The ports of Santo Tomas and Puerto Barrios are also within this free zone limit.

Directly opposite Livingston the water of the River Dulce is sufficiently deep for vessels of any draft to anchor within a short distance of the beach, but beyond the town to the northward a few hundred yards the mud from the winding river forms a long, narrow bar that reaches to the opposite bank of the river, is quite wide and carries but about six feet of water. It is dangerous to cross in the afternoon when the cool and refreshing sea breeze sets in about 2 p. m.

The bluff upon which the little town is built is in no place less than sixty feet high. On the river side, near the wharf, it ascends abruptly up to the height of at least 100 feet.

The port derives its name from an English gentleman who, some decades ago, was the British consular agent at the Island of Ruatan, Spanish Honduras. Tradition hath it, that the climate of the Caribbean Island not agreeing with his health, he removed to this port and lived for many years. His grave is pointed out to the traveler by the grateful Caribs, among whom he passed his time, teaching them how to read and write. Such, in brief, is the only information that can be elicited why this little Spanish-American settlement bears an essentially American name.

By far the greater part of the inhabitants of Livingston are Caribs, at least so they are called and so they style themselves, but it is doubtful if a single drop of Indian Carib blood courses through the veins of many among them, for the miscalled Caribs are seemingly of pure negro origin, and they possess all the characteristics, as well as the features, of the black race; not of the Guinea negroes, however, but of the tribes that once roved the wilds of southern Africa. Their complexion is rather lighter than that of the unmixed Southern negro, nor are their noses as flat or their foreheads so retreating. They resemble, in fine, the pictures of the Zulos, but are by no means as fine a race, physically, as the latter are represented to be.

As far as the genuine Caribs are concerned, but little doubt exists in the minds of the English officials at Belize of their almost total extermination by the Spaniards within thirty years after the discovery of the Antilles by Columbus, in 1492. They possessed villages along the entire coast of Central America, from the northern extremity of British Honduras to the Isthmus of Darien. They were a brutal and a ferocious race, ever at war with their neighbors or with each other, for the Carib nation was sub-divided into several tribes, who united their forces only when attacked by the warriors of some other nation. It is said that they stubbornly and successfully resisted the attempts of the monarchs of the ancient Indian kingdoms to subdue them, while they met the Spanish " conquistadores " man to man on the shores, or beside the rivers of their native land, and continued their resistance until the greater part of their people had fallen under the swords of the invaders, when a small remnant of their once large nation retreated to the mountains and joined the inhabitants of those inaccessible sierras in an eternal warfare against the Spaniards.

They were undoubtedly cannibals, or at least they ate the prisoners they captured in battle, while so terrible was the reputation they acquired among their foes that the Spaniards dreaded to encounter them, and out of respect to their prowess and undaunted courage named the vast sheet of water that washed their inhospitable shores " El Mar de Los Caribes"— the sea of the Caribs. Such were the indigines of the eastern coast of Central America during the sixteenth century.

It has been asserted that some of the present race of negroes who live on this coast and who are miscalled Caribs, are principally Jamaicans, who have emigrated since the emancipation. The greater part of them, however, are said to be the descendants of a cargo of slaves. The ship in which they were brought from Africa, and which was directed to the Jamaican slave mart, was driven into the Caribbean Sea by a terrible easterly gale, and was wrecked on the coast of British Honduras. Whether this latter information is correct or not, one fact is certainly self-evident, these people are not Caribs, but are almost full-blooded negroes.

They inhabit the entire coast from the southern extremity of the peninsula of Yucatan to the Isthmus of Darien, and may number in all about 20,000.

They are a quiet, indrustrious and peaceful race of people, but when roused are capable of long and untiring resistance to tyranny, and make excellent soldiers, for when well treated they are extremely docile and susceptible to discipline.

In Guatemala they are possessed of privileges which are denied the half-castes and creoles of that republic, for before Livingston was declared a free port they were permitted to import whatever they needed for the use of their families at but 12 per cent ad valorem duty. Such is the strictures with which they kept their faith with the government, that but few instances occurred of their attempting to evade the tariff or of their selling the goods they entered for their own use to foreigners or to their half-caste neighbors.

The men are of medium size and are very stout and muscular, while the women appear to be a shade or two lighter than the males, are generally short, but are remarkably well formed, as well as exceedingly graceful in their movements.

While not more than one-half of them understand Spanish they all speak English; that is to say, the same mumble-jumble kind of language spoken by the Barbado and Jamaica negroes, for it is as unintelligible to an American traveler as is the dialect of the miners of Cornwall.

Several careless or superficial observers have asserted that these poor people are loose in their morals and that they never marry. These writers are wofully mistaken, for this singular people are exceptionally chaste as compared with the peasantry of almost any European country.

The young girls, as they approach maturity, are watched with jealous care by their parents, and are seldom allowed to associate with the opposite sex of their own years. Upon arriving at the proper age they are given in marriage, and this simple ceremony is considered as binding between the contracting parties. When a Carib sees a girl he fancies he

at once asks her to unite fortunes with him. If the girl likes
him she will answer: "Have you a plantation ready for me?"
That is sufficient. The Carib goes earnestly to work, and clears
and plants an acre or two of land with yuca, plantains, bananas,
etc., builds a hut, and then returns to claim his bride. The
latter, with one of her friends, goes and examines the new plantation. If it suits her she so informs her dusky admirer, and
then, in the presence of their friends, they drink a cup of coffee
between them. This is generally all the marriage ceremony
that takes place, but it is considered binding and irrevocable.
From that time forward the woman is the owner and absolute
mistress of the little plantation, and from its products she
generally supports her lord and children.

It is probable her husband may have other wives, for poly-
gamy seems quite common among these strange people. In
such case the tawny Don Juan lives stated periods with each
of his wives during the year.

These so-called Caribs are very intelligent, and are fairly
industrious. The men occupy their time in fishing—for they
are essentially a race of waterman; or in building dories—
canoes. These boats are of different sizes, from the small
dory that can easily be carried on a man's back to the boat of
ten or twelve tons. They are fashioned out of the trunks of
trees, and are similar to our southern dugout. Strange and
incredible as it may appear to an untraveled reader, some of
these boats are very large. The author has seen vessels, constructed out of single trees that were large enough to carry
twenty-five beef cattle. Such boats are common on the Pacific
side of the Isthmus of Darien.

The female Caribs are yet more industrious than their husbands, fathers and brothers, for they are the agriculturists of
the settlements, and when not engaged in their household
duties are either working in their fields or accompany their
husbands on their fishing expeditions.

So stalwart and hearty are they that they can accomplish as
much work in a day as their brothers, and when they "work
out" obtain the same wages as the men. Since the Guate-

maltecans have been induced to establish fruit plantations, the Carib laborer has advanced from 18¾ to 50 cents per day.

They invariably demand their pay in advance. If a foreigner hires a laborer for fifteen days he must first give him. or her, $7 50 before a stroke of work is done. Then the workman goes happy and contented to his labor. When one breaks his contract—which is seldom—the justice of peace, besides punishing him with a fine, compels him to fulfill his bargain.

Although beef cattle are very cheap, and the adjacent forests abound in various kinds of game, these people seldom eat meat. Their principal diet is composed of fish, of plantains, which are boiled and roasted; bananas, which are generally eaten raw; pineapples and other fruit, while the bread of the country is the cazabe, and is made from a species of yam, called by the people yuca.

This root is ground fine and is then subjected to a severe pressure, for it contains a semi-poisonous juice. When properly prepared, the cazabe bread is very palatable and nutritious, while the yuca root from which it is made is as great a blessing to the Caribs as is the bread-fruit to the islanders of the Pacific.

The commerce of Port Livingston has increased wonderfully during the last few months. Its imports for 1880 were: 6000 packages of miscellaneous merchandise, a total of 574,000 pounds; 1839 barrels of flour, 5646 sacks of salt—a total of 1,139,200 pounds.

The exports during the same period were: 17,000 sacks of coffee (2,125,000 pounds), 2000 hides, 650 bales of sarsaparilla, 100 bales of skins, 20,000 pounds hule (caoutchouc) and $6000 worth of tropic fruits.

This traffic, both export and import, has increased at the rate of 20 per cent for 1883 and 40 per cent for the year 1884. Lately the gold mining excitement that prevails on the banks of the Motagua river has caused the little town of Livingston to assume quite a lively appearance.

The coffee traffic of Livingston may be said to be principally in the hands of the English and the North American merchants. Several invoices have been sent to New Orleans, but for some unknown reason the results were not as favorable as the shipments to other ports have proven. The price in England ruled a very little higher than that obtained in New York, while the sales in New Orleans fell far below those of England.

It is barely possible that the shipments sent to our city may have been of an inferior quality, but merchants of Livingston assert that the article in each case was identical, and that for some unknown reason Guatemala coffee seems to be better appreciated in the North and in Europe than in New Orleans.

Some of this coffee has been lately sampled in New Orleans, and was pronounced superior to the ordinary grades of Rio that come to this maket, and nearly, if not quite, equal to the Mexican Cordoba staple. Nearly four years ago two enterprising young Americans, Messrs. Anderson and Owen, established steamboat communication on the river Poliche and the Golfo Dulce. Thus almost all this coffee and freight traffic passes through their hands, for such is the confidence they have inspired among the merchants of the interior that they are permitted to ship it when and how they please. This enterprise has greatly influenced the increase of traffic from Port Livingston, and it is said that the firm will soon need more boats.

The port of Champerico, on the Pacific coast, has lately become quite important, for a large quantity of coffee is shipped to foreign countries. The port is connected with a town twenty-eight miles in the interior by a well-constructed narrow gauge railroad. This road passes through a most prolific agricultural region.

CHAPTER VII.

While more than a hundred flourishing cities and towns are found within the limits of Guatemala, a city of the same name is the capital of the Republic, and the principal centre of population that exists throughout the extended territorial area of Central America.

Three different cities bearing the same name were founded by the Spaniards during their occupation of the country. The first, or la Ciudad Vieja, was situated upon the site of the ancient capital of the aboriginal kings, which had been partially destroyed by Alvarado during the conquest. The new city boasted many fine buildings and imposing churches, monasteries and convents. It was suddenly overwhelmed, early the morning of the 11th of November, 1541, by a torrent of water that burst from the side of the tall mountain of Hunahpa. For two or three days before this catastrophe occurred, floods of rain fell from the surcharged clouds, and terrible squalls of wind, at intervals, burst over the devoted city. Near the summit of the volcano a vast lake or natural deposit of rain water had gradually collected. About two o'clock, that fatal Sunday morning, a series of earthquakes were experienced; the shocks were both prolonged and severe. Of a sudden, "a great noise like the simultaneous firing of a thousand cannons" was heard by the terrified inhabitants. The porphyritic ribs of the great mountain were torn asunder by the earthquake's convulsions, and the waters of the vast aereal lake, released from its confinement, poured down the steep side of the tall mountain and deluged the adjacent plain. The beautiful city was instantaneously overwhelmed. The moiety of its solid edifices and all the houses of the

Aborigines were swept away, while the majority of the inhabitants were submerged by the deluge. Among those who
perished was the beautiful but haughty and imperious Beatriz
de la Cueva, the wife of the impetuous and chivalrous conqueror, Pedro de Alvarado.

The few surviving Castillians determined to found a new
city. A site, about three miles from the former, was chosen,
and in a few years the "proud Ciudad de los Caballeros de
Santiago," adorned with magnificent churches and proud
monastaries and convents, graced the edge of a verdant valley whose southern boundary was formed by the volcano
which had destroyed La Ciudad Vieja.

This new city, or as it is now called, La Antigua Guatemala,
existed 232 years. It was equal in size and wealth to any of
the great capitals founded by the Spaniards in the New World,
excepting that proud city of the lakes, the Tenoctitlan of
the Aztecs, Mexico, the metropolis of the vast province of
New Spain.

In the year 1773, this second colonial capital was destroyed
by a series of earthquakes which followed each other with
astonishing rapidity. Several of its proud churches, whose
ruins to-day attest their vast strength and architectural beauty,
were overthrown, while not one of the numerous chapels,
monastaries and convents escaped the devastating effects of
the earthquake. Almost all the private residences were destroyed, while numerous of its unfortunate inhabitants were
swallowed up in the huge chasms that yawned open for awhile
and then suddenly closed. To-day a few people inhabit the
ruined city, but its streets are almost deserted, while the
mouldering ruins of its famous religious edifices indicate to
the awe stricken tourist what it once had been.

The situation of this formerly flourishing centre of population is extremely picturesque. Its convent yards, spacious
squares and beautiful gardens have been transformed into
coffee groves, while half-naked Indian laborers, of both sexes,
stare with stupid wonder upon the immense piles where once
holy monks murmured their daily orisons. They patiently
gather the harvest which timidly hides from the fierce glare

of the tropic sun, under the deep green foliage of the coffee trees, that flourish in the once spacious gardens where gentle nuns chased the gaudy butterfly which in all its tinted glory flitted from branch to branch and from flower to flower.

Two tall mountains guard the approach of this magic valley. The water volcano, inactive since the epoch of the destruction of the first city, rears its bold summit 13,350 feet above the level of the sea; while the fire volcano, which at times sullenly emits huge volumes of mingled fire and smoke, attains an attitude of 12,900 feet.

The present capital of the Republic, the far-famed city of Guatemala, was founded in the year 1794 by the terrified inhabitants of the lately destroyed Ciudad de los Caballeros de Santiago. That is to say, numerous of the most wealthy inhabitants of the former city fled to the site of the present capital immediately after the destruction of La Antigua.

It was some time, however, before the home government permitted the removal of the provincial government to the present city. Guatemala, therefore, in comparison with some of its sister centres of population—Escuintla, for instance—is one of the most recently founded cities of the Republic. It is situated on the edge of a vast plain, which on all sides is surrounded by high mountain ranges, and contains a population of at least 60,000 souls.

The site of the capital was formerly known by the name of El Valle de los Vacas, from the fact that the plain was occupied by one of the companions of the conquerer, a certain Hector de la Barreda, as a stock farm, where were collected he first cattle introduced into the province, in the year 1529.

This locality enjoys one of the most delightful and healthy climates of the known world. Although the valley attains an altitude of but about 3000 feet above the level of the sea, the calenturas and other malarial fevers, so prevalent along the sandy shores of the Pacific slope never surmount the mountain barriers that guard the entrance to the wide plain.

The small pox, that loathsome and dread disease which was introduced into Mexico in 1520, by a negro who followed the forces of Pamfilio Navaaz, rapidly spread among the tribes and

nations of the New World. For 350 years it has periodically
made its appearance in different localities of Mexico and Central America. In 1884 it ravaged the aboriginal settlements
of Guatemala and San Salvador. At different periods it has
become epidemic in the capital. Under the present enlightened
and truly paternal government, the sanitary condition of the
capital has been vastly improved, thus whenever sporadic cases
of the disease appear the utmost care is taken to prevent its
spread. Isolated cases of Typhus and Typhoid fever have
occasionally occurred but the fever has never assumed the proportions of an epidemic. Upon the whole the capital may be
pronounced an exceptionally healthy city. Foreigners who
take up their residence in it enjoy excellent health.

An excellent system of cleanliness prevails; every day early
in the morning the streets are swept while no garbage of any
kind is allowed to remain on the sidewalks or in the gutters.

The city is supplied with excellent water, from the different
localities by aqueducts built in the old Spanish style, about
five miles long. Thirty public fountains adorn the public
squares and plazas from which reservoirs the poorer inhabitants
draw their daily supply of the precious fluid. A few years ago,
Gen. Barrios granted a franchise to a company to establish a
" water works " for the purpose of supplying the growing demands of the capital with water from the river Zapote.

Several of the churches of Guatemala would adorn the proud-
est city in the world. The cathedral, although of modern construction, is a truly grand edifice. It faces the principal plaza.
On one side of the square are the offices of the municipal government, and the telegraph and railroad departments. Directly
fronting the cathedral is the Federal palace which occupies an
immense square and contains all the numerous departments
and offices of the general government. On the left side, as one
stands in front of the church, with his back to it, is a row of
fine stores where foreign and domestic manufactured merchandise is exposed for sale. The cathedral and the bishop's palace occupy the front of an entire square.

This grand edifice is over three hundred feet long and is
nearly as wide as it is long. It contains five naves, while the

stone portal is exquisitely sculptured. A short distance from the main entrance, fronting the plaza, stand colossal statues of the four evangelists, while within the spacious edifice, in the tall columns and the high walls, hang some of the finest paintings that can be found on the continent. The churches of San Francisco, La Merced and Santo Domingo, are also fair examples of Spanish-American architecture.

The former contains the celebrated NEGRO CHRIST whose votaries number legion, and whose miracles have shed a glory over the one universal religion and the church of Central America. While other images may enjoy a local reputation, this one in particular is famed throughout the extensive area of Latin America as one of the most potent of the numerous sacred statues that grace the niches of the various edifices dedicated to the worship of the Redeemer of mankind. An impartial Christian might well hesitate were he called upon to decide as to the superiority of the claims to miraculous power advanced by the enlightened devotees of the three famous images of the Virgin of Guadeloupe of Mexico; that of Remedios; or the famous Cristo Negro of Guatemala. There are at least a score of other fine churches that might be mentioned but the above noticed four are most remarkable on account of their architectural beauty and superior reputation for sanctity.

The heretical government administered by the great reformer Don J. Rufino Barrios, has taken possession of the principal of the grand monastaries and convents and transformed them into government offices. The new post office is an example of this kind. Other monastic edifices have been turned into private dwellings, and no few of the elite of the capital have incurred the penalty of excommunication by having purchased, repaired, altered and lived in buildings that once were the property of the church.

The National Theatre is a fine edifice of modern construction. It is situated in the centre of a vast square, which is walled in and provided with benches of solid masonry. This theatre will compare favorably, as to size and convenience with most of the buildings of the same kind in Christendom. The pit, or orchestra, is generally reserved for gentlemen. Around the

vast area four tiers of boxes capable of holding many spectators
are arranged. The first two tiers are specially devoted to the
wealthy descendants of the chivalrous conquerors, the third
row is occupied by the bourgeoise, while the fourth and last
tier is the exclusive domain of the masses. As the opera and
theatre are the principal public diversions of the Guatemaltecans, the government, through the medium of one of the federal departments arranges for all theatrical representations.
Some of the best companies of Italy and Spain are lured thither
by the heavy subsidies paid them from the treasury, nor would
it be an exaggeration to assert that the paternal government
of Gen. Barrios, has, within the past twelve years, paid in
theatrical subsidies, a large enough sum to build and equip a
half a dozen fine gun-boats.

The people of the city, boast with pride of the numerous
benevolent institutions they possess. The general hospital is
a vast structure where seldom less than five hundred patients
are daily treated. A special fund is set apart for its mainten-
ance, while skilful native physicians, many of whom are grad-
uates of the most celebrated medical colleges of the United
States and of Europe, attend to the vast number of sick committed to their charge. The military hospital, in the southwestern portion of the city, (or rather in the suburb of that
quarter) is also a most admirably conducted institution. The
sick are well cared for while the convalescents are furnished the
most nourishing and nutritions diet that money can purchase.
A gymnasium for the exercise of the most advanced convalescents, has been established while pleasant walks and beautiful
gardens adorn the grounds in which the edifice is situated. The
Hospitium is an institution for the reception of crippled children and confirmed invalids. It is divided into two separate
departments, one of which is devoted exclusively to the male
and the other the female patients. The children undergo a
thorough course of primary education during their stay in this
humane institution. There are also two maternal asylums
where indigent mothers can leave their offsprings while employed in their daily labor.

Almost immediately after he assumed the reins of government, the great liberal chieftain, Gen. Barrios, conferred upon

his country an admirable public school system, exclusively devoted to secular education. Before his advent to power the education of the young was almost entirely in the hands of the priesthood. The result may easily be imagined. The pupils were compelled to devote no small portion of their time to purely theological studies, while even the children of the poor, whose opportunity for study and improvement was necessarily very limited, were more thoroughly grounded in the catechism, doctrines and dogmata of their religion than the secular elementary branches which certainly were calculated to prove of more material benefit to them in their temporal career. The new system of education being purely secular, as was above stated, has certainly brought about a great change in the sociology of Guatemala. The masses are gradually becoming elevated to a higher grade of civilization, while every insigni·ficant little Indian village boasts at least one primary school.

The capital possesses the most celebrated and best appointed higher educational institutions in Central America. The legal college is a splendid and spacious building where numerous law students receive a first-class training. Its library contains more than ten thousand volumes. The medical college, the school of engineers, and the Politechnique, are in every way peers with their sister institute the legal college.

The National Institute, devoted to secondary instruction may fairly be considered one of the most perfect institutions of its kind on the continent. More than five hundred students from all parts of Central America are daily instructed within its walls. " It is endowed with a zoological museum, a well appointed cabinet for physics and chemistry, an astronomical observatory five storys high, together with numerous out-building·ings which complete the establishment."

The Deaf and Dumb asylum, to which is added a school for the unfortunate inmates, is conducted on the same liberal principle as its sister charitable institutions. The moiety of its regular occupants are the offspring of the indigent class of inhabitants.

The Belen Female Seminary occupies the principal appointments of the old convent of the same name, and is well attended.

The pupils receive an excellent education. In this institution Mr. Batres assures us nothing but English is spoken.

Besides these institutes of learning there are numerous public schools devoted to primary instruction in the different quarters of the city. As education is compulsory these latter schools are invariably well attended.

The private residences of the wealthy inhabitants are noted for their elegant appearance. They are invariably furnished in a most luxurious style, while their spacious courtyards are adorned with flower gardens which contain the most exquisite exotics of the tropics. As the capital is the residence of the most wealthy and enterprising planters, mine owners and merchants of the republic, the number of beautiful and costly private houses may be readily imagined.

Numerous public squares furnish walks and promenades for that class of inhabitants whose means will not permit the luxury of horses and carriages. On certain evenings of the week the members of the elite of Guatemaltecan society frequent these squares and listen to the music of the military bands, while promenading along the flower bordered walks.

Several lines of street cars furnish ample transportation for the inhabitants of the city. One line from the Palacio Nacional to the Hippodrome, or race course, is particularly patronized by the middle class who every evening ride down the spacious Prado to the terminus of the line.

The city of Guatemala possesses the best organized, appointed and efficient police force of any city in Latin America. During his visit to the United States, three years ago, President Barrios was greatly pleased with the appearance of the New York police force. He determined to organize a similar body in his own capital. He engaged the services of an experienced New York police officer, Capt. Pratt, and put his intention into immediate execution. This officer has succeeded in carrying out Gen. Barrios' idea to perfection, and has already done wonders with the crude material given him to mould into shape.

If it possesses no grand manufactories like New York, Philadelphia or Chicago, Guatemala contains numerous forges, carpenter shops, and small factories of various kinds which have flourished under the present liberal administration. The native artisans of all classes are skilful and patient workmen, and with better tools and some further practical instruction would rank peer with any of their class in the world. As stone masons they are unrivalled. In some branches of this work they are superior workmen to their fellows of the United States and Europe.

With its clean, well paved streets, its numerous grand public buildings and its finely appointed baths; its spacious military barracks and its grand and beautifully adorned squares, Guatemala, the proud capital of the prosperous and go-ahead Central American republic, is truly one of the finest cities within the extended limits of Latin America.

CHAPTER VIII.

Mountain Ranges and Foot-Hills—The Cochineal Insect—Coffee District of Retalhulen—Mr. Batre's List of Agricultural and Forest Products —Torrents, Rivers, Lakes and Watercourses—The River Dulce and the Golfite—The Coffee Regions of Alta Paz—Coffee Production in Gautemala a Complete Success.

The surface of the republic is corrugated by numerous mountain ranges, by their spurs and also by chains of tall foot hills which divide the country into numberless plains, savannas, and valleys. On the Pacific coast the mountain flanks slope abruptly downwards, leaving between them and the sea a vast fertile plain in which are situated the cities of Retalhulen and Escuintla. They are the centres of promising and flourishing agricultural districts. This plain—or rather, as the country is broken by mountain spurs here and there—these valleys are noted for their prolific yield of sugar cane, indigo, corn, rice and cochineal. The latter valuable article of commerce, is a very minute insect which thrives on a species of the nopal or prickly pear. Vast plantations of this cactus are cultivated. When the harvest approaches, sheets are placed under the plants, which are violently shaken, and the insects by thousands fall upon them. As soon as they leave the parent and life sustaining leaves they immediately die, and losing their bright crimson color, turn to a dingy hue. The color returns, however, in the process of transforming the insect into the brilliant dye which, for a long time, superceded in the markets of Europe the Tyrian purple that for more than thirty centuries was the most valuable and famous dying extract known to the world.

The entire Pacific slope, from the mountain bases to the ocean, is susceptible of being brought into the highest grade of productiveness, but its climate is hot and arid, and its products are essentially those of the torrid zone. Retalhulen, which is situated at an altitude of about 2000 feet above the sea, is the centre of a great coffee growing district. It is also the present terminus of the Champerico railroad.

The agricultural and forest products are numerous, valuable and varied. The following list furnished by Mr. Batres in his " Sketch of Guatemala" may be considered as complete, as far as the present knowledge of the subject extends, for there are vast stretches of territory in the northeastern portion of the republic where the foot of white man has never trodden, and where most probably hitherto unknown species of medicinal and other valuable plants will yet be discovered.

" Who, then, can for a moment doubt the dazzling future of this portion of the New World? It is sufficient to take into consideration its geographical position, its fertile soil, its valuable productions and all the natural riches it contains. Both oceans bathe with their crested waves the hot sands of the extended coast-lines of Central America. The variety of climate is so extraordinary that this fertile region furnishes the greatest diversity of forest and agricultural resources. While on the one hand exist inexhaustible deposits of gold, silver, lead, opals and coal in deposits, hitherto but superficially worked, we, on the other hand, encounter virgin forests abounding with valuable woods. The coffee shrub exhibits its white blossoms and ruby-colored fruit; indigo (añil) is cultivated on a vast scale. Thus over a vast expanse of territory we find growing wild the balsam tree, baptized by naturalists with a great many names (the myroxilon Sonsonatense, myrospermum pereiræ, myroxilon punctatus, miroxilion robinia-folium, myrospermum Salvatoriense); there are entire forests of the India Rubber tree (Siphonia elástica), at present a source of incalculable wealth; there are waving fields of the sugar cane; the most exquisite textile plants, like, for example, the maguey (Agave Americana), the saltwort, the soft rush (carludovica palmata), the capulin (tidia argentea), the soft aloe (furcroya gigantea), all capable of becoming the basis for remunerative industry; resins, gums and balsams are met with on all hands, like, for instance, the liquid amber (styracifera), the mángle (rhizofera), the guapinol (himenea courbarie), the copal tree, the estoraque or officinal storax, the turpentine fir, vegetable wax (myrica cerifera), vegetable soap tree (myristica sebifera), the sarsaparilla root (smilax zarzaparrilla), the nanacascalote

(Divi-divi) tree, and the chan (salvia-chio), quinine bark, vanilla beans, cocoa (theobroma cacao), the Chiapas pimento tree (Eugenia pimenta), the tamarind tree, and a great many other valuable trees indigenous to those latitudes.. Over broad fields the golden wheat and tall Indian corn undulate in the wide expanse, while at the same time the fruits of all zones are exhibited in the same market. Thanks to the extreme variety of temperature, all of them are in a small extent of territory. Cochineal, cabinet and dye-woods, vie in abundance and excellence in Central America, together with hides, skins of numerous animals, etc., etc.

While the native writers of Guatemala dwell with just enthusiasm upon the number of beautiful rivers that water the soil, there exist but few worthy of the name. The Polochic and Motagua, the Passion and the Dulce, the Usumacinta and the Michatoya are the only ones that are navigable for small boats. The other rivers of the republic are mere mountain torrents or watercourses.

On his journeys through the country the traveller notices many small bodies of fresh water which are denominated lakes by the people of the vicinity. But four of them in reality deserve this imposing title. These are the lakes of Atitlin, Yzabal, Petin and Itzal, and are situated in localities widely separated from each other.

The little Guatemaltecan port of Livingston is washed on one side—the southern—by the waters of El Rio Dulce, the river of sweet water. This winding river, at its mouth, is very wide and deep. After a course of fifteen miles to the west, it spreads and forms a wide but deep sheet of water, called by the natives, " El Golfite," which is about nine miles wide by fifteen long. A short distance to the west it spreads out much wider than before and becomes the "Laguna de Yzabal" the Lake of Yzabal, which body of water is navigable for vessels of deep draft. Lake Yzabel covers a superficial area of about 65,000 acres. During the rainy season severe wind and rain storms not unfrequently visit this usually calm region, and vent their fury on the unprotected lake, whose waters are lashed into foam by the irresistible squalls that sweep down from the contiguous mountain summits.

On the right side of the lake, as one journeys from the mouth of the river towards the interior, is situated the little town of Yzabal, which is again the single port of entry for the eastern coast of the Republic. A trip from the port of Livingston, as far as the town of Yzabal, is one long vista of beautitful tropical scenery. At one place, about five miles from where the river flows into the "Golfite," its waters have burst through a vast rocky barrier and cut a passage to the sea through this flinty obstacle. On either side the rocks rise high and precipitous over the rushing flood beneath, and form a long line of palisades, far superior in scenic effect to those of the Hudson, while the fantastic shapes, assumed by the rocks which were torn apart at some remote geologic period, strike the eye of the beholder as the work of Titanic sculptors. At one place the statue of a woman is seen, clearly cut and defined standing on a pedestal, while the figure must be at least forty-five feet high. As the tourist nears the statue it loses its faultless outline, but at the distance of a mile or so it has the appearance of a perfect work of art. Temples and palaces, domes and towers, crowd upon the bewildered vision of the traveler as his craft follows the turns of the winding river, and it is only when the boat passes directly under them that he dis-covers the palaces, domes and statues he saw are the mere vagaries of his fancy, which had been conjured into existence by the fantastic shapes assumed by the surface of the rocky barrier.

From the mouth of the Rio Dulce to the Lake Yzabal is full thirty miles. The lake is twenty-six miles long, thus the hither end at the mouth of the Rio Polochic. which might be termed a continuation of El Rio Dulce, is fifty-six miles from Port Livingston. The Polochic river runs a generally eastern course, from its source in the vast mountain range that cuts the re-public from north to south, of about eighty miles before it min-gles its waters with those of Lake Yzabal.

About forty miles from its mouth is situated the little town of Panzos, the head of navigation and the commercial centre of all Eastern Guatemala. The actual distance from Panzos to Lake Yzabal is much greater by water, in consequence of the serpentine course pursued by the Polochic. This river is deep in places but is often along its entire course obstructed by shoals, yet it is in reality navigable far above Panzos for large dorys. Not far from Panzos is situated the town of Coban, which is the centre of the great coffee region of Guatemala, for Alta Paz is not far from Coban, and at this former locality the principal coffee plantations of Eastern Guatemala are congregated.

It is safe to assume that the coffee industry of Alta Paz will represent a capital of at least $10,000,000. As each of the planters are annually setting out more trees, the yearly increase of the acreage of the staple is estimated at about 150 manzanas, or 300 acres. Four winters ago, for the first time since the conquest of the country by the Spaniards, frost visited Coban, and blighted millions of the younger plants.

Some of the farmers pruned the trees thus injured close to the ground. They have grown up again, and in two years bore equally as well as an ordinary five year old tree. Those injured plants that were not thus treated invariably died. Their places have since been filled by young trees which have begun to bear. Notwithstanding this misfortune, the ensuing coffee crop was even larger than the one that preceded it. The harvest of 1884, produced 3,500,000 pounds for export, besides a large quantity consumed in the country.

The coffee trees of Alta Paz flourish in an atmosphere and in a soil in every way congenial to the perfect development of their fruit. The neighboring mountains covered with luxuriant growth of forest timber, attract rain and conduce to moisture, and as the coffee tree is an essentially tender shrub, it shrinks from the intense glare of the tropic sun and thrives best in moist and humid localities.

For several years even after it has begun to bear, it requires protection from the sun, and is generally planted between rows of trees or under the protecting shade of the huge leaved banana. An hour's exposure to the vertical tropic sun would most probably greatly injure, if not destroy, a four year old tree, thus, it may be seen if the cultivation of coffee is profitable, the planter must be ever on the lookout and guard his precious trees from any sudden exposure to the heat.

The eight year old trees of Coban, or rather Alta Paz, will, so it is asserted, yield an average of two and a half pounds per tree each picking season. Those of Cordova, Mexico, are even more prolific and will give about three pounds, under favorable circumstances. The coffee plant of Costa Rica and San Salvador, of Nicaragua and Brazil will not average more than one pound and a half per tree. There is one locality, however, at Uruapan, Mexico, where the coffee tree grows larger and yields more than in any other part of the world. From some as yet unexplained cause, the plant assumes the appearance of small apple trees, while numerous of them have several times yielded from twelve to forty-eight pounds per harvest.

But if no such phenomenal growth and production of the coffee plant takes place at Alta Paz in Guatemala, its growth is steady, and it arrives at maturity at the age of five years, from which period it will produce a constant yield of about two and a half pounds yearly until it reaches the age of, perhaps, forty years. This industry is destined to become one of the most important of the agricultural enterprises of Eastern Guatemala. If at times the price has ruled low, in the end its cultivation is extremely profitable, for it has been estimated that if the staple sold on the place for but six cents per pound, it would pay 12 per cent on the actual money invested in its production.

The following is a list of the principal merchants and coffee growers of Coban. A glance at it will satisfy even the most careless observer as to the nationality of these same planters and merchants.

Sarg Hermanos, Duseldorff & Co., Pablo Surra & Co., Francisco Planos, Van Nostiz & Co., W. A. Duseldorff, D. H. Turkheim, D. M. Connell, Henry Littlepage, S. M. Slattern, Julius Wolter, Herman Helmrich, L. Castelano.

Of these houses, seven are either German or bear German names, three are Spanish or native, while but two are English.

It will be safe to calculate that although two-thirds of the products of Central America go to England, two thirds of the merchants of the five republics are German or are of German descent.

Notwithstanding these gentlemen are extremely patriotic, and at their social gatherings drink deeply to their dear "fatherland," they are not so patriotic as to send their produce to Germany if they can get a better price for it in England or in the United States.

In their capacity of planters they have to feed many thousands of laborers, and they need American produce to enable them to do so. By consequence they are very anxious to enter into closer trade relations with the United States. If the merchants of New Orleans ignore this promising traffic, those of New York and Philadelphia do not.

Last month three steamers from the former port, and two from the latter touched at all the Central American ports, from Belize southward along the coast to Costa Rica, while certain English ocean tramps regularly take cargo at Livingston.

As was said before, the giant range of mountains that separate Guatemala into two parts, about equally wide, is an almost impassable barrier between the two sections of the Republic. It will be several years before the enterprise of man will unite the Pacific ocean and the Caribbean sea by a railroad. Until the *desideratum* is accomplished, Eastern and Western Guatemala will be virtually separated; at least commercially so. Thus the entire commerce of Eastern Guatemala is destined to centre at or near Panzos. From this point communication with the sea is easy and safe and is rapid, while the Government has ordered the construction of large receiving warehouses at Port Livingston to accommodate the growing commerce of the locality.

While New Orleans can put coffee in Philadelphia for $\frac{1}{4}$c. per pound, she has made no effort to secure the control of the flourishing coffee traffic of Guatemala. The crop this year will amount to about 3,500,000 pounds, of which a million pounds is consumed in the country, the remainder of which will be freighted to Europe, to New York and to California. The coffee crop of Alta Paz should seek this market by consequence of the contiguity of New Orleans to the producing centre, in comparison with New York and Europe, for the Crescent City is but 900 miles distant from Port Livingston and the latter is about 100 miles from the plantations of Alta Paz. Thus New Orleans is just 1000 miles distant from the eastern coffee fields of Guatemala; New York about twice as far and England is, in round numbers, say, 6000 miles distant. This coffee trade should be enjoyed by the merchants of the Mississippi valley, and might be, were the dealers in the article to make as sincere efforts to secure it as their Eastern and English rivals do to retain it.

The coffee crop of Central Guatemala is very abundant this year. For some time the low price at which this staple has ruled in Europe and America has had a most depressing effect throughout the coffee-producing centres of the hemisphere. While the planters of Brazil, Colombia, Venezuela, Costa Rica and Nicaragua have been constantly losing money for the last three years, their more fortunate brethern of Honduras, Guatemala and Mexico have managed to make somewhat more than their expenses. In the three last mentioned countries the rate of wages for agricultural labor yet rules comparatively low. In Brazil the gradual emancipation of the slaves will, doubtless, decrease. the acreage of coffee planting. In Venezuela, Colombia, Costa Rica and Nicaragua (all of which republics are in direct and constant communication with the Isthmus of Panama) the labor market is seriously affected by the comparatively high rate of wages paid laborers by the Panama Canal Company. This latter enterprise employs thousands of workmen at an average price of $1 50 per day. Coffee planters cannot afford to pay such extravagant prices for labor, and, by consequence, these four republics are experiencing an alarming shrinkage in their coffee-producing area.

Another advantage, beside the low rate of wages that obtains in Guatemala, is experienced by the planters of the latter country. Its enterprising and enlightened President, Gen. Barrios, has several times issued decrees regulating the labor supply. Criminals instead of being carefully housed, fed on the fat of the land and maintained at government expense, are compelled to work on railroad enterprises and plantations. In a population of 1,500,000 souls are found 950,000 of the working class. But this aboriginal race hates to labor for the patri-

cian caste, and will only work when necessity compels them·
Gen. Barrios, by suppressing and enacting severe laws against
voluntary pauperism, has driven a vast number of hitherto non-
producers into the coffee groves, the cane and nopal fields and
the mahogany forests. In rural centres of population the most
incorrigibly lazy adults are pressed into the army, and the
rest are compelled to labor in the coffee fields for a certain
number of days per annum. But while thus rendering labor
compulsory, the health, well-being, comfort and wages of the
laborers receive the strict attention of the government, and
in no case has the just complaint of the workman against his
employer been unheeded. The beneficial effect of this legisla-
tion was remarkably apparent during the last two years. The
railroad enterprises were at a stand-still for want of laborers.
Hundreds of idle Indians were drafted and put to work on the
Guatemala Central and Champerico roads. The coffee trees
were growing wild and neglected; sufficient agricultural laborers were dispatched to the plantations to insure the safety
of the harvest and the plants.

Thus the high rate of wages that rules in other coffee-producing centres, and the comparatively low price that obtains
in Guatemala, together with the ample amount of either voluntary or enforced labor disposable, seems to render the future
success of the coffee producing industry of Guatemala beyond
question.

CHAPTER IX.

Few Wagon Roads and Bad Bridle Paths—Mule and Donkey Pack Trains—Unique System of Transportation—The Guatemala Central and Champerico Railroads—The Northern Line—The Shea and Cornick Contract—The Lyman and Gordon Concession—Mahogany Cutting—Mining Industry—Manufactures—Future of the Country.

While there are several fine roads, leading from the capital in different directions, they degenerate into mere bridle paths at the distance of a few leagues from the city. The road to Escuintla is a fair highway; that to Coban was constructed at a vast expense. The road to the old cities of Guatemala passes through a broken and rugged mountain country. The rest of the republic is traversed by mountain and bridle paths. The system of transportation employed is naturally slow and expensive, pack mules and donkeys being principally employed in this industry.

If, as political economists assert, the prosperity of a nation depends upon its cheapness of transportation, Central America is far from being a prosperous territory. But the present energetic and patriotic ruler of Guatemala, Gen. Barrios, has turned his attention to this important problem, and quick and cheap passenger and freight transportation has been decreed. A few years since he started a subscription to build a railroad from the Pacific port of San José to the capital. A line was eventually constructed from the coast to Escuintla, a distance of about twenty-eight or thirty miles. For a long time the enterprise hung fire, but about two years ago Messrs. Crocker, Stanford and Huntington, of San Francisco, bought the line from its original owners and continued it to the capital city. This syndicate has entered into arrangements for the construction of several other Central American railroads, while the principal of their undertakings have their scene of operations within the limits of Guatemala and San Salvador.

About four years since, Messrs. Lyman & Fenner, two enterprising American gentlemen, obtained a concession to construct

7

a line from the little Pacific port of Champerico to the city of
Retalhuelan, a distance of some twenty-eight or thirty miles.
Mr. Bell, a well known Californian banker, provided the funds
and the Government furnished a liberal subsidy besides a large
grant of land. If the assertions of the Guatemaltecan statesmen may be credited, the subsidy, which is being paid with
the utmost regularity, will cover the entire expenses of construction. This arrangement, which certainly must meet the
approval of the owners of the line, seems also to suit the
Government and the people, for if the former advanced their
money at a time when Guatemaltecan securities were at a low
figure, and took what at that epoch seemed a great risk, the
planters of the Retalhuelan coffee district are contented with
the simple circumstance of having secured quick and certain
transportation to the coast.

Shortly after construction work was commenced on the road,
Mr. Lyman, for some reason not explained, withdrew from the
enterprise, which, since that epoch, has continued under the
sole management of his partner, Dr. D. P. Fenner.

This little enterprise has proved to be extremely remunerative to all concerned. Quite a quantity of mixed freight is
daily shipped at the several stations and numerous passengers
are constantly traveling between the port of Champerico and
Retalhuelan. During the coffee season, business is unusually
brisk, and the Pacific Mail Steamship Company's vessels
touch at the port once a week.

It will not be long before this enterprise is extended to the
capital, for the Government has offered its manager extremely
liberal terms. Thus another grand agricultural region will
be opened to commerce and immigration, and flourishing
plantations, now virtually cut off from the capital and the sea
port, will be placed in rapid and regular communication with
both.

The golden dream of both the government officials and the
people in general is to secure rail communication between the
Pacific and Caribbean coasts. The prolongation of the Guatemala Central from the town of Escuintla to the capital has
solved the first portion of the problem. No sooner had Gen-

Barrios made arrangements with the Huntington syndicate for the continuation of the Escuintla branch to Guatemala City than he turned his serious attention towards the realization of the remaining part of the plan. After mature deliberation he determined that all the inhabitants of the Republic should bear a portion of the burden, and that the proposed road should be the property of the people as well as of the nation. Two years ago he issued a decree which constituted each male and female inhabitant of the Republic who earned the sum of *eight dollars* per month a shareholder. Each person so situated is required to pay $40 in ten years for one share, or rather more than four per cent per annum on his or her gross earnings. He at once subscribed and paid cash for five hundred shares. All of the principal military and civil officers followed his example and took as many shares as their means warranted. Many who occupied subordinate positions, and who took but one share, paid for it at once. All the rest are compelled to make quarterly payments of $1 at a time.

Contrary to the expectations—and perhaps the hopes—of the remaining political enemies of the administration, who predicted that the promulgation of this, in their eyes, arbitrary and unconstitutional decree, would culminate in a disastrous revolution and the overthrow of the government, the measure, instead of rendering Gen. Barrios odious, has, if possible, increased his popularity. The merchants of the capital, and the planters and land owners whose property lies contiguous to the proposed route of the new road, have subscribed liberally. The military and civil officials are proud of the opportunity offered them of thus sustaining the project of their beloved chieftain; while the Indian rancheros, storekeepers, arrieros, artisans and laborers, whose monthly earnings bring them within the limits of the decree, pay their quarterly instalments with the utmost promptness, and seemingly with corresponding pleasure, for their vanity is gratified by being stockholders in the great undertaking. This new line is known as the Northern Railroad, and the president or manager of the concern is the famous Don Angel Peña, a gentleman whose name has long been looked upon as a synonym for honesty and integrity by his fellow citizens.

The entire cost of the undertaking from Guatemala City to the coast, a distance of about 206 miles, was estimated at $12,000,000 by the government engineer, Sylvanus Miller, Esq., an American gentleman, who for many years has been identified with the railroad movement of Central America. This engineer has carefully surveyed the country from the capital to the coast, and has chosen the definite direction of the line. The route runs from Guatemala City in a general northeasterly course and strikes the Motagua river at a point near Zacapa. From thence it runs to El Mico, not far from the hacienda of Gen. Rascon. From this latter point it proceeds directly to the coast, and terminates at Port Barrios, the site chosen for the eastern terminus.

Within a few months after the decree was promulgated, the rapid payment of subscriptions, by the wealthier inhabitants, swelled the railroad fund in the coffers of the President to at least $500,000, and bids were asked for the construction of the first division of the road, from Port Barrios, on the Caribbean coast, to El Mico, a point some sixty-two miles in the interior.

An American citizen—resident of Guatemala, named Millen, entered into a contract with the government for the construction of the first division of the road. This gentleman made his own terms with the management of the enterprise who accepted his figures and specifications without comment. But it was soon apparent that Mr. Millen had been remarkably unfortunate in his calculations, for the excavation and other construction work cost much more than his estimates, and he was in a short time compelled to suspend further operations.

Meanwhile the attention of the well known railroad contracting firm of Shea, Cornick and Shea, of Knoxville Tenn., was drawn to this enterprise. In March, 1884, Mr. Cornick and Mr. Tim. Shea, accompanied by the author of this work, proceeded to Guatemala city, and assisted by the influence and advice of Dr. D. P. Fenner secured a most favorable contract for the construction of the first division of the road from Port Barrios to El Mico. This work has proceeded very favorably up to date. The principal difficulty encountered by the contractors has been the labor supply, which is inconstant and not over good. They have been compelled to rely principally on imported labor, several hundred of negroes having been sent to the scene of operations from New Orleans alone.

Within a few days after Shea, Cornick & Co. secured their contract, and before they had begun their work, the government entered into still another arrangement for the completion of the proposed road from El Mico to the capital city, with Messrs. Lyman and Gordon of New York. The Lyman in question is the same gentleman who was interested for a period in the Champerico railroad, and his partner is the celebrated ex-Confederate general, J. B. Gordon. As far as can be ascertained, these gentlemen have fulfilled all their preliminary engagements with the government, such as filing their bond and making surveys, etc., and will soon begin construction work at the city of Guatemala.

There are several other different railroad enterprises spoken of in government circles which may soon be undertaken. One in particular, although a comparatively small affair, would prove very profitable to the parties owning it. The coffee district of old Guatemala city is practically cut off from the coast during the rainy months. A line from the destroyed city to tap the Guatemala Central would drain this entire district and could be constructed at a minimum cost.

The other important enterprise spoken of is a line to connect the port of Belize, British Honduras, with the capital of Guatemala. This road would cut directly west, through the English Colony, and then taking a general southwesterly direction would drain the richest and fairest portion of the country. Several well known capitalists have had this matter under consideration for some time, and but little doubt is entertained that when the concurrence of the two governments is obtained that the enterprise will be undertaken.

Even under the present defective transportation system that obtains, the republic enjoys a fair domestic and foreign traffic. The former may safely be set down at $75,000,000 per annum and the latter, in imports and exports at $9,000,000. With better wagon roads and the completion of the present projected railroad system the general traffic of the republic will increase at a rapid ratio, and Guatemala will become one of the most prosperous, wealthy and powerful among the Latin American sisterhood of nations.

The republic has never enjoyed as high a reputation for forest products, as either British Honduras, Spanish Honduras, or Nicaragua. Yet several parties are now busily engaged in mahogany cutting on the banks of the Motagua river. Messrs. Ford, Anderson and Owen and the Saarg Brothers have at different times shipped large quanties of furniture woods to the United States and Europe.

The fruit planting industry has been treated of in another chapter. The government has fostered and protected it and has invariably assisted indigent persons who have started the cultivation of bananas. The principal scene of this industry is in the neighborhood of Port Livingston. The vast stretch of unoccupied land along the banks and contiguous to Lake Yzabal will eventually be occupied by banana and sugar plantations, while the fruit planting industry of Eastern Guatemala is destined to assume imposing proportions.

About a year since a Boston syndicate begun the cultivation of bananas, plantains and pine-apples on a large scale near Port Livingston. Up to date their enterprise has been remarkably successful, and hopes are entertained by its sanguine promoters that they will soon have a large supply of fruit ready for shipment.

Since the epoch of the independence the mining industry of Guatemala has steadily declined until within the past five years, when the discovery of valuable gold placer deposits on the Motagua river and several of its branches gave it a new and vigorous impulse.

During the Spanish regime a vast quantity of gold dust was shipped by Guatemala to the mother country, while several famous silver mines were also worked. It is now a conceded fact that numerous valuable silver deposits have been discovered and located in the mountains near the Honduranean frontier. When the fortunate owners can procure capital to work these lodes the district will probably prove a second Potosi. Mr. Sanchez, the secretary of treasury, showed the author a piece of crude silver that weighed 160 ounces, which was the result of a working assay of 2500 pounds of rock taken at hap-hazzard from his mine. Competent judges have proved this property to be extremely valuable, so Mr. Sanchez proposes to form a company to work it.

About sixty miles from Yzabal are situated the rich placer mines of the Rio Bobos (a tributary of the Motagua), upon which are located the auriferous lands of the Friedman Mining Company of New York. The manager, Mr. Edgar Friedman, has opened a good wagon road, seven miles long, and is now busily engaged in getting up machinery and in piping and opening the main ditch for his supply of water. On the opposite side of the river are the hydraulic works of Messrs. Papadophul, Paximo and Arias. This company bring their water in ditches and flumes, a distance of about two miles. They have sufficient pressure, and are working very successfully. Adjoining these are the lands of Messrs. T. J. Potts and John W. Knight, formerly of Louisiana. These gentlemen have had preliminary surveys made preparatory to putting up hydraulic works on a large scale. Water is plentiful and conveniently situated, and it is calculated that the ground will yield twenty-five cents of gold dust to the cubic yard.

The gold extracted is of a very fine quality; worth about $18 40 per ounce troy at the United States Mint. Another American syndicate has recently denounced a placer near Lake Yzabal. There are also rumors of the discovery of lead and mercury in the same vicinity. These reports, however, as yet lack confirmation.

The republic boasts but few manufactories worthy of the name. The principal supplies of textile goods come from England, notwithstanding the fact that American cotton goods, particularly calicoes, are highly thought of in Guatemaltecan markets. If American manufacturers of this class of goods would consult the taste and customs of their purchasers, they could not only acquire the dry goods trade of the republic but of all the other Latin American markets as well.

There are numerous articles of domestic manufacture that as yet may be considered as unknown beyond the limits of the

republic. Certain localities furnish fine straw hats, others are
famous for tule and straw mats, while in others a warm woolen
cloth is made, which furnishes the poorer classes of the higher
altitudes warm and comfortable clothing.

The departments of the interior possess numerous mountain
streams which can be readily utilized for moving machinery.
Thus when the manufacturing era—which the numerous natural products of the republic indicate will soon be inaugurated
—dawns upon Guatemala a thousand perennial mountain
watercourses will furnish a cheap method of manufacturing to
the future mill kings of the country.

The author has often been asked if he could conscientiously
advise American capitalists to invest their money in the development of the forest, the agricultural and the mineral resources
of this republic in particular, and of Central America in general. In answer he has pointed to the different enterprises
that have been undertaken upon the information imparted by
him to the interested parties, all of which have up to date,
proved remarkably successful. These enterprises will necessitate the eventual employment of several millions of dollars.
Among them the Shea, Cornick & Co.'s railroad construction
work, in Guatemala, and the Honduras timber and fruit planting companies in Spanish Honduras may be cited as examples.

As far as the natural resources of Central America are concerned it is impossible to exaggerate their importance or estimate their value. The cane plantations of Guatemala, average
a yield of 4000 pounds of crude sugar to the acre. Cotton products, 1250 pounds of lint fiber to the same area of land, while
in various localities upland rice returns the grateful planter a
harvest of 250 barrels for one planted. The steep hill sides
yield the simple Indian who merely drops the corn in a hole
and draws the earth over it with his bare toes, sixty bushels
per acre, while the fertile valleys return almost fabulous harvests of wheat, rye and other cereals.

Mr. Hawley, an English traveler who explored the hitherto
unknown portion of the republic, in the Peten region, discovered grand forests of mahogany and tropic cedar, and vast
stretches of land covered with the valuable Brazil tree. In

one of his elaborate political essays, the deceased Guatemaltecan historian, Don José Milla, estimated the market value of the different classes of furniture wood trees, fit to cut, now standing in the primeval forests of Central America, at the vast sum of $700,000,000. This estimate excludes trunks of less than fifteen inches in diameter. When the immense quantity of dye woods and construction timber is added to the above estimate, the curious enquirer may manage to conceive a faint idea of the great value of the forest productions of this fortunate land.

Of the mineral resources of Central America no just estimate can be made. Each of the five republics contain almost innumerable deposits of gold and silver ore. In some localities of Honduras paying placers of silver dust have been discovered. In the same republic a majority of the streams and rivers course over beds that are literally impregnated with golden particles. Throughout the wide area of the Yoro and Olancho Departments it is almost impossible to turn over a spade full of earth without finding "color." This assertion sounds like a tale of the Arabian Nights, but it is nevertheless borne out by stubborn facts.

If, in several cases, American miners have gone thither and have not succeeded, a thousand reasons might be advanced to account for their failure. Overflowing with vanity and pride; considering themselves superior in all things to the natives of the country, they imagine they know everything and only awake from their delusion when they find that their woful ignorance has undone them. They prosecute their work in the rain or under the rays of an intense tropic sun, and when their reckless exposure culminates in sickness, they blame the climate, but lose sight of their gross imprudence. Their failure simply proves their inferiority to their Spanish predecessors, who, with less advantages, and by the employment of the simplest and most primitive methods, for nearly three centuries, forced the unwilling earth and rocks to yield rich tributes of precious metals. If, for the first few decades of their occupation of the country, the Spanish conquerors forced the unwilling natives to work for them, the labor supply was soon exhausted, and their successors were generally compelled to work with their own hands and amass their fortunes by the sweat of their brow.

The American emigrant invariably follows the pernicious example of the American miner. He wishes to introduce the system of farming that obtains in his own country, and often fails where his neighbor, a native of the locality, is rewarded for his judicious management by profitable harvests.

By studying the peculiarities of the climate, and grafting certain American farming principles upon the native system of cultivation, foreign emigrants, if they are prudent and persevering, can scarcely help but succeed. One great drawback to their advancement has been commented upon by the natives. As a general thing they reach the scene of their future labor almost penniless. Many cases may be cited where having planted large areas of sugar cane and cotton, they have been unable to harvest their crops for want of means to purchase sugar machinery, or to pay for the picking of their cotton.

As far as Guatemala is concerned it seems destined to enjoy a brilliant future, under the rule of its able and patriotic President, Gen. Barrios. It is already the wealthiest and most prosperous of the Central American republics. A new generation of statesmen, imbued with liberal sentiments and privileges, has grown up around him; thus ,when he resigns the reins of power, or if death should suddenly strike him in the midst of his glorious career, there are many able to succeed him and carry out the great work of reform he has so ably inaugurated.

With its immense and valuable forest resources, its salubrious climate, and remarkable fertile soil; with its numerous rich deposits of gold and silver ore, and vast placer diggings as rich as the auriferous fields of California or Australia. Guatemala is destined to command the attention of foreign capitalists. Then its fertile soil will be cultivated, its grand forests utilized and its valuable deposits of precious metals be forced to yield their rich tribute. Thus, wealthy, prosperous and happy Guatemala will, before long, assume a proud position among the sisterhood of Latin American Nations.

REPUBLIC OF HONDURAS.

CHAPTER I.

The Discovery of Honduras—Columbus' Adventurous Voyage—Origin of the Name of the Country—The Man Hunters of the Caribbean—Destruction of the Aboriginal Inhabitants of the Antilles and the Introduction of Natives from the Continent as Slaves.

Twelve years had transpired since that memorable day, October 12, 1492, on which the famous navigator, Cristobal Colon, viewed for the first time the shores of the Western Hemisphere.

During these twelve years this extraordinary man had experienced all classes of vicissitudes. His life was often endangered by the tempests of the ocean, or the rage of his exasperated companions; while, on the other hand, he had been greeted with the praise and distinction of his sovereigns and the enthusiastic eulogies of the entire people of Europe, upon his return to his native country, after his astonishing discovery of a new world. Later on he was calumniated and met with cruel treatment and persecution, which indignant public opinion loudly condemned; while his sovereign, who, if he did not authorize these wrongs, gave ground for them by the plenary powers with which he invested those who had carried them into execution. He afterward rendered the illustrious man tardy justice. All these circumstances had tried that great soul, but, without for a moment diminishing the confidence he entertained in his destiny, which he believed yet called him to open new and still unheard of paths of fortune to the human race.

Although his body was racked by physical sufferings, at the advanced age of 76 years, the admiral started upon his fourth and last voyage. He left Cadiz the 9th of May, 1502, in command of five small vessels, the largest of which was scarcely seventy tons' measurement, manned by one hundred and fifty adventurers.

He was accompanied by his brother—the "Adelantado" Don Bartolome Colon, an intrepid and experienced mariner and a man of excellent judgment—and his younger son, Don Fernando, a mere child in years, but whose tender age was supplemented by great strength of mind, which he undoubtedly inherited from his illustrious father.

A terrible tempest, that Colon had predicted and provided against, placed his fragile vessels in imminent danger, when off the Island of Santo Domingo, whose Governor, obeying the instructions he had received from court, refused an asylum in these critical circumstances to him who had years before discovered the same island. The storm dispersed and nearly destroyed the vessels, and it was some days before they collected again, at a port on the western coast of Santo Domingo, where they were repaired.

Continuing his journey, the admiral touched at several small islands and cays which he had seen on his former voyages, and on the 30th of July arrived at Guanaja, which he named the Isle of Pines. This was the first land discovered by the Spaniards in Central America in the sixteenth century.

Don Bartolome Colon, with some of the crew, having disembarked on the island, witnessed the arrival of a canoe of large dimensions, made of the trunk of a single tree. To protect its passengers from the sun and rain it had in the centre a sort of a cabin, formed of mats. In this enclosure were women, children and merchandise. It is supposed that the canoe and cargo belonged to Indian traders, who had loaded it on the coast, a short distance from Yucatan.

The admiral regarded the people of these islands as much more civilized than those of the Antilles, discovered by him during his anterior voyages. The fact of their not being frightened or astonished by the Spanish vessels, nor afraid to approach the strangers; their being better dressed than the West Indians and the class of goods in which they traded, gave force to the admiral's opinion.

The diary of the historian (or notary) of the expedition, Diego de Porros, and the narrative of this voyage written by Colon for the sovereigns of Spain, are sterile of details, and make no mention of meeting with this canoe. But the indefatigable historian, Herrera, who, when writing his interesting "Decades," had access to the works of the first discoverers and conquerors of the New World, says "that those Indian merchants carried copper hatchets, metal plates, and a species of crucible in which to fuze metals. They also possessed superior arms to those common to the West Indies; such as wooden swords, with canals on the edges of the blades, in which were secured sharp, strong pieces of flint, that were held in their places by a kind of cement, or else were fastened with stout cords. They also had vases and other utensils of earthenware, of marble, and of hard wood; and sheets, dickies and overshirts, without sleeves or collars; chocolate in abundance, corn, yams and other alimentary roots, and likewise a beverage, which, from the description given of it, seems to have been a local drink called *chicha.*"

Proceeding onward, the squadron reached the main land on the 14th of August. The admiral and some of his followers landed, and on that day, for the first time, mass was celebrated on Central American soil. This was an event well worthy of record, for it was the commencement of the establishment of a new religion, which was to substitute that false and sanguinary worship which for centuries had cursed this portion of the planet. That place, which was called, then, Caxinas, is the same locality where the port of Truxillo was afterward established.

Against contrary winds the squadron continued advancing along the coast, but without going far from it, and anchoring at night under its shelter. At fifteen leagues from the point of Caxinas a deep river (the Tinto) emptied into the gulf. The boats went a short way up it. The admiral landed with some of his people. On the 17th of August he raised the royal standard of Spain, and took possession of the country in the name of the Spanish sovereign. In Caxinas a new religion was inaugurated, and at the river Tinto, a domination that

was destined to last three hundred years. These events were
the points of departure of the civil and religious transforma-
tion that these countries have since experienced.

A number of Indians, who differed from the people of the
Antilles in language and physiognomy, visited the Spaniards
at the Possession river (which was the name they then gave
the Tinto). Neither did these Indians dress alike. Some
covered half the body, others wore cotton jackets without
sleeves, and the chiefs cotton caps, either- painted or white.
Some went entirely naked, but had their bodies covered with
streaks of paint and figures of animals of divers colors. They
offered the Spaniards provisions, and in return the latter gave
them some objects of but little worth, but the natives regarded
them as of great value.

For many days Colon and his companions coasted that land,
to which they gave the names of *Guaymura*, of *Hibueras* and
of *Honduras*, which latter it retains to this day. They called
it Guaymura because that was the name of an Indian town on
the coast. Hiburas, on account of having found in the sea a
great number of pumpkins, called, in Santo Domingo, tribures;
Honduras, because having sailed a long distance without finding anchorage, when they came once more upon soundings
they exclaimed, "Thank God, we have at length passed these
honduras," (*i. e.*) deep places. A fearful storm endangered
the safety of the vessels and the precious lives they carried.

"The ships were leaking, the sails torn, the anchors, portions of the rigging, cables, boats and much provisions were
lost." Thus the admiral wrote to the sovereigns, adding:
"Other hurricanes I have seen, but none to last so long, nor
so terrible."

The narrative expresses in plain terms the bitterness that
stirred that grand soul. Not because the noble old mariner
thought of his personal peril. The fate of his son, of thirteen
years, and of his brother, who sailed in the worst of the ships,
and who had, against Colons's desire, come with him simply because of the great affection he bore him, painfully affected his
spirit. On the other hand, to find himself far from his country,
soon probably to perish in the solitudes of the ocean, whose

waves threatened to sepulchre, from one instant to the other, his dreams of glory and his hopes of further distinction. He sorrowfully thought of the misfortunes of his family, to whom he could not leave even a poor roof to shelter their heads, and he expressed, in his letter to the sovereigns, the confidence (which perhaps he did not entertain) that they would restore to his eldest son, Don Diego, the honors and the treasures they had dispossessed him of.

Wearied with physical sufferings, unable to rise from his bed, he caused a little temporary cabin to be built on deck, from which he directed the movements of the squadron. But the danger became so extreme that the sailors confessed to each other, and thus prepared for death.

At length, after a long and weary struggle with the elements, on the 12th of September they rounded a cape, the tempest calmed, and a fair wind carried the vessels toward the south. Colon, overcome with gratitude and religious devotion toward the Supreme Being, gave the name of *Cabo Gracias a Dios* (Cape thank God), to the point of land where he experienced the favorable change of wind.

The squadron proceeded along that shore, which afterward received the name of the Mosquito coast. The natives called it Cariay. Being compelled to obtain wood and water, the boats entered one of the several rivers that empty into the Gulf. On their return a stiff breeze began to blow. The sea rose and dashed against the boats, upsetting one of them whose crew was drowned. In memory of this unfortunate event the name of "Disaster" was given to this river by the admiral.

Notwithstanding the bad condition of the vessels, they slowly and with difficulty proceeded, and at length anchored off a small island which the natives called Quiribiri. The Spaniards, however, gave it the name of *Huerta*—orchard—in consequence of the numerous fruit trees they found on it.

The inhabitants of the contiguous coast were greatly frightened at the sight of the ships and the singular beings aboard of them, and made preparations to defend themselves. Colon managed with great prudence, and endeavored to inspire them with confidence. He would not embark that day nor the next, but occupied the time in repairing his vessels, examining his provisions, and resting his worn-out crews.

The Indians perceiving that the strangers had no intention of injuring them, began to make signals of peace, by displaying their white cloaks, and eventually swam to the ships, bringing with them some cotton cloths, and a few pieces of inferior gold, which they offered to the Spaniards, calling it *guanin*. The admiral refused to accept their gifts, but on the contrary wished to present them some European articles he thought might please them. But the rejection of their presents wounded their feelings, and they likewise refused the admiral's offering. The next day the Spaniards found on the beach the playthings they had given to the Indians strung on a line.

The natives, however, continued evincing the greatest desire to have the strangers, who had so excited their curiosity, come on shore, and made various attempts to induce them to do so. One day an old man came to the beach, and shook a white flag to attract the Spaniards' attention. He was accompanied by two young girls, whom he offered as hostages. Colon received them on board with kindness; dressed them in European clothes, and then returned them to their conductor. On their part they were greatly pleased with the welcome they met with.

At length the admiral, accompanied by some of his people, went on shore, but wishing to procure information regarding the country, began to question the natives by signs, and ordered the notary to take down their answers. But the moment the latter brought out his tablets and made preparations to write, the Indians became alarmed, and doubtless attributed that operation to witchcraft. They ran away, but quickly returned with some powders, which they burnt, and waved the smoke over the Spaniards. The latter being no less superstitious than the natives, thought also that the latter were endeavoring to bewitch *them*. Even Colon, who was so superior to his contemporaries, paid tribute to the ideas of his epoch, and believed in the supposed witchcraft of the Indians.

The admiral made excursions into the interior, but without finding what he sought—gold. The Spaniards procured only some jewels, made of inferior metal, but which were unable to satisfy the avarice of those who had abandoned their country and exposed themselves to the greatest dangers to obtain the longed-for precious metal.

In certain of the houses they found corpses. Some were embalmed, while others were perfectly preserved in cotton cloth and covered with ornaments. On the boards of which the coffins were made, were engraved figures of animals and portraits of faces which were pronounced the likenesses of the parties interred.

The admiral, on his departure, carried with him two Indians to serve as guides, to the great grief of the people, who sent to beg him to return their companions. The admiral succeeded in pacifying the messengers, but was not equally successful in calming the alarm of the rest of the natives.

The remainder of this last voyage of the great navigator took him beyond the limits of Honduras. He soon returned to Europe, and died believing that he had merely reached the shores of India. He never imagined nor appreciated the vast results that were destined to flow from his discoveries. On his deathbed he exclaimed with bitterness: "I have only opened the door for others to enter."

Shortly after their occupation of the principal islands of the Antilles, the Spaniards divided the natives among them, and reduced the poor unfortunates to the most galling slavery.

The chieftains were, in some exceptional cases, exempted from this fate, but in other instances they shared the same destiny as their former vassals, and, urged by the cruel lash of their unfeeling task-masters, moistened with their bloody sweat the soil that had descended to them as their patrimony from many generations of ancestors.

In a few years the cruelty of their masters, the arduous and unceasing labor, from sunrise to sunset, and often later, had so thinned their numbers that the Spanish colonists of the Antilles were compelled to search elsewhere for more slaves. They sent vessels to cruise along the lesser islands and the numerous cays that dot the gulf, and in a short while almost depopulated them. The discovery of the continent opened a

new field for the enterprise of these man-hunters, and it was
not long before they plowed along its extended coasts, and
filled their vessels with the shrieking captives whom they
ruthlessly tore from their families and their beautiful tropic
homes.

CHAPTER II.

Expedition of Pedro de Alvarado into Guatemala--Cortez Sends a Force into Honduras—He Journeys Thither by Land Himself—Conquest and Occupation of the Country by the Spaniards—Later History of Honduras.

The five fragments of the former Central American republic bear such an intimate relation with each other that the historian will find it almost impossible to compile the history of one of these little republics without constantly referring to that of the other four. The entire country was conquered by the Spaniards about the same time, for the mail-clad soldiers who destroyed the Indian natives of Nicaragua and Costa Rica, met on the northern confines of the former province their fellow-countrymen who had overthrown the aboriginal empires and kingdoms of Honduras, Guatemala and Yucatan.

The conquest of the Aztec empire achieved, Cortez, the stern " conquistador," like another Alexander, sighed for more worlds to conquer; but, unlike the " Macedonian madman," he did not sigh in vain. For on three sides of his possessions, to the north, to the south and to the far west, great kingdoms, whose plains groaned under the weight of their rich harvests, whose mountains teemed with veins of silver and gold, and whose streams, arroyos and rivers coursed over sand impregnated with gold dust, invited his soldiery to invade and possess them.

Scarcely had the dense clouds of smoke that lowered over the smouldering ruins of Mexico—the famed island city of the Montezumas—been dissipated by the pure breezes that descended from the adjacent mountains and refreshed the desolated plains, when the restless and avaricious conqueror sent formidable expeditions out in all directions to explore and to conquer the country, in the name and for the glory of Charles, the Emperor King of Spain, and to bring the millions of the idol-worshipping natives of these *terras incognitas* to a knowledge of and an inheritance in the one church universal.

An army of these conquistadores, under the command of Pedro de Alvarado, one of the most gallant and chivalrous of the captains formed under the eye of that great commander, Hernando Cortez, penetrated to the far south, crossed the wild jungles, climbed the tall mountains of Chíapas, and passed the boundary line which separates that State from the present republic of Gautemala. The brave captain was informed of great kingdoms which existed to the south of the point he had then reached—of kingdoms whose sovereigns possessed immense stores of gold, silver and precious stones, and who were, in point of riches and power, but little inferior to the powerful Mexican monarch, whose empire had been lately overthrown and whose capital had been so recently entered, sword in hand, by the same ruthless conquering adventurers.

The conquistador immediately retraced his steps and returned to Mexico. Here he obtained the necessary authority to raise a sufficient force to conquer these powerful Indian kingdoms. So with the title of captian general and governor of countries he should discover, conquer and occupy, he started on his adventurous journey, nor was it long before he had overcome the Indian nations who vainly attempted to arrest his progress. After a series of sanguinary combats and battles, he reduced the greater part of that territory which is known as Guatemala, and also a portion of Honduras, to subjection to the crown of Spain.

In the meantime Cortez himself had sent an expedition along the coast, southward from Vera Cruz, to colonize and conquer that section of Central America at present known as Spanish Honduras. After a series of adventures, the commander of the expedition planted his colony and then sent expeditions into the interior to explore and conquer the country. As usual, the brave and reckless but mail-clad soldiers of Spain prevailed over the naked hordes of Indian patriots who sturdily attempted to bar their progress. nor was it long before the colony and province of Honduras was added to the already vast American possessions of Spain.

From that period, until the cry of independence resounded over the mountain tops and careered over the wide plains of

Spanish America, the enslaved Indian peoples who were sunk into the depths of hopelessness and despair, toiled in the mines or cultivated the fertile lands for the descendants of the rapacious conquerors. Millions of the indigenes were swept away by the small-pox and other terrible diseases introduced into their country from Europe. Millions more fell under the keen swords and the sharp lances, of the "conquistadores" during the wars of the conquest, but millions more wore away their weary lives in the mines that were hidden deep in the bowels of the tall mountains, or patiently wasted away on the cane, and indigo fields, under the burning sun that shone down upon the plains from a cloudless tropical sky.

But after three centuries of oppression and cruelty the cry of independence, raised by the intrepid priest, Hidalgo, in Mexico, 1810, was wafted over the provinces of Oaxaca and Chiapas, and fell upon the ears of the long-suffering and enslaved Indians and half-castes of Central America. It was also gladly welcomed by the indignant creoles, who, if they individually loved their Spanish fathers, hated the Spanish race with an intensity equalled only by the indigenes, who had three long centuries of sanguinary oppression to avenge. The result of the struggle is well known.

The revolted colonies eventually gained their liberty. All Central America was united under one government, and the Republic of Central America took its place among the nations of the earth.

But in 1838 the nobles and the clergy succeeded in overthrowing the Liberal party, and the republic was destroyed. It separated into five parts, which are to-day known as the republics of Guatemala, San Salvador, Honduras, Nicaragua and Costa Rica.

Until within a comparatively recent date Spanish Honduras was the least known and mentioned of the several fragments which comprise that geographical division known as Central America.

Upon the disintegration of the republic, each fraction established a separate government. Then the Honduraneans founded their little republic, which is comprised within the following limits: It is bounded on the north by Guatemala and the Caribbean sea, on the east by the latter, on the south by the Republic of Nicaragua, Pacific ocean and the Republic of Salvador, and on the west by Guatemala and Salvador. It contains 48,000 square miles and a population of about 500,000 souls. The two principal cities are Comayagua and Tegucigalpa. The latter, since 1880, has been declared the capital of the country. It contains about 12,000 inhabitants.

The republic is divided into twelve departments, each of which is under the jurisdiction of a Governor. The names of the departments are as follows: Copan, Gracias, Santa Barbara, La Paz, Comayagua, Yoro, Colon, or Mosquitia, Olancho, El Paraiso, Tegucigalpa, Choluteca, Islas de Bahia (Bay Islands).

Honduras enjoys a liberal republican government, which was established and carried into effect by the late President of the republic, Lic. Marco A. Soto. In the year 1876 this gentleman was chosen by the people of Honduras to re-establish the government. He assumed the functions of provisional President at Amapala, on the 27th of August. In the year 1880, after having restored peace and prosperity to the country, he was elected constitutional President, which position he held until ill health compelled his resignation in August, 1883.

The present constitution of the republic is one of the most liberal and perfect that ever emanated from human wisdom. The articles which may be deemed interesting to Americans are in whole or in part as follows:

Honduras should be considered as a portion of the disintegrated republic of Central America; in consequence, it recognizes the duty and urgent necessity of returning to a union with the other separate fragments of said republic. * * *

ART. 2. The Honduras nation is a sovereign, free and independent republic.

ART. 6. The Constitution guarantees to all the inhabitants of the republic, natives or strangers, the inviolability of human life, individual security, liberty, equality and rights of property.

ART. 7. The republic recognizes the guarantee of the *habeas corpus*.

ART. 8. The slave that treads the soil of Honduras shall be forever free. Traffic in slaves is a penal offense.

ART. 10. Before the law, neither privilege of caste nor class can exist.

ART. 13. All foreigners possess equal privileges, and shall enjoy the same civil rights as the Honduraneans. By consequence they can buy, sell, locate, exercise industries and professions, possess all kinds of property, and dispose of it according to law; visit with their ships the ports of the republic *and navigate in its seas and rivers.* They are exempt from extraordinary contributions (or forced loans), and are guaranteed entire liberty of conscience. They may erect churches and establish cemeteries in any place in the rebublic. Their matrimonial contracts cannot be invalidated *by not being in conformity with the religious requirements of any sect or creed.*

ART. 16. Service in the army is obligatory. Each Honduranean, between the ages of eighteen and thirty-five years is considered a soldier of the active army, and each from thirty-five to forty years of age a soldier of the reserve. Naturalized citizens are exempted from military service for ten years.

ART. 24. The State considers it a sacred duty to foment and protect public instruction in all its diverse branches. Primary instruction is obligatory, is secular and is gratis. *
* * No minister of a religious sect shall be permitted to direct any school or college maintained by the State.*

ART. 26. *The navigation of the rivers of the republic is free to all flags.*

The government is divided into three branches—the executive, the legislative, and the judicial.

The executive power is exercised by a citizen who is styled the President of the Republic. He must be a native of Central America, of thirty years of age, and must be in possession of all the rights and privileges of citizenship at the time of his election. He is chosen by the popular vote. The term of office is for four years. He is eligible to re-election, but cannot be chosen for a third official period until a lapse of four years from the termination of his second term of office.

The members of the Cabinet have the power to be present at the sessions of Congress and to take part in the debates but have no vote. They are compelled to answer any question put by a member regarding any subject that comes within the jurisdiction of Congress, excepting in matters relating to foreign relations and war when the President considers secrecy necessary.

The legislative branch of the government is invested in a single chamber of deputies, or representatives, in the National Congress. This body possesses somewhat similar functions to the combined powers of the Senate and Congress of our country. One deputy should be elected to represent every ten thousand inhabitants, but as the congressional districts have not yet been declared, each department elects three representatives, excepting the Bay Islands, which is allowed but one.

Congress may transact business provided three-quarters of the whole body, which constitutes a quorum, are present. A simple majority determines the resolution of a question. Each member of Congress is inviolable, and at no time, either in the present or in the future, can be called to account for ideas written or spoken by him in the course of his duty.

This constitution was promulgated on the first of December, 1880. The executive and the governors of the departments have earnestly endeavored to carry out its provisions, and have so well succeeded that peace, prosperity and the partial development of the resources of the republic have attended their patriotic efforts.

Upon the resignation of President Soto, Gens. Bogran and Delgado and Mr. Arias were candidates for the high office he was compelled to vacate. The elections were held for three consecutive days. Out of 45,000 votes cast, Gen. Luis G. Bogran received 42,000; the remaining 3000 being about equally divided between his two competitors.

Gen. Bogran enjoys the reputation of being one of the most gallant and skillful soldiers Central America has produced since the death of Morozan. At an early age he entered the military service of his country, and during the interminable civil wars that have devastated Honduras, took part in many combats and battles. He is but 36 years old and has been in public service twenty years.

Although he has filled the executive chair but little more than a year, he has already inaugurated and carried out several important measures of reform. If he lives until the end of his term of office, he will have accomplished more to bring about the complete regeneration of his country than any of his predecessors.

CHAPTER III.

The famous traveler and scientist, Baron von Humbolt, remarked that Mexico was the garden of the world, but that the province of Valladolid (the State of Michoacan) was the Eden of Mexico. If the great geographer was right, then Honduras, which in many respects resembles Michoacan, may justly merit the appellation of the Eden of Central America.

The republic is about two hundred miles wide. Its entire northern coast is bathed by the generally placid waters of the island-dotted Caribbean sea, while a small portion of its southern and western limits are washed by the long rolling billows of the Pacific ocean. For a few leagues from the coast, on either side, the land is low, and, in some places, marshy and damp. Here lurk the fever germs, which very often attack the traveler. But the fevers of the coast are easily cured and are but seldom fatal. With the adoption of slight precautions, combined with temperance in eating and drinking, the foreigner from a colder climate is seldom troubled more than once by the insidious disease, and then the attack is usually very light.

At a distance of about fifty miles from the northern coast the land gradually begins to rise, and the traveler soon reaches an altitude where the soft zephyrs which sigh amid the foliage of the plantain, palm and cocoanut groves are met by and are tempered by the cool fresh breezes which almost constantly blow down from the adjacent mountain tops. A few miles west and south from San Pedro Sula the rank dense vegetation of the tropics ceases, and gives place to the arboreal exuberance of the semi-tropics. In this happy locality fevers are but seldom known, while the various pulmonary diseases that are at present making such ravages in the homes of our own country are never experienced by the Honduraneans of the interior. The word consumption is not found in the "medica" of Honduras, while bronchitis, diphtheria and rheumatism have never yet been heard of by the healthy natives of the republic.

At Sehuatepeque, some thirty miles northeast of Comayagua—the ancient capital of the republic—the climate is cool, refreshing and bracing. The wide plain of the same name is inclosed by tall mountains, which are covered to their summits with a rich growth of pine, larch and oak forests. The sides of these mountains, in many spots, are singularly fertile, and produce admirable crops of corn, barley, wheat and rye, while the valley beneath groans under the weight of profuse crops of cotton, sugar cane and coffee.

The topography of Honduras presents a scene as broken and as diversified as is witnessed in the Island of Jamaica. In fact, the greater part of the territory of the republic is corrugated by the numerous spurs into which the great mountain range of the continent is here divided. Huge hills and tall mountains inclose thousands of beautiful, fertile and pleasant little valleys, which are covered, during the rainy season and several of the months that follow it, by a rich carpet of nutritious grass, which provides subsistence to thousands of fat cattle.

When the extreme heat of the tropic sun parches the grass and literally kills it, the copious dews that fall on the mountain slopes moisten vast patches of a species of wild Guinea grass, which is also very good food for cattle. During periods of drouth, when even the dews cease to fall, and when all classes of vegetation seem to gradually disappear, the cattle find a sufficient and an excellent kind of nourishment among the undergrowth that flourishes in the grand primeval forests. •

For nature seems to have showered its richest blessings upon this glorious country and has produced an infinite variety of shrubs, plants and trees that sustain animal life equally as well as grass. There is one tree in particular, vulgarly called by the people the horse tree, whose foliage fattens cattle and other stock even better than the best grass or corn. The preservation and increase of the number of these singular trees has always been considered of paramount consequence by the government, therefore the destruction of a single specimen is punished by a rigorously enacted fine of three dollars. Thus, notwithstanding the constantly recurring drouths that afflict the republic by consequence of the absolute neglect of irrigation and the culpable ignorance of the natives of the simplest laws that govern agriculture, the cattle of the interior never suffer for want of food, and even during the most protracted drouth present a fat and sleek appearance.

The country to the north and east of Tegucigalpa—the capital of the republic—is extremely well watered. The various mountain-spurs contain numerous springs, which flow down their sides, and, as they near the plains, aggregate and form rushing torrents of pure cold water, which fall tumbling and foaming into the valleys below. Thus the irrigation of the plains and valleys is not only practicable, during the dry seasons, but is extremely feasible; while thousands of eligible sites are presented for the erection of saw, grist and stamp mills in every one of the mountain districts of the country.

To the south of Tegucigalpa, after the tourist has crossed the high mountain range that environs the capital, he descends into a long irregular valley which reaches to the coast. This locality presents a different aspect than is witnessed in the northern districts. Perennial streams and rivers are few and far between, while none of the so-called rivers are navigable during the dry months; in this season the mountains present a brown and parched appearance; but few of the trees which grace the plains retain their foliage, while the ground is arid and dry, and in many places cracked wide open. These fissures occur often and render traveling over the plains very dangerous after nightfall, in case the tourist should wander from the road.

Yet this very soil which presents such a parched aspect, is remarkably fertile and productive. Could the inhabitants rely upon a fairly wet season they would ask no further favor from providence. The few months of rain would mature their crops to such a degree that they would ripen almost as soon as the dry season sets in. But, unfortunately, the rainy season is often retarded, while, frequently, scarcely enough rain falls to quicken the grass into growth. Then the inhabitants suffer for want of a sufficiency of corn—the staple cereal—while the lack of pasture endangers the well-being of the cattle.

But the mountains that divide Honduras, on the Pacific slope, are remarkably rich in metal bearing ore, principally silver. There are numerous valuable mines in the neighborhood of Tegucigalpa, some of which are, even now, being worked in a somewhat primitive manner. Thus, while nature has prevented this locality from developing into a profitable agricultural region, she has been prolific of other gifts. The climate, up to a short distance of the coast, is healthy. The forests abound with valuable woods, and the mountains groan under their burden of precious metals.

While the northern and southern coasts abound in precious woods, such as mahogany, cedar, vera, san juan, rosewood, ebony, sandal-wood, an infinite number of different kinds of palm trees, etc., the interior, where the land attains an altitude of from 3000 to 8000 feet above the level of the sea, produces all the various kinds of timber that are found in the more temperate regions of this hemisphere. Live oak forests are common in the semi-tropic zone, while the huge proportions of the trees and their rough, gnarled branches indicate their value as ship-building material.

The pine forests which adorn the mountain and hill sides of the temperate and the cold zones are equal to any found in our own country. In fact, they cover the principal portion of the republic. The trees are large and tall, and are, in many cases, near to the winding branches of the Ulua, Blanco and Chamilicon rivers.

From the accessibility of Honduras to the great lumber marts of Mexico, the West Indies, and South America, it is evident that the manufacture of lumber in this country is destined to become a very important Honduranean industry in the very near future. Already these vast virgin pine forests have begun to attra the attention of foreign capitalists.

The great drawback to the progress and the prosperity of Honduras has hitherto been the total lack of cheap transportation between the ports and the cities of the interior. The country is so mountainous that the principal roads are mere bridle-paths, over which the imports and exports are carried on muleback at vast expense. It costs at least $100 a ton to transport freight from Puerto Cortez to Tegucigalpa, a distance of 175 miles.

In 1876 the country could not boast a single mile of telegraph. To-day the principal ports on either ocean are united to the capital by iron wires, and 1800 miles of telegraphs enable the government to communicate with the most remote limits of the country.

The ancient Spanish system of jurisprudence obtains in Honduras. Government has improved all branches of the judiciary and has issued the following codes : The civil and penal ; the laws that govern mining and commerce ; the military code ; regulation of public instruction and the code custom duties.

There existed no army nor regular military organization. Recruits were brought to the barracks in bonds, and were forced to serve at the dictation of each petty chief. Dreading the anarchic period that obtained prior to August, 1876, a complete military system has been organized and the republic to-day can call to arms a fairly disciplined army of 41,992 men. This National Guard is a guarantee for public peace and interior tranquility. The republic also possesses sufficient elements of war for the defense of her rights and her territory.

The establishment of the postal service on a firm basis was one of the late President's principal efforts of reform. He succeeded in carrying it into effect. Honduras was the first republic of Central America to enter into the postal union. The constitution of 1880 may be justly considered as one of the most liberal and progressive documents ever submitted to a people.

The public school system is remarkably efficient and practical. Notwithstanding the fact that the last famine affected the attendance of pupils at the schools, the government in 1881 sustained 356 boys' schools, and in 1882 440 ; in 1881 110 girls' .

schools, and in 1882, 133; in 1881, 13,463 boys attended school in 1882 15,720; in 1881 the girls's schools numbered 3852 pupils, and in 1882 4430. The expense attending these efforts in 1881 amounted to $63,946 and in 1882 $73,646.

During the past and the present administration several foreign companies have invested quite large amounts of capital in various enterprises connected with mining and agriculture.

During the era of peace brought about by the triumph of liberal principles, the agricultural interests have greatly improved both in system and value, while all other industries have progressed to such a degree that the future development of the country seems to be secured.

Commerce, both in importation and exportation, has wonderfully increased during the last five years. The last six months of the year 1882 the imports at Amapala reached $401,453, and the duties collected amounted to $182,660. The exports were $162,964, and the export duties $1691. In September and October of the same year the imports at Truxillo amounted to $118,211, and the duties to $8391. The exportation during the same months reached $245,755, and the exportation duties to $31,379. At Puerto Cortez and Omoa, from March to November, the imports reached $422,247, and the duties to $85,650. At the same ports for the same period the exports amounted to $542,751, and the export duties to $9060.

The domestic or interior commerce of the country may amount to $20,000,000 per year while its foreign traffic—imports and exports combined—will reach to about $4,000,000; thus the entire traffic of the republic will aggregate $24,000,000 per annum, or to almost $50 per capita. This may be considered as a very small estimate, for even the veriest drone in the great national hive will certainly earn and spend that sum per annum, while many thousands, of course, gain and expend much more.

Some idea of the anomalous condition of this traffic may be derived from a presentation of the fact that in a particular locality a fine steer or fat cow will not sell for more than $6 or $8, while some leagues distant the same cattle are worth from $12 to $15 per head.   A good beef hide sells for from $1 to $1 20 at Santa Barbara; at Seguatepeque for eighty cents, but at the coast the article will readily bring from $3 to $3 50.

While much of this stagnation of traffic may be attributed to the total lack of good roads, and the consequent high rate of freight tariff which obtains between the centres of production and the ports of the coast, no small part of the blame must be attached to the people themselves, who have never made any very serious attempts to improve their highways.   Many of the mountain paths might be made more practicable.   This subject has, however, attracted the serious attention of Gen. Bogran, the present enlightened President of the republic, who has called upon Congress to provide ways and means for the establishment of a better system of public highways.

Honduras boasts of but one small railroad of which a description will be given in another chapter.   Several lines, however, are projected.   Certain New Orleans parties have obtained from the President a franchise to construct a railroad from Puerto Cortez along the coast to Truxillo.   This projected line will open a vast region to commercial and agricultural enterprise.

The people of Honduras, of whom a moiety are pure Indians, are extremely hospitable and do not appear to entertain that jealous sentiment toward foreigners so common to the Latin American people.   The better class are intellectual and are as a rule finely educated.   Most of them have traveled extensively in Europe and the United states, and are consequently zealous promoters of all projects which have for their purpose the development of the vast natural resources of their country.

The Indians of the interior are a pure and unmixed race. They are peaceful and docile and are excellent laborers.   They possess intellectual faculties of a high order, as no few of the lawyers and statesmen of the country are of that race.   Under the present efficient and liberal public school system the status of the Indian people is being gradually improved, while in all localities where it is possible to do so, primary schools for the education of children have been established.

On either coast the people are more mixed. In many localities a new race has been created by the inter-marriages of the blacks and Indians. The mingling of the whites with this unique race instead of improving seems to deteriorate it. In a few generations this miscegenated stock dies out, for the males are weak and sickly, and the females, as a general case, give birth to unhealthy offspring. Colonies of Caribs—so called— are established at different points on the Caribbean coast, while to the east of Truxillo, Zambos, Mestizos and Mosquito Indians are the principal Inhabitants of the country.

Although the Honduraneaus claim to be Roman Catholics, they by no means seem to constitute religion a serious business of their existence. The principles of liberalism have swept over the republic, and, to say the least, the better class are remarkably liberal in their religious sentiments. The priests possess but little influence, are not overwell paid and do not seem to be so universally respected as their caste was under the Spanish and Conservative regimes. Some parishes have been entirely abandoned, while the rural churches, as a general case, present a dilapidated appearance.

9

CHAPTER IV.

The beautiful and spacious harbor of Puerto Cortez derives its name from the celebrated Hernando Cortez, the conqueror of the Indian empire of the Montezumas.

In the year 1524 a Spanish adventurer, named Gil Gonzales de Avila, set sail from the Island Santo Domingo, armed with authority from the good monks, to whom the Emperor Charles V. had given jurisdiction in such matters, to pacify and conquer the heathen people who inhabited the *tierra firme*. A favorable breeze wafted his little squadron safely over the long rolling billows of the gulf and the placid waters of the Caribbean sea, and after some days of pleasant navigation he sighted the high mountains of Spanish Honduras. In a few days he anchored in a wide bay, whose southern shore was lined with pretty little Indian towns, that were surrounded with luxuriant plantain, banana and mango groves.

During the following night some of his horses sickened and died. When the tide receded he threw their carcasses overboard for fear the Indians of the vicinity, who were in deadly fear of these animals, should discover that they were mortal, and afterwards hold them in less esteem. This circumstance impressed the conqueror's mind so profoundly that he gave the bay the name of Puerto Caballos, or Port of the Horses. Gil Gonzales deemed the loss of these animals such an evil omen that he refused to form a settlement in the locality, and left the bay next day. He sailed further on to the Cape of Tres Puntas, or Manibique, where he established a colony, to which he gave the name of San Gil de Buena Vista.

A few years after this occurrence the conqueror, Hernando Cortez, who went to Honduras for the purpose of chastising his rebellious lieutenant, Cristobal de Olid, explored that port which was so distasteful to Gil Gonzales.   His quick, military eye at ouce noted its superior advantages as a harbor, and he gave orders for the establishment of a town, which he marked out himself, near the site now occupied by the village of Cieneguita.   From that date the Spanish colonists have called the harbor Puerto Cortez, thus ignoring the name given it by Gil Gonzales.

This fine bay is wide and long.   At the further end a lagoon runs to the westward and almost connects with the river Chamelicon.   In fact, it may not be long before a short canal will be cut from the river to the lagoon.   If this is accomplished, another cutting about three miles long would connect the river Uloa with the Chamelicon.   The two canals would bring the entire country, watered and drained by these two long rivers, in direct communication with the town and harbor of Puerto Cortez, thus cutting off the ugly bars at the mouths of those waterways, which are at times absolutely impassable.

As the steamer enters the bay the land to the right hand is low and flat, and is covered with numerous detached groves of cocoanut trees.   Some distance around the right hand point, which is washed by the Caribbean, is situated the town of Omoa, which was, during the Spanish regime, strongly fortified.   A large castle was constructed for the purpose of protecting the roadstead, while several water-batteries were erected whose fires flanked the harbor.   Behind this town, a short distance into the interior, are several well known placer mines which were worked, but not exhausted, by the Spaniards at intervals for more than 250 years.

If we may give credence to the tales of certain Carib fruit cultivators, the Spaniards, notwithstanding their thirst for gold, passed by or neglected large areas of auriferous earth in this vicinity, which now lie waiting capital and enterprise to develop them.   The true reason the placers were not worked more vigorously may be attributed to a want of labor.   The Spaniards tasked their Indian slaves to such a degree that they rapidly decreased in number.   Thus only the most prolific gold lands were worked from the era of the first conquerors down to the epoch of the independence of the country.

The flat land noticed on the right hand, as the traveler enters the harbor, is remarkably fertile, as well as very easy to work. Within the past three years the fruit-planting industry has received a vigorous impulse from the regular communication established between Puerto Cortez and New Orleans through the medium of the Macheca and other lines of steamers. Each month the supply of fruit is greater than the one preceding, for the people are constantly planting. So the steamers and the numerous schooners that frequent the port, can now count on full cargoes of bananas each trip.

It is reported that parties at Cieneguita have lately set out many thousands of cocoanut trees, while others have gone quite extensively into rubber and cacao planting. There is no reason why these branches of agriculture should not be established in this vicinity, for it is a well-known fact that extensive cacao plantations are being laid out at or near Port Livingston, Guatemala, and that many thousand rubber trees have, within the last three years, been planted at San Pedro Sula.

Almost directly opposite Puerto Cortez, but separated from it by the entire width of the harbor, is situated the pretty little native village of Cieneguita. This place is fast assuming importance as a fruit producing centre. One negro planter is now cutting at least 1000 bunches per month; that is to say he furnishes each of the Macheca steamers 500 bunches per trip. The fruit is cut green, and is generally brought off to the vsseles in dories or dugouts. Some of these boats are quite large and will carry 100 bunches. The majority of them, however, will not bear more than twenty-five or thirty. Many of the Ladinos and Caribs at this place have little banana patches, and sell the steamers from five to fifty bunches per trip. Occasionally steamers from New York, Philadelphia and Baltimore run into the harbor and purchase cargoes. If a Macheca steamer happens to be in port at the same time the price of fruit advances, for the latter vessels cannot afford to lose time and are compelled to load quickly. Some pineapples and cocoanuts are purchased each trip by the regular line from the fruit producers of this place.

Messrs. A. Mueller & Co., also do a thriving fruit traffic with this port. Notwithstanding the many cocoanut trees that line the shore of the harbor, but little, comparatively speaking, of this fruit is exported. Most of the existing trees are old, while those which bear, yield small and very inferior fruit. But if, as is reported, the people of the coast are actually planting cocoanut groves, in eight or ten years the exportation of this class of fruit will assume considerable importance.

The land, from Cieneguita around the shore to the lagoon, situated near the head of the bay, is also extremely fertile. The greater part of it has been pre-empted by the enterprising Ladinos and Caribs of the locality.

The little town of Lagoona is the largest place in the harbor. It contains about 1200 inhabitants, and possesses quite a number of wooden edifices. The majority of the houses, however, are built in the usual style of the country and are heavily thatched with palm leaves. The stranger who enters one of these dwellings will be surprised at the number of places where daylight shines through the roof, and doubtless will sympathize with the occupants during the rainy season, yet from some undiscovered reason, the water never, even during the heaviest and longest rains, penetrates through the openings. Some of these thatches are three feet thick ; a completely new one will last for five years without needing repairs.

Notwithstanding the dry and combustible materials these houses are made of, and the careless manner the occupants use fire, it is but seldom conflagrations occur. The traveler who crosses the continent from this port to the Pacific may see on his route some ruined or deserted huts, but it is seldom the charred remains of one of them meets his sight.

Puerto Cortez, the little town where the railroad depot and the government customhouse are situated, is located on the north or left hand side of the harbor, as the traveler enters the bay. It contains about 800 inhabitants and extends along a sandy neck of land, which is but a few yards wide. Indeed, the houses on the left of the railroad track are often in danger of being overflowed during the wet season by the water that floods the bayou which leads from the lagoon. Yet, strange to say, although the water in the marsh, back of the town, stagnates during the dry months, Puerto Cortez is remarkably healthy. While the calenturas and chills and fever are prevalent at Cieneguita and the villages across the harbor, this little hamlet is comparatively free from both.

The villa of Puerto Cortez is the head of the municipality, and the other towns of the vicinity are tributary to it. It is the residence of the collector of the port, who also controls the custom-house at Omoa, of the jefe politico, of the justice of the peace, of the postmaster and the other members of the munic- ipality. The principal business firms are De Brot, P. Arnoux, W. C. Merrilles, Chas. Caron, G. Collier and J. Tolaso. The well known and esteemed Mrs. Berard keeps the Washington Hotel, which institution is deservedly very popular with travelers.

The railroad edifices were once quite imposing. But all of them, the locomotive and repair shops, have become dilapi- dated from the effects of time and lack of care.

The total import and export traffic of Puerto Cortez will aggregate somewhat more than $1,200,000 annually. The im- ports are machinery, Western produce, cotton goods, hard- ware and general articles of merchandise. The principal exports are tropic fruits, sarsaparilla, hides, rubber, mahog- any, cedar, rosewood, ebony, dye woods, etc.

The exports of precious woods will undoubtedly increase greatly within the next twelve months, by consequence of the wood-cutting privileges President Bogran has granted Ameri- can companies. The fruit planting industry is in such a pros- perous condition that a remarkable augmentation in the in- crease of the exportation of tropic fruits may also be relied upon. Puerto Cortez is at present the principal port of the republic, as its import and export traffic is now greater than that of Amapala on the Pacific coast.

Tela, an important fruit producing centre, will soon be de- clared a port of entry. The principal business firm and fruit planting corporation, the Honduras Fruit Company, is not only doing a fine general traffic, but is cultivating a vast banana plantation. Mr. Chas. Mills, of Grand Rapids, Mich., is the president of the syndicate and its business manager at Tela.

While there are several flourishing fruit planting localities on the coast, such as Belfate and Ceiba, the country contiguous to the port of Trujillo is the most important. This seaport carries on a large import and export traffic with our country and Europe, besides its constantly increasing fruit trade with New Orleans. Bonaca, Ruatan and Utila are the principal ports of the Bay Island.

The enterprising S. Oteri has several steamers constantly plying between these ports and the Crescent City. He probably carries on a larger fruit traffic than any other house in the South.

As a great influx of people from the Spanish main may be expected this winter, the various steamers on these routes will be strained to their utmost capacity to carry all the freight and passengers offered them.

The principal seaport on the Pacific coast is Amapala, which is situated on Tiger island, in the bay or gulf of Fonseca. This grand sheet of water presents one of the safest and most extensive harbors, not only on the Pacific coast, but on the planet. Three considerable rivers, the Choluteca, the Nacaome, and the Guascaran, discharge their turgid currents into its capacious bosom and discolor the deep clear blue waters which flow into it from the tranquil Pacific ocean.

The gentle swells of this gulf wash the coast of three independent nations, San Salvador, Honduras and Nicaragua, each of which possesses a port of entry within its limits. La Union is the seaport of Salvador, and is situated at the head of a subordinate bay of the same name. Estero Real, on the margin of a long, deep estuary, which runs far into Nicaragua, in a general northerly direction, is the seaport of that republic, while Amapala, situated on the northern slope of a mountainous island, is the Pacific seaport of the progressive republic of Honduras.

The gulf of Fonseca is fifty-two miles long by about twenty-nine wide, and would, were it not for the numerous islands that dot its surface, and shelter its havens from the force of the trade winds, which sweep the vast area of the Pacific, contain nearly 1500 square miles. It is not only famed for its extent and security but for its depth of water. There is but one shallow spot, towards the north, which reaches from the island of Martin Perez to the low northern shore of Honduras. Ships of the deepest draft may anchor within a stone's throw of the town of Amapala, while between it and the island of Esposicion, the water is very deep and the entering and returning tides often flow through the strait with great violence.

The entrance from the sea is about twenty miles wide, but immediately across it lie two huge islands, named Concha-guita and Mianguera, which belong to San Salvador. These islands break the entrance into three separate channels, and thus serve to protect the wide expanse of the bay from the long high swells that roll before the force of the trade winds which blow steadily across the wide Pacific for nearly the entire year from the same direction. The island of Concha-guita is 1562 feet high, and that of Mianguera is nearly 1200. At the entrance to the bay are two volcanic mountains named Conchagua which is 4000 feet high, and Cosiguina which is 3000 feet above the level of the sea.

The site of Amapala is a narrow strip of level ground on the northern coast of Tiger island. It contains about 3000 inhabitants and boasts of a fair share of commerce. Ships from the eastern ports of the United States and from Europe via Cape Horn, after a passage of from 120 to 150 days, cast anchor off the port. The Pacific mail steamers touch several times a month, in their trips up and down the coast, while, occasionally, small boats from Nicaragua and Salvador visit the port.

Amapala is almost destitute of coast trade and possesses no vessels of any kind, save a few primitive looking launches and Indian doreys or canoes. Its only commerce, therefore, is foreign, nor can it be said that this traffic is augmenting to any satisfactory degree. The town boasts several houses which trade direct with Europe and the United States. The Casa General de Agencies, which does the business of the mail steamers, is at present in charge of Gen. Carlos Roloff, an adventurous Pole, who distinguished himself in Cuba during the late revolution.

The houses of Amapala are mostly of wood and are thatched with tiles made on the main land. The lumber of which they are constructed comes from abroad, although a few miles inland the sides of the mountains are covered with a vigorous growth of sturdy yellow pine trees.

The population of Amapala fluctuates; at times, 5000 people crowd the little town, while probably, three months latter, not more than 3000 souls can be found within its limits. Good wages in Salvador or Nicaragua will cause quite an exodus to those republics, while a failure of the corn crop invariably brings about an immigration of the most enterprising laborers.

The women are clean and neat in their dress and person, while each morning the children are scrubbed and bathed until their little copper-colored hides shine. The men are generally dissipated but are hard workers and excellent and intrepid watermen. Although the bay abounds in fish, but few specimens are seen in the markets, while fruit and vegetables, from the neighboring islands and the main land, and corn, the staple food of the people, fill the stalls and form the principle objects of domestic traffic. The chief exports are hides, tobacco and woods.

The Honduraneans are possessed with a deep faith in the future great importance of this port, and rely on the much-talked-of interoceanic railroad to elevate Amapala into a great commercial depot. Mr. Squier advanced the same favorable opinion. It would be difficult to furnish substantial arguments to sus · tain this supposition, for the very railroad which is relied upon as the source of Amapala's future greatness, will certainly prove its death blow. At present, Tegucigalpa and the towns and Pueblos south of it are supplied with their foreign merchandise through Amapala. Should the railroad be built the traffic line will change and all the markets from the northren coast to Tegucigalpa will obtain their supplies direct from Europe and the United States via Puerto Cortez. That the railroad, sooner or later, will be built is, of course, certain, and then the importance of the Pacific seaport of Honduras will be sensibly diminished.

The only hope for Amapala is that the vast fertile plains from Savana Grande to the southern coast may be cultivated and made to yield their rich tributes of cocoa, fruit, coffee, sugar, indigo, etc., and that the numerous mines which exist among the mountains may be worked by enterprising "miners."

The rocky hills might be made to yield large and profitable annual harvests of henequin or sisal grass, while the forests contain almost inexhaustible quantities of valuable woods. When these natural resources of the country south of Savana Grande are developed, then and only then, can Amapala hope to regain that wealth and importance it will certainly lose upon the completion of the much-talked-of and even more longed-for Honduras interoceanic railroad. The amounts of the import and export traffic of this port are given in another place.

CHAPTER V.

The Grand Valley of San Pedro Sula—The Rich Forest Resources of this Vast Plain—Marvelous Yield of the Cotton Plant—The Celebrated Interoceanic Railroad—The Flora of Honduras—Opportunities for Investment of American Capital—A Fertile Soil and Prolific Harvests.

To the east of the villa of San Pedro lies a plain commonly known as the Valley of Sula. It extends from the coast toward the south for about sitxy miles, and averages from thirty to fifty miles in width. It is traversed by the rivers Chamelicon and Ulua.

This immense plain is densely wooded, for the most part with a beautiful palm the *attalea cohuina*, which covers thousands of square miles along the rivers, and also the northern coast of Honduras. This tree grows nowhere but on the most fertile soil.

At localities amidst this enormous palm forest are found inexhaustible quantities of mahogany, cedar, fustic and rosewood, which are cut for exportation along the banks of the aboved-named rivers.

The India rubber tree, (*siphonia elastica*) grows luxuriantly, and furnishes the rubber exported from Puerto Cortez. Also, the sarsaparilla (*smilax officinalis*) is found in abundance and furnishes a valuable article of export.

All the wild growing fruit trees are found which are indigenous to tropical America. The corozo palm, which is produced in countless numbers, funishes drupes weighing from eighty to 100 pounds, consisting of nuts, resembling diminutive cocoanuts, which yield a very superior oil.

The terminal bud of the corozo palm, as well as of the cabbage palm (*euterpe montana*), furnishes a culinary vegetable which compares favorably with cauliflower.

Vanilla abounds in the forest. Near the banks of the rivers and rivulets grows the pita (*bromelia fibresta*) in paying quantities for commercial purposes. The fruits of the wild fig tree and breadnut, or masica, as well as the leaves of the latter tree, serve to feed and fatten stock.

All kinds of tropical fruits grow here to the highest perfection. Those cultivated are plantains, bananas, pineapples, oranges, limes, lemons, aguacates, maugoes, guanabanas, or sour-sops, chirimoyas. matasanos, rose-apples, akee, or vegetable eggs (*cupania sapida*). The other productions are cacao, coffee, sugar-cane, corn, which gives from three to four crops in the year, rice, of a very good quality, and cotton, which, instead of being an annual plant, as it is in the United States, is here perennial, and growing much larger, yields more than twice the amount it does in the most favored locality of the former country.

Together with these tropical plants may be seen many of the vegetables of the temperate zone, which are cultivated with facility, and can be produced the whole year round. Cabbages, turnips, radishes, lettuce, eggplants and tomatoes grow luxuriantly. Vines have been tried and yield very fine grapes, which fact, considering that the grape is here indigenous, was to be expected. Olives and almonds would grow here to perfection, the soil and climate being just what they require.

This beautiful valley is watered by the rivers Ulua and Chamelicon, both of which may be navigated for some distance by light draught vessels. It is sparsely inhabited, only a few small villages and establishments of mahogany cutters being found over the whole of its extent.

The villa of San Pedro is situated on the eastern border of the valley of Sula, which plain, extending about three miles further east from the town, is closed in by a chain of mountains running from north to south, which separates it from the great valley of Quimistan, famous for its gold mines since the early days of the Conquest.

San Pedro has about 2500 inhabitants and is a thriving little town. The foreign element is well represented, the principal merchants as well as planters being foreigners. Two saw-mills are running; one cotton-gin is erected, and the town is surrounded by banana, plantain, cane, cotton and India rubber plantations. An American company proposes to establish a central factory for the manufacture of sugar, having obtained liberal concessions from the government.

Apart from the Americans and Europeans established here, miners and prospectors are passing through continually, on account of the proximity of the gold fields of the valley of Quimistan ; thus the traveler is agreeably surprised to hear everywhere the English language spoken.

The old town of San Pedro was founded in the year 1536 by the famous conqueror, Pedro de Alvarado, about two miles to the west of the present villa. It was destroyed in the seventeenth century by buccaneers, when the few remaining inhabitants commenced to build on the site where the villa now stands. The opening up of the country by the railway drew a number of foreigners to the town, and since that time it has been steadily growing.

The temperature throughout the valley rises from 62° Fahrenheit in November, December and January, to 95° Fahrenheit in the shade in April and May, these two last being the hottest months in the year. However, even in these months the thermometer rises very seldom above 92° Fahrenheit. The nights are always cool and pleasant, which is caused by the vicinity of the forest-clad mountains, the altitude of the town above the level of the sea being about 900 feet.

At the time of the conquest by the Spaniards the whole valley of Sula and surrounding country was thickly inhabited by Indians. Everywhere through the forest and on the banks of the rivers are found relics of that unfortunate race, which in such an incredibly short space of time was exterminated by the ruthless conquerors. The Indians were taken by thousands, branded like cattle and divided among the Spaniards, who treated them with the utmost cruelty. Believing the supply to be inexhaustible, they forced them to toil beyond their strength at the plantations and mines, where death from privation and overwork soon relieved them of their suffering.

Of the amount of labor then at the disposal of the Spaniards one may judge by reading, in Jose Milla's History of Central America, that Pedro de Alvarado, when he landed at Puerto Caballos (now Puerto Cortez), in the year 1539, on his return

from Spain, to assume again the government of Guatemala,
conquered by him a few years before, had a road made from
Puerto Caballos to San Pedro. This highway was wide
enough to permit two trains of loaded mules, if meeting, to
pass each other. It was completed in the short space of ten
days, so that he, his wife, Dona Beatriz, and her maids of
honor, as well as his numerous followers, with their cumber-
some luggage, armaments, etc., could pass with ease and
comfort.

As the only railroad in the country runs through this valley
a brief description of the enterprise might be interesting to
the American public. Its history may be briefly summed up
as follows:

The government of Honduras, naturally emulous of the
prosperity and the material progress witnessed in the sister
republics of Central America, determined to construct a railroad from ocean to ocean, across the territory of the republic,
a distance, in round numbers, of 244 miles. Certain English
speculators offered to undertake the enterprise. The government granted them a most favorable franchise for the construction of a narrow-gauge road from Puerto Cortez, on the
Caribbean sea, to Amapala, on the Pacific ocean. This concession virtually put the vast and valuable forest resources of
the republic in the hands of the company. In fact, what with
wood-cutting and mining privileges, and the grant of ten
square miles of land for each mile of road constructed, the
franchise gave the constructors so much valuable property
that they would have been able to build the road, equip and
run it for twenty years without a cent of income upon the
mere sale or development of the lands—the forest resources
and the mining property carried in the grant.

But in its haste to see the good work accomplished and
likewise in consequence, perhaps, of a want of experience in
such matters on the part of the Honduranean officials, the
government granted the company the privilege of issuing
bonds, on the completion of a certain number of miles of road
and the acceptance of the same by the government engineers.
Unfortunately no stipulation was made as to the amount of

bonds to be issued. The government depended upon the good faith' of the constructors, and the latter relied upon this generous confidence as a means to feather their nests most effectually.

Under these happy auspices the British company set earnestly to work to carry out their designs. Some hundreds of tons of light iron rails and other construction materials were dispatched to Puerto Cortez; an imposing wharf was constructed at the latter place, and the breaking of ground and the laying of the first few sleepers was the signal for a grand barbecue that lasted several days, and which resulted in the permanent occupation of the country by several enthusiastic young English engineers, who never recovered from the effects of that fatal carouse.

The route located by the company presented no engineering problems, from the coast to the further end of the great plain of San Pedro Sula. This latter point was some miles within the stipulated distance to be finished before the company could issue its bonds. But the English speculators were equal to the emergency. By their orders the locating engineers so twisted and turned the route that the required number of miles were made up within the desired terminal point, and the company at once proceeded to issue its first bonds.

But these first bonds proved to be the last also, for they were issued so thick and so fast that some $30,000,000 worth were placed before the company wearied of issuing. It is true that when the issue reached high up among the millions, the bonds were sold at a very low figure, but as long as they sold at all the company flooded the market with them and—then desisted from further efforts, including all work on the unfortunate road as well.

As but sixty miles of track were laid, over a route that extended across a long level plain, the enterprise, if the assertion of the British company may be credited, cost the modest sum of $500,000 per mile.

Of course, the Honduras Government refused to acknowledge such a fraudulent debt. Then the British bondholders appealed to their government. The members of that govern-

ment sympathized with their unfortunate countrymen, but
plainly intimated to them that their enterprise being of an
entirely speculative nature, government would not interfere
in the premises, and they must settle the matter as they best
could.   Thus, for many years, this so-called debt has hung,
like a dark cloud, over the Republic of Honduras, preventing
the influx of foreign capital and the consequent development
of its vast natural resources.   But of late the British bondholders have shown signs of relinquishing a great portion of
their preposterous demands, for, two years ago, their agent
proposed to scale this debt of $30,000,000 to $2,500,000.

While not exactly acceding to their proposition, President
Bogran has not refused to entertain it.   The settlement of this
unjust claim has long been one of his dearest hopes.   It is
more than probable that he will enter into a favorable arrangement with the holders of these bonds when the opportunity
presents itself.

During the past few years this road has been under numerous managements.   In 1881 a Mr. Hayden contracted with
the government to run it, but the unfortunate gentleman, after
he had sunk about all he possessed, was drowned in a vessel
that foundered near the coast.   The elder Mr. Merrilles then
took charge of it and retained control of the property until a
company, represented by Messrs. Waterbury and Hance, of
New York, obtained a concession from the Honduranean
Government to continue the line to the Pacific coast.   As this
firm, never, if we may credit the assertions of the Honduranean
government, carried out any portion of its contract, President
Bogran took it out of their hands and turned it over to the
management of Mr. Edward Kraft, an enterprising American
resident of San Pedro.

This latter gentleman since he has had charge of the enterprise has laid out a large sum of money for repairs and rolling
stock.   The road is at length in fair working order, while Mr.
Kraft's management seems to give general satisfaction.

The valley of San Pedro Sula, with the adjacent high lands,
contain a fair representation of the flora of Honduras, which
also may be considered as general throughout Central America.

The names of the principal forest trees and medicinal plants of the Republic are as follows.

HARDWOODS.

1. *Madre y Padre* (mother and father)—A small tree, from eight to twelve inches in diameter ; principally used for fence posts. It should be cut when green. When dry is is so hard that no ax can make an impression on it. In wet or damp land it will outlast iron.

2. *Mora*—The *fustic* of commerce; is used for dyeing purposes and for house and fence posts, etc. House posts that have been interred not more than ten feet from running water, on being taken out, after fourteen years, had not lost their bright golden color. There are two kinds of *mora* or *fustic*. One is all yellow ; the other has a hard, stringy heart, of dingy black color.

3. Laurel—called *Laurel* in Spanish, and in botany *Laurel guindo* or *Laurel regio.* This wood (the black laurel), like the *fustic* or *mora*, will equal iron for posts in damp localities, if cut at maturity and under favorable circumstances. There are three kinds, black, yellow and white. The first is the only kind used for out-door purposes. It will eventually become a valuable export.

4. *Sempisqui*—A large tree, which often reaches from eighteen to twenty-two feet in diameter in various localities. It is of regular form and also of imposing appearance. The sap is pale yellow, the first formation is rose-red, and the heart, or hard wood, dark brown. It is very hard and fine-grained.

5. *Silimere*—Of medium size, and regular form. The wood is hard and fine-grained, its color dark rose red and its heart dark brown. It is very durable.

6. *Sile*—Of medium size, hard, fine-grained and durable. The color of this wood is a dark rose-red. The heart is deep brown. It is very hard, fine grained and heavy to handle,

7. *Frijolio* (called by the Belize and Jamaica negroes Billy Webb)—It is of large growth and very superior quality. The color of the wood, from the bark to the heart, is light lead. The heart in very old specimens is a deep dark red color; of fine grain and very heavy.

10

8. *Madre Cacao*—This wood is equal, if not superior, on account of the many uses to which it can be put, to mahogany. Its color is a bright yellow, its grain fine. It is very heavy and not liable to crack or split.

9. Oak (*Encima, S.*)—There are four varieties to be found in various localities, viz: white, red, black, and live oak—the moss oak of Louisiana.

10. Pitch pine and yellow pine, with the same qualities as the pure timber of the temperate zone. There are immense quantities all over the country.

11. *Almendro*—A heavy, solid, fine-grained wood. The color of this timber is a pale yellow.

12. *Cortez*—A large tree, very durable. Color of all the wood—a pale yellow. Very fine grain.

13. *Balsamo*—A large tree; qualities same as the former. Color of wood, yellow; heart, red.

TIMBER USED IN HONDURAS FOR BUILDING PURPOSES.

1. Laurel—Yellow and white, is much used for inside work, such as beams, rafters, door and window frames, etc. It is strong and durable.

2. Mahogany—Too well known all over the world to require any particular notice. In Honduras it is not used for building purposes with but few exceptions.

3. Cedar—Is very plentiful, and reaches a large size.

4. *Manacapa*—Superior to the yellow or white laurel or mahogany for general building use, etc.

5. *Calan*—A heavy, fine-grained wood, which is equal to mahogany in durability. Its color is yellow.

6. *Yaya*—Has all the appearance and qualities of lancewood, of which, probably, it is a variety.

7. Yellow Pine—Is but little utilized in Honduras, except in localities where it is abundant and other kinds of timber are scarce.

8. *Manteca*—(Lardwood)—Used for the same purposes as yellow pine. It is a heavy, close-grained wood, much stronger than pine and more elastic.

9. Bloodwood—(*Palosangre*)—This is believed to be the zebrawood of Europe, as known in commerce. Is seldom used.

10. *Jabon*—Is not so durable as the before-mentioned hard woods, but still is quite lasting. What it lacks in durable qualities it makes up in color, being of a very rich, bright-orange tint, and is heavy and close-grained.

11. *Maquelize*—This wood is like mountain ash and is used for like purposes. It can be readily bent, when green, into any desired form.

12. *Ciruelia*—A species of wild plum tree, very much like the zebrawood. It is occasionally used to make furniture.

13. Rosewood—Is found in various localities, but the quality is said to be somewhat inferior of that of Santo Domingo.

There are many other varieties of durable woods, suitable for building and other purposes.

MEDICINAL TREES AND PLANTS.

1. *Jiole*—A large tree of very pretty appearance, growing to the height of seventy and eighty feet. It possesses medicinal qualities. The bark and leaves are used as a beverage, like tea or coffee. It is pleasant, agreeable and slightly aromatic. The fresh juice is used to close and cure wounds; as a poultice to the feet, in fever and ague, or fever; to ease the head; in cases of sick headache the leaves are placed on the temples. The bark and leaves are used in water for sickly, weak persons to bathe in.

2. *Ramon*—A medium sized tree of common appearance. The sap of this tree is used as a remedy for bites of venomous insects.

3. *Mato Palo*—A very curious tree; the juice taken fresh from the bark, spread over a piece of strong calico or thin leather, is applied to reducing inflammation, swellings and what is also commonly called windy swellings. It is good for man and beast, and is celebrated all over the country.

4. *Sansapote or Oraca*—The kernel of the fruit is used as a remedy in summer for bowel complaint and dysentery.

5. *Chicalaca*—This is a tree of medium height. The flowers are used in combination with elder flowers (called *flores de sauco*) in fever and ague and for fevers generally.

6. *Chichapate*—The bark of this tree is used in the above mentioned disease.

7. *Carlos Santo*—A small plant; the seed and root are used as a remedy in dropsy.

8. *Orozul*—An herb; all the herb is used in combination with senna as a cathartic for colds and catarrh.

9. *Chillindron*—This is a tree of medium size; the seed is used to cure toothache by being put in the cavity of the tooth.

9. *Guaco*—A vine used as antidote for the poison of snake bites.

10. *Contra Yerba*—A small herb used in a great many sicknesses, viz: Fever and ague, fever, snake bites, stings of insects, etc.; and also as a tisane in fevers.

11. *Escorchinera*—An herb used as a remedy for sick headache, inflammation in the throat, and to bring on the catamenial periods.

12. *Nawapate*—A plant used as a remedy for boils, ulcers, etc. It is taken in decoction and applied as a powder and poultice, and also as injections for pains of the bowels.

13. *Ariana*—An herb used as a remedy for dysentery, etc.

14. *Candala*—An herb used as a poultice for boils, etc.

15. *Ojo Puerco*—A plant used as a remedy for snake poison.

16. *Yerba el Toro*—Used in painful inflammations, etc.

17. *Siwapate*—A tree; the bark is used as a tisane in flatulent colic, etc.

18. *Ojo Sierra*—An herb; used as a tisane to cool and purify the blood.

19. *Suntul*—Herb; used as a tisane in colds, catarrh, coughs.

20. *Vivoran*—Herb; used as a powerful vomit, taken to break up colds, catarrh, etc. In some districts it is known by the name of "leaf of the wind," and "leaf of the air."

21. *Malva*—Herb; used for injections, fomentations and poultices.

22. *Escobilla Amarga*—Herb; used as malva, etc.

23. *Frijolio*—Herb; used with malva sylvestre and malva castilla, in the same diseases as the two former, and often as a beverage.

24. *Cinco Negritos*—A medium sized tree; the bark used as tisane in fever and ague. It is a powerful sudorific.

25. *Palo Quesillo*—A plant; used as a remedy for private diseases.

26. *Pericon*—A medium sized tree; the juice of the leaves is used to relieve afterpains in child-bearing and for wind colic, coughs, etc.

27. *Ditimo*—A small plant; the leaves are utilized as a tisane to stop bleeding from the lungs and anus. It grows in abundance.

28. *Sueldo con Sueldo*—An herb; the leaves are bruised and applied as a poultice in sprains, dislocations, etc.

29. *Limoncilla*—A plant or shrub; the bark is used as a tisane, or a vomit, but it is very powerful, and for this reason is seldom used.

30. *Chuchilo*—A tree of more than medium size; the bark is made into a tisane. As a cathartic, its effects are powerful.

31.—*Guacuco*—A tree; the fruit is used as a tisane in the localities where it is found.

32. *Orejuela*—A large tree; the shell which covers the seed is the part used. An ointment is made of it to close the soft part of the heads of infants. It is applied to the child from the age of six weeks to two months.

33. *Michoacan*—An herb; the bulbous root is the part used, and is taken as a cathartic, like the Carlos Santos.

34. *Redoma* (commonly called *Esponga*)—The fruit of a vine which contains a round, soft, fibrous matter or substance, from which it takes the name of sponge. It is used as a quick, easy vomit.

34. *Chiamora*—A vine; its seed is used as a strong cathartic; is given to infants particularly to chew on, for the purpose of cleansing and strengthening their stomachs, care being taken that they do not chew too much.

CHAPTER VI.

The system of agriculture followed by the inhabitants of this
country is as primitive as that employed by the grandsons of
Noah, while it may not fairly be considered as effective. The
ignorant husbandman clears a small space on the most convenient mountain side, opens the soil, at intervals, with an iron-
shod stick, drops a few kernals of corn in each hole, which he
covers by drawing the soil over it with his bare foot. Such
fields constitute the celebrated *milpas* or maize patches, which
supply the greater part of the people with corn from which
they manufacture their indigestible tortillas or so called corn·
bread.

The plains although the most fertile and productive localities,
are seldom cultivated. When they are, the ground is merely
scratched by a steel-pointed stick, called by habit a plow. Yet
fields thus prepared produce bountiful crops of wheat, rye and
barley. There is a vast quantity of land, in the higher valleys,
that are hidden amid the tall mountains which corrugate the
surface of the country, where cereals of all kinds may be produced in the utmost profusion. When the country is occupied
by immigrants, and the application of modren agricultural implements is made, these little valleys will become blooming and
productive farm lands, competent to furnish a large population with breadstuffs.

The peculiar topographical formation of the country renders
its climate extremely diversified. While the people of the
mountains, in the morning, crouch over their fires, or smother
themselves under several blankets, their brethren in the valleys
distant but a few thousand feet from (below) them, are swel-
tering under the fierce rays of the tropic sun that beats down
upon them from the brazen cloudless sky above.

By consequence of these singular local extremes of heat and cold the flora of the republic is remarkably varied and extensive. Every plant, tree and shrub that flourishes in any part of this hemisphere can be produced within the fertile limits of Honduras. The sturdy dwarfed pine that braves the cold blasts of the winds that come rushing down from the mountain tops may, while casting its long shadow down the hillside at evening, darken the spot where the tender fern or the sensitive shrub of the semi-tropicl vegetates. Thus there is no limit to the nature of the production of this fertile soil, while many landholders embrace within a single tract of their territory the cold, the temperate, the semi-tropic and the tropic climates.

Honduras produces all the spontaneous alimentary food found within the limits of the tropics, beside some species peculiar to Central America alone. The cherrimoya assumes a size and possesses a flavor equal to the Mexican species. The aguacate is large, mellow and well-flavored. Orange trees develop into large proportions, while their uncared for and unpruned branches bend under the weight of a profusion of golden fruit.

The hill and mountain sides are covered with rare plants and shrubs, which bear luscious and to us literally unknown fruits. Even the forests yield their tribute, while a huge specimen of the banyan, or wild fig, bears a succulent bulb, which is greedily devoured by cattle, horses and mules.

Coffee flourishes in various localities. The departments of Santa Barbara and Copan are noted for their tobacco and coffee farms. Numerous profitable plantations exist in the vicinity of Chinda and Santa Barbara, which now, in consequence of the prompt opening of the river Ulua by the Shears enterprise, may export their crops to the outer world. The coffee of Honduras is large and is exceedingly well flavored, while by consequence of the cheap tariff of wages for the agricultural labor that can be obtained in the locality, it is produced at a much less cost than is the general rule in Central America.

The cotton plant grows to perfection in the numerous tropical and semi-tropical plains that dot the country. Its fibre seems as large and as fine as the best Louisiana staple. Some months ago, Mr. W. A. Coleman, a planter of San Pedro, sent some fine specimens of cotton-bolls to the *Times-Democrat* office. A letter which accompanied the samples, and which fully described the wonderful productiveness of the plant, was published in the columns of that journal.

It will not be long before the cotton fields of Honduras (which may be made to produce at least 1200 pounds of ginned cotton per acre) will enter into competition with the Egyptian cotton lands in the marts of Europe. Labor is so cheap that it can be produced and picked at a minimum cost; thus the price of its cultivation will not ascend to more than one-third the cost that obtains in our Southern States.

Sugar cane attains a size and yield scarcely to be imagined by the Louisiana planter. The crop is perennial. There are numerous fields on the coast that have not been cultivated or replanted for twenty-five years, yet their minimum yield is stated to be about 2500 pounds per acre. Where care is taken in the cultivation of the crop, the yield will reach 3500 pounds per acre of ratoon or old cane. There are various localities in this highly favored country where the cultivation of sugar cane might become a flourishing industry.

A great many farmers of the country have begun to culti-vate Guinia grass. The foot-hills of the tropics and semi-tropics are chosen as the localities most favorable for the production of the grass. Its cultivation bids fair to become a most valuable branch of agriculture, for it is stated that beef fed on it possesses a superior flavor to any other. The seed was originally imported from Jamaica, but the plant thrives better in Honduras than in the West Indies.

Every class of vegetables found in the markets of the United States can be produced in Honduras. Onions, cab-bages, carrots, beets, turnips, etc., when cultivated grow to a prodigious size, while pumpkins, squashes, melons of all kinds, cucumbers. etc., yield fabulous returns to the patient hus-bandman. Potatoes of the finest quality thrive in the valleys of the temperate belt, while the gardens adjacent to the city of Tegucigalpa supply the local markets with a superior speci-men of this valuable table esculent.

When the railroad penetrates the Tegucigalpa valley and connects the interior with the coast, a thriving traffic in vegetables will be carried on with the people of the tropical districts of the republic, while the same fertile lands will furnish the tropic marts with apples, peaches, plums, pears, cherries, currants and all the varied fruits and vegetables of the colder zones.

Tobacco is cultivated in many parts of the republic, but that of Copan enjoys a just pre-eminence over all others for flavor. While it cannot be said to equal the Mexican leaf, or possess its exquisite aroma, the Honduras tobacco will compare very favorably with the average plant produced throughout Latin-America.

The government possesses a monopoly of the tobacco trade. It buys the leaf and sells it at retail. No one can sell cigars without a license, or manufacture them without permission. At the same time the export of both the manufactured article and the leaf is free, and tons of both are sent to Guatemala and Salvador annually. The government also enjoys a mono-poly of the liquor trade, thus no small portion of its revenue is derived from these sources.

The forests of the tropics abound with hule or rubber trees; or rather not long since did; for their number, by consequence of the vandalic system employed by the Indians in extracting the precious gum, is gradually decreasing. Some years ago Mr. Edward Kraft, together with several other enterprising foreign residents of the valley of San Pedro, inaugurated the rubber planting industry. Mr. Kraft possesses several thousand trees, from one to six years old; Mr. Jose Soube, 4000; the Coleman brothers an equal number, perhaps, while numerous natives have planted many thousands more.

The rubber tree should not be tapped until it has attained the age of ten years, when it will yield annually twenty-five pounds of excellent caoutchouc. A tree will readily net its possessor $6 a year; thus Mr. Kraft's trees will return him a large income in the course of a few years. An acre of ground produces 160 trees; thus 100 manzanas or 200 English acres will yield 32,000 trees.

This industry is destined to assume great proportions in the course of the next two decades. Meanwhile the spontaneous production of the rubber tree is still going on. It will be many years before this natural supply will be exhausted. It is safe to assume then, that the rubber industry of Honduras will form an important factor in the future traffic of the republic.

Bananas of various kinds, together with several species of the plantain thrive luxuriantly on the tropic plains of San Pedro and La Paz, and also along the extended northern coast. The cultivation of these valuable fruits for exportation has long been a chief *desideratum* with the present truly liberal government, which, on its part, has made every endeavor to foster and encourage this nascent industry.

Hitherto, the energies of the people have been principally directed to the wood cutting and mining industries. But the establishment of the Oteri and Macheca lines of steamers, and the marvelous development of the tropic fruit traffic in this country, have brought about a corresponding development of the fruit planting industry along the Caribbean coast. At Puerto Cortez a fair amount of capital is invested in this interest, and flourishing plantations are established at the Lagoona, Cieneguita, and other points along this pretty bay, while around the point, in the neighborhood of Omoa, banana and plantain raising has become the principal industry of the inhabitants.

Within the past six years several foreign and native residents of the Sula valley at or near San Pedro, have established extensive fruit plantations. The miserable condition of the railroad has prevented the planters from freighting their fruit to the coast. The Macheca Bros. and Oteri, have often lost money by accidents on the road. Several instances have occurred where cars laden with bananas have jumped the track; before they could be replaced the fruit was spoiled. As the planters were aware of the uncertainty attending transportation over this route they refused to furnish fruit unless they were paid for it before the cars left San Pedro station. The loss consequently always fell upon the shippers, who, after having been bitten several times refused to run any further risks. For quite a period, then, the San Pedro fruit planting industry languished. Thousands of marketable bunches of bananas rotted monthly on the trees, while the farmers not only took no further steps to increase their acreage of cultivation, but even neglected the land already planted.

But the new management of the railroad, under Mr. Kraft's supervision, has repaired the track and rendered passenger and freight traffic tolerably certain The planters have recovered their courage, have again begun to bestow more attention upon their almost deserted plantations, and once more trains loaded with bananas, for shipment may be seen leaving the San Pedro depot.

There are numerous steamers and a number of schooners engaged in freighting fruit from Central America to the Crescent City. Yet six years ago three or four small schooners sufficed to carry on this traffic. But the business spirit of the elder (S). Oteri, and the enterprise of the Macheca Bros. and C. A. Fish & Co., has developed the tropic fruit traffic into vast proportions. The business manager of the Macheca's on the Caribbean coast, Capt. James Leitch, has, if he was not chiefly instrumental—greatly influenced the development of the fruit planting interest along the Caribbean coast from Belize southward and eastward as far as Tela. He encouraged the natives to plant and in many instances assisted them with means. While at times the simple people have treated him with absolute injustice, have deliberately broken their contracts, and have given fruit, which he had bought, and which certainly belonged to him, to occasional New York or Philadelphia steamers, they cannot cite a single instance where he has dealt unjustly with them. But by fair dealing and strict adherence to his contracts, Capt. Leitch has won the confidence of this people and is deservedly popular with them.

It is fortunate, however, that the Honduras coast is so extensive and that so much unoccupied land may be utilized, for banana planting This crop is even more deleterious to the soil than tobacco. In five years a plantation is worn out, and the planter must prepare new land for further crops, while the wasted soil, on the lately occupied place needs years of rest before it can thoroughly recuperate.

President Bogran has declared his intention of creating Puerto Cortez, Omoa, and the territory contiguous to them a free zone. If this plan is carried out a most favorable impetus will be given to the fruit planting interests. The results of such experiments have proven so favorable at Port Livingston, Guatemala, that the present government of Honduras, will, when some arrangement can be made toward carrying out the inter-oceanic railroad enterprise certainly favor Gen. Bogran's project.

CHAPTER VII.

The Wood Cutting Industry—Its Importance—Description of Mahogany Cutting Methods—The Honduras and Grand Rapids Timber Company—Origin of its Establishment—Its Admirable Success—Stock Raising—Tobacco Planting—Manufacture of Rum, Hats and Other Articles—Cities and Towns.

Ever since the first appearance of the buccaneers on the Caribbean coast, furniture wood cutting has been one of the principal industries of the native and foreign residents. It was this traffic that brought about the first settlement of British Honduras, which ultimately culminated in the conquest and permanent occupation of that province by our transatlantic cousins. The principal furniture woods are mahogany, cedar, ebony, rosewood, and amarillo. There are numerous other kinds of Central American hard timber, as yet unknown to foreign commerce, but which are destined to become, before long, both known and appreciated. The dye woods—fustic, brazil, logwood and bragillito—are valuable objects of commerce.

Camps are formed for mahogany logging at the beginning of the dry season. Experienced men select the proper trees, which are felled, hewed into shape and the floatable logs are cast into the rivers and streams to be carried to the sea. The dye woods will not float, and are consequently transported in crates. The methods employed in getting out timber could be improved upon, but are at the same time very good, labor being abundant and cheap, and the appliances simple. On account of the hard work required in cutting mahogany trees close to the ground, the natives direct their axes to a point from six to eight feet above it, leaving an average of probably from 300 to 500 feet of the best part of the tree, so far as beauty of grain is concerned, on each stump, besides the roots which are gnarled and twisted, and bear the same proportionate additional value to the body of the tree that a walnut root does, being admirable for veneers. The bottom of the tree is wide and spreads out. Two thousand feet is a modest estimate of the amount secured from an average trunk, irrespective of the waste. A tree lately cut in Honduras made three logs which were sold in Europe and brought over $11,000. The mahogany tree ranges from one to seven feet in diameter, is often sixty feet to the first branches, and frequently exceeds ninety feet in height, the cedar averages about the same in diameter. The Honduras mahogany comes to market in logs from two to four feet square, and twelve to fourteen feet long, planks sometimes being obtained that are seven feet wide. Its grain is very open, and often irregular, with black or grey specks. The veins and figures are often very distinct and handsome, that which is of golden color and free from specks being considered the best. It is said to hold glue better than any other wood. The weight of a cubic foot of mahogany varies from thirty-five to fifty-three pounds. As compared with oak, which is called 100 per cent, the strength of mahogany is between sixty-seven and ninety-six, its stiffness is from seventy-three to ninety-three, and its toughness from sixty-one to ninety-nine per cent. The dye woods are generally small, and are cut into small pieces.

The government engineer of Honduras estimates the total value of the trees, such as are regarded fit to be cut, at $200,-000,000 while the smaller trees not ready to cut are also worth a large amount.

Europe possesses few furniture woods, and has held the imports from Honduras and other countries in high esteem. This appreciation, born of the necessities of the case, has resulted in securing better prices for mahogany and other valuable woods in the European markets than can be obtained in the ports of the United States. However, these conditions are likely to change, and a more direct business will grow up with the commercial centres of the United States. The railroads are beginning to be interested, and are making overtures favoring international traffic, and it is expected it will not be long before Honduras woods will be shipped in large volume to New Orleans, and thence to Chicago, thus reaching a main western distributing point direct, instead of drifting in a circumnavi-

gable manner to New York city, and thence westward, as
heretofore. .

Regarding means of transportation, there are several lines
of steamers running between Honduras and New Orleans. The
cost of freighting mahogany, for instance, from Honduras to
New Orleans is more than to London, England. The average
cost to the latter port from $5 75 to $10 per ton, while to New
Orleans it is about $12. These are given as bottom figures.
The schooners being small craft, find it more profitable to carry
fruits and other lighter cargo than to load with heavy timber.
On account of the scarcity of many of the hard woods of the
United States, consumers are forced to seek foreign supplies.
Hitherto, or until within a recent period, this country has not
been impressed with the necessity of going heavily into the
importation of fancy woods, consequently the traffic has been
comparatively moderate. Moreover, a large home investment
of capital has been called for in developing the internal traffic
of our own country, and with vast resources of her own, the
United States has not until lately been required to go abroad
to seek a market for her surplus manufacture.

But within the past five years our home industries have begun to produce more than a sufficiency to furnish our domestic supply, thus, the manufacturers have been compelled to
seek foreign markets for their surplus wares. Central America has hitherto exchanged the products of her vast and valuable forests for European manufactures. If our merchants
are only true to their interests and display the same untiring
energy towards building up our foreign commerce as they
have evinced in developing our domestic traffic, this *desideratum* can readily be accomplished.

To prove this assertion, the following instance might be
cited: When ex-President Soto was in Chicago, somewhat
more than a year ago, he informed the author that he was desirous of establishing closer trade relations between the Great
Republic and his own beautiful inter-tropical country. He
mentioned the Honduranean wood-cutting interest and expressed a hope that American capitalists would find it to their
advantage to invest in it. This conversation culminated in

the purchase by the author of a valuable wood-cutting franchise in the name of the firm of Robinson & Lacey, of Grand Rapids, Mich. These gentlemen formed a company in their native city which immediately proceeded to carry out the conditions of the grant, one of which was the absolute possession, with the right to export free of duty or any charge whatever, 10,000 first-class mahogany trees, together with the privilege of cutting cedar trees at a minimum rate for stumpage. The syndicate, under the able management of Mr. Jas. D. Lacey, has already accomplished vast results, and has nearly, if not quite, 1,500,000 feet of first-class mahogany timber ready for transportation to our markets.

Stock raising may fairly be estimated as the next important Honduranean industry. In fact, if proper steps were taken towards its development it would most probably become in a few years the most important. On the Pacific coast, where the rainy season seems neither as prolonged nor as consistent as on the Atlantic slope, stock raising is less profitable, for it is attended with more risks. There are few perennial streams in that locality, and during the dry season the parched arid plains yield but scanty provision for the starving herds. Often hundreds of cattle die before the rain sets in, while numerous cases occur where they become so debilitated that they cannot endure the scouring effect produced by the new grass, and die in the most intense agony. If on the vast plains that lie between the Naocame, the Guaarcarin and the Choluteca rivers the grass is rich and plentiful and the cattle are sleek and plump in the rainy months, the barrenness of the same localities during the dry months, unless irrigation is employed, will forever preclude the probability of this region becoming a great cattle producing centre.

On the Caribbean—or Atlantic—slope the situation is vastly different. The country, while corrugated by mountain ranges, spurs and foothills, is reticulated by numerous perennial streams. Between these watercourses the land is generally level and liable to overflow in many localities. It is true that the water quickly subsides, probably in a few hours; yet the soil has been sufficiently irrigated to revivify the grass, the shrubs and the other herbage that cattle depend upon for their subsistence.

At Sehuatepeque, for instance, the wet season lasts from eight to nine months. During the height of said season it rains almost constantly; thus the high table lands, the mountain slopes and the foothill sides of this locality always furnish sufficient herbage not only to sustain the cattle, but to keep them in good condition for the market. On the wide plains of Olancho, and beyond to the eastward in the Department of Mosquitia, cattle raising may safely be considered the prime industry. Vessels loaded with fat steers are constantly sailing from Trujillo to Cuban ports, while the Departments of Santa Barbara and Comayagua supply both the Belize and Havana markets with well conditioned beeves.

While even the most enthusiastic admirer of Honduras cattle would not affirm that this stock equals the improved breeds that roam the vast plains of Texas and California, yet the Honduranean beeves compare favorably with the so-called Spanish cattle of Florida and Northern Mexico.

President Bogran has taken steps to procure some blooded stock for his own ranche. Capt. Arnoux, Mr. Zuniga, Mr. Zelaya, Mr. Alonzo Valenzuela, and several of the ranchmen of the Northern coast, either have, or purpose, to follow his example; thus in a few years the present breed will be vastly improved.

But little can be said in favor of Honduranean horses and mules. They are as a general case small, but at the same time are exceedingly wirey. The freight transportation of the country is carried on, almost in its entirety, by pack trains of mules and donkeys (burros). This transportation system is extremely expensive, but is the only one that can obtain until railroads become more general and cart roads are opened in the most important localities.

Vast herds of goats and sheep abound in the semi-temperate and cool regions. In all seasons of the year these hardy animals find ample subsistence where larger cattle would die of starvation. Wool producing has not yet arrived at the degree of an important industry, although it well might, if

11

steps were taken to promote its development. Both sheep and goats are raised principally for their meat. In many cases their hides are not even preserved.

While tobacco planting is a flourishing industry in the department of Copan, the plant is generally cultivated throughout the entire country. The leaf, for lack of proper curing, is not equal to the prime Mexican staple, but is, nevertheless, of a very fine grade. Thus the manufacture of cigars and cigarettes is carried on in every town, village and hamlet. It must be admitted that the common Honduranean cigar is not a first-class article, yet it is very cheap. Good ordinary cigars, equal to those exposed for sale in this country for five dollars per hundred, are bought at retail for seventy-five cents per hundred; cigarettes are correspondingly cheap.

The government monopolizes the sale of tobacco, that is to say, all tobacco in the leaf; cigars and cigarettes sold within the limits of the republic are retailed by persons duly authorized by Government, and who buy from the national deposits the leaf for cash. The dealers are not allowed to charge more than five per cent over the government price. This monopoly yields quite a revenue to the national treasury.

The manufacture and sale of rum is also a government monopoly. This liquor is extracted from molasses and is called *ron de cana* and also *aguadiente*. In some localities a species of rum is extracted from the mescal, a plant of the aloe family. This liquor is much superior to cane rum, and justly merits the appellation of mescal brandy. Rum, of a fair quality, but of singular flavor, is extracted from the banana. Several parties along the coast have lately inaugurated this business, which, in time, promises to assume very fair proportions.

There are other minor classes of native industries which, while they may exert some local influence, are but little known or appreciated beyond the limits where they are practiced. Thus certain towns are famous for the palm leaf hats made by their inhabitants; others for the manufacture of pottery and earthenware; others for preserves and prepared fruits, and others yet, for the various kinds of mats exposed for sale in front of the houses, etc., etc.

As stated in another chapter, the interior lands situated at a high altitude above the sea are admirably adapted to the cultivation of wheat and other cereals. In these fortunate regions the intense heat of the tropical sun is partially lost in the extremely rarified atmosphere and is also tempered by the cold winds that blow from the adjacent bleak mountain tops. At night, the dense clouds which during the day cling pertinaciously to the tall summits of the mountains, descend to the low lands, and—during the dry months—shed a copious fall of dew over the plains and valleys. Thus, where in the hot regions near the coast the vegetation assumes a dry and parched appearance, in the higher altitudes, it is invariably fresh and green, and the crops produced in the latter localities are remarkably plenteous.

The unexperienced traveler often notices with astonishment that while in one locality the people enjoy a plentiful supply of Indian corn—which is the staple food of the masses—at another point, situated perhaps but sixty or seventy miles distant, they actually suffer from a lack of this, to them, indispensible cereal The cause for this anomalous situation is easily explained. The districts where famines temporarily prevail have experienced a drouth during the rainy season. The parched soil has refused to return its usual prolific yield of the cereal, and, as the mountain bridle paths are almost impassible during certain seasons of the year, and as transportation is always extremely costly, the price of corn by the time it reaches the district where a scarcity prevails, is so exorbitant that the poorer classes in many cases are totally unable to pay for it. An example to prove this assertion may be cited.

In the years 188 and 1882, the districts on the Pacific slope, between the capital city, Tegucigalpa and the coast, experienced an unusual and prolonged drouth. The corn crops utterly failed twice in succession, and the starving people were compelled to substitute the seed of the broom corn for the accustomed cereal. On the Atlantic slope, and also on the eastern table lands, the crops were unusually prolific, but the cost of transportation from this locality to the Pacific slope was so great, that when Government was compelled to come to the rescue of the starving people, and furnish them with Indian corn, it was found much cheaper to purchase the article in San Francisco, pay freight on it to Amapala, and thence to Nacaome, the centre of the famine afflicted reigon, than to draw upon the ample domestic supply in the eastern districts. Thus while corn sold for $1 50 a fanega—400 ears—in San Pedro Sula, at Nacaome it readily brought from $5 to $6.

The same lack of transportation methods prevents the wheat and flour of the interior table lands from being sent to the coast on either side, and the natives of San Pedro on the Atlantic slope, and Nacaome, and Guascaran on the Pacific side, find it much cheaper to purchase their supplies of this important food stuff in the New Orleans and San Francisco markets.

While there are several primitive grist mills in the republic which turn out very fair flour, their products exercise but a limited influence, which is felt only in the markets of the localities where they are established. The condition of the roads and the high price of transportation will account for this singular situation. Two years ago a young German planted a vegetable garden, and a large quantity of wheat near the Potosi mining company's property. He depended upon the demand at the mines for a market for his produce. The flour furnished from his wheat field also finds a ready market in the neighboring pueblos. He intends putting up a small grist mill and planting a larger area of wheat.

The gigantic "Tabor" enterprise on the Patook river has also established a grist mill on one of its properties. As some of its lands produce a very fine quality of wheat, the syndicate proposes planting a vast area of this cereal during the present season. The local superintendent, Alonzo Hicks, Esq., has put several saw mills into operation and is getting out furniture and construction timber for transportation.

The Pacific slope is partially watered by four streams, or rivers, which in the dry months contain but little water. They are the Guascaran, Nacaome, Choluteca and Black rivers. The latter is the boundary line between Honduras and Nicaragua. On the Atlantic coast nature has been more prolific of her gifts in this direction, for besides numerous little streams that irrigate the country there are several navigable rivers. The Ulua, Chimalicon, Blanco, Santa Barbara, Patook, Stephens and the Wanks are fine rivers which, with their branches, drain the entire Atlantic slope. The Patook river is navigated by the boats of the Tabor syndicate, the Ulua by the Sheers company, and the Tinto by the Trujillo and Puerto Cortez Railroad Co.

Comyagua, the former capital city, contains about 8,000 inhabitants and is situated in a vast plain watered by the Comyagua river. This latter contains a perennial supply of the precious fluid, but it is only navigable in restricted localities.

Tegucigalpa, the present capital of the republic, is situated on the edge of a wide valley, close to the base of a tall mountain range. It contains 12,000 inhabitants and boasts several imposing churches and edifices. It is the centre of a rich mineral region. Its wealthier residents are all engaged—more or less—in mining operations.

While there are numerous centres of population of from 3,000 to 6,000 inhabitants in the republic the two aboved named are the principal cities. Santa Barbara, the capital of the same name, may also be considered as important, as it lies in the centre of a rich mineral and agricultural region.

CHAPTER VIII.

Within the past five years the mining industry of Honduras has been partially revived, and several American, French and native companies have begun the development of various valuable deposits. Ex-President Soto is at the head of á syndicate which is working several mines in the Yuscaran district. A Chicago company is developing the vast Potosi mineral property in the Department of Santa Barbara. A French association is taking ore out of the Santa Cruz deposit, and a New York company has made considerable progress towards developing the Camalote mine. A Colorado syndicate is in possession of a most valuable mineral property at, or near, Juticalpa, while Messrs. Collyer, Conners and Don Abelardo Zelaya are working profitable mines near Tegucigalpa on their own account. Gen. Bogran, the President of the Republic, is the possessor of several paying placer gold, and, strange to say, one placer silver mine. Edward Kraft owns some six square miles of placer diggings that were formerly abandoned by the Spaniards. This valuable gold deposit was rediscovered by him. Numerous natives are operating placer gold mines in a quiet and unostentatious manner in different localities of the republic.

During the three hundred years the Spanish crown held Tropic America in subjection, Honduras was esteemed one of the most valuable of its transatlantic possessions. Numerous profitable silver and gold mines were opened and worked, while notwithstanding the badness of the roads and the primitive methods employed to extract precious metals from the ore, each mule train that wended its way to either coast carried large sums in silver and gold in bars.

But besides the inexhaustible ledges of silver and gold-bearing rock that seam the mountain sides, vast plains lying between the principal rivers, and the beds of the numberless smaller streams and mountain torrents, were found to contain paying quantities of gold dust. Many of these placer diggings were worked by the avaricious Spaniards, but a majority of them are still virgin, although their existence is known to most of the natives who live in their vicinity. The Department of Olancho may be regarded as a vast placer mine, while there are many other localities in the republic where still richer placer deposits have lately been found.

Unlike California and Lower California, Sonora and Chihuahua, Honduras is reticulated by numerous rivers and streams of water admirably adapted to gold-washing purposes. Travelers seldom take the trouble to carry water with them, for every two or three miles of their journey they pass perennial streams of the precious fluid. The placers of Honduras can therefore be worked at a minimum cost.

There can be no reasonable doubt entertained as to the value of the mineral resources of this little republic. All that has hitherto retarded their development has been the lack of capital and enterprise. Both these wants have lately been filled. Foreign capital is investing heavily in the mines already known, while American enterprise is pushing into the neglected mountain districts, where a number of sturdy experienced prospectors are engaged in searching for hitherto undiscovered mineral deposits.

One of the most prolific gold-bearing regions in Central America is found near the centre of the extensive Department of Olancho. The cream of these placers, consisting of a well watered locality containing sixty-seven square miles, is owned by an enterprising Chicago gentleman named Dr. Osgood. The doctor bought the property from a Cuban prospector, who had located the mines but failed in forming a company to work them.

In the spring of the past year, Mr. Osgood succeeded in overcoming the usual difficulties that all pioneers of mining enterprises always seem destined to encounter, and formed a company to carry out his vast plans. He first went to Honduras and carefully examined his property. Several experts accompanied him and thoroughly prospected the locality. Their reports were in the highest degree favorable, and might be termed unanimously so, for the lowest estimate, of the yield of the gold bearing soil, was forty·five cents to the cubic yard of earth

Before he returned to Chicago the doctor organized several working parties who are at present engaged in taking out paying quantities of gold dust. When the necessary placer working machinery is on the ground and in operation, the work will be carried out on a grand scale. From the knowledge now possessed of this enterprise it seems destined to become one of the most valuable mining properties south of the Rio Grande.

The Tabor syndicate, mentioned above, has received valuable mineral and navigation franchises from the Honduranean Government. One concession grants them the exclusive privilege of the navigation of the Patook river, for a long period of years. The president of this company is Senator Tabor, of Denver, Colorado. The general manager is Captain Burrows, a gentlemen well known in the mining circles of Colorado, Arizona and New Mexico. The superintendent of the several camps is Mr. Alonzo Hicks, of Flushing, Long Island.

The syndicate has placed two little steamboats on the Patook river and is busily engaged in removing the obstructions that impede navigation in the upper part of this water course. Captain Burrows is sanguine regarding the ultimate success of his navigation enterprise and has announced that, in a few months, the river will be navigable for his steamboats for 150 miles from its mouth.

Besides this enterprise, the Tabor syndicate is busily engaged in developing several valuable mining properties. Mr. Hicks writes that he has already got out 600 tons of fine ore, which he will immediately proceed to mill. Captain Burrows has purchased, and sent to the locality, all the mining machinery necessary for present operations, so this entire grand enterprise, in all its different branches, may safely be pronounced already on a promising footing.

As an indication of the great and valuable mineral resources possessed by the republic, the following extract from the official report of Dr. Fritzgaertner, the government geologist and mineralogist, may prove interesting to the American reader:

"The government of Honduras has adopted similar mining laws to those of the United States, in their main features. Mining property is not taxed, and there is no duty on the exportation of ores or bullion. The government will tender all assistance in its power for the transportation of machinery, and will admit it free of importation duties.

Native gold in nuggets, scales and dust is found in numerous placer grounds, also in fissure veins, and occurs often in the form of wire gold. It is likewise found in combination with ores of copper, iron and tellurium. Platinum is found in numerous river beds in scales and in grains. Silver is very abundant, and exists principally in the following forms: Native silver in plates and wires, chloride and bromide of silver, argentile, silver glance, ruby silver, argentiferous grey copper and galena.

Tin is known to me in paying quantities in two localities. Bismuth and antimony are also very frequently found. Copper has been discovered in many parts of the Republic. The quality is excellent and the quantity inexhaustible, while the ore, as a rule, contains a very large percentage of silver and gold. Lead is found in large deposits and fissures. This metal is not worked for its intrinsic value, but only in case the ore contains gold and silver in paying quantities. Whole mountains of fine magnetic iron exist both near the coast and in the interior. The natives use clean and fine ore directly in their forges. The iron produced is of a very superior quality and greatly resembles steel in all its characteristics. Coal is very abundant on the Atlantic coast, near the river Ulua, the quality being a semi-bituminous kind. As the quantity seems to be quite considerable, this mineral will, in the near future, become a valuable article of commerce along the Caribbean coast. There are numerous old mines of historical fame, formerly worked by the Spaniards. There are in Honduras a great many abandoned mines which were worked, as far as the water level, by the conquerors, while local traditions speak of the

12

fabulous sums taken from many of them. In this paper I will take the provinces in their order and give a list of the most noted of these old workings.

Province of Chaluteca; the extreme southern department of Honduras, contains many deposits of high grade silver ores. The most famous of the old Spanish mines, in this section, are the Corpus, the Cuyal and the St. Martin. The province of Gracias, in the southwestern portion of Honduras, possesses a most salubrious climate. The ore of the Coloal copper mines contains 50 per cent of copper and from 50 to 200 ounces of silver per ton. The historical mine of Sacramento contains chloride of silver in large quantities. The district of Evandique is known for its fine opals, which command high prices in London.

The province of Tegucigalpa, abounds in fissure veins. Almost everywhere old Spanish workings are encountered; nearly all are abandoned and partly caved in. The most noted mining localities are Yuscaran, with about 120 mines including the once famous " Guavabillas " which sixty years ago produced $400,000 in six months, and " La Veta de Paraiso " " Guadalupe " " Mercedes," " El Roble," etc. The veins at Yuscaran average from three to six feet in thickness, and the ores are all high grade.

Not far from Yuscaran is located San Antonia, a once celebrated mining camp. It contains four horizontal beds of argentiferous galena and carbonate of lead. The four layers are stratified, lying one above the other. Another rich camp is " Santa Lucia," with many old mines, of which I will mention only " La Mina Grande." This vein is in many places ten feet wide, and is composed of colespar and galena, with chlorides and sulphides of silver with copper. Two other well known mines, at present worked by natives, are " Veta Azul," and " La Mina de San Bartolo," both containing chloride of silver. The mine of Guasacaran, with a productive silver ore deposit, is well worthy of notice.

The province of Comayagua forms the centre of Honduras. The Honduras Interoceanic Railroad will pass through this section and thus render some of its mining districts more accessible. The principal of these are "Aramacina," "Lanterique," "Las Piedras," and "La Paz." Tin ore was found by me in this province in combination with copper. On this section many old dumps exist which contain thousands of tons of valuable ore.

Province of Olancho—a district of 11,000 square miles, but with very few inhabitants. In this district are numerous placers containing gold in paying quantities. Olancho is the historical ground on which Gil Gonzalez and his followers reaped their golden treasures.

The mountains of Olancho have never been practically explored, although numerous veins of gold quartz have already been discovered.

While traveling through the province of Yoro, I found shot gold in many water courses. The latest information I have received is that gold gravel has been discovered in this locality that pays one and a half ounce per day, to the pan workers.

The province of Santa Barbara borders on the Atlantic. Gold placers have recently been discovered that have attracted considerable attention abroad. This auriferous ground is near Quimistan and extends to the bay of Ysabal, Guatemala.

There are in the valley of Quimistan, three valuable mines; Santa Cruz, Camalote and Monte Cristo. They are being actively worked by foreign companies and will shortly have fifty stamps in operation. The gold ore is of a free milling character and is both abundant and fairly rich.

During my sojourn in Honduras I was authorized to organize the National Museum. I exhibited in the rooms of the museum, specimens from 580 different localities, which were forwarded to me or collected personally. A list of mines, both ancient and modern, showed 410 working. About sixty mines are at present operated, fifty of which are worked in a most primitive and wasteful manner.

The Rosario Mining Company, of New York, has lately taken possession of an old mine and will, without doubt, receive large returns if the property is properly managed. By order of ex-president Soto, I took charge, for two months, of the Lonia Larga mine. It was caving badly at the time and was partly filled with water. There were no ladders and their place was supplied by poles, with notches cut in them, the ore having to be carried in rawhide sacks from the bottom of the mine. The result of my two months' work was gold and silver bullion to the amount of $45,000, at an outlay of $15,000.

The foregoing lines clearly demonstrate the fact that in former days mining was carried on to a very considerable extent in Honduras. We know from the reports of the conquerors that immense deposits of the precious metals wore brought to light in that country. The old excavations left by them verify their glowing accounts. The records of the mints of Guatemala and Tegucigalpa show the amount of $6,004,242 as being coined during the period between the years 1795 and 1825, from bullion reduced in Honduras. We must remember that this was only a small portion of the actual gold and silver product of that period, as the greater part of it found its way into the marts of the world as bullion in bars.

After the victorious war of independence against Spain, the Spanish aristocracy, the then owners of these rich mines, left Honduras, and their property reverted to the government. A number of their mines were taken up by the natives, but from want of knowledge and lack of industry and capital, together with their crude and wasteful way of reducing the ores, the profits were small, and they gradually abandoned the claims, or most of them.

At present a moiety of the natives are engaged in agricultural pursuits, and consequently a large number of valuable mines are lying idle. The introduction of modern methods of mining and reducing, with a small amount of capital, would certainly bear good results.

The attention of the mining world is already again being directed toward Mexico, and will no doubt soon get down to Honduras, which will in a short time become one of the world's greatest mining fields.

In conclusion, I would state that in my capacity of geologist of the government of Honduras, I visited all parts of the country and was thereby furnished an excellent opportunity of examining most of this abandoned mining property, together with many localities where placer diggings and gold and other mines were known to exist, but which as yet have never been even located or appropriated by mining corporations."

The greater portion of the grand valley of San Pedro Sula is as yet unoccupied. Its fertile soil is covered by immense tracts of cahoon palms, mahogany, cedar and ceiba trees, and the winding streams that water it are the home of the wild fowl that nightly come in from the sea.

President Bogran is anxious to see this vast tract of land settled by foreign emigrants, and has offered every inducement to heads of families and young couples to make their home in the country. Land will be furnished all who really desire to cultivate it. Every moral and material aid that can be extended them, emigrants may expect from his government, while the Honduras people will be glad to welcome them as fellow-citizens.

About fifteen leagues—forty-five miles—to the westward of San Pedro, is situated a large sheet of water called lake Yojoa. The country surrounding this lake is not only remarkably beautiful but its soil is fertile and its climate is that of perpetual spring. A portion of the lands of this locality are at the disposition of emigrants, for as this situation is central and near the route of the proposed interoceanic railroad, President Bogran is anxious to see it occupied as soon as possible.

The short space allowed by the plan of this little work prevents the author from entering into further details regarding the vast, the varied and the valuable forest, agricultural and mineral resources of this truly wonderful tropic republic. If it is impossible to describe their infinite variety and estimate their value, it is none the less impossible to exaggerate their future importance in the commercial world.

In company with its sister republic Guatemala, Honduras is blessed with a truly liberal system of government. Gen. Luis Bogran, the President of the country is one of the most brilliant young statesmen as yet produced by Central America, and he labors earnestly to bring about the thorough social and material regeneration of his country. He has wisely eschewed the traditions, the sentiments and the customs engendered• by 350 years of Spanish misrule and five decades of anarchy and revolution; he ignores the sullen system of conservatism engrafted upon Government methods by nearly 400 years of theocratic rule; and has boldly taken the precepts of Morozan, Ocampo and Juarez, as his guides in the path of reform he has marked out and entered. His life is exceedingly precious to his country, for if he lives until the expiration of his term of office, he will surely accomplish the regeneration of his country.

As it may be some time before the Interoceanic Railroad is constructed, Government has given a franchise to certain Americans to build a line from Trujillo to Tegucigalpa, a distance of nearly 200 miles. This road, in conjunction with the McConnico system, will open a vast stretch of territory to enterprise and commerce. As the latter will eventually connect with the Guatemala Northern Railroad, the capital of the land of the Quiche will be placed in regular, but somewhat roundabout, communication with Tegucigalpa.

With its vasts forests of precious woods, its fertile soil which returns such prolific crops, its tall mountains laden with rich mineral deposits, its wide plains where the bed-rock has collected and upheld the particles of gold that for countless centuries have washed down from the adjacent mountains, with its rapid rivers whose beds are impregnated with golden sand, Honduras is not only the most promising division of Central America, but it is probably the most valuable mineral territory for its extent on the planet.

SAN SALVADOR.

The object of this little work is to present to the people of
this section and of the Mississippi valley a brief account of
the natural resources of Central America. For that reason
the Caribbean coast and the territories contiguous to it, or in
communication with its ports by railroads, wagon roads or
bridle paths, as the case may be, have been accorded as much
space as the plan of the work permitted, while the Pacific
coast, with its superior ports, its wide cultivated savanas and
its industrious and prosperous people, has been little more
than briefly mentioned. The author's reason for the adoption
of this plan is obvious. New Orleans (and also the Mississippi valley through this port) is in direct communication
with the centres of the commerce of the Caribbean coast
by the Oteri, Macheca, Muller & Co., Miller, and C. A. Fish
& Co.'s lines of steamers. The first three lines communicate with the ports of the republics of Guatemala and
Honduras, and also those of British Honduras, every few
days, while the Miller and C. A. Fish lines touch at the ports
of Nicaragua, the Mosquite Reservation and the Republic of
Costa Rica, every month. The steamship Lucy P. Miller extends her trips to Aspinwall (Colon), Isthmus of Panama.

Central America, from the boundary line that separates its
territory from Mexico, on the north, to the Isthmus of Panama,
may be divided into two almost equal portions; which are
known as the Atlantic—or Caribbean—and Pacific slopes.
These two grand divisions are virtually separated by an im-

mense mountain chain called the Central Cordillera. As the
mountains are tall, rugged and very broken, the roads that
lead over them are mere bridle paths, and, for a great portion
of the year, are almost impassible. The difficulty of transporting effects over the Cordillera, and the high rate of freight
tariff that in consequence obtains, has virtually resulted in a
commercial separation between the two slopes, rendering them
almost totally independent of each other as far as traffic is
concerned. This situation will continue until railroads, that
connect the two oceans, are constructed.

The Republic of San Salvador, although one of the most
enlightened, prosperous and wealthy of the numerous Latin
American Nations, as it lies exclusively on the Pacific coast,
and is cut off, by the mountain range above mentioned, from
all commercial communication with the Caribbean seaboard,
excites comparatively little interest in the American people,
east of the Rocky mountains. While it carries on a profitable
and constantly augmenting commerce with San Francisco
and Europe, per steamers to Panama, thence across the isthmus by rail, and then again by steamers to the east, from the
very nature of things has no communication with New Orleans,
nor does a dollar's worth of trade with our port. 'A mention
of this republic then will suffice for the plan of this work.

The history of San Salvador, from the epoch of the conquest
of the country by the Spaniards, is incorporated with that of
the rest of Central America. The first mention of it we find
in the archives of Hispano-Americo-Central History is, that
the first explorers found the country thickly settled by a
powerful and industrious race of indigenes who were excellent
miners and most successful agriculturists. They were known
as the Pipiles, were divided into several nations and were
ruled by wealthy and powerful caciques—kings.

As soon as he had subdued the Cakchiquel Kingdom of
Guatemala, the intrepid but sanguinary conquistador, Pedro
de Alvarado, advanced against the city of Atehuan, one of
the most eastern centres of population of the great and powerful Kingdom of Cuzcaltan, which comprehended a great portion of modern Salvador. The king and nobles had made

extensive preparations for the reception of the Spanish commander as a friend. At Atehuan, Alvarado was met by a commission of nobles who were charged to offer him obedience and to acknowledge themselves as vassals of the Spanish crown.

The conqueror immediately procceded to the capital where he and his followers were received in the kindest and most hospitable manner. Good quarters and an abundance of excellent provisions were provided, and the king came in person to pay his guest a ceremonious visit. But the infamous and ungrateful conduct of the Spaniards and the ravages committed by their auxiliaries soon drove the disappointed and ill treated natives to desperation. They deserted their beautiful city, and fled to the woods and mountains. The poor people captured by the conquerors were immediately *branded* and sold as slaves.

Alvarado sent envoys to the fugitives, with a threatening message ordering them to return immediately, and acknowledge vassalage to the monarch of Spain. The king justly indignant at the treatment his people had met with at the hands of those whom they had received as guests, answered that he knew no other monarch than himself and neither was, nor ever would be, vassal to any one; that if he wanted him and his people he must come and seek them, and he would be received on the points of their sharp lances. The general sent an expedition against them, which was defeated with terrible loss. Eleven horses were slain in this combat. Alvarado, upon the return of his shattered forces, resorted to pacific measures. He sent another envoy " with a honeyed message," but the king refused to receive him. He then marched against " the rebels" with all his forces but was unable to subdue them. Irritated at this unexpected turn of affairs Alvarado instituted "*a legal process*" against the fugitives. They were declared in a state of rebellion against their *natural sovereign*, the king of Spain. The king and principal nobles were sentenced to be hung, while the whole population of the country were condemned to be publicly branded and sold as slaves.

He continued seventeen days at Cuzcatlan, but was unable to come to terms with the people who refused to treat on any pretext whatever with the ferocious invaders of their country. As the rigor of the season prevented further military operations in the mountains, he was compelled to retreat, deferring for a period the conquest of this rich and populous country.

In the year 1525, the Spanish commander sent another expedition against the Cuzcatlan king, who had returned with his people to his capital. The natives, who foolishly encountered the invaders in the open field where the cavalry could manœuvre with facility, were defeated in several partial combats and, at length, in a pitched battle. The conquerors entered Cuzcatlan in triumph and immediately carried out the sanguinary provisions dictated by Alvarado during his first expedition.

In a short while the whole territory was entirely subdued by the indefatigable, but ruthless conquerors, who divided the lands among them, while the natives, like so many cattle, were branded and parceled out with the soil they were forced to cultivate.

In 1522, the territory which is now comprised within the limits of the modern republic of San Salvador contained a population of more than 3,000,000 industrious and contented natives; some of the tribes had elected and deposed their chiefs or caciques at will, and it was only when the immediate ancestor of the king who so gallantly repulsed Alvarado's first attack, conquered the various tribes and united them under his dominian that an aboriginal feudal system was established in this locality.

For three hundred long years San Salvador continued a Spanish province. The few aborigines that remained, in the capacity of serfs or peons, tilled the fertile soil or toiled in the mines situated deep in the interior of the giant mountains. Meanwhile the deep hatred the natives bore their oppressors was inherited by the Ladinos, or that mixed race which sprang from the intercourse of the conquered and the conquerors. This sentiment was entertained in a greater degree, if possible, by the Creoles or pure blooded descendants of the Spaniards, who treated their children born in the province of Spanish mothers as inferior beings to themselves and the other fortunate mortals who first saw the light in Old Spain.

When the day of reckoning came, the Indians, Ladinos and Creoles united and bitterly avenged the three centuries of oppression they and their ancestors had groaned under; and after a series of sanguinary conflicts, the Spaniards were mostly driven out of the country.

During the long years of anarchy, revolution and civil strife subsequent to the declaration of independence, San Salvador suffered all the ills and misfortunes consequent upon such a situation. The mines were deserted, and in the course of time even the localities of the most valuable were forgotten. Commerce, both external and internal, was paralyzed, while the little traffic that yet survived was almost entirely in the hands of strangers and aliens. Agriculture was but faintly carried on, and a thousand flourishing plantations, farms and ranches were abandoned.

This unfortunate condition continued until the year 1876, when Barrios, the reformer of Guatemala, the chief of the Liberal party of Central America, could no longer shut his eyes to the retrograde policy that swayed the administration of President Valle, and demanded an interview with that functionary. The parties met at Chingo and formed a plan for the regeneration of San Salvador and Honduras. But Valle had no intention of carrying out the compact. He merely wished to gain time to prepare for war, which was soon afterwards declared.

In the spring of the same year Barrios entered Salvador at the head of a large, well-armed and finely disciplined army. He totally defeated the Salvadorean forces and entered the capital in triumph. Thus the little republic was entirely at his mercy, while the Liberals of Honduras, weary of anarchy and confusion, were ready to enter into any arrangement he chose to propose to them. Then Gen. Barrios might have realized the ambitious dream of his life, the reunion of the old Central American republic. But he threw away the opportunity, and after pacifying Honduras and binding Salvador to him by a treaty of alliance, he withdrew his victorious troops from Salvadorean territory and returned in triumph to his capital.

Since that epoch San Salvador has been indirectly under his dominion, while his potent influence is felt throughout the wide area of Central America. But Salvador has greatly gained by the change. No revolution can change her tranquility while the protecting arm of Barrios extends over her. In fact, the very political existence of the great Liberal depends upon the situation in San Salvador, for in the very nature of things Salvador must either be a friendly and allied power or a conquered province. Barrios cannot for a moment permit the existence in Salvador of a dominant party which is, or might become, inimical to his interests. It is probable, therefore, that while he lives his voice will have paramount influence in the administration of the public affairs of this republic.

There seem to be but few persons in this country or in Europe who really understand the political status in Central America. The subject is worthy the study and attention of American statesmen, who, in case of further complications in Central America, should be better posted on the political situation that obtains in that to them almost *terra incognita.*

San Salvador is the smallest of the Central American republics. It is bounded on the north and east by Guatemala and Honduras, and on the south and west by Honduras and the Pacific ocean. It possesses an area of 7226 square miles, or 4,624,640 square acres. The population is somewhat more than 600,000; that is, if we may believe the assertions of prominent Salvadorean statesmen. It now possesses a republican form of government, although the spirit of conservatism is indicated in the constitution, which prohibits suffrage to persons of no stated occupation and to servants. The executive, with the title of President, is chosen by popular vote—with the restrictions specified by the constitution—and serves for a term of four years. The Senate is composed of twelve members and the Houses of Deputies of twenty-four. Complete toleration in religious matters is guaranteed, but the constitution is not as liberal as that enjoyed by the sister Republic of Honduras. The expenditure of the government is somewhat less than the revenues, while the national debt, which is now very small, is being gradually extinguished.

Salvador is one of the most flourishing of the Latin American nations. Its commerce, both internal and external, is constantly augmenting. In 1883 its exports amounted to somewhat more than $5,000,000, and its imports to $3,500,000. The principal exports are coffee and indigo, but sugar is also exported to a small extent, while rubber, gums, skins, hides, tan bark, etc., are shipped to California and Europe. In fact, England enjoys more than half the foreign commerce of the republic.

Quite a lively traffic is carried on between Salvador and the neighboring republics. Honduras sends vast quantities of tobacco in the leaf, mats and straw hats to her sister republic, while the latter exports coffee, indigo and certain gums to the markets of the former. Guatemala receives a large annual amount of cattle from her thriving neighbor, and in return sends back to its markets numberless articles which find a ready sale.

The country is corrugated by numerous mountain spurs that spread out fan like, from the great range that divides Central America. In several districts along the coast, the tall foot-hills come down to the very ocean that bathes with its long rolling billows their rocky bases, while wide verdant plains and beautiful tropic valleys are burdened with prolific crops of indigo, sugar-cane and nopals, whose pale green leaves give life and food to the purple cochineal which, even comparatively recently, was such a valuable article of commerce.

The cultivation of indigo has become the principal industry of the country. Experience has proved it to be a prolific crop and a great deal of money is invested in its production. It is prepared for export on the haciendas and is principally shipped from the port of Acajutla, in sailing ships to Europe via Cape Horn, and per steamers north to San Francisco, Cal., and south to Panama, where it is transported across the isthmus to Colon and from thence transhipped to the Atlantic seaboard and Europe.

The cultivation of coffee is fast assuming imposing proportions. It is true that last year Guatemala shipped more of the precious staple than either Salvador or Costa Rica, but it is no less true that the quantity cultivated in either of the two last named republics far exceeds that produced by Guatemala. The higher regions, where the table lands spread out into wide expanses between the bases of the giant mountains, and attain an altitude of between 2000 and 3500 feet above the level of the sea, are the chosen localities for the cultivation of this valuable article of commerce. In those fertile districts, where the cool bracing winds that career down from the summits of the contiguous mountains, encounter the hot breezes of the tropics which are tempered by its refreshing currents, the coffee plant attains its highest degree of productiveness, while the dews which nightly fall heavily in these regions enfold in their humid embrace the younger plants and refresh and invigorate them after the hot ordeal they have passed through during the long tropic day. For the coffee plant is ranked among the most tender of all the numerous specimens of the tropic flora. After it is placed in the ground it requires constant and perfect protection from the intense heat of the sun. It thrives best in damp places and under the grateful shade of neighboring trees, while it is invariably planted, on the Atlatic slope, between rows of the huge leaved plantains or bananas.

In Western Guatemala and in Salvador, the trees are set out during the rainy season and generally, by the time the dry months set in, have acquired sufficient strength to live through that trying period. Yet sometimes before the wet period arrives the young plants assume a sickly yellowish appearance and they must be irrigated with the greatest regularity, or they will certainly die. The coffee industry in 1881, was remarkably prosperous and more than 20,000,000 pounds were shipped from the ports of the republic. This quantity represented somewhat more than $2,000,000 in the currency of the country.

The low price lately obtained for the article, in foreign markets, has had a depressing effect on this industry. The planters, for the last three years, have done little towards increasing the acreage of cultivation, and have, in a measure, turned their attention and energy to the production of other crops.

.Thus indigo planting has received a new impulse, while stock raising has become a promising industry.

Although there are several famous mining localities in the republic, agriculture has always been the principal occupation of the people. Shortly after the conquest the Spaniards extracted a large amount of silver and gold dust from the rocks, river beds and gulches, which they of course sent to the mother country. But the mining industry soon flagged, for on the warm, sultry Pacific slope, the natives quickly died under the lashes of their cruel task-masters, and the Spaniards, unable to endure the hardships entailed upon the prosecution of this industry, were forced to abandon it almost entirely.

The tropic fruit traffic has excited but little interest in San Salvador. The republic lies too far from the great Pacific market to render the shipment of bananas, plantains and oranges, either safe or profitable. As their is no demand, there exists no reason to produce a supply, so this branch of industry is limited to furnishing the domestic market.

Quite a profitable trade has been done in dye woods and furniture timber since the regeneration of the country under the Zaldiva regime. Ships frequent even the little out-of-the-way roadsteads that indent the coast, and receive on board valuable cargoes of precious woods. The ports of the republic again witness the arrival of vessels destined to carry on this traffic. They generally bring outward freights of European manufacture for the supply of the interior markets.

The improvement of the breed of cattle, and increase of the herds, has lately received increased attention from the agriculturalists. Vast stretches of territory which had lain idle and fallow since the epoch of the conquest, and fertile mountain slopes and foothills that had never been disturbed by the hand of man since the primitive inhabitants were exterminated by their oppressors, have lately been transformed into cattle walks, and furnish vast herds with excellent pasturage. President Zaldiva has offered premiums for specimens of improved breeds of native stock. The farmers and stock raisers have entered into a friendly emulation, while hopes are entertained that it will not be long before cattle raising will be considered one of the principal industries of the country.

There exist several flourishing cotton factories in different localities which turn out a coarse cotton cloth. There are many kinds of domestic manufactures, which of course are not known to the outside world.

The wagon roads and bridle paths of this republic are by far the best constructed and kept in repair that can be found in Central America. The roads that connect the principal cities with the coast, and with each other, are either paved or mac- adamized, while those of the interior are kept in repair by the municipalities they traverse.

Some three years ago the Huntington syndicate of Califor- nia obtained concessions which virtually put all the projected railroad system of the republic in their power. They have surveyed the principal lines and have done considerable work on some of them.

There are numerous fine cities, towns and villages within the boundaries of the little republic. San Salvador is the capital. It contains many imposing churches and public and private edifices. It is not situated far from the coast, to which it is as yet unconnected by rail.

Three principal seaports, two of which may be considered mere roadsteads, are the receiving depots for the foreign traffic of the country. They are La Union, La Libertad and Aca- jutla. The latter was founded about the same time as San José de Guatemala, and carries on quite a promising com- merce.

Altogether, San Salvador may be looked upon as a promis- ing, progressive and enterprising little republic. But it can never, until both its own and the Honduranean and Guate- maltecan railroad systems are completed, hold direct commer- cial communications with this city and section.

NICARAGUA.

CHAPTER I.

Belief in a Natural Passage Between the Two Oceans—Gil Gonzalez'
Journey Through Costa Rica and Nicaragua—He visits Nicoya and
Nicaro—Discovery of the Great Lakes—Expedition of Cordoba—Gra-
nada, Leon and Segovia Founded—Cordoba Declares Against Pedra-
rias--Is Defeated and Executed--Death of Gil Gonzalez and Pedrarias—
Cruel Treatment of the Natives by the Spaniards.

The Emperor Charles V. at the very commencement of his
reign, evinced the greatest anxiety to know the exact where-
abouts of the much talked of strait that was said to connect
the Atlantic and Pacific oceans. The conquest of Mexico
once achieved, he ordered his victorious captain, Hernando
Cortez, to send expeditions along either coast, both north and
south, to search for the much longed-for passage. Pedrarias,
the Spanish governor of Darien, received the same peremptory
orders and at once set about carrying them into effect.

About this time a certain Spanish *caballero* named Gil Gonzalez de Avila, arrived at Darien. He had been commissioned
by the emperor to fit out an expedition to explore the Pacific
coast for a distance of 200 leagues. Pedrarias sent with him as
pilot, Andrés Niño, who had accompanied Hurtado when the
latter discovered the gulf of San Lucar. Gil set sail the 21st
of January, 1521, from the gulf of San Miguel.

After a voyage of about 100 leagues to the northwest, he
discovered that his vessels had sustained some damage and
hauled them out for repair. He took advantage of this circumstance to penetrate into the interior with 100 infantry and
four horsemen. But he suffered terribly. The country was
marshy and overflowed and he was compelled to cross several
rivers on rafts.

During this adventurous expedition he passed through numerous Indian villages belonging to a cacique named Nicoya.

13

The latter informed Gil that the name of the country was Orotina, and that some distance further to the north he would find several large lakes of fresh water. Nicoya consented to submit to the ceremony of baptism, and his example was followed by 6000 of his countrymen and vassals. The Spanish commander having made many inquiries regarding gold and where deposits of it might be found, the cacique presented him with a quantity of the precious metal that amounted to $60,000, together with six good sized idols, also of pure gold.

When his followers were rested and in condition to proceed, Gil again took the field accompanied by porters and interpreters, and shortly afterwards arrived in the country of the Niquirinos. This people had made preparations to attack him, but the interpreters sent with the expedition by Nicoya assured them of the good intentions and peaceful disposition of the Spaniards, so they threw down their arms and received the strangers with shouts of welcome.

Nicarao, the cacique of the country, a much more powerful potentate than Nicoya, entertained the adventurers at his court and also made them many presents, among which was a quantity of gold valued at $100,000. Gil Gonzales de Avila gave him in return some silk dresses and other European articles, and then set himself earnestly to work to convert the Indian monarch to christianity. The questions asked by Nicarao regarding the Catholic dogmata, and his conversations with the missionary who had undertaken this important conversion, prove that he was a man of great talent. At length, the monarch having succeeded in convincing his council of güegüe—ancients—of the truth of the christian religion, he and his principal military and civil officers, with 9000 of his vassals, were solemnly baptized and received into the bosom of the Catholic church.

Gil soon left his hospitable host, accompanied by an Indian *tapaliqui*—general—who served him as interpreter, and halted not far from Nicarao's capital, which was situated in the midst of the great lake of Cocibolca, on a mountainous island called Ometepe. The Spaniards gave this lake the name of Nicarao-agua, or the waters of Nicarao. From this incident the

word Nicaragua is derived, which has since been bestowed
upon the whole republic.

Gil had learned that the lake Cocibolca discharged its surplus waters into the Atlantic, but that it had no direct communication with the Pacific. Yet his new friends informed him
that it was connected with another lake, further to the west,
which latter might possibly empty into the ocean. The object of his present expedition was to ascertain the truth of this
information. Unfortunately he was unable to reach the locality
where the lakes were said to unite, in consequence of a sanguinary war that was going on between Diriangen, cacique of
Diriambra, and Tenderi, cacique of Nindiri. He was compelled
to make a wide detour to the west to the district of Nograndans
and saw lake Xolotlan (now lake Managua) from Jubila, the
capital of the Nagrandanos. In this city he was received by
the *Monexia*—the united military and civil councils—who were
in session at the time and were about to proceed to the election of a new cacique.

Further to the north Gil discovered a great gulf that was
known as the Chorotega, but which he thought was a third
large lake. From this point of observation it was impossible
for the Spaniards to ascertain with certainty if this arm of the
Pacific really did communicate with lake Xolotlan. Some of
the Indians told him a river from this lake communicated
with the gulf; others pretended that this river, or strait, had,
just before, been closed during a terrible convulsion of the
earth caused by an eruption of a volcano—Momotombo—situated near its edge, and since that occurrence the lake Xolotlan empties into the Cocibolca.

Relying upon the statements of his new found friends, Gil
made no further attempt to explore in this direction. One of
the principal Indians informed him that the gulf of Chorotega
(now the Fonseca) communicated directly with the Atlantic
through a strait situated behind the great volcano Conchagua
and the range to which this latter peak belonged. Delighted
with having discovered the secret of the existence of the long
desired and sought-for strait, and fearing that some of his followers might obtain the same information, Gil hastened away

from the locality. After having collected his scattered people
at the capital of Nicarao, he proceeded to Orotina, where he
found his pilot, Andrés Niño, who in his absence had navigated along the coast for 350 leagues and had reached the
limits of Guatemala. The Spaniard embarked at this point
with all his people and returned to Panama, having been ab-
sent nearly two years.

From this epoch may be dated the long series of misfortunes
that overwhelmed the gallant discoverer of Nicaragua. Gil
Gonzalez de Avila was of a frank, communicative and generous disposition, and was greatly beloved by his subordinates.
Pedrarias, the Governor of Darien, was valiant, audacious
and intelligent; but he possessed a tyrannical and jealous disposition. He was very ambitious, but he was also cruel and
sanguinary. Gil having solicited the future government of
the regions he had just explored, Pedrarias, desirous of appropriating to himself the results of said expedition, refused Gil's
just demand under the pretext that the territory in question
was not that which Gil had been authorized by the king to
conquer, but the same that had been discovered by his (Pedrarias') lieutenants, Ponce and Hurtado. Irritated at such
injustice, Gil embarked for Santo Domingo and laid his grievances before the REAL AUDENCIA. This body, enchanted
with the relation of his discoveries, and desirous, above all, to
expedite the discovery of the connecting passage between the
two oceans which Gil assured them existed, gave him the full
and legal title of Governor of Nicaragua.

According to a map which was drawn up from information he had received from the Indians, Gil thought that the
Gulf of Fonseca could not be far distant from the Bay of
Honduras. He departed for the latter with the ships, men
and horses which had been furnished him in Santo Domingo.
He arrived without accident, but when about to disembark a
terrible tempest arose; and his horses becoming sick, he was
compelled to throw them into the sea. Shortly afterwards he
disembarked in a fine bay a little to the north of the scene of
his misfortunes and founded a settlement which he called San
Gil de Buenavista.

In the meantime, Pedrarias, whom the story of Gil's former expedition had inspired with an unconquerable desire to add Nicaragua to the provinces under his jurisdiction, resolved to send an expedition thither, to form an establishment. But to realize this object it was necessary to find a commander who, with the valor to conquer and the talent to establish a colony, should lack the ambition and enterprise to declare himself independent.

There was at Panama, among the unemployed adventurers who swelled the little court of the governor, the same Francisco Fernandez de Cordoba, who had explored Yucatan before Grijalva's expedition thither. He was a gentleman of good family and had been one of the first settlers of Cuba, where he had made a fortune. His expedition to Yucatan, which he had undertaken at his own cost, had ruined him. He was not able to continue his discoveries in that direction for want of means. He had, therefore, been compelled to seek for employment. Cordoba was past the middle age. His vast experience had dispelled the illusions of youth and he was noted for his philosophic temperament. He was sufficiently brave to conquer, and disinterested enough not to inspire fears of his appropriating what he had conquered.

Pedrarias therefore hastened to offer the command of the expedition he intended to send into Nicaragua, to Cordoba. Upon the latter's acceptance of the trust he furnished him with a sufficient force, well fitted out, and also sent with him the same pilot who had guided the fleet of Gil Gonzalez de Avila. Cordoba, who came originally from Andalusia, chose for his followers from among Pedrarias' soldiers, all who were natives of that part of Spain. These adventurers were the forefathers of the principal Nicaraguan families of to-day.

After having disembarked at Orotina, he founded a city at the mouth of the Salto, which he called Bruselas, in memory of the recent military achievements of the Spaniards in Flanders. He then marched to the territory of Nicarao and entered into an alliance with him. He shortly afterwards, but not without some difficulty, entered the country of the Dirianes, where the king—cacique—permitted him to found a city close to Subteba. He named it Granada, after one of the principal cities in Spain. As he found this locality very healthy he resolved to make the new city the centre of his future operations. He fortified it and erected a magnificent church, which he dedicated to his patron, San Francisco. Desirous of exploring the lake as soon as possible, a brigantine was brought, in pieces, from Bruselas, on the backs of the Indians, porters of the neighborhood. He soon discovered that the lake (Nicaragua) communicated only with the Atlantic.

Gil Gonzalez, who had been engaged in exploring the country to the north, in search of that strait which constantly seemed to elude him, learned from certain Nicaraguan Indians that the country had been invaded by one of Pedrarias' lieutenants. He immediately gathered his people together and accompanied by numerous Indian auxiliaries marched against the invaders.

The distance was greater and the country more broken than he had imagined, and while he was slowly penetrating the district of Olancho, Cordoba heard of his intentions and advanced to meet him as far as the country of the Nigrandos, where he founded Leon, not far from the margin of lake Xolotlan, near Imbita.

Here he fortified his camp and calmly awaited Gil's approach. After some time had elapsed he was informed that his adversary had flanked his position and entered the country of the Chontales. He marched out to find·him. At length the forces met near Toreba. The battle was deadly. Cordoba, almost victor in the first combat, was utterly defeated in the second and lost many men, all his horses and almost $425,000 in gold.

Gil made preparations to pursue him and reconquer all Nicaragua, when he was informed that a Spanish fleet had appeared off his settlement of San Gil. Deeply impressed by this fact, he preferred to lose the results of his victory, and resolved to return to his northern conquests. His greatest fear was that the intruders intended searching for the strait, which he constantly imagined he was about to discover himself. Cordoba took advantage of this retreat to follow him, at a distance, as far as the river Coco, where he stopped short and founded a city, which he named Nueva Segovia.

The quarrels that arose in Honduras between Gil, Las Casas, Olid and Cortez, irritated the Real Audiencia of Santo Domingo to such a degree that this body at length sent a hidalgo named Moreno to Central America, with instructions to pacify the country. Moreno disembarked in Trujillo, deposed Las Casas, and appointed Juan Ruano governor *ad interim* of Honduras and Nicaragua. Having installed the new functionary, Moreno commanded Cordoba, who was then at Leon, to submit to Ruano, to obey the orders of the Real Audiencia, and ignore the instructions of Pedrarias.

Cordoba resolved to take advantage of the situation and declare himself independent of all parties save the King of Spain. But Pedrarias had in Granada numerous relatives and friends who opposed this movement. Cordoba endeavored to force them to submit, but the Granadans rebelled against his authority, and under the command of Captains Soto and Campeon marched to encounter him. The ancient feud between the Indian nations of Nagrando and Diriamba swelled the ranks of both combatants. The rebels of Granada were compelled to retire before the forces of Cordoba. Soto and Campeon fled to Bruselas and afterwards to Chiriqui. From this latter locality they sent word to Pedrarias of all that had taken place.

This latter chieftain, enraged at the treachery of his former obedient lieutenant, resolved to chastise him. He collected an ample force and set sail for Bruselas. He from thence proceeded to Leon, which he captured, and immediately ordered the unfortunate Cordoba to be beheaded. He marched afterwards to Trujillo, raised the whole province against Ruano, and obliged him to flee for his life.

Ruano returned to Santo Domingo followed by Gil, who had remained quiet in the hope of eventually succeeding him in the government. The Audiencia resolved to send him to Spain with a detailed report of the events that had lately taken place in Central America, and Nicaragua in particular. They also petitioned that Gil might be appointed Governor, as he was the only man, in their estimation, who could pacify the country.

Gil was well received by the court and was appointed to fill the post he had so long struggled for. But scarcely had he triumphed over his enemies, and obtained his just rights, when he sickened and died at Valledolid in the beginning of the year 1526.

With the execution of Cordoba and the untimely death of the chivalrous Gil Gonzales de Avila, ends the romantic and adventurous era of the conquest of Nicaragua. The cold blooded Pedrarias in person took an active part in the subjugation of the country. The two former adventurers were kind and friendly to the natives, who readily followed them on their various expeditions and fought valiantly under their orders.

Meanwhile the King of Spain (Charles V.) had appointed Diego Lopez de Salcedo Governor of Honduras and Nicaragua in place of the deceased Gil Gonzales. On his arrival at the scene of operations, this functionary found Savaadra, a lieutenant of Cortez, in command. He immediately deposed him, put him in prison for awhile, and then, after confiscating his property, exiled him to Cuba. But Pedrarias, who had waited quietly at Leon until Cortez returned to Mexico, sent his lieutenant, Rójas, against Salcedo. The latter was able to maintain his pretensions; so, after a series of sanguinary conflicts, Rójas entered into a compact with him by which Pedrarias was recognized as Governor of the Nicaraguan territory as far as the jurisdiction of Nicarao extended. Pedrarias, who was dissatisfied with this arrangement, refused his consent to it, and determined to go to Spain and petition the king for a legal title to his conquests.

After a prosperous voyage, Pedrarias reached the peninsula and immediately proceeded to the court. He was well received by the king and succeeded in obtaining the title of Governor of Nicaragua, with instructions to leave Salcedo in charge of the government of Honduras.

The news of this arrangement having reached Leon, the municipality of that city laid hold of Salcedo and reduced him to prison. When Pedrarias arrived he had him tried for having destroyed Bruselas, and kept him prisoner for eight months, when he eventually released him and allowed him to proceed to Honduras, where he was soon after poisoned by his enemies.

Pedrarias who had treated the Indians with the utmost severity and had suppressed the least sign of resistance to his power with the most bloody reprisals, on his return to Panama encountered a change in the situation. Taking advantage of the quarrels between their oppressors, the Indians had broken out in open rebellion But Pedrarias was equal to the situation, and fought the Indians without cession. Numerous combats, and six battles took place. At first the Indians obtained many advantages but they were eventually defeated, with terrible loss, and finally, submitted to Pedrarias in 1529.

This latter chieftain inaugurated a system which he denominated the " *Period of organization.*" The chiefs of the Indian rebels were thrown to the bloodhounds which tore them to pieces. The survivors were forced to embrace the Catholic religion under the penalty of death. The masses were subjected to heavy tributes and severe tasks. The repartaminto system of labor was introduced, and generalized, and the natives were divided like cattle among the cruel conquerors. Those individuals who resisted were ruthlessly tortured, and when communities rebeled, their towns and villages were destroyed, and the miserable inhabitants put to the sword. The Indians were reduced to the most abject slavery. Their property was taken and they were branded like cattle with red-hot iron. The Antilles having been depopulated through this system of cruelty, the Spanish residents sought slaves on the main land. Thousands of the unfortunate natives were chained and sent to Trujillo to be transported to Cuba and Santo Domingo to be sold as slaves.

Pedrarias died, as he had lived, in harness, in the year 1531. Through his own personal efforts and those of his Lieutenants he achieved the conquest of that vast stretch of territory extending from the equator, north, to the southern limits of Guatemala. But his cruel system of government prevailed for a long period after his death, and the miserable remnant of Indians, he still permitted to exist, moistened their native soil with their bloody sweat, or dragged out a brief and painful existence in the mines or gold placers.

CHAPTER II.

When the adventurer, Gil Gonzalez de Avila, first landed on the coast and penetrated to the borders of the great lakes, Nicaragua contained within its limits a happy and industrious Indian population of 3,000,000 souls. In less than ten years, more than two million and a half of the natives had perished in battle, were worked to death in the mines, or had starved amid the mountain fastnesses which proved their last refuge from Spanish oppression. The very year of Pedrarias' death, 1531, a terrible famine prevailed. The small-pox and scarlet fever followed in its train, and at least 250,000 more of the miserable Indians perished. Thus, in 1810, when the first movement towards realizing the independence of the country was made, an impartial observer unhesitatingly estimated the entire aboriginal population of the province at but 90,000 souls.

The history of the long Spanish rule in Nicaragua comprises but little more than a series of combats with Indian rebels and of quarrels between the two rival cities of Leon and Granada. The home government oppressed the descendants of the conquerors almost as much as the latter did their Indian vassals. The inter-marriage of the first conquerors and settlers with the daughters and female relatives of the aboriginal caciques brought about the creation of a new race who were indifferently called Creoles and Ladinos by the Spaniards. But the Spanish fathers treated their half breed children with contempt and their native wives with a good humored assumption of superiority. The issue of these marriages naturally feared their fathers and loved their mothers;

and invariably sympathised with the oppressed aboriginal population. None but native Spaniards were permitted to fill the public posts or hold commissions in the army, thus the half castes were relegated to a life of toil or idleness.

Meanwhile the English had landed at various points on the Atlantic slope, and eventually formed permanent establishments. The Mosquito tribe and the Zambos joined their standard and waged a ferocious and interminable war against the Spaniards and the Indians who remained faithful to them. The English entered into a vast contraband trade with the Ladinos and also with many disaffected Spaniards, and promised them material assistance whenever they saw fit to make a bold strike for their independence. In the beginning of the present century the English were virtually masters of the entire Caribbean coast, while the restless Creoles and Ladinos, of the interior, and the entire Indian population were ready to avenge the long dark period of Spanish misrule and made secret preparations for revolt.

At length, in 1810, the news arrived and was promulgated, that in 1808, the armies of the Lion of Corsica had entered Spain and had deposed the taciturn Ferdinand VII.; that Quito had raised the standard of liberty over her public buildings and that the Mexican priest, Hidalgo, had proclaimed the independence of Mexico.

The patriots of Leon followed the example of the so-called rebels of Mexico and New Grenada and deposed their governor, José Salvador. The Spanish Cortes, upon information of this event, decreed that Nicaragua should be governed by a council composed of the deputies of Leon, Costa Rica, Granada, Rivas, Segovia, Matagalpa and Nicoya. This council met in 1812 and decreed the promulgation of the liberal Spanish Constitution.

But the patriots were dissatisfied with this arrangement. The people of Granada took the initiative. They deposed all the Spanish functionaries and demanded independence. Troops were sent from Leon to suppress the revolt, and several sanguinary conflicts took place. Various patriots, among whom were Arguello and Cerda, were sent prisoners to Spain.

Upon the fall of Napoleon, Ferdinand reascended the throne of his ancestors and the liberal Constitution was abolished. But many of the Spanish functionaries in Central America deprecated this restoration of absolutism. The Creole and Ladino patriots endeavored, in conjunction with this new element of opposition, to bring about an entire separation from the mother country, but their efforts were fruitless and much precious blood was shed in vain.

In 1820, the successful conspiracy of Gen. Riego, the fall of the absolute party and the new promulgation of the Constitution of the Cortez decided the fate of Guatemala. The exiles of 1814, returned and the patriot party pronounced openly in favor of complete independence. Gainza, the Captain General, favored this movement hoping to direct and manage it for his personal benefit. At length Guatemala was solemnly declared free and independent on the 15th of September, 1821.

An election for deputies to Congress was immediately held, but before the Congress in question met, the new republic was annexed to the ephemerel empire established by Iturbide, in Mexico. Then two political parties divided Central America. The one in favor and the other against annexation The larger cities adhered to the compact, but those of second order—Granada, for instance—demanded separation from the empire. The patriot inhabitants, under the leadership of one Ordoñez, refused to submit and arnachy and civil war prevailed until the fall of the Iturbide regime, in 1823.

June 24th 1823, a Congress was held in Guatemala, which is known in history as the National Constitute Assembly. On the 1st of July the united provinces of Central America were declared free and independent, and from that date may be reckoned the actual emancipation of the country.

On the 17th of October, the same year, a constitution was submitted to Congress, for discussion. The 17th of April, 1824, slavery was abolished. At that epoch there were not more than a thousand slaves in Central America. The owners were immediately paid their full value. At length the First Federal Constitution was promulgated on the 22d of November, 1824. Each province was elevated to the position of a sovereign state, with its independent Congress or legislature, while a National Congress was to hold its regular periodical sessions at Guatemala the capital of the republic. The new Constitution was sworn to by the public officials April 15, 1825, and the first federal Congress met on the 1st of the following September. This Constitution, notwithstanding the numerous revolutions that menaced its existence, was considered the fundamental law of the entire country until 1838, when it was overthrown and the republic was destroyed by the triumphant serviles.

While the Constitution was being drawn up and the republic founded, Nicaragua was the prey of factions whose struggles converted the state into a theatre of battle and bloodshed. The ancient rivalries of the cities of Leon and Granada broke out afresh. The residents of one city favored the federation of the five republics; those of the other declared for the absolute separation of the provinces and their entire independence of each other. The Federalists became known as the liberal party and the anti-annexionists as the serviles.

In the beginning of the year 1824 the province was governed by an administrative council, which substituted the government of Sarabia. But it scarcely had time to pass a few measures, among which was the abolition of slavery, when its authority was destroyed by the terrible struggle between the two parties. On the 4th of July a revolution broke out. On the 22d of the same month, after a sanguinary conflict, Léon was captured and sacked by the enraged Liberals.

In March, 1825, Honduras and Nicaragua seceded from the federation; and on the 10th of April a Congress, presided over by Zamora, met and gave a constitution to the free and sovereign State of Nicaragua. On the 22d of the same month Cerda and Arguella, who had been exiled in 1811, were elected, the one a supreme chief and the other vice chief of the State.

But this attempt at political organization was made too late. The parties had committed such excesses against each other that their reconciliation was impossible. But the principal cause of further troubles was the quarrel that took place between Cerda and Arguello. Each became chief of one of the two parties that divided society. A cruel civil war broke out. During its course the subject of dissention was completely lost sight of, and a terrible conflict, that lasted years, devastated the country.

From this epoch may be dated that strange Nicaraguan custom which made it incumbent upon each member of society to declare himself a partisan of one of the political parties which were constantly striving to obtain possession of the government. The females were as bitter and rancorous as their male relatives and contributed, in no small degree, to the intensity of the conflict. The idea of submitting to the political supremacy of the opposite party was too humiliating to be borne by the high minded people, thus as fast as one faction gained the upper hand the other rebelled and strove to overthrow it.

According to the historian, Levy, "this unfortunate situation brought about a corresponding corruption of morals   Each ambitious man strove either to govern or take part in the government. Those who occupied the principal posts sought to enrich themselves. Property was violated and individual liberty ignored. Justice was prostituted and only the phantom of a government existed, The conquered party was the object of inhuman reprisals, and, desirous of avenging those of its numbers who had been shot like dogs, grasped the first opportunity to renew the strife. Treason, hypocrisy, seduction, conspiracy and assassination were introduced into politics, and the country became the prey of the most horrible disorders." This terrible condition of affairs prevailed until the death of Cerda, who was shot at Rivas, in 1829.

About this time the Liberal General, Morozan, attempted to reorganize the government and put an end to the civil wars that desolated each of the five states of the federation. For a period his efforts were successful and the serviles were about to give over the struggle in despair, when the brutal and ferocious Carrera of Guatemala appeared in the political arena. Morozan's star paled before that of the fortunate ladino, and he was driven into exile. He returned to Costa Rica in 1840, but was defeated, captured and shot at San José. With him fell the Central American republic.

In 1838, the federal Congress dissolved the federation, declaring the states free, to govern themselves as they saw fit, with the single restriction that the form of government should be republican. On the 30th of April, 1838, Nicaragua proclaimed her absolute independence, and promulgated a new Constitution. Each state assumed its proportion of the debt contracted by the federation.

But before the declaration of the state's independence the internal disorders had continued. The rivalry between the cities of Leon and Granada served as a pretext for the most bloody struggles. The poorer politicians established a situation of war against all who owned property, without distinction of party. Zepeda was cruelly assassinated at Leon, and the vice governor, Nuñez, assumed the functions of chief of the nation.

The last Federal Congress closed its sessions on the 30th of June, 1838, and Pablo Buitrogo was elected the first supreme director, with instructions to establish the Constitution of April 30th. He was soon succeeded by Don Manuel Perez.

The federal cause was totally lost. The dictator, Carrera, held the key of the situation and by his declaration of Guatemala as a separate and independent republic definitely dissolved the federation. Then Perez, the supreme dictator of Nicaragua, endeavored to bring about a union of the three States of Salvador, Honduras and Nicaragua. A convention was held in 1842, but the exalted passions of the different political parties soon put an end to the deliberations of this body, and the plan of partial federation fell to the ground.

Left to its fate, Nicaragua continued the prey of the most complete anarchy, and for five years a continuous situation of civil war obtained. In 1844, Malespin invaded Leon and overthrew Perez. José Leon Sandoval assumed the functions of supreme dictator. This gentleman endeavored to reform his country but was unsuccessful. He sent an agent to England to attempt the solution of the Mosquite question and to solicit assistance for the Nicaragua canal, which had been projected by Baily, in 1838. This mission failed and, in 1847, Sandoval resigned and José Guerrero was chosen to fill the position he had vacated.

As early as 1836, the Nicaraguan Government resolved to dispossess some English fillibusters who had captured Greytown in 1824, and had even gone so far as to establish a customhouse at that point. Colonel Quijano was sent with sufficient forces to oust them. He succeeded in his mission. The English retired but sent an envoy to Belize to ask assistance from Governor McDonald. This latter official acceded to their petition, sent forces to the scene of operations and retook the port, which was, however, evactuated shortly afterwards.

When the English troops retired Quijano immediately reoccupied the place. The English and Nicaraguan Governments from that moment entered upon an angry correspondence. The former claimed jurisdiction along the entire Caribbean coast. The latter naturally demanded that England should repress her fillibustering subjects and leave Nicaragua in peace. Then the English incited the Mosquito Indians to attack the port, but government soldiers repulsed them time and again until Captain Lock, by order of the Governor of Jamaica, Sir Charles Grey, at the head of a large force, took possession of the port, ascended the San Juan river and occupied Granada. He held possession of this city until he made a formal arrangement with the Nicaraguan Government, on the 7th of May, that it would no longer interfere with the sovereignty of the Mosquito Nation over the Atlantic coast. The foreign residents of the port, in gratitude for the action of the Governor of Jamaica, gave it his name, and since that epoch it has been generally known as Greytown.

This disgraceful circumstance had—temporarily at least—a very beneficial effect upon the people. The fact that a small body of foreign soldiers had, almost without resistance on their part, captured their principal Caribbean seaport, penetrated far into the interior of their republic and occupied their second city in importance and wealth, humiliated them to such a degree that they dropped their arms and put an end to their interminable civil wars.

In 1849, Norberto Ramirez succeeded Guerrero. This year was marked by the arrival of the American Minister Plenipotentiary, Mr. Squier, and Nicaragua entered into a treaty of peace and friendship with the great republic. About the same time an American named Brown entered into a contract to construct the canal, and Vanderbilt, the great American ship-owner, obtained permission to transport freight and passengers, for California, through the country from Greytown, on the Caribbean coast, to the Pacific.

But these measures, although a step forward in the right direction, were far from satisfying the irritated state of feeling consequent upon the repeated violations of national territory, and the Central Americans again demanded possession of the Bay Islands and the port of San Juan del Norte—Graytown. The English, upon these manifestations, immediately occupied Tigre Island, in the gulf of Fonseca. Then the United States interfered and demanded the recognition of the Monroe doctrine. At length the Clayton-Bulwer treaty was entered into. The absolute independence of the Central American republics was assured as well as the neutrality of all future canals that might be cut through this territory. But the American statesmen, in their anxiety to prevent the further extension of slavery and the acquisition of territory to the south that might be utilized for that purpose, lost sight of the Mosquito coast question and foolishly entered into a stipulation which virtually rendered American influence null in Central America. Thus, if the ratification of this treaty was a glorious event for the little Latin-American republics, it was an ignominious compact for our own country to be bound by, and cannot be abrogated too soon.

On the first of January, 1851, the first Vanderbilt steamer arrived at Greytown. The supreme director, Laureano Piñeda, placed at the disposition of the enterprise the two ports of La Virgen and San Juan del Sur. This step was taken for the purpose of diminishing the length of the transit, as hitherto the route led through Realejo and Granada.

14

The same year the town of Managua was declared the capital of the republic, for the purpose of putting a stop to the disastrous rivalry that still existed between the cities of Leon and Granada. A third convention decreed the union of the three States—Honduras, San Salvador and Nicaragua. In 1852 a national assembly was held at Tegucigalpa for the purpose of conferring a constitution on the new federation, but no result was arrived at, and the plan of the confederation was definitely abandoned.

In 1853 Don Fruto Chamorro was elected Supreme Director. This gentleman was one of the most intelligent statesmen and accomplished scholars that Central America had as yet produced. He was a sincere patriot and entertained liberal, but not radical, sentiments. He set himself earnestly to work to pacify his country and regenerate society. In 1855 a constituent assemby abolished the constitution of 1838, changed the title of state to republic, and that of supreme dictator to president. The chieftains of the radical faction fled to San Salvador, but soon returned to Nicaragua at the head of a party of ardent followers, and at Leon were joined by a great number of recruits. Chamorro placed himself at the head of the army and stood a siege of nine months in Granada.

The radicals then invited the American filibuster, Walker, to join their ranks, and in 1855 the latter disembarked at Brito and attacked Ruas. But the young Nicaraguans, irrespective of party, banded against him and he suffered a total defeat. This adventurer again returned to the country. The sequel of his romantic career will be given in another place. For five years he disturbed the country and prevented the prosecution of the plans of reform meditated by the patriot Chamorro.

The death of Walker, and the final dispersion of the unpatriotic Nicaraguans who had followed his desperate fortunes so faithfully, inaugurated a new era of peace and reform. Under the Presidents Martinez, Guzman and Quadra, and somewhat later Zavala and Cárdenas, Nicaragua has slowly but surely entered upon a new political existence.

The war for the conquest of the country by the Spaniards, which has been marked by so many sanguinary scenes and heart-sickening atrocities, and the long, dark, sullen Spanish regime, which brutalized the indigines and terrorized and embittered the creole and ladino population, were the causes which eventually led to the cruel wars and bloody emeutes which devastated the country for five long decades after its independence. When the oppressed creoles and ladinos rebelled against their former masters, the lessons of the past three centuries had been well digested, and, when victorious they turned against each other the arms they had taken up to battle for their freedom. But liberty is a coy damsel who can only be won by force, while her conduct is so capricious and her principles so ambiguous that their true meaning is difficult to be ascertained. She so much resembles license that many of her votaries mistake it for her, and, enveloped in error, commit a thousand excesses before the truth dawns upon them. A people before they can achieve liberty must be purified by a baptism of blood, while the capricious goddess is only reached after wading through a sea of slaughter. Such has been the history of every people who have striven for independence, and such was the history of unfortunate Nicaragua for a period of nearly fifty years.

It would seem almost impossible then that a people who had for so long a period been surrounded by such corrupting influences could even seriously undertake, and eventually achieve, the political, social and material reformation of their country. Yet the Nicaraguans have accomplished all this within the brief period of a decade and a half. The good work of regeneration was begun by President J. Vincente Quadras. His successors, particularly Zavala, the last president and Dr Cárdemas the present enlightened Executive, have faithfully followed his example and have at length fairly solved the problem he first undertook. In fact Nicaragua in some respects has progressed further on the path of political and material reform than her northern sisters. She has extinguished her foreign debt, and has inaugurated a grand railroad system which will in a few years net-work the entire republic with iron bands. Steps have been taken to restore the port of Graytown to its former condition and improve the navigation

of the rapid river San Juan, and the government, desirous of
filling the waste lands with industrious settlers, has offered
advantageous terms to foreign immigrants.

The reader will observe, therefore, that the terrible lessons
of the past have not been unheeded by the people of Nicaragua,
and that in a comparatively brief period they have reformed
the abuses that obtained in their system of government. They
have regenerated the republic. They merit the respect and
esteem of their fellowmen and deserve to be classed among the
most progressive and liberal of all the people of Latin America.

CHAPTER III.

Thirty years ago the Republic of Nicaragua was better
known to the civilized world than any other portion of Central America. A band of brave American filibusters, under
the command of the famous Walker, for several years waged
a war of conquest on Nicaraguan territory. After a series of
sanguinary combats and romantic adventures, the intrepid
Walker, assisted by a few discontented Nicaraguan chieftains
and their followers, eventually prevailed. He seized the reins
of power and for a brief period controlled the destinies of the
country.

Notwithstanding the avowed hostility of the British Government and the undisguised enmity of the people of the
northern section of the great republic to his person and projects, hundreds of volunteers flocked to the standard of the
filibuster chieftain. Thousands more would have cast their
fortunes with him and his success would then have been fully
assured, when he was betrayed into an impolitic act which
speedily brought about his downfall. The moiety of his forces
were natives of the Sunny South. They were naturally deeply
imbued with the political sentiments and the traditions current in that section. Their greatest ambition was to bring
about the establishment of a slavocracy in Central America,
and they induced the reckless adventurer to declare slavery
an institution of the new Americo-Latin Republic.

From the moment that imprudent resolution was taken,
and the decree establishing slavery promulgated, the fillibustering movement was doomed. The British Government
openly interfered and supplied the patriot chieftains with
arms and money. The abolitionists of the northern section

of the United States denounced the new slave-holding power
and the Government was compelled, by the voice of popular
opinion, to prevent all further shipment of material of war,
and of volunteers to Nicaraguan ports.

Deprived of reinforcements, of munitions of war and of supplies, surrounded on all sides by a hostile and irreconcilable
people, the gallant but misguided American chieftain, after
almost superhuman efforts to sustain his sinking cause, was
delivered by the English into the hands of his implacable enemies and was executed as a filibuster. He met his fate calmly
and courageously ; but before he died he is reported, in the
bitterness of his disappointment, to have uttered the following significant and prophetic remarks :

" I have been deserted by countrymen. They promised me
means, arms and reinforcements. I fought their battle in a
foreign country, but it will not be long before the struggle
will be renewed in my own southland and the forces of pro-
slavery and abolition will contend for political supremacy on
the cane fields and cotton plantations of the South."

The deep significance and great importance of the problem
Walker attempted to solve was not at the time comprehended
by the world at large, nor did he himself appreciate, to its full
extent, the work he had undertaken. Walker was not a mere
adventurer. He was an acute observer and had, notwithstanding his assertions to the contrary, arrived at the conclusion
that the institution of slavery had reached its apogee in the
United States. Several of his old comrades at arms who yet
survive have said that his intention was to found a new slave
empire where the soil, the climate and all the surroundings
warranted the success of his grand enterprise.

Nicaragua once subdued and his army reinforced with thousands of adventurers from every land, but particularly from
the southern section of the United States, he would have proceeded northward, and Honduras, Guatemala and San Salvador would in turn have been subdued. These conquests
consolidated, he would have added Costa Rica and the isthmus
to his vast domain, and then, but not till then, would have
declared himself emperor of United Central America.

But to carry this grand enterprise to a successful issue would have required vast sums of money and large armies. The gold and silver mines found in the mountains of Guatemala, Honduras and the Department of Segovia could have supplied the former; the reckless and adventurous youth of the south the latter; and had he not betrayed his pro-slavery tendencies too prematurely, he might have succeeded. In this case, the war of secession in the United States might have been delayed, if not altogether averted, for a more congenial clime for the permanent establishment of slavery would have been furnished, while the institution would naturally have become unprofitable in our own Sunny Southland.

But Walker's grand project fell to the ground, and the soldier paid with his life the penalty of his failure.

But the romantic career and subsequent martyrdom of Walker solved one problem that had sorely perplexed the statesmen of both Europe and America. He struck a fatal blow at English supremacy in the Caribbean sea. When the British delivered him over to execution, they fondly imagined that the greatest foe to their ambitious designs was thus removed. But they were mistaken. The United States and France at last awakened to an appreciation of England's insidious Central American policy and remonstrated against its continuance. The result of this interference was the treaty between Nicaragua and England in 1860, which restored to the former country the territory which had been wrested from her by the latter power. The Cape Gracias and Graytown districts were returned to Nicaragua in full sovereignty. Yet certain commercial restrictions were maintained which even the most prejudiced enemy of Great Britain must confess have proved beneficial to the localities in question. The Mosquito reservation was established, and England, ostensibly at least, renounced her absurd pretentions to political supremacy in Nicaragua. A treaty between Honduras and Great Britain restored to the former the possession in full and absolute sovereignty of the Caribbean archipelago commonly known as the Bay Islands.

As England's designs on Central America eventually assumed such significant political proportions, and as Nicaragua

was the principal victim of that insidious policy, a brief sketch
of the history of Great Britain's endeavor to acquire absolute
political preponderance in Central America might be interesting to American readers.

In the year 1589, a pirate, or filibuster, named Blanveldt
founded a colony at Bluefields.   Other pirates established
themselves at Pearl Lagoon and other different points ; and in
a few years acquired such strength that they openly defied the
majesty and power of the Spanish monarchy.   They soon convinced the surrounding Indian tribes that they were most implacable enemies of the red man's deadly foe, the Spaniards,
and eventually acquired an unbounded influence over the untutored sons of the forest.   Through their intermarriages with
the Indian woman, and the subsequent miscegenation of
ladinos, negroes, caribs, Indians and their own parti-colored
issue, a new race of people was created whose descendants
live still at different localities along the extended Mosquito
coast.   `

As the majority of these pirates were English—(their leaders
almost invariably were)—they naturally looked to the mother
country for moral, if not for material, support to consolidate
and increase the number of their conquests.   For two centuries these ferocious and brutal, but at the same time reckless
and desperate adventurers, harried the islands of the Antilles
and the vast stretch of coast along the Spanish main.   Their
piratical ships infested the Mexican gulf, the wide Caribbean
sea, and even extended their incursions as far east and south
as the mouth of the Rio de la Plata.

A filibuster craft of ordinary tonnage would unhesitatingly
attack a Spanish vessel of triple its size.   The ferocious pirates
were generally victors in these sanguinary combats.   The
Spanish crews, and male passengers, were either slaughtered
immediately, or were reserved and afterward compelled "to
walk the plank" for the amusement of their blood-thirsty
captors, but the female captives were doomed to an even
more terrible fate.   While a portion of the filibusters, pirates,
buccaneers, or whatever they should be styled, were the masters of the southern seas, their companions made long and

victorious incursions into the interior of Guatemala, of Nicaragua, and of Costa Rica, and devastated the country for miles on either side of their line of march.

Thus amid such constantly recurring scenes of murder, of rapine, and of license, the blood cemented foundations of England's future commercial and political predominance in Central America were laid.

In the year 1655, Cromwell dispatched a powerful fleet to the Antilles. His intention was to wrest Cuba, Puerto Rico, Jamaica, and in fact all the West Indian possessions of Spain, from the degenerate successors of Charles V. and the absolute and all powerful Phillip II. The commanders of the land forces and the fleet quarreled, thus the conquest of the Island of Jamaica was the only result accomplished by the expedition. But the sullen Protector was greatly dissatisfied with his incapable subordinates and was meditating the dispatch of another and more formidable expedition to the Antilles, when death put an end to his ambitious projects.

Had this wonderful man, this indomitable spirit, controlled the destinies of Great Britain a decade longer, or if his immediate successor had possessed a tithe of his talent and patriotism, the English flag would to-day wave in the gentle breezes that sway the cane fields and wanton over the wide savanahs of Cuba, Puerto Rico and Hayti, and fly on the summits of the tall mountain ranges which enclose the fertile valleys and elevated table lands of Central America.

From the epoch of the conquest of Jamaica, British influence was predominant on the coast of the Spanish main from Campeche, south and east to the reeking fens and tropic jungles of the distant Isthmus of Panama. The paw of the British lion pressed heavily upon the Bay Islands. The government laid claim to that territory since known as British Honduras and, in 1798, achieved its ultimate conquest. The entire Caribbean coasts of Guatemala, Honduras, Nicaragua and Costa Rica were virtually subject to English rule, while the savage and yet unconquered tribes of Southern Yucatan, of Eastern Honduras and of Nicaragua, looked to Great

Britain for material support against their common enemy, the Spaniards.

Although the courts of Madrid and London were seldom at enmity during this long period of British oppression in Spanish America, the subjects of both waged an unremitting war in the seas that washed the Spanish possessions and along their extended coasts. If the Court of St. James disavowed the piratical acts of the filibusters, the most successful of their leaders were welcomed at Whitehall and even enobled by the degenerate Stuarts. It was not until the buccaneers began to prey upon British commerce that any attempt was made by the island sovereign to repress them. Then the British Government awoke to a sense of their crimes and assisted Spain to annihilate them.

While retaining their hold upon their numerous settlements along the Caribbean coast, the English people adopted a new method of aggression in Central America. If the most ferocious and abandoned pirates were destroyed, the most humane gradually became peaceful merchants and civilized smugglers. If the sullen roar of piratical cannon and the sharp rattle of British musketry no longer sounded in the ears of the terrified Spanish-Americans, the gaily dressed English "contrabandists" defied the rigor of the Spanish authorities and flooded Latin American marts with British manufactured goods.

The Caribbean coast of Nicaragua was the favorite resort of these gentry, while Graytown, Bluefields and Corn Island were their principal headquarters. Again and again were they assailed by the Spanish naval and military forces, but they generally succeeded in beating off their assailants, and became more aggressive after each victory.

During the Napoleonic wars the fleets of Great Britain swept triumphantly over the gulf of Mexico and the Caribbean sea, and Trinidad and several other important Spanish American possessions were permanently annexed to the British empire. Upon the assumption of the Spanish crown by Joseph Bonaparte, the Spanish colonies, incited by British emissaries, refused to acknowledge his authority, and after his fall rebelled against the mother country. Aided by the moral influence, and in many cases by the material assistance, of Great Britain, the rebellion was successful, and from the year 1821 a majority of the present Latin American nations date the epoch of their independence.

The disentegration of the vast colonial empire of Spain rendered its feeble fragments an easy prey to European avarice. The enunciation of the Monroe doctrine and the jealousy of thè great powers prevented the conquest of Latin-America by England, France and Prussia, and the reconquest of portions of it by Spain. But England never relinquished her hold upon Central America until the successful termination of the Americo-Mexican war warned her that the young colossus of the West was then her equal in power, and was destined in the very near future to entirely overshadow her and eventually succeed to the heritage of her American possessions.

Then the British government sullenly relinquished its pretentions to political predominence in Central America. In their ignorance and simplicity, American statesmen were gulled into entering into the disgraceful Clayton Bulwer treaty; and by this act of supreme folly the spread of true republican institutions was retarded, and the political influence of the United States in Central America was shattered for thirty years.

During the sixth decade of the present century the violence of the abolition agitation in the North, the birth of the Republican party and the promise it indicated of political supremacy in the near future, gave rise to a renewal of British aggression in Central America. The English statesmen foresaw the approach of that terrible civil war which eventually devastated the fairest section of our country, and in alliance with the ambitious monarch of France determined to make a permanent European impression upon Latin-America. France was to have Mexico, and England the entire eastern, or Caribbean, coast of Central America.

But that combat of the Titans, the battle between the Confederate ironclad Merrimac, and the Federal Monitor, in Hampton roads, March 9, 1862, taught England that none of the magnificent war ships she possessed at that epoch were able to cope with vessels of the construction of either of the two American ironclads. That memorable naval combat eventually shattered the triple alliance that sought to subvert Mexico, while the success of the Federal Government in the war of secession forever destroyed the fond hopes entertained by England of the appropriation of Central America.

Since 1885, Great Britain has faithfully carried out the provisions of her treaties with the Central American republics, but jealous of the growing power and influence of the United States clings with desperate tenacity to the Clayton—Bulwer treaty which documents many of the American people now justly regard as so much waste paper.

Such in brief is the history of past British aggression in Central America. The filibustering expedition of Walker, in Nicaragua first opened the eyes of our people to its significance, the Federal successes, in 1865, shattered Great Britain's future political influence in Central America forever.

At least so thought the American statesman of that era, but events which have subsequently occurred have proved that once more they had become the simple dupes of astute English diplomists. The treaty entered into, between Great Britain and Nicaragua, in 1860, was so cunningly worded (notwithstanding the deep interest America took in this treaty) that innumerable pretexts might be seized to warrant further aggression. In fact England has several times interfered with the tariff arrangements at Cape Gracias and Graytown, while the existence of Mosquito Reservation is a constant menace to the Monroe doctrine, and an insult to Nicaragua sovereignty.

No matter how much an American might sympathize with the efforts made to civilize his people by the present Mosquito chief (and hereditary king) of the Mosquito Indians, politically speaking, the United States should never have permitted England's interference in the matter. Great Britain had no just right to claim jurisdiction over any part of the Caribbean coast, while the treaty of 1860 leaves that power the actual protector of the Mosquito Reservation.

By the terms of this famous treaty, over 7000 square miles have been wrested from the jurisdiction of the Republic. If

the latter is guaranteed ostensible sovereignty over the territory in question, the Reservation is virtually independent, and
under the rule of an ambitious chieftain might be the cause of
serious complications, if not a sanguinary war, between the
Indian tribes and the Republic.

The present chief, or king, as many style him, George William
Albert Handy, is untutored as far as books are concerned, but
is naturally sharp, shrewd and diplomatic. He has shown
neither as much ambition nor skill as a warrior, as his dead
brother Sula displayed, but having on several occasions evinced
both courage and determination, there is no knowing what
steps he might take were he assured of the material aid of Great
Britain. He could render his little capital at Bluefields, or,
his residence at Pearl Lagoon, impregnable to the assaults of
the government forces, while 6000 brave warriors would as-
semble at his call, who could occasion infinite trouble and bloodshed before they were subdued.

Meanwhile the Mosquito Reservation, with its large commerce, and the constant influx of immigrants, might eventually
become the weak flank of the Nicaragua government. In case
of war with any foreign power, it would prove an excellent base
of operations, while the capture and occupation of the ports of
Graytown and Cape Gracias would effectually cut Nicaragua
off from all communication with the Caribbean coast.

CHAPTER IV.

If the small space Nicaragua occupies on the globe seems to warrant the cause of its present apparent political insignificance in the sisterhood of nations, the vast natural resources found in its fertile soil, its grand forests and its prolific mines point it out as a locality destined to become more and more important as the wants of the commercial world become more importunate and varied.

The Republic of Nicaragua comprises that portion of Central America found between the limits of 10° 45′ and 15° 10′ north latitude and 83° 11′ and 87° 38′ west longitude from Greenwich. Its boundaries are the Atlantic ocean, or that part of the Atlantic between the West Indies and the continent, commonly called the Caribbean sea, on the east; on the south the Republic of Costa Rica; to the west the Pacific ocean, and on the north the Republic of Honduras.

The dividing lines that separate Nicaragua from the neighboring republics have never been fairly determined. As far as the line on the Honduras frontier is concerned, ancient documents prove that the boundary between the two provinces on the Atlantic coast terminated at Cape Camaron. A capitulation made with the King of Spain, by Diego Guiterrez, dated November 29, 1540, for the conquest of the locality now known as the Mosquitia, plainly says so. It is a well known fact that all the country comprehended between the Tinto and Coco rivers was subdued by Rójas, a lieutenant of the Governor of Nicaragua, in whose name he founded the City of Natividad, at Cape Gracias á Dios.

Yet Juarros in his geography of the kingdom of Guatemala says that "the province of Honduras is limited on the east

and southeast by Nicaragua, and that the last of the Honduranean rivers is the 'Platenas'." On both modern and ancient
maps this is a little river situated between the Black river and
the Patook. Thus according to this authority Honduras never
extended further to the east and south than the Patook.

The same Juarros says that on the Pacific coast Honduras'
ancient limit never passed the mouth of the Choluteca river,
which empties into the Gulf of Fonseca. All the old documents that bear on this question say the same. Therefore the
former boundary between Honduras and Nicaragua might be
considered as lying directly on a straight line drawn from the
mouth of the Patook river on the Atlantic to that of the Cho
luteca on the Pacific coast.

Not long since a commission from either republic was directed to re-establish the proper boundaries. Nicaragua
claimed the line just mentioned; Honduras demanded as her
limit the Coco river in all its extent, and the Black river on
the pacific slope. The Honduras commission never for an instant denied that the original limit of their republic was near
Cape Camaron, but they said that none of the country from
Cape Camaron to Boca del Toro (to the south of Costa Rica)
ever belonged to the Spanish, but to Indians, who were always
under the protection of the English. Therefore, the day that
England *ostensibly* renounced said protectorate, a portion of
this country belonged to each of the three republics, Honduras,
Nicaragua and Costa Rica, and that Honduras claimed as far
south as the river Coco on the Atlantic side, and the Negro
river on the Pacific side.

The commission eventually decided upon the following boundary :

The line on the Bay of Fonseca to be located at a point 13° 3'
north latitude, on the margin of the Negro river, and to follow
that river until its union with the Guasaule, the Guasaule until
its junction with the Torondano, and the Torondano up to its
head. From thence over the mountains to the point where the
range of Dipitlo separates. The line follows this range to the
northeast as far as the plains, and from thence in a direct course
to False Cape, to the north and east to the mouth of the Coco

or Wanks river. The most eastern point of this dividing line is situated in latitude 15° 11' north, and longitude 83° 25' west.

By this arrangement Nicaragua was deprived of more than 3000 square miles of territory. On the west it lost some very valuable mineral lands, and on the east the beautiful lake of Carastaca. The Nicaraguan Congress has never ratified this treaty, thus the dividing line between these two republics has never been fixed.   ·

Nor have the Governments of Nicaragua and Costa Rica yet settled their boundary question with satisfaction to either, while the subject still gives rise, from time to time, to angry disputes. Nicaragua claims the territory of Guanacaste, which certainly was under her jurisdiction until 1825. Costa Rica maintains: First, that both Guanacaste and Nicoya belong to her as far as La Flor river, which stream, in times past, divided Nicoya from Subtiaba; second, that the margin of Lake Nicaragua and the right bank of the San Juan river, along its entire course, as far as El Castillo, belong to the jurisdiction of Guanacaste, and as the latter by right pertains to her, so does the territory claimed by Nicaragua; third, that the right bank of the river San Juan, from El Castillo to the port of Graytown, belongs to her, legally, in virtue of various ancient documents, but above all, by the "real cedula" of the 18th of February, 1574, which named Diego de Artieda y-Chirinos, Governor of Costa Rica, and defined the limits of his jurisdiction. The Costa Rican officials also point to the "Capitulacion" of the 29th of November, 1540.   ·   ⁓

To these specious arguments Costa Rica adds those that she derives from her geographical position, according to which her natural limits are the banks of the San Juan river, the southwestern bank of Lake Nicaragua and the Sapoa river, as far as the Bay of Salinas, and the fact of the annexation of Guanacaste to Costa Rica in 1825, which was legalized by the Federal Congress of the united Central American republic—since destroyed—of the same year.

Such was the situation in 1857.

In 1858, very shortly after the expulsion of the American filibusters, the two governments entered into a boundary treaty·

on the 15th of April. The government of Nicaragua has since rejected this treaty. The terms of article 2 of this compact are as follows :

The boundary line of the Caribbean coast begins at the point of the castle at the mouth of the river San Juan, and follows the right bank south of the Castillo, at a distance of three miles from the fortifications. From this locality it forms a curve, the centre of which is said fortifications, but the curve constantly maintains the distance of three miles from the fort up to a point above the castle, and two miles from the bank of the river. The line continues parallel to the turns of the river and the southern bank of the lake, at the distance of two miles from same to the river Sapoa. From this point, which is well determined, that is, two miles north of the lake, an imaginary line is drawn to the centre of the Salinas Bay, on the Pacific.

At the epoch of the independence the province of Nicaragua claimed to possess about 58,000 square miles. The treaties with Honduras and Costa Rica have reduced its territory to somewhere about 40,000 square miles. The modern republic, then, is 200 miles long by about the same width. Its shape very much resembles an isosceles triangle, whose base is the Caribbean coast and whose apex is the cone of the volcano of Coseguina.

The Caribbean coast, from Cape Gracias à Dios south to Graytown, is 300 miles long. Of this extent, 150 miles north and south and fifty miles into the interior is set apart for the Mosquito reservation, which latter comprises some 7500 square miles. The Pacific coast, from northwest to southeast, is about 200 miles long, and possesses two fine ports. Corinto is situated on a pretty little bay, and is the terminus of the railroad. San Juan del Sur is a fine, safe harbor, but is comparatively unimportant at present. The Caribbean ports are Gracias, Pearl Lagoon, Bluefields, Corn Island and Graytown.

The central knot of the Honduras-Nicaraguan chain of mountains is situated at, or near, Sulaco, in the centre of the Republic of Honduras. The principal range follows a southwestern course, and under the name of the Sierra de Macuelizo or San Marcos, reaches as far south as Frijolillo. From thence

15

it suddenly turns to the southeast and follows this general
course amid many turns and windings as far as the valley of
the San Juan river. This last extension may be divided into
four principal sections. The first extends from the hill of Frijolillo to the mountain of Jinjajapa, or Boete. It commences
in the Sierra de la Botija, whose principal peaks are the Va-
riador, the San Sebastian and the Caguasca. Then follow
two notable necks, the Portillo Liso and the Portales, and
afterwards the Sierra de las Tablas.

The second section extends between the hills of Jinjajapa
and the barranca of Tamarindo. It is more irregular and merits
special attention. It at first takes a northerly direction, passing by the hills of Yuscaran as far as Moropotente. At this
point it turns to the east passing by the Rodeo and the mountain of Yali, and from thence proceeds to the south and widens
into a tableland between San Rafael and Jinotega, dividing the
waters of the San Rafael river, which empties into lake Managua, from the river San Gabriel. Between Jinotega and
Matagalpa it bears the name of the Sierra of Guaguali or
Robles, and takes a general southwesterly direction, up to the
valley of San Salvador, from whence it turns towards the south
passing by the hills of Piedra Colorada and Picota. This last
forms a neck—or isthmus—which unites with the hill of
Pando.

Such is the line of the Cordillera in Central Nicaragua notwithstanding volcanic convulsions posterior to its formation,
disturbed the primitive harmony of the mountain system and
its spurs; but more than all in the section first described. The
watercourses of the department of Matagalpa, which undoubtedly should find their way to lake Managua, have been
violently diverted from their course by a formidable obstruc-
tion, the mountain of Guisisil— 4500 feet above the plain—
which is situated in the tableland of Totumbla.

The third section commences at the cerro of Pando and terminates in the mountain of Quimichapa. Its most notable
elevations are, the range of the Ojos de Agua, the hill of Cer-
badilla, the mountain of Siguatepe—dominated by the hill of
Pans—the Portillo de das Lajas, the Oluma, the Tablazon,

the table of Camoapa, the neck or collar of the Paso Real, that of the Puerto at the foot of the hill of Buenavista, the peak of Santa Bula and the hills of Tierra Colorada.

The fourth section reaches from the mountain of Quimichapa to the neck, or collar, of the Castillo, in the valley of the San Juan. This chain, which has several peaks that range from 3000 to 4000 feet above the plain, gradually descends to an elevation of but 600 to 700 feet. It traverses a mountain which has never been explored on account of the deep chasms and fissures that seam its sides.

There are several famous volcanoes in Nicaragua which of late years have shown signs of activity. They do not form a chain of mountains nor do they belong to any particular range, but rise lone and isolated, high above the plains and table lands. Their peaks form regular cones and present two especial features: First, all their summits are in the same rectilinear direction. Second, this direction is, at the same time, almost parallel with the Pacific coast and with the central Cordillera. For that reason the great valley of Nicaragua to the Pacific should be divided into four distinct lines. 1. The coast line. 2. The foot-hills, which are the spinal column of the neck, that separates the lakes from the ocean. 3. The line traced by the volcanos, and 4. the Cordillera itself which forms the limit of the grand valley that contains the lakes.

The volcanic peaks of Nicaragua may be seen by the mariner, who skirts the Pacific coast, a long distance from the shore and serve as land marks. As their latitude and longitude is well known, the sight of their tall summits indicates to the navigator their precise position in the watery waste.

The first Nicaraguan volcano in the long chain south, is La Madera. Its peak, which attains an altitude above the plain of 4190 feet, is truncated. It has a common base with its near neighbor Ometipe whose summit is 5350 above the tableland. Both these volcanos are situated on an island in the great lake of Nicaragua. Their craters show no signs of even comparatively late activity, nor are any traditions extant concerning past eruptions.

The peak of Zapatera, although properly speaking is not a volcano, yet presents undoubted evidence of volcanic origin. Higher up but on the main land, near the city of Granada the truncated peak of Mombacho rises 4588 feet above the surface of the lake. It has for a long time been quiet, but during the period of its activity, the aspect it presented must have been grand and sublime. A short distance from Mombacho is situated the truncated peak of Masaya, 3000 feet above the level of the plain. It was in a state of activity a few years since. Its last eruption took place on the tenth of November, 1858; on the sixteenth of March, 1772, it vomited forth a torrent of lava two miles wide, which to-day covers with unsightly heaps of scoria all the northeastern side of the mountain, presenting a huge, black, desolate stain in the wide zone of vegetation which on three sides surrounds it.

The peninsula of Chiltepe advances from the southern bank of Lake Managua, near the capital, far into its waters. It is similar to the island of Zapatera, a volcanic mole whose position in the general line of Nicaraguan volcanoes will not permit one to doubt its volcanic character. Its highest elevation is 2800 feet.

In the northeast angle of Lake Managua the majestic sharp peak of Momotombo rears its tall summit 6121 feet above the surrounding waters. A short distance to the right is situated its miniature or counterpart, the Momotombito, which forms an islet on the bosom of the lake. Momotombo, for a long period inactive, awoke from its lethargic slumber in 1852. But up to date its eruptions have not been formidable, although it constantly emits more or less smoke. At times a rumbling sound is heard within its vast interior and slight earthquake shocks invariably follow.

After Momotombo, the line traced by the volcanic chain inclines to the west. The cones that compose it are united at their bases and form a range called la Serra de los Marrabios. It occupies a centre of a general geologic elevation whose most perfectly known portion is the plain of Leon. The slopes of this table incline insensibly downward on the northern side, but to the south present a series of stony branches, broken by

numerous chasms which extend to the sea, between the neck—
or isthmus—of Nagarote and that of Rama Gacha, and the
volcanoes of Santa Clara. The principal of these volcanoes are
Asososca, Las Pilas, two peaks 4000 feet high; Orota 2,700,
Telica 4190, Santa Clara and El Viejo, which latter is a sharp
peak 6266. To these might be added the Chonco, which follows the sierra of the Marrabios, although physically it does
not form part of it. There are in this region numerous other
volcanic peaks, but they are insignificant when compared with
the aboved mentioned volcanoes. ·

Forty miles to the northeast of the Viejo rises the truncated
cone of Coseguina, 3835 feet in the air. This volcano is
famous for its terrible eruption in 1835, when it threw ashes
over a circle of 1500 miles in diameter. It occupies the centre
of a peninsula that extends far into the southern side of the
gulf of Fonseca. On the north side of this gulf is the volcanic
cone of Conchagua, 3866 feet high. It is situated near the
port of La Union, San Salvador. From this point the volcanic chain extends almost to the southern limit of Mexico.

These two gigantic mountains guard the entrance to the
grand gulf of Fonseca and present admirable opportunities for
triangulation, which will certainly be taken advantage of
when an exact topographical map of the country is made.

In that portion of Nicaragua situated between the great
lakes and the central Cordillera, it seems evident that another
line of volcanoes was once in process of formation. A vast
number of elevated cones run almost parallel with the volcanic chain just described, notwithstanding in certain places
their proximity to the Cordillera proves that they are not exactly isolated, but rather form part of the spurs of that chain,
whose physical condition has often been completely modified
as far as its western slopes are concerned. These latter extend over a region that is eminently volcanic. Many of the
hills are visible from the lake, the most important being Ven-
tanillas, from which flows the river Tule.

There are several small lakes without outlets which seem to
owe their origin to the volcanoes—at least such bodies of
water only occur in Central America in regions that indicate

volcanic disturbances.   The first is called the Apoyo or
Diriomo, near Granada.   The surface of its water is 780 feet
above the level of the sea.   It is picturesquely situated in a
vast amphitheatre, whose wall rises 900 feet high.   It contains an area of four square miles and is said to be very deep.

Near Masaya is situated the lake of the same name.   It is
340 feet lower than the city, which is 750 feet above the sea.
It has an area of ten square miles ; and as it has never been
properly sounded, the ignorant people of the neighborhood
think it has no bottom.

A short distance from the city of Managua is found the
little lake Tiscapa.   It is but a half mile in diameter, with a
depth of 80 feet at its edges and 160 in the centre.   Near it
are situated the ponds of Nejapo and Asosasca.   This region
seems to have been the scene of numerous geological changes.
The volcanic hill Motastape, located between these two small
lakes, is the result of some such convulsion.   These two ponds
are each about a half mile in diameter and possess a depth of
from 250 to 300 feet.

In the peninsula of Chiltepe is the pond Jilua, and in the
hills of Los Marrabios are several other small ponds, such as
El Tigre and the Moyotepe.

While many of the volcanic mountains, mentioned, are bleak
and bare, the bases and far up the sides of those which may
be considered as extinct are covered with an exquisite and
varied growth of vegetation.   The little valleys at their bases
are carpeted with luxuriant grass, intermingled with flowers
and flowering shrubs, while in certain localities, vast numbers
of giant tropical trees strike their huge roots deep into the
fertile soil.   At the bases of the mountains the mahogany,
cedar, ceiba and tamarind mingle their frondose foliage.   Further up their sides, the oak, the beach and the sycamore find
a congenial soil and climate, while still further upwards the
hardy pine thrives in the cold breezes that career downward
from the bleak summits of the volcanic peaks.

These mountain slopes and foot-hill sides produce extended
areas of grass which furnishes excellent pasturage for large
and small cattle ; vast herds of fat steers roam amid the cha-

paral that follows the forest growth, while in the region where the oak thrives best, hardy goats and sheep find perennial herbage that affords nutritious subsistence. These localities are destined, in the near future, to furnish an ample supply for the beef markets of the West Indies and, perhaps, those also of Europe.

A thousand little valleys lie snugly ensconced within the mountain chain and its numerous spurs and ramifications. Constant streams of water net-work their surface, and irrigation may be employed with perfect success. But the majority of the little tropic paradises are unoccupied and lie idle, awaiting the hand of man to develop their productiveness. Their soil has lain fallow and untouched for 350 years, for the ruthless sword of the conqueror and the deadly march of famine and pestilence have swept away the millions of happy and industrious natives who once harvested prolific crops, where, to-day, the cry of the wild bird is the only sound that breaks the funereal silence that reigns in these lone localities.

Lake Managua, which was known to the aboriginies by the name of Xolotlan, is about thirty-seven miles long by twelve miles (average) wide, and contains an area of 444 square miles. Its altitude is 169 feet above the level of the Pacific ocean. Two points from the opposite sides advance far into waters and give it the appearance of a figure 8. The northern point is low and may be considered a continuation of the hill Guisisil, the other is the volcanic peninsula Chiltepe. The only island within its limits is that which serves as a base for the peak of Momotombito.

This lake is rather shallow and contains numerous movable sandy bars which render its navigation somewhat dangerous for fair sized vessels. Several small steamers, at present, ply over its waters, while a daily line affords communication between Leonviejo, the present terminus of the Central railroad, and the city of Managua, the capital of the republic.

The margins of the northern side are almost unoccupied; on the southern bank are found the cities of Mateares, Managua and Tipitapa. There are numerous little rivers and streams which discharge their waters into its bosom, but they are generally dry in the summer season.

The river Tipitapa is the outlet, or rather strait, that connects the two great lakes. It is sixteen miles long, but is not navigable on account of the rapids and rocks that line its bed. Its average width is 125 yards.

The great lake Nicaragua, is ninety-six miles long and forty miles wide in one place. As its average width is twenty miles it possesses an area of about 2000 square miles. Its depth is irregular; in some places the surroundings are forty-five fathoms, in others from twelve to twenty-five and thirty feet. Currents are visible but their direction is uncertain, while strange to say its waters are infested with huge sharks which are exceedingly voracious. It is 129 feet above the Caribbean sea at its lowest stage. During the dry months its waters are from five to seven feet lower than in the height of the rainy season.

A great many rivers and streams, some of them constant, empty into the lake, while numerous islets, the most of them inhabited, dot its calm bosom. The port of Granada is formed by a curve in the beach and is protected by a group of more than 100 little islets. It carries from twenty to twenty-four feet of water with a sandy bottom that proves excellent holding ground for anchors. The island of Ometepe is twelve miles long. Its northern portion is rocky, but the southern half is extraordinarily fertile and contains two little villages.

The city of Granada, the second centre of population in size and in importance in Nicaragua, is situated on its margin and is connected with the capital by an excellent wagon road.

The western coast is quite close to the Pacific, being separated from it by only a narrow isthmus but seventeen miles wide. This neck of land presents but few obstacles to the construction of a canal which would unite its waters with the great ocean.

CHAPTER V.

The eastern slope of the great Nicaraguan Cordillera carries to the Caribbean coast the waters of numerous rivers whose copiousness is derived from the length of their course, the number of their affluents, and the great quantity of water that falls on the wilds they traverse. Four of these rivers are of the first order and are navigable for a considerable distance. They are the Coco or Wanks, the Rio Grande, the Mico and the San Juan.

Generally the course of these rivers may be divided into three parts. The first portion waters the high lands and the mountain slopes and are not navigable. It comprises numerous little streams and watercourses, of but little individual importance, but which unite and form the principal river. The second portion is navigable only for small boats, but the bed is obstructed and in many places rapids and falls impede the way. The third portion is quite deep and is navigable for fair sized steamers from the last rapid or fall to the sea coast. The freshets that occur during the rainy season, which swell the violence of the current, tears immense trees from the banks which sink and in time the accumulated debris forms little islands, or shallow bars, that more or less obstruct navigation. This is invariably the case at the mouths of each of the rivers of Central America, for even the mouth of the Mico or Bluefield river has a bar that carries but twelve feet of water.

The Coco is the least known of all the Central American rivers, yet it has often been navigated by buccaneers, tourists and missionaries. The filibuster Ravaneau published a fair account of it. The Jesuit father, Navarro, and the English captain. Haly, have also described it. The Coco is three hundred miles long, but as it runs through a narrow valley and has but few feeders, it does not contain the volume of water warranted by its length. Its general course is from the west to the northeast. It rises at the Portillo Liso, where is is known by the name of the river Tapacac, and a short distance to the east receives the waters of several little streams. Where it unites with the Macuelizo it takes the name of Ocotal. On its further course it is swelled by the contents of numerous mountain torrents, and when it joins with the Jicaro, it is known as the Telpaneca river. Many miles further to the northeast it passes through a wide plain called el Llano Coco. From this point it takes the name of the Coco river, and thus it is generally called by the natives of the country.

But this river possesses a vast number of other names by which it is indifferently called by foreigners. The English mahogany cutters always style it the Wanks or Benks. The mariners of the same nation know it as the Cape river. The buccaneers, who ascended it as high as Segovia, which place they several times sacked, called it the Segovia river. The Spaniards invariably mention it as the Gracias river, and the missionaries, as the Phantasm or Encuentro, while the Indians invariably style it the Yoro. This last is probably the true name, or at least that which it bore at the period of the conquest.

Four miles above the mouth a creek, that flows from lake Gracias á Dios, empties into the right side of the river; on the west side of this lake is situated the port of Gracias or Cape town. Two hundred years ago this lake, or rather little bay, which now has an area of six square miles, was an excellent port. It has but twelve or fifteen feet of depth while the entrance is not more than twenty yards wide, with from seven to eight feet of water on the bar.

The Rio Grande, or the Matagalpa, river rises in the sierra of Guaguali; eight miles from its source it passes by Matagalpa, the capital of the department of the same name. A little below the town of Sebaco it takes the name of Chocoyas and runs in a southerly direction—receiving by the way the waters of numerous rivulets and streams—to the little town of Esquipulas, and from this point is known as the Rio Grande. From its source to its junction with the Oloma, at Vulvul, its length is but eighty miles. On this stretch of its course it is not navigable. At Vulvul ends the civilized portion of the country, and the river's banks, as far as Tooma, are dotted with the habitations of aborigines. But these natives are harmless and peaceable, and assist the traveler in every possible manner suggested by their simple views of hospitality. From Vulvul to Tooma is sixty miles. From Tooma to the sea the distance is about 100 miles. Along this portion of the river the scenery is majestic. It averages 300 yards wide and fifteen feet deep in the channel, while navigation is unobstructed. About ten miles from the bar it widens into a little lake, on the northern end of which is situated the Mosquito town of Walpa.

The bar is very dangerous and seldom carries more than eight feet of water. It was at this place Columbus lost a boat and its crew. He baptized the river by the name of El Rio del Desastre. With exception of the difficulties presented by the bar, the last ninety miles of the Rio Grande is a magnificent water highway, and offers the most excellent advantages for agriculturists and emigrants.

The river Mico or Bluefields rises in a sierra near the town of Libertad, in the centre of the mineral district of Chontales, and in the course of a few miles receives the waters of the Bala, the Jabali, Salto, and many other rivers and streams of more or less importance, all of which, with their rapid currents, furnish excellent water power. Its general course is from west to east. About fifteen miles from La Libertad it enters the uncivilized region and is navigable for the small boats of the aborigines, who call it the Rushwass. It waters a vast region covered with virgin forests interspersed with flowering plains. For fifty miles its course is frequently interrupted by rapids and snags, and this condition continues until its junction with the Wapee or Escondido.

This latter is formed by the two rivers, Murra and Siquia, which form their currents at the foot of the hill Wapee. Its scenery is very beautiful and varied, and at Kisilala are found the falls of the same name which are 100 feet high. The valleys of the rivers Murra and Siquia present extraordinarily excellent opportunities for the establishment of various kinds of enterprises.

Below its junction with the Wapee, the Mico is navigable to its bar, a distance of forty miles, for vessels of twelve feet draft. It empties into the Bluefields bay, and besides its principal mouth, has more than twenty others, which may be entered by small boats.

The lagoon, or bay, of Bluefields, in the Mosquito reservation, possesses an area of 100 square miles. Its principal entrance is just five miles south of the mouth of the Mico. The bar that separates it from the Caribbean sea is never dangerous, but it seldom carries more than twelve feet of water. The lagoon, in some places, is quite deep, but it is gradually filling up with sediment brought down by the Mico and several other small rivers which empty with it. In the centre of the entrance to the bay is the islet of Casada, and in front, on the opposite margin, is situated the Mosquito city of Bluefields at the foot of the hill Aberdeen.

The San Juan river is probably the most important watercourse in Central America, for it is the outlet for the great lakes of Managua and Nicaragua and carries their surplus waters to the sea. In consequence, Mr. Levy, the French engineer who so thoroughly explored Nicaragua and published an interesting work regarding the republic in 1870, considers the valley of the San Juan as extending from the western bank of Lake Managua to the sea at the Graytown bar. He divides it into four sections, which he separates as follows:

1. Lake Managua and all its tributary rivers.

2. The river Tipitapa, which unites the two great lakes.

3. Lake Nicaragua and all rivers that enter into it.

4. The outlet through which is discharged the waters of the vast hydraulic system of Central Nicaragua.

The lakes have been described briefly in the foregoing pages. The outlet so called by Mr. Levy is a large river that under any and all circumstances is destined to be always utilized as the principal transportation via of southeastern Nicaragua. It flows from the southeastern extremity of the lake, between San Carlos and the river Frio. Its length is 120 miles and its general aspect is that of a great river, with an average width of 150 yards. Its banks are covered with extensive virgin forests.

From San Carlos to El Castillo the San Juan may be justly considered as a mere prolongation of the lake. At this point the waters flow over a species of rapids into another bed, nine feet below. At San Carlos, which is commonly considered the end of the lake, the San Juan is about a quarter of a mile wide and seven or eight feet deep during the dry season. Thus, when the waters are lowest the volume that passes over the rapids is at least 4800 cubic yards per minute.

At Toro, a distance of four miles from San Carlos, the river is obstructed by a collection of rocks, which have on one side a channel of eight feet depth. With the exception of rocks at El Toro, the bottom of the river is sandy. From this point to the sea it is navigable for small steamers the whole year round. At its mouth is situated Graytown, the principal port on the Caribbean sea.

Within the memory of the present generation of American seamen, San Juan del Norte, or, as it is styled by foreigners, Graytown, was one of the best and most spacious seaports on the Caribbean coast of Central America.

During the early years of the sixth decade of the present century, the celebrated American ship owner, Com. Cornelius Vanderbilt, established a weekly line of steamers between New York City and Graytown. This enterprise was undertaken for the purpose of facilitating the transportation of adventurous Americans to the gold fields of California. They were landed at Graytown and carried by small steamboats up the grand river San Juan to the lakes, and from thence to San Juan del Sur, on the Pacific side, where they re-embarked in steamers for the port of San Francisco. This system of light freight and passenger transportation proved very convenient to travelers and profitable to the steamship lines, until the successful opening of the Panama railroad to passenger and freight traffic, in the latter part of the year 1855. Vanderbilt then directed his steamers to the new port of Aspinwall, since denominated Colon, by the authorities of the republic of Colombia, and the Caribbean port of Nicaragua was virtually deserted.

In the same year—1855—the mighty mass of water that forms the current of the San Juan river burst its left bank near the Colorado, and discharged a vast portion of its volume over the adjacent lowlands into that little stream. The bar at the mouth of the San Juan, which until that epoch had carried thirty feet of water at low tide, no longer experiencing the scouring effects of the former quantity of water that had hitherto poured over it, began gradually to receive the muddy deposits that came down held in solution by the water. The wide expanse fronting the port also began to fill, and grew shallower as years passed, until to-day, where twenty-five years ago vessels of the deepest draft swung safely at anchor, a long, low island covered with bamboo cane and willow trees, stretches out to the thither side of the river.

The unfortunate political condition of the republic, the Walker troubles, the interminable emeutes and revolutions that desolated the country for the succeeding decade prevented the government from taking any steps toward restoring the port to its former condition and improving the navigation of the river. In the words of Mr. Theodore Hocke. who lately surveyed the San Juan from its source in the lake to Graytown :

"The San Carlos river brings in tremendous quantities of silt, which has almost entirely filled up the old bed of the San Juan to Graytown, and with great damage done to the port by shifting bars, it has made navigation almost an impossibility, as the vast mass of the San Juan water is directed into the channel of the Rio Colorado and lost to Nicaragua. This will be remedied by cutting a canal from the head of San Carlos river entrance along the San Juanillo to Graytown, and by there building a breakwater. With some dredging it is expected to form a harbor of sufficient depth to receive the Royal Mail steamships of twenty-six feet draft.

"The surveys for this work are under way and will soon be completed.. The government will advertise for bids to do the work by contract. The approximate cost is estimated at from $2,500,000 to $3,000,000. To secure payment the government will soon make a loan in Europe."

A Nicaraguan envoy was last year in England watching the money market. He received fair propositions from various syndicates, but as Nicaragua's credit is unsurpassed, from the fact of her well known solvency, this gentleman refused to enter into any arrangement, basing his action upon the hope of obtaining still better terms than those offered him.

It will be safe to assume that early in the year 1885 the work of re opening the San Juan river to navigation will be commenced.

On the Pacific slope the distribution of perennial water-courses is less diffuse, while but few of the rivers are navigable even for small boats. The Pacific coast of the republic is about 200 miles long, from the gulf of Fonseca to that of Salinas. The water is bold up to the very coast, while neither reefs nor shallows render navigation dangerous The waves dash high on the steep sandy beach, while the surf, which is denominated "La Tasca" by the natives, is remarkably violent and constant. The two extremities of the coast terminate in bays. These latter form first-class harbors, which as yet are unfrequented. The distance between the coast and the foot-hills being very short, the water-courses which drain this region are inconstant and of but little importance.

The bay, or gulf, of Fonseca has every appearance of having once been an interior lake, but some grand convulsion of nature tore the huge coast line of mountains asunder and left an opening eighteen miles wide and of vast depth, which communicates with the ocean.

The first river of importance on this coast is the Choluteca, which courses through a territory claimed by both Honduras and Nicaragua. It rises in the mountains of Ule and Lepaterique. Its course is remarkably serpentine, and it receives so many affluents that its volume is considerable. It passes close to the city of Tegucigalpa, in Honduras, and empties into the gulf of Fonseca. About ten miles from its mouth, on its left bank, is situated the city of Choluteca. The mouth forms a wide, deep creek, through which the ocean tides penetrate a long distance into the interior.

The Rio Negro, or Black river, rises in the foothills of Caguasca, and during its course receives the waters of numerous little streams, the principal of which is the Queso. It flows for a short distance to the south and then turns to the west. Its course forms a small semi-circle. One of its branches, the Guasaule, is as large and important as the main river, and has been proposed as the boundary limit between Honduras and Nicaragua. At the village of Amatillo the Rio Negro formerly flowed in a direct course to the sea, but its bed below this point was entirely filled up with ashes during the famous eruption of the volcano Coseguino in 1835. It opened another way towards the northeast and emptied in a wide marsh called Salinas Grandes. This new course was closed in 1844, in consequence of an earthquake. Then the river crossed its old bed and flowed towards the southeast. This bed filled up in 1853 during an unusual freshet, and the river forced its new course to the south and empties into a marshy lagoon called Los Peregilos. The river Palo Blanco also empties into this lagoon.

At the southern extremity of the gulf of Fonseca a wide, deep creek extends some fifty miles into the interior. It is 300 yards wide, and thirty miles from its mouth carries three fathoms of water. It is known as El Estero Real.

The peninsula of Coseguina contains several safe ports. The port of Rosario is quite spacious. Eight miles to the westward is a group of rocky islets named Los Farallones.

Several small rivers empty into the harbor of Corinto, which is one of the best protected anchorages on the coast. The little town of Corinto is the principal seaport possessed by Nicaragua on the Pacific slope and is the terminus of the railroad from Lake Managua.

Between Corinto to Cape Desolado, a distance of forty-five miles, are the mouths of the rivers Leon and Tamarindo. The entrance to the last named river forms a pretty little port, which carries deep water close to the shore on either side.

Between Cape Desolado and Point Caseras, numerous small rivers empty into the sea. The greater number of them are dry in the summer season, but their outlets form deep creeks into which vessels of fair draft may enter and seek shelter from the storms that, in the wet months, often rage along this coast. Point Casares shelters a fine anchorage. Between this place and the Bay of Salinas—a stretch of thirty-five miles—are the ports of El Brito, Nacascolo and San Jaan del Sur. This latter is small but deep and safe. It is connected with the Great Lake by a macadamized road which was made by Vanderbilt, when his ships touched at Greytown, from 1851 to 1855.

The Bay of Salinas forms a beautiful deep port, of circular shape, which contains an area of about eight square miles. No river enters into it, thus, in consequence, it receives no sedimentary deposits. In the middle of the bay is an island which marks the western terminus of the boundary line, between Nicaragua and Costa Rica, according to the treaty of 1858. The valleys that open upon the bay are extremely fertile and possess a remarkably healthy climate. It is difficult to comprehend why such an advantageous locality should be neglected. While emigrants from Europe are seeking homes in cold Canada and dry and arid Australia, it seems strange that lands so happily situated, so fertile and, above all, blessed with such healthy climates, should continue abandoned and desolate while millions of human beings, in the Old World, scarcely manage to gain a miserable living, by the sweat of their brow, cultivating a worn out soil that, even with the use of the best fertilizers, scarcely returns paying crops.

A general impression prevails that Central America is a vast region whose surface is dotted by unsightly bleak and barren mountains, and whose few plains are watered by rivers whose banks are marshy and reek with malaria and pestilence. A few Americans who have visited San Jose, Acajutla, Corinto, San Juan del Sur, Salinas and Punta Arenas, on the Pacific coast, and Trujillo, Gracias, Bluefields, Pearl Lagoon, Gray-

16

town and Port Limon, on the Caribbean side, where malarial fevers of a light type are prevalent in the summer, season as a general case, return their homes and report Central America as being an unhealthy territory, where deadly fevers rage, in epidemic form, the year round.

As these self-styled travelers have seldom penetrated into the interior, they are utterly ignorant of the sanitary situation in Central America. There are numerous officers of steamers sailing out of this port to the Central American coast and the Bay Islands who circulate the same doleful accounts of the climate of Guatemala and Spanish Honduras. As they have never been any distance into the interior, they know as little of the climatic condition of those republics as a person who has touched at Port Eads, but has not ascended the river does of the climate and surroundings of the Crescent City.

The fact is almost two-thirds of the entire territory of Central America, from the Sarstoon river to the southern limits of Costa Rica, is blessed by as healthy a climate as the most favored locality on the planet. At from thirty to fifty miles from the Caribbean coast the land suddenly rises until it attains an altitude of from 2000 to 4000 feet above the level of the sea. At this elevation the exuberant vegetation of the tropics ceases and is superseded by the exquisite flora of the semi-tropic zone. If certain fruits of the extreme tropics languish and will not develop there are other species that still thrive well, while the coffee plant, the orange, the lemon, the citron, the lime and other fruits of a hardier nature are produced in a soil and fostered by a climate in every way conducive to their perfect development.

At a distance of 3000 feet above the level of the sea the mahogany, brazil, cedar, tamarind vera and amarilio disappear, and the oak, the larch, the sycamore and giant laurel mingle their foliage with the zapote and the ahuehuete, and at an elevation of 4000 feet the southern pine reaches a size and height far superior to the stunted specimens seen in northern climes.

The City of Guatemala is situated at an altitude of 4500 feet above the sea. San Jose, Costa Rica, is 4000 feet. Tegucigalpa, Honduras, is 3000 feet. Segovia, Nicaragua, is 5000 feet. Thus all these .cities, although lying in the extreme tropics, enjoy a semi-temperate climate.

At an elevation of 2500 feet above the level of the sea malarial fevers, chills and fever and all the sickness incident to a low latitude and hot climate are entirely unknown. As bronchial and pulmonary diseases never visit such localities, these regions may safely be pronounced even healthier than most of our Northern and Eastern States.

It is safe to assume that two-thirds of Guatemala, Honduras and Costa Rica, and at least one-half of Nicaragua and San Salvador, are situated at an altitude of from 2500 to 7000 feet above the sea. The climate of these localities varies from semi-temperate to fairly cold; thus it is just to assert that by far the greater portion of Central America possesses an exceptionally bracing and healthy climate.

CHAPTER VI.

The Republic of Nicaragua is divided, politically, into seven departments, which are as follows :

	Area in Miles.	Population
Granada	2,500	65,000
Leon	2,500	45,000
Rivas	1,000	25,000
Chinandega	1,500	25,000
Chontales	3,000	35,000
Matagalpa	2,500	31,000
Segovia	3,000	32,000
Uncivilized Region	24,000	40,000
	40,000	298,000

DEPARTMENT OF GRANADA.

This is the most important department of the republic, both on account of its commerce, its population and the proportion of its cultivated lands in ratio to its area. It is situated in the civilized portion of the republic and possesses coasts on both lakes, as well as on the Pacific. It is in direct communication, by fair wagon roads, with the departments of Leon, Matagalpa, Rivas and Choutales, without taking into consideration the route via the lake and the river San Juan to Graytown, which latter port is in monthly communication with New Orleans per steamer Lucy P. Miller.

The portion of this department that borders on the Pacific lies between the bay of San Martin and the mouth of the river Escalante. This coast is forty miles long, and the water that washes its beach is bold and without reefs or any other impediments to navigation. It possesses little ports at the mouths of the rivers San Diego, Sitalapa, San Rafael, Masachapa, San Pablo, Calero, Achiote and Escalante. These watercourses are inconstant and during the summer are generally dry. They water an exceedingly fertile territory which unfortunately has been neglected since the date of the conquest.

The lake coast presents notable characteristics. In front of the mouth of the Ochomogo river lies the great island of Zapatera. Between the latter and the coast is situated the fine port of Charco Muerto. This excellent harbor is almost unfrequented, although it is spacious enough to admit a large squadron. It carries from seven to eight fathoms of water. The island of Zapatera is separated from the coast, on the south, by a narrow channel called the Boquete. To the north and south are numerous islets, all inhabited save one called La Ceiba.

A short distance from the harbor of Charoco Muerto is a group of small islands, the majority of which are remarkably fertile. The length of this portion of the department on the borders of the lake is about forty miles.

The stretch of coast along the margin of lake Managua is fifty miles, or twenty-five miles each side of the ancient fall of Tipitapa. The expression "ancient fall" is here used because the waters of the river or strait of Tipitapa no longer *fall* into the lower bed, but filter through under the rocks.

The general aspect presented by this department is that of a vast tableland whose slopes decline gradually toward the lakes, but are broken and abrupt in the direction of the Pacific. A central mountain range divides it in nearly two equal portions The scarcity of water in the region of former volcanic disturbances, naturally causes one to wonder why this locality was chosen by its primitive inhabitants, in preference to other contiguous places more adaptable for farming. The hillsides alone are cultivated and almost invariably return excellent crops.

The department of Granada has no navigable rivers. Those on the Pacific are intermittant, while on the lake side the Ochomogo is the only one that merits mention. Between the city of Granada and the strait or creek of Panaloya, are two marshy lagoons named Tisma and Jenicero. They are formed by the surplus waters of the Tipitapa before it enters the lake. The climate of the central tableland is hot but is tempered by the northeast winds. On the higher lands it is quite cool. Jinotepe, one of the most important centres of population is situated at an altitude of 2513 feet above the sea.

The department contains twenty-two cities and towns of consideration. The four principal are:

Granada, with a population of.....................12,000.
Managua, with a population of.....................10,000.
Masaya, with a population of...... ....14,000.
Jinotipe, with a population of...... .... 5,000.

Granada, the second city in size and importance in the republic, is situated at the northwest extremity of Lake Nicaragua, near the foot of the volcano of Mombacho, at an altitude of 218 feet above the sea. It was founded in the year 1523 by the gallant, but unfortunate, Francisco de Cordoba, between the lake and the Indian city of Salteba, which now forms one of its suburbs.

During the epoch that the filibusters flourished and later still when the country became the prey of factions during the interminable civil wars that followed the era of independence. Granada suffered more than any other Latin American city, not excepting Panama. It was totally destroyed by the English pirate Edward David, in 1665, and was attacked and partially ruined by the English buccaneer Gallardillo in 1670. Both pirate chieftains entered the country by the river San Juan. It was also burned by a large body of pirates who disembarked at the Pacific port of Escalante. It was after occupied and partially destroyed by different political factions during the long period of anarchy subsequent to the declaration of independence, and at length was almost ruined by Walker, the American filibuster, November 22, 1856.

The city contains a population of 12,000 souls, mixed castes and creoles. It has almost arisen from its ruins, yet several blocks remain covered with ashes over which grows a vigorous vegetation. The principal church has never been rebuilt. It contains numerous fine public and private edifices and in consequence of the advantages offered by the topography of the neighborhood might be readily and effectually fortified. Its commerce with foreign countries and the other departments is quite important and valuable.

Managua, the capital of the republic, is 220 feet above the level of the sea. It is situated on the margin of the lake of the same name on the site of a great aboriginal city that was totally destroyed during the war of the conquest. Although it now contains 10,000 inhabitants, it was a mere village when it was chosen—on account of its situation about midway between Leon and Granada—as the seat of government. This measure was adopted with the hope that the sanguinary rivalry which existed between the great cities would cease, when the inhabitants of neither could claim precedence.

The situation of the capital is picturesque in the extreme. Behind it rises a range of foothills whose soil is admirably adapted to the cultivation of coffee. In fact this region boasts more than 200 coffee plantations with an annual yield of 1,500,000 pounds of the precious berry. The coffee industry bids fair to assume great importance, particularly when immigration flows into the district and a permanent supply of labor can be obtained.

Managua can boast of but few imposing public or private edifices. The government palace is probably the largest and best appointed building in the city, while the parish church presents the finest appearance of the several places of worship. The capital is the head, or centre, of the sub-prefecture of the same name. This political arrangement renders it in a measure independent of the departmental government. The centres of population on the banks of the river San Juan, although they are virtually dependent on the department of Granada, are independent as far as their elections are concerned, which they hold in conjunction with the perfection of Acoyapa.

DEPARTMENT OF LEON.

This department is bounded on the north by those of Matagalpa and Segovia, on the east by Chinandega, on the south by the Pacific ocean and the west by the department of Granada. It is watered by several rivers which empty into Lake

Managua, or the Pacific. The coast extends from Boca Falsa to San Martin bay. The most notable points, are First, the mouth of the river Leon, at which is situated a small port, where considerable salt is deposited by the sea; the river Tamarindo, with its well conditioned port, and Cape Desolate, which might be considered a promontory. It contains eight cities, towns and villages of importance. The four principal are :

Leon, with a population of .... 28,000.
Subtiaba, with a population of .... 7,000.
El Sauce, with a population of .... 2,000.
Telica, with a population of .. .. 2,000.

The portion of the lake coast that belongs to this department has an extension of about thirty miles. At Imbita, or Moabita, one found the ruins of the old city of Leon, close to which is a fine port on the south side of the volcano Momotombo, but whose entrance is partially closed by the volcanic island Motombito. Further around to the east is the semi-circular bay Maboto, in whose bosom two important rivers, the Encuentros and the Rio Grande empty. These watercourses are navigable for quite a distance from their mouth.

The topography of this department is less mountainous and broken than its sister political divisions, yet in its centre rises the tall sierra of Marrabios. Its climate is rather hot, yet to the north the slopes of the Cordillera enjoy a fresh and bracing atmosphere.

The city of Leon is the seat of departmental government. It contains 28,000 inhabitants, of mixed race, and is situated in the centre of a vast plain which is well watered and extensively cultivated. The first city of this name was founded on the banks of Lake Managua, in 1523, by Cordoba. In 1610, the inhabitants frightened at the threatening aspect presented by the volcano Momotombo, deserted the town and founded a new city close to the ancient Indian capital, Subtiaba. As the new city increased in size it gradually approached the Indian town, from which it is now separated only by the width of a street. These two centres of population have separate municipal government.

Leon was the ancient capital of Nicaragua and the residence of the Spanish authorities. Although it has passed through many vicissitudes it has never been entirely destroyed like Granada. It is therefore the monumental city of the Republic. Its streets are well paved and lighted. The principal public edifice is the great cathedral which was commenced in 1746, by Bishop Martin B. Figueroa; was finished by Bishop Carlos Cabrera in 1774, and was dedicated by Bishop Esteban de Tristan. It is said that the plan of the building was furnished by a British traveler and that its construction cost $5,000,000. This edifice occupies an entire square, but its height is too low to correspond with such a vast base. In former years it possessed many valuable ornaments, but having been pillaged several times during the civil wars it now boasts but few articles of value. In the sacristy is a collection of portraits, said to be genuine, of all bishops who have filled the See of Nicaragua. From the summits of the towers a glorious panorama is presented to the view. The Bishop's palace, the National palace, the barracks and the old convents of La Merced, La Recoleccion, San Francisco and the Hospital of Saint John of God, are the few other buildings worthy of mention.

The Indian town, or suburb, of Subtiaba boasts one of the finest sacred edifices in Nicaragua, which is also the most ancient in the republic. It possesses many valuable and curious ornaments. At the epoch of the conquest this Indian capital contained more than 100,000 inhabitants, who were engaged in commerce and agriculture, and were celebrated for their industry as well as pacific inclinations. Both Leon and Subtiaba are noted for numerous springs of excellent drinking water in different localities.

DEPARTMENT OF RIVAS.

This department is bounded on the north by that of Granada, on the south by the Republic of Costa Rica, on the west by the Pacific ocean as far as the bay of Salinas, on the east by lake Nicaragua. The sea coast of the department extends from Salinas bay to the mouth of the Escalante river and has the following ports: Caseras bay, the port of Brito, the mouth of the Rio Grande de Tola, the port of Nascascola, San Juan del Sur and Cape Natau.

The lake coast is broken by the mouths of many little unimportant rivers which rise in the volcanic regions of Costa Rica. The other principal localities are Tortugas point, the mouth and port of the river Sapoa, those of the rivers Santa Clara, La Lajas and the Gil Gonzalez, the port of La Virgin and the two points or Capes Del Palmar and El Menco. The large island of Ometepe also belongs to this department.

The Department of Rivas is situated between the Pacific ocean and lake Nicaragua and forms a narrow isthmus remarkably fertile, and watered by numerous little streams and rivers. It is therefore, in ratio to its size and the number of its inhabitants, the most progressive locality of the republic, as far as agriculture, the amount of its exports and its industries are concerned—and even for the development of its system of public instruction. The different routes marked out for the Nicaragua canal pass through its territory. Thus its future will be remarkably brilliant should this grand enterprise ever be carried out.

The climate is damp, but the evening and morning breezes are so fresh that the region may be considered fairly healthy. The population is mostly collected around the city of Rivas, the capital of the department. It contains ten considerable towns and villages. The four principal are:

Rivas, with a population of........ 10,000
San Jorge, with a population of........ 3,000
Potosi, with a population of............... 2,500
El Obrage, with a population of.................... 3,000

The city of Rivas possesses an altitude of 177 feet above the level of the sea and contains 10,000 inhabitants, of mixed blood. It was founded on the site of the ancient Indian city of Nicarao, and was called Nicaragua until the beginning of the present century, when the name was changed to Rivas.

It contains no edifices worthy of mention. This city has been several times partially destroyed by earthquakes, and was nearly ruined during the war of the filibusters. It is noted as the place where Walker sustained a siege of five long months during the year 1856.

The lake port of Rivas, San Jorge, contains about 2500 inhabitants. The principal port on the Pacific is San Juan del Sur, which carries on quite a large import and export traffic, but does not contain more than 400 inhabitants.

The principal locality of note in this department is the island of Ometepe, which is washed by the calm swells of the Great lake. From the summit of its tall volcano may be witnessed one of the most beautiful panoramas presented to human sight in any region of the World. The ascent is quite easy, as it is gradual and very little broken. This island contains many antiquities, the most of which are found in tombs many centuries old.

An idea of the importance of this little department may be gleaned from the fact that besides its numerous stock raising establishments and coffee plantations, it possesses more than a million and a half cacao (chocolate) trees, and 175 indigo vats, which produced, in 1880, 275,000 pounds of this costly article.

DEPARTMENT OF CHINANDEGA.

This district is bounded on the north by the department of Segovia, on the east by that of Leon, on the south by the Pacific ocean, from Cape Coseguina to Boca Falsa, and on the west by Honduras.

The department is most admirably situated. In its centre extends that vast plain which is watered by the Estero Real and its affluents. In the south are numerous little rivers which water that portion which lies between the Pacific and the foot hill range of Marrabios; and in the north rise the slopes of the temperate lands from which flow the Black river and its branches. The southern district is admirably adapted for all kinds of agriculture, and the northern portion for stock raising purposes and mining enterprises. The various products of the soil, the forests and the mines may be readily exported from the numerous little ports, on the Pacific coast, belonging to the department.

Chinandega has seven considerable cities and towns, the principal of which are:

Chinandega, with a population of...................9,000
El Viejo, with a population of............... 4,500
Chichigalpa, with a population of............. 3,500
Realejo, with a population of.....................1,500

Chinandega, the capital of the department, is built on the site of an ancient Indian city. It contains a mixed population of 9,000 souls and has an altitude of 121 feet above the level of the Pacific. In times past it was quite an important business locality, but the gradual filling up of the port of Realejo, upon which it depended, and the opening of that of Corinto, which is connected with Leon by a fine wagon road, caused its traffic to revert to the latter city. The completion of the rail-road from Leon Viejo to Corinto, which passes close to Chinandega, has in a measure revived commerce and it is now quite a flourishing business centre.

It possesses no fine edifices, but its houses are generally situated in the midst of cultivated plots of ground, which gives the town the appearance of a vast orchard. Its neighborhood is quite picturesque, while it is surrounded by numerous plantations of sugar cane and cotton.

The port of Realejo was founded by Alvarado, in 1534. It was sacked and burnt several times by the buccaneers, and also by the filibusters under Walker. It once boasted 15,000 inhabitants, but now contains but one tenth that number.

Corinto is an admirable little port. Since the completion of the railroad it has become the principal sea port of the republic. It has two deep entrances. Ships of the greatest tonnage may anchor close to the beach.

DEPARTMENT OF CHONTALES.

This department is bounded on the north by that of Matagalpa, on the east by the Caribbean sea, on the south by the river San Juan, and on the west by Granada. ,

The civilized region of this department presents the aspect of a series of almost circular valleys, separated by the western spurs of the Cordillera, excepting the northern portion, which might be considered a knot of irregular mountains. The climate is temperate on the plains but cold on the higher lands. The principal products are cattle and gold.

It contains nine towns and villages, the four principal of which are:

Acoyapa, with a population of..................................7,500
Juigalpa, with a population of................................3,500
La Libertad, with a population of............................ 3,200
Boaco, with a population of,..................................5,000

The capital, Acoyapa, is a mere collection of adobe houses and Indian huts, and is connected with the lake by a bad bridle road, which terminates at the port of San Ubaldo.

The soil is remarkably fertile, while the climate of the table lands is bracing and healthy. There is no finer spot on the planet for the establishment of a colony of American emigrants, were it only connected with the Caribbean coast by a good wagon road.

. DEPARTMENT OF MATAGALPA.

This region is bounded on the north by the Coco river, on the east by the Atlantic and the uncivilized portion of the republic, on the south by the Departments of Granada and Choutales, and on the west by those of Leon and Segovia.

The country is broken by irregular mountain spurs that hold in their embrace numerous fertile valleys, which are watered by many perennial water-courses and streams. The climate is not only temperate, but is absolutely cold in the higher table lands. Fine wheat crops are produced, together with all the vegetation of the temperate zone.

It contains twelve towns and villages. The four principal are:

Matagalpa, with a population of..........................10,000
Jinotega, with a population of............................ 7,000
Metapa 4,500
Sebaco, with a population of.............................. 2,500

The principal industry is stock raising; yet several valuable mines are worked on a small scale.

Matagalpa, the capital, is situated 2000 feet above the Caribbean sea and is surrounded by high mountains, that shut out the horizon on all sides. It has been several times destroyed by the Zambo and Mosquito Indians.

DEPARTMENT OF SEGOVIA.

Is bounded on the north and west by Honduras, on the east by the Uncivilized Region, and on the south by the Departments of Chinandega and Leon.

Many of the rivers that empty into the Coco have their sources in this department, but none of them are navigable—not even the Coco, until its junction with the Jicaro. The principal industry is cattle raising, although a small quantity of coffee and indigo is produced. It contains seventeen towns and villages, the principal of which are:

Ocotal, with a population of.........................12,000
Condega, with a population of........................ 3,000
Somoto, with a population of......................... 1,500
Esteli, with a population of......................... 3,000

Ocotal, or Segovia, is situated in a picturesque locality on the banks of the river Telpaneca. It was founded in 1524 by Cordoba, and has been many times destroyed since that date by the pirates and Mosquito Indians, who ascended the Coco river in small boats. It contains no fine buildings, but boasts a population, together with its suburbs, of 12,000 souls.

The climate of this department is cool and remarkably healthy. Its soil is very fertile and is watered by many constant rivers and water-courses. It contains some of the richest silver and gold mines in the World, but they were mostly abandoned during the struggle for independence.

THE UNCIVILIZED REGION.

This district is divided into two parts; the Mosquito reservation and that portion of the republic inhabited by native tribes. The latter are harmless, inoffensive and remarkably friendly. The author lived with the Smoos for two months, in 1874, and was treated in the kindest and most hospitable manner. They readily yield their lands to English or Americans. When their country is settled by immigrants it will be one of the most flourishing districts of the republic.

CHAPTER VII.

The system of government administered in Nicaragua may
be designated as moderate republican. If the actual administration of public affairs is undoubtedly conducted in as democratic a manner as is practiced in any of the other republics, the
constitution is by no means as liberal as those which have,
comparatively lately, been promulgated in Honduras and Guatemala.

The Constitution, which was modeled upon that of the.
United States, is supposed, by the framers, to avoid certain
dangerous or equivocal declarations which they seemed to think
darkened the pages of the immortal work of our forefathers.
With exception of the slavery clause—the cause for which has
since been abolished in this country—it would be difficult to
find a single passage, in which the Constitution of the little
republic expresses more enlightened or liberal sentiments than
may be found in its great model.

Yet, the Constitution of Nicaragua is an admirable document and is well worthy of being carefully studied and examined. If it is more conservative than that of Guatemala,
or of Honduras, it is certainly more practical. Under the
two latter, liberty, fraternity and equality are carried almost
to the verge of socialism, while the Charter of Nicaragua,
like that of Salvador, stops short at qualified suffrage.

The government of the republic is separated into three distinct branches; the Executive, the Legislative and the Judicial. The first is exercised by a citizen who must be in entire
possession of all the rights and attributes of citizenship. He

must be a married man and at least thirty years old. Under the title of President, he is the chief magistrate and holds office for the term of four years. The legislative power is vested in a Congress whose members are elected by the popular vote. The judicial functions are vested in magistrates, whose office is also elective.

The present chief magistrate is Dr. Adan Cardenas. This gentleman is a profound scholar and speaks several modern languages fluently. He, for several years, represented his government at Washington, and is, therefore, well known and highly appreciated in this country. He has occupied numerous public positions, and is one of the shrewdest and most consummate diplomats in Central America. Dr. Cardenas belongs to the conservative party, yet his so-called conservatism might rather be termed rational liberalism, for he is as liberal in his principles as any other Central American President. If he is not constantly descanting on the sublimity and beauty of equality or fraternity, his public acts prove that he entertains wise and enlightened sentiments, while he certainly has shown himself a sincere promoter of the material interests of his country.

With his vast experience in public affairs, his enlightened ideas and his profound patriotism, Dr. Cardenas is essentially the right man in the right place; it is safe to assume that if the rest of his term of office is marked by as many wise public acts, as the period he has already exercised his official functions has been, his name will occupy a bright place in the future history of his country.

The late civil wars and revolutions which so devastated Nicaragua left among other burdens a large debt for posterity to discharge. That indebtedness has been fully paid, while the citizens of the republic justly boast, that theirs is the only Latin American nation that owes neither a foreign nor a domestic debt. The *Gaceta Oficial*, in its issue of December 12, 1884, published the following article, which is reproduced in full:

" For eight years government certificates, called state notes, have been in circulation. They are of the first and second order, with privileged six per cent bonds, all required to be paid in fines and custom duties.

The cancellation of orders for custom duties proved a complicated and confused business, because a moiety had to be paid in money, and a certain percentage in these certificates. The merchant was compelled to procure this paper to enable him to pay his custom duties, or else to obtain security that he would pay the value of the certificates. The press cried out against these different classes of certificates which circulated in commercial transportation, which caused confusion therein and also in the accounts of the national treasury. Many of these certificates were issued without proper care or formality, thus giving scope for forged utterances of the same, with grave injury to the interests of the state as well as of individuals.

For these reasons President Vincente Quadra proposed to Congress in 1871, the consolidation of all these certificates into one debt. This proposition was rejected, doubtless because the necessity of such a measure was not clearly realized then, or because, as often happens with all innovations, an opposite financial result was feared to that held in view.

But the course of time proved the correctness of President Quadra's views and the desired conversion took place March 24, 1867. The new certificate was circulated under the name of the "consolidated bonds," which bore five per cent interest from the first of December of the same year. This law decreed that custom duties should be paid; in the hundred, at sixty-five cents cash, and the rest in old certificates, or in fifty cents cash, and fifty cents in consolidated bonds. As may be seen this last arrangement resulted in obliging all to indirectly adopt the converted paper as the law dictated.

At first the new paper was greatly depreciated and sold at thirty-five per cent; but the regularity with which the interest was paid, and the bonds gradually canceled inspired confidence. The increase of importations raised year by year the value of these bonds until they reached par and eventually a very high premium. This result proved to the world the value of government promises. But at length it became a serious question with merchants who had to buy these bonds at a high premium,

17

for they could not compete in the sale of their goods with those who had bought them up at a cheap rate some time before. To remedy this evil, Congress, September last, passed a law, authorizing the payment of these bonds, with accrued interest, in ready money, granting government the power to raise a loan, if necessary, on those conditions it deemed the most favorable. But the government could not realize the required loan as the terms offered were too severe. As the amount of the consolidated loan became gradually less, the government no longer needed a loan, and, on the first of the present month, Congress passed a law withdrawing the bonds and authorizing their payment, with interest up to date, in ready cash. Thus the interior debt is cancelled and Nicaragua has neither foreign nor native creditors nor owes a single dollar to anyone.

The history of this interior debt is very interesting. The total value of the consolidated bonds was $1,751,732 50. Taking this sum with the amounts paid in the former certificates, we find that the total interior debt, acknowledged and paid, amounts to the large sum of $3,503,465 60.

 This plain statement clearly indicates the present financial situation in Nicaragua; add to this, that commerce is flourishing, railroads are being constructed, new plantations are established, and mining and stock raising being pushed, it will be seen that Nicaragua, if not as rich as San Salvador for instance, is in an equally prosperous condition.

In the foregoing six chapters the author has endeavored to furnish a brief account of the past history of the republic, as well as a description of the topography of the country. Mention has been made of the several departments, their natural resources, their rivers, plains, mountain slopes, mines and above all, the climate and the nature and productiveness of the soil. As the plan of this work will not permit any detailed account of these various interesting subjects, the author deems that enough has been said to draw the attention of the American public to a country but little known to or understood by them and to prove that the Republic of Nicaragua, with its liberal laws, its cordial invitation to immigrants, its fertile soil and rich mines, is one of the best localities where

parties possessing little capital, but plenty of energy and
enterprise, may not only find a fortune in agriculture but a
happy home and the climate best suited to their health or
habits.

Nicaragua can boast of but few manufactures, while those
are of a simple and primitive order. The numerous mountain
torrents that descend to the plains afford thousands of opportunities for the establishment of factories and quartz mills,
when the time comes to utilize this vast hydraulic motor
power.

The railroad construction system adopted by the republic,
and which is being pushed gradually forward, is as unique in
its conception as it is practical in its methods. Government
has undertaken the construction of the proposed roads. It
owns and runs the line already built, whose earnings last year
not only paid all expenses, but an interest of six per cent
clear on every dollar thus far expended on the work. This
line is about seventy miles long. Its Pacific terminus is the
pretty little port of Corinto. It passes through one of the
most productive agricultural regions on the planet; skirts
the two great cities of Chinandega and Leon, and strikes lake
Managua at a point near Leon Viejo. The city of Managua,
which is distant, by land, from Leon Viejo, about forty-two
miles, will soon be connected with it by rail, as the proposed
line, to skirt the lake to the capital city, is now in course of
construction and will be finished in two years. From Managua to Granada, which is thirty miles, the road will be built
in 1887. But meanwhile the government intends, as before
mentioned, to restore the port of Graytown, or San Juan del
Norte, to its former favorable condition, and also to render
the San Juan navigable for vessels drawing eight feet of water,
from Graytown to the Great lake. All this work is expected
to be accomplished by the end of 1887. Thus, in three years,
the people of the republic confidently expect to be able to
cross from ocean to ocean, by rail and water transportation,
in a comparatively brief period of time.

The principal industries of Nicaragua are foreign and domestic commerce, precious wood cutting, agriculture, stock raising

and mining. The total foreign traffic for the year 1883, excluding the traffic of the Mosquito reservation, was: imports $1,600,000; exports $2,200,000. The domestic commerce may be estimated at $25,000,000 per annum.

Coffee planting has become a staple industry, while labor on the coasts is both scarce and costly; in the interior and particularly in the distant departments it rules reasonably low as yet. Within the past five years not only have numerous new plantations been established, but on the old ones the area of cultivation has been greatly increased. Although the coast, on either side, is lined with fine cocoanut groves, but little attempt has been made to increase the acreage of this valuable product.

The fruit planting industry has been totally neglected. If on the Pacific coast the fruit producing centres are too distant from San Francisco to enable a traffic in bananas and plantains to become profitable, the Caribbean coast is but five days' distant from New Orleans, and the fine lands on the Coco, the San Juan and the Matagalpa rivers, might be utilized to great advantage in this industry. The banks of the Mico, or Bluefields, river, in the Mosquito reservation, are now crowded with flourishing banana plantations. The fruit produced in this latter locality is the best that finds its way into our markets, so there is no reason why the other river banks which possess equal advantages, should not produce as fine fruit.

Tobacco, indigo, vanilla and numerous other tropic articles of commerce are produced in the *tierra caliente*, while wheat, rye, oats, barley and many kinds of vegetables and fruits grow to perfection on the temperate table lands. Indian corn and broom corn flourish in all localities at less than 10,000 feet above the sea.

Stock raising has, within the past five years, excited considerable attention. The supply of the Guatemala, West Indian and Isthmian markets has created a demand for beef cattle along the entire coast. In the northern departments, near the Honduranean line, the number of cattle has been greatly increased. There is sufficient land in Northern Nicaragua and Southern Honduras, at present entirely unoccupied, ·

to furnish 5,000,000 beef cattle annually, without withdrawing from agriculture the most fertile lands. Yet Texas undoubtedly contains more cattle than the Central American republics combined.

On the Texas and Northern Mexican cattle ranges the average pasture allotted each beef is three acres. In Honduras and Nicaragua it is no exaggeration to assert that the pasturage found on the mountain and foothill sides, and the banks of the numerous streams and water-courses which irrigate the country, is so varied and so plentiful that one acre will not only maintain, but will fatten, one beef for market.

The peculiar topographical formation of numerous portions of Central America renders them particularly adapted to cattle raising. It is true the American people do not either know, or seem to care to know, this fact; but the time will come (indeed the time is not far distant) when the meat supply problem will attract the serious attention of our statesmen. The Mexican states of Sonora, Chihuahua, Tamaulipas, Nuevo Leon and Coahuila have already been drained to meet the demands of our market. The central and southern states of Mexico have large and constantly augmenting populations to feed, and cannot be relied upon even to make good the annual drafts drawn upon our domestic supply. Thus, Central America and Colombia and Venezuela will soon be called upon to fill the demands of the beef markets of these United States, of the West Indies and Europe.

Notwithstanding that many of our patriotic statisticians may deny this statement, it is nevertheless true. Already our Atlantic ports are engaged in shipping vast quantities of refrigerated beef to Europe, while Florida and Texas annually send great numbers of beef cattle to the West Indies in general, but Cuba in particular. These latter demands of cattle upon our production of beef cattle are already being felt, nor will it be long before the advanced price of the article in our home markets will seriously effect this new traffic.

Meanwhile the governments of the beautiful and fertile inter-tropical Republics of Nicaragua and Honduras invite American stock raisers to come and occupy their waste lands.

They desire them to bring blooded stock to improve the breed of the domestic cattle. The same opportunities are offered sheep farmers, and millions of acres of land admirably adapted to the raising and feeding of sheep and goats can be easily and readily obtained.

Since the Walker troubles the wood-cutting industry on the Caribbean coast has dwindled to comparative insignificance. Years ago the banks of the Wanks, the Matagalpa, the Mico and the San Juan rivers were crowded with mahogany and cedar cutters' camp, and a great amount of timber was shipped from the different ports of the coast. To day but few mahogany camps are in operation, for the rubber industry has drawn away the greater part of the disposable labor.

On the Pacific slope a vast annual quantity of dye woods are shipped at Corinto. Fustic is the principal object of commerce, while Campeche and Brazil—for there is a difference between the two—come next. On the Estero Real and other watercourses and rivers some mahogany and cedar is occasionally cut, but not enough to make much impression on European markets.

In the very near future the wood-cutting industry on the Caribbean coast will again revive. The available mahogany and cedar trees in Honduras and British Honduras are being thinned out, and the magnificent forests of Nicaragua will be called upon to yield their tribute until the younger trees of the two other localities shall have grown sufficiently to cut.

The Department of Segovia contains some mines whose names were once famous. They are mostly abandoned or are worked in the most primitive manner. The author visited several of them last May and was presented with numerous remarkably rich specimens There is one lode whose ore averages $540 per ton of gold, while a silver lead was pointed out to him whose average working yield was $266 per ton. Neither of these mines are being operated—at least not in form —as the owners only work them at stated periods, merely to comply with the law and retain their possession.

It may read like a fable to assert that there are in the Department of Segovia at least sixty mines equal to any that have yet been worked in Nevada, California, Colorado or New Mexico. Yet such is undoubtedly the case, while the names of fifty-four can be cited whose ore averages more than $150 to the ton, *working assay.*

Should the curious reader ask why these, to him, fabulously rich mines are not worked, numerous reasons might be advanced, anyone of which would answer his question. The hitherto unsettled and revolutionary condition of society, the natural apathy and indolence of the creoles; the former insecurity of life and property; the lack of capital to inaugurate enterprises; the bad condition of the roads and the great cost of transporting mining machinery over the tall and rugged mountains are a few of the causes that might be cited to show why these mines have not lately been operated. To-day Nicaraguan society is no longer revolutionary but is inclined to peace and pacific pursuits. The people are arousing from their long lethargic slumber and have begun to manifest a deep interest in the material progress of their fertile and rich country. The lack of capital will soon be supplied from foreign money markets. Foreign arms will assist native muscle to cut good roads from the mines to the central railroad system, while to-day, both life and property are as safe (if not actually safer) in Central America, as in any of our southwestern territories. These are not merely assertions 'they are stubborn facts and are borne out by irrefragible testimony.

While American miners are satisfied with the possession of property that will turn out $25 to the ton, and are making large investments, in their utter ignorance of the mineral resources of Honduras, and the Nicaraguan department of Segovia, they refuse to believe in the disinterested statements of travelers. Let those who doubt, but yet have money to invest in mining enterprises, go to the department of Oláucho, Toro and Tegucigalpa in Honduras, and Segovia in Nicaragua, and their own eyes will speedily convince them of the vast mineral resources of those localities.

For two decades the greater number of the people of Eastern Nicaragua, including the inhabitants of the Mosquito Reservation, have bended their entire energies to gathering rubber.

It would be impossible to estimate the quantity of this valuable article, supplied by the forests contiguous to the Caribbean coast within the past twenty years. It must have aggregated to several millions of pounds annually. But lately the price of rubber, in consequence of the many substances that are employed in adulterating the pure gum, has seriously declined. The cost of gathering it is almost as great as the price it obtains on the spot. If this situation continues much longer the rubber gatherers will be compelled to seek other employments. In this case the wood cutting industry will be revived and· fruit planting on a large scale inaugurated.

The Caribbean ports of Nicaragua are virtually free ports; at Gracias and Graytown ten per cent duties are collected on imports, at Bluefields and Corn Island, Mosquito Reservation, but three per cent on imports are levied. This anomalous condition obtains by consequence of the treaty of 1860, with Great Britain, which defined the extent of the Mosquito Reservation and the tariff duties to be collected at the Caribbean ports of the Republic.

On the Pacific coast the government tariff of customs prevails. As the greater portion of the import and export traffic of the republic is carried on in that locality, the federal treasury suffers but little, while the inhabitants of the Eastern coast are greatly benefited by the arrangement.

So much has been said and written concerning the proposed Nicaraguan inter oceanic canal that it is almost needless to mention it here. The Americo-Nicaraguan treaty lately discussed by the American Senate, and which treated of the eventual construction of said canal, failed ratification by that body. Whether some other foreign nation or individuals may undertake the great enterprise or not is more than can now be conjectured. But one thing is certain: sooner or later the canal will be constructed, and then future American statesmen will severely censure the timid or conservative policy that permitted the control of the great artificial strait to pass beyond the pale of American influence.

Sufficient information regarding Nicaragua has been furnished in the preceding pages to give the reader a faint idea·

of the vast agricultural possibilities and the forest and mineral resources the little republic possesses. It has been shown that the lands are marvelously fertile and at least one-half of the country enjoys a climate as healthy and agreeable as that of any other portion of the planet. If Nicaragua, three decades ago, was the prey of revolutionary factions and life and property were insecure, two decades of peace which have been employed in pushing the material advancement of the country has brought about a new condition of affairs. Life and property are respected in Nicaragua as much as they are in the Crescent City, while money invested in agricultural, mineral or wood-cutting enterprises returns an almost fabulous profit as compared with general investments in this country. It is safe to assume, then, that those who wish to better their fortunes, who have a small amount of capital to invest, could find no safer or more promising locality than Nicaragua, the scene of the exploits of the chivalrous Gil and Cordoba—the native land of Cardenas and Zavala.

COSTA RICA.

CHAPTER I.

Priestly Theories Regarding the American Indigines—Dr. Plongeon's Discoveries in Yucatan—America the Older World—The Yucatecan Story of Adam and Eve, and the Death of Abel—The Lost Atlantis—Ruins of Ancient Cities in Costa Rica—First Spanish Expedition—Journeys of Gil, Cordoba and Pedrarias—Combats with the Indians—Pizarro's Campaign—Invasion of the Territory of Urraca—Gallant Defense Made by Him—Battle With Pedrarias—Subsequent Death and Defeat of Urraca—Subjugation of the Province.

Notwithstanding that many learned theologians have, during the past three centuries, published ponderous tomes to prove that the continent was originally populated by colonies from both Asia and Europe, their adversaries have successfully refuted their arguments and assert that America is the *older* World and was most probably peopled long before any portion of the Eastern Hemisphere.

The researches of Dr. Aguste Plongeon, who, accompanied by his accomplished and scientific wife, spent several years in examining the ruined cities of Yucatan, have resulted in bringing to light many historical facts that had long been buried in the mists of ages. He found inscribed on the columns, obelisks, mural ornaments, and temple walls of the ancient city of Uxmal, the story of Adam and Eve, with a detailed account of the killing of Chaakmol (Abel) by his worthless brother Ake, while Cay (Cain), the high priest, in vain endeavored to save him. Engravings of Abel's wife (and sister) Moo, and his mother, father, sisters and brothers, weeping over his ensanguined corpse, are sculptured on the facades of several ruined temples, while deep in the interior of a huge mound were found his (Chaakmol's) statue, the urn which once contained his heart, together with some primitive ornaments and the knife (made of light colored flint) that killed him.

If the orthodox reader may doubt the truth of Dr. Plongeon's revelations, the facts of the case are to-day accepted by numerous scientists and antiquarians. Egypt was the scene of the early childhood, the school days (if such term may be used) and the manhood and prime of the Hebrew law-giver, Moses. It is a well known fact that this great reformer and natural leader of men, was skilled in all the learning but, particularly, in the theology of the Egyptians. Dr. Plongeon believes he can prove that this latter people received the light of civilization probably 150 centuries ago, from Yucatan. In this case the subjects of Chemi were taught the story of the creation of the world, of Adam and Eve, of Abel (Chaakmol), Cay (Cain), and Ake, by the learned priests of the great Maya temples of Uxmal.

During his visit to Uxmal, the scientific explorer made a still more remarkable discovery. He deciphered hieroglyphical inscriptions, he found engraved on the temple walls of the ruined capital, which furnish an account of the submergence of the lost continent, Atlantis. Thus the narrative of Herodotus, the father of history, is in every essential correct, and thousands of feet below the troubled surface of the stormy Atlantic lies a vast territory that once was the scene of human greatness and of an elevated civilization, far superior to that which confronted the truthful ancient traveler in Egypt, 2300 years ago.

If we may believe the assertions of Central American newspapers, the truth of Dr. Plongeon's statements regarding the lost continent, has recently been attested by a fortunate discovery, of which the Caribbean coast of Nicaragua was the scene. In excavating a deep hole some workmen came upon a large rock, forty feet below the surface. This huge stone is covered with hieroglyphics and engravings, which give a brief account of the sudden submergence of the vast territory which once was situated in the wide space that is now covered by a great portion of the Atlantic ocean. This event, according to Egyptian records, took place some 7000 or 8000 years before the Christian era. The hieroglyphical accounts of the history and subsequent assassination of Chaakmol (Abel) speak of Atlantis several times. Later inscriptions also mention it, thus it is safe to assume that the statue of Chaakmol is at least 12,000 or 13,000 years old.

Dr. Plongeon discovered many other curious facts, among them the last words of Christ, "Eli Eli lama sebach thani are pure Maya and literally mean, *It is finished and darkness comes over my face.*" This is almost the precise meaning of the phrase, given by one of the Evangelists. Again, the scientist says that the names of many of the letters of the Greek alphabet, are Maya, while the appelations of numerous objects and also various Egyptian phrases are undoubtedly of genuine Maya origin.

Accordingly the learned Doctor believes that Yucatan was the cradle of human civilization and from that once densely populated land emanated the knowledge, the sciences and arts which rendered ancient Egypt so famous, while the religion of the land of Chemi, and the mysteries practiced by the white robed priests of Thebes, were first preached to the world in the spacious temple of the Sun, at Uxmal.

Of course theologians have pronounced the Doctor's assertions as utterly false and denounced him as a madman. As the gentleman in question is undoubtedly sincere, as he is inclined to persist in his opinions, had he lived in the good old days of the Inquisition, when burning, branding and other ingenious methods of torture, were employed against all who presumed to utter a word against the dogmas, the teachings and the precepts of the Church, he would beyond doubt long ere this have been handed over to the mercies of that saintly institution. But he fortunately lives in an era of enlightenment and investigation, thus his life at least is safe, even if the priesthood of all sects deride his opinions. As far as his being a madman is concerned, the learned Boucher de Perthe was for a period of fifteen years considered a poor, harmless lunatic by the Galic Church, and even by those learned parties the members of the French Institute, because he asserted that the flint knives, arrows and lance heads, he discovered imbedded in the clay at Abbeville were the workmanship of pre-historic men.

Sufficient facts have been elicited to prove that Southern Mexico, (Yucatan in particular) Guatemala, British Honduras, Spanish Honduras, Nicaragua, Costa Rica and the Isthmus of Panama, were once the cradles of a high order of civilization. But nothing more is known of the dynasties and kingdoms which flourished at that remote age than is told by the hieroglyphical inscriptions, and the carved engravings found on the columns, monuments, and temple walls of the ruined cities of Central America.

Certain localities of Costa Rica are strewn with ruins of undoubtedly great antiquity. Positive proofs exist that centuries upon centuries anterior to the Spanish conquest—certainly before the first Egyptian pyramid was built—the whole extent of the territory now known as Costa Rica was inhabited by a race of men who were much more highly civilized than the inhabitants of Nicaragua, who welcomed the mail-clad Spanish warriors of Gil Gonzales to their hearts and their homes. Several ancient tombs found in remote localities, whose crumbling sides were overgrown with tropic bowers, lately gave up the secrets contained in their hidden interiors for æons of ages. Pottery of singular shape but of skilled workmanship, stone hatchets, axes, and cooking implements, and *penates* made of gold, were found resting side by side with huge stones covered with inscriptions and hieroglyphics of a nature and form far different from the pictures and carved signs that cover the temple walls of Uxmal and Chichen-Itza. Until some future savant shall decipher these mysterious inscriptions nothing can be known of the history of those who carved them, but the belief is gradually gaining ground that the mystery that shrouds these monuments will yet be dispelled and that many authentic pages will be added to the past history of this continent.

In that portion of this work relating to Guatemala, three chapters of the ancient history of the aborigines are given. The reader has seen that authentic records furnish the history of several flourishing aboriginal kingdoms that were governed by dynasties of monarchs for centuries anterior to the conquest. They teach us that Votan, 400 years before the Christian era, founded the great empire of the Votanides, whose capital city was Palenque. The ruins of this ancient metropolis cover many square miles of area, while in its apogee it must have contained at least 2,000,000 inhabitants.

The Votanides were eventually driven to send out colonies, which penetrated to the south and founded kingdoms in Guatemala, Honduras, and probably in Nicaragua also. The traditions relative to these occurrences, as well as the Cakchiquel and Popul Vuh manuscripts, distinctly aver that wherever this conquering people emigrated they always found people more or less civilized.

At the period of the Spanish conquest neither Nicaragua nor Costa Rica was the seat of a powerful aboriginal kingdom, like the monarchies of the Montezumas, the Quiches and the Cakchiquels, or the empire of the Incas of distant Peru. While their people were highly civilized, were noted astronomers, agriculturalists and goldsmiths, and lived in large and populous centres of population, they were more democratic and were ruled by caciques. With some of the nations the office of cacique was elective. The people chose their rulers and in certain cases deposed them at will. With other nations the cacique was the hereditary head of the government, and in some isolated cases possessed absolute power.

If the indigines of Costa Rica, shortly anterior to the conquest, were more divided than those of Guatemala and Yucatan, if no powerful monarch had united them into a great kingdom by conquest or persuasion, the system of division and government cannot fairly be set down as merely tribal. If one hundred caciques drew out their forces, and in a stubborn battle contested against the valiant Spanish captain, Pedrarias, there were but four principal caciques present on that occasion; the others were merely subordinate chieftains or head men of villages and towns.

Costa Rica was discovered by Colon, during his last voyage to the New World, in the year 1504. Several years passed before other navigators followed in his traces, and it was not until the year 1513, that the famous but unfortunate Vasco Nuñez de Balboa, from the summit of a tall mountain peak, saw the long rolling billows of the Pacific ocean.

The news of the discovery of a vast sea to the westward of the Isthmus of Darien, infused a new spirit of enterprise in the hearts of the intrepid Spanish adventurers, who languished at the little settlement of Darien, on the Caribbean coast of the isthmus. They longed for an opportunity to push their discoveries still further to the north and south, along the coasts washed by both oceans.

About this time a celebrated Spanish caballero, named Pedro Pedrarias Dávila, was appointed Governor of the Spanish settlements of Darien, and Captain-General of the vast south sea. He arrived at Darien about the year 1514, accompanied by numerous Spanish gentlemen who, having wasted their fortunes in an unfortunate Italian expedition, were only too anxious to seek a fresh field of enterprise in the New World.

The gallant Nuñez de Balboa married his daughter, but the ferocious chieftain, jealous of the fame acquired by his new relative, accused him of high treason against the crown, and the hero was beheaded in the presence of his relentless enemy.

But, as is mentioned in that portion of this work relative to Nicaragua, if Pedrarias was cold-blooded, avaricious and ferocious, he was one of the most skillful captains and intrepid soldiers formed during the wars of the Spanish conquest of tropic America. As a general he ranked second only to Cortes on the list of heroes who won so many kingdoms, provinces and countries for Spain. As an audacious and successful soldier, he may be considered as peer with either Cortes or Pizarro, and during the eighteen years that he commanded on the isthmus, he added a vast area of territory and millions of people to the proud colonial empire of Charles V.

In the year 1516 he sent a fleet towards the northwest, which coasted along the shores of that territory now known as Costa Rica and Nicaragua. The expedition was commanded by two Captains, named Hernan Ponce and Bartolomé Hurtado. On the beach of a little bay in Costa Rica, they saw drawn up in battle array a long line of natives, but, declining the combat, the Spaniards held on their way to the north and west. The people who so readily assembled to defend their native coasts, were known as the Chinchires, a brave and gallant nation of indigines, which afterwards gave the Spaniards infinite trouble and annoyance before they were definitely subdued.

The Spanish chieftains at length reached a port that bore the name of Chira, which they called San Lucar, but which was afterwards known as Nicoya. As gallant and patriotic as their neighbors, the Chinchires, the aboriginies of Chira assembled in their canoes and fearlessly attacked the large vessels of the explorers. They filled the air with the sounds of martial music, and made menacing signs at the strangers. When they had approached near enough to use them with effect, they bent their long bows and discharged a cloud of arrows at their foes. The Spaniards answered with their light cannon. Several of the canoes were sunk and many natives slain by the first broadside. Terrified by the noise of the cannon and at the deadly effect produced by their discharge, the natives lost heart and without waiting to pick up the crews of the destroyed canoes, who were struggling in the water, turned and fled towards the shores.

The Spanish vessels moved nearer to the beach and fired at the Indian troops who, drawn up in columns of battle, had witnessed the signal defeat of their fleet. A few broadsides served to disperse them and they fled into the interior.

The Spanish captains not liking the looks of the coast any more than the hostile aspect of the natives, and at the same time anxious to return to the isthmus, turned in their tracks and soon reached Panama. Although Pedrarias was greatly dissatisfied with the meagre results obtained by the expedition, he afterward claimed jurisdiction over the coast skirted by these two adventures and eventually obtained the governorship of both Costa Rica and Nicaragua.

This chieftain was admirably seconded by several gallant Spanish captains whose names already were, or afterwards became, famous. Among these were Ponce, Hurtado, Cordoba, Soto, Ojeda, Olid, Rojas, Pizarro, and the Licenciate Gaspar de Espinosa, who it seems was more devoted to a military life

18

than to his professional labors. This latter caballero, during one of his excursions penetrated as far as Orotino, or some two hundred leagues to the northwest.

In 1520 Espinosa conducted an expedition of two small ships, in search of a group of islands, called by the natives, Cebaco, which was situated about seventy leagues northwest of Panama. Meanwhile, the future conqueror of Peru, Francisco Pizarro, advanced in the same direction by land. All that is known of Pizarro's campaign is that he fought many combats, and succeeded in finally subjugating the natives.

The Islanders, (inhabitants of the Cebaco group), although very numerous, were utterly disheartened by the successes obtained by Pizarro on the main land, and warned by the terrible treatment experienced by the brave Chinchires at the hands of the conquerors hastened to enter into peaceful relations with Espinosa. During his stay at the Islands the Spanish captain was unwearied in his search for gold. One of the native caciques informed him, that the mountains, gulches and rivulets of the contiguous main land contained numerous deposits of the precious metal, and that the locality, in question, was dominated by a powerful cacique named Urraca, and was called Burica.

But Urraca was a gallant chieftain who, ever since the expedition of Ponce and Hurdado, had been preparing means of resistance when, as he foresaw, he should be visited by the hated strangers. He sent all the women, old men, and children to the fastnesses of the neighboring mountains, and when his spies informed him of the approach of the Spaniards he marched forth to meet them.

The vanguard of the Spanish forces, composed of friendly Indians, was totally destroyed before the white men could come to their rescue. Then Urraca hurled his forces on the little Spanish army. The powerful bows of the natives discharged long, sharp arrows, which wounded the horses and in many cases penetrated the steel armor of the invaders. The Spaniards, almost disheartened, were slowly retreating toward their ships when they were unexpectedly reinforced by Hernando de Soto, who had shortly before been sent by Pizarro on an excursion towards the coast. This timely assistance reanimated the invaders and they again advanced and slowly forced the Indians backwards until they came to a locality so broken by rocky chasms, and wide arroyos, that the cavalry could no longer manenver. The natives rallied and fought desperately. While a portion of them defended the new position they had taken, other bodies attacked the flanks and rear of the Spanish forces and reduced them to the greatest extremity. At length Espinosa was compelled to retreat. During the ensuing night he endeavored to reach his ships, but the Indian cacique was on the alert and again hurled his columns upon the tired fugitives. The latter fought with the courage of despair, and at length succeeded in breaking through the enemies lines and reached their ships.

Espinosa landed at different points along the coast and fought several more actions with the natives. He captured many of the latter whom he carried to Panama and sold as slaves. Before he departed from the neighborhood, however, he left at Burica, a small detachment of Spaniards under the command of a captain named Compañon.

When Urraca was informed that all the Spaniards had left his coast save a small detachment, he at once determined to destroy it. He collected his forces and laid siege to the fortified post occupied by Compañon. The latter defended himself for several days but would have eventually fallen into the hands of his implacable enemy, had not reinforcements, under the command of Hernan Ponce, arrived in time to succor him. Urrica, without attempting to dispute the disembarkation of the new comers, retired in good order to his mountain fastnesses.

Pedrarias deeming the occasion worthy his own efforts determined to go in person and destroy the indomitable Indian cacique. He set out from Panama at the head of 140 Spaniards and numerous auxiliaries. Francisco Pizarro commanded his advance guard and the artillery.

Urraca meanwhile had made arrangements to meet this new and more formidable foe. He entered into an alliance with a neighboring cacique named Exquegua. The combined American forces occupied a most advantageous situation, and the relentless Urraca was appointed commander-in-chief. When Pedrarias discovered the Indian position he halted and examined it carefully before attacking. For awhile he hesitated, but upon reflection determined to make the attack, for he well knew that were he to retreat without striking a blow, after coming so far in search of his enemy, he might lose prestige with his own followers and would certainly incur the contempt of the aborigines.

The battle lasted nearly from sunrise to sunset. The Spaniards lost many men and horses and Pedrarias was compelled to exert his greatest skill to avoid a serious disaster. At length an opportunity was afforded to use his artillery. The balls made huge gaps in the ranks of the assailants who eventually retired about night fall. During the three ensuing days Urraca attacked the Spanish camp various times but was invariably repulsed. He at length retreated into the mountains where he selected and fortified an admirable position and defied Pedrarias' efforts to dislodge him. The Spaniard subdued the neighboring country, divided its inhabitants among his men as slaves, founded the town of Natá, and leaving his lieutenant Diego de Albitez in command returned to Panama.

Shortly afterwards Francisco Campañon was again placed in command of the dispirited district. Despairing of being able to subdue the persistent Urraca by force he resorted to stratagem. He invited the chief to a conference. The latter relying upon the captain's "safe conduct" proceeded to Natá, where he was immediately imprisoned by the treacherous Spaniard. He managed to escape after a few months confinement and fled to his people who welcomed him with the wildest demonstrations of joy. He again raised a large army and marched to Natá. Against his usual policy he met the Spaniards in the open field. The battle was sanguinary and was most stubbornly contested. Many of the invaders were killed and wounded, while the wide plain was literally covered with the bodies of slain Indians. European arms and valor eventually prevailed. The natives at length sullenly retired to their mountain fastnessess leaving the Spaniards master of the open country.

For a period of nine years the courageous Urraca waged a relentless war against the invaders, until the majority of his people, worn out by so many efforts, abandoned their cacique and submitted to the conquerors. Urraca, accompanied by a few faithful followers, fled to the confines of Nicaragua, but the Spaniards who respected his valor and constancy made no attempt to follow him. A few months afterwards he died heart-broken and was, in accordance with his earnest instructions, buried in a mountain cave far beyond the reach of his implacable enemies.

After the death of this heroic leader the Spaniards quickly consolidated their conquests. The Indian warriors who had deserted their gallant chieftain were compelled to labor as porters, delve deep in the mountain sides in search of precious metals, and with the sweat of their brows to moisten the soil they had formerly possessed themselves. Before the death of Pedrarias, which occurred in 1531, Costa Rica was completely pacified, and the province was held in the tenacious grasp of Spain until the descendants of the conquerors and of the Indian followers of Urraca, broke the galling chains that fettered them, and won their independence in 1821.

CHAPTER II.

Costa Rica, is the most southern republic of Central America,
and, until recently, was, with the exception of Salvador, the
most prosperous. It is bounded on the north by Nicaragua,
on the east by the Caribbean sea, on the south by the Pacific
ocean and the isthmus of Panama, and on the west by the
Pacific ocean. It contains an area of 21,500 square miles or
13,700,000 square acres of territory and about 230,000 inhabitants, mostly of Spanish descent.

The form of government is republican. The Executive power
is vested in a President who holds office for a term of four
years. Two vice presidents are elected at the same time the
President is chosen. The senior of these two officials assume
the functions of the Executive office during the disability, or
absence of the President. The deputies to the national congress are also chosen for four years and hold annual sessions.

The present Constitution was promulgated in the year 1871,
but since that date has been several times slightly modified.
Its provisions are extremely liberal.

The republic is divided into seven provinces, and one district, or territory, namely:

	Population.	Capital.	Population.
San José, province	60,000	San José	25,000
Cartago, province	45,000	Cartago	15,000
Heredia, province	40,000	Heredia	12,000
Alajuela, province	35,000	Alajuela	8,000
Guanacaste, province	12,000	Santa Cruz	2,000
Liberia, province	6,000	Liberia	2,500
Punta Arenas, province	8,000	Punta Arenas	2,000
Limon, district	4,500	Limon	2,000
	210,500		68,500

Besides the number of inhabitants shown by the above table, the northeastern portion of the republic contains an uncivilized aboriginal population amounting to at least 14,000. The number of civilized Indians, of pure aboriginal descent, may be computed at somewhere in the neighborhood of 6,000. Thus the entire population of the republic may safely be estimated to be at least 230,000.

While the western slope of Costa Rica is comparatively thickly settled, the Atlantic, or Caribbean side, is as yet a vast and untenanted wilderness. There are large tracts of territory where the foot of white man has seldom trodden, while certain almost inaccessible regions were avoided by the hardy followers of Cordoba and Gil Gonzales, of Pedrarias and Rojas during the war of the conquest. The inhabitants of these *terras incognita* steadily met the Spanish conquerors on the borders of their rivers, streams and lagoons, man to man, and almost invariably came off victors in the combats that ensued. They often enticed their enemies into the depth of their mountain, and forest fastnesses, and slaughtered them in detail.

PUNTA ARENAS.

This province is situated on the western slope and is but thinly inhabited. The coast is washed by the long rolling billows of the great Pacific, and is marked by two mountainous peninsulars which reach far out into the ocean and enclose the two pretty little bays or gulfs, called respectively, el Golfo de Nicoya, and el Golfo Dulce.

For a short distance from the coast the land is low and sandy, and during the rainy season is converted into a vast marsh. The forest growth is insignificant, from the beach, eastward into the interior, up to the banks of the turbulent and inconstant Rio las Barrancas. There the scene changes as if by magic. The acasia, and the date, cocoa and caboon palms, give place to the tall spreading ceiba, the frondose mahogany, and the gigantic cedar, while the mountain slopes, and the foothill sides are covered with a dense growth of dyewood, live oak, laurel, zapote, amarillo, and vera trees, whose thick foliage shelters a thousand different kinds of creeping plants, beautifully tinted flowers and aromatic shrubs.

This tropic paradise is inhabited by a hardy, brave, fine-looking and contented race of ladinos, who, as far as personal appearance is concerned, certainly rank peer with any of the mixed races of the continent. In Honduras, Guatemala and San Salvador, the ladinos, who are the dominant class, retain much of the dark complexion, and many of the characteristics of the former aboriginal occupants of the country, from whom they are descended. In Nicaragua, particularly, on either coast slope, the people are an essentially miscegenated race. The white, black and red branches of the human family, having each contributed their quota of blood. If the members of this race retain few of the striking characteristics of either of the three castes from which they sprang, they still possess the pride and courage of the whites, the patience, indolence and tenacity of the Indians, and the stalwart proportions, and crisp hair of the negroes. But their complexion is neither white, red, nor black. It might better be described as a bright, but not disagreeable yellow, while the skin is softer and smoother than that of the eastern or mongolian people.

On the western coast of Costa Rica, while there are many specimens of the same class of yellow people, that is met with on either coast of Nicaragua, the majority of the inhabitants have a soft, light nut-brown or brunet complexion like the rosados of Mexico and the peninsula of Yucatan. In this instance the white blood seems to have predominated over the other streams with which it has mixed, and the people are almost white. Tradition also hath it, that the aboriginal inhabitants, the followers of the tenacious king Urraca, possessed much lighter complexions than the people to the north and south of them. Be this as it may; the fact that the inhabitants of the western and central portions of Costa Rica are of much lighter complexions than their northern and southern Latin American neighbors, is both well known and generally acknowledged.

The males are tall, well formed, and are also active and intelligent. They make excellent soldiers, being particularly famous for their courage, constancy and patriotism. They proudly assert that one Costa Rican soldier is equal, in combat to five men from any other portion of Central America. They are opposed to the union of their little republic with its four northern neighbors.

The women of this caste are, as a general case, remarkably handsome, fascinating and engaging. They are almost white, while their hands and feet are small and faultlessly shaped. Their hair, which it is their delight and pride to dress and adorn, is of a rich brown color, and when unconfined hangs far down the back and almost sweeps the ground. Even the married women, although their forms have never been compressed by the corset, retain, to a great degree, their fine figures to an extreme old age. They are very clannish and almost invariably marry with members of their own caste. Their features are regular, the face oval, mouth small and filled with white well shaped teeth, while their eyes are large, deep brown or black and are full of expression. This race of people, although in social position they occupy the same grade as their ladino neighbors, of the same caste, to the north and south of them, occupies the entire territory, from the Rio de las Barrancas on the west, to Carillo on the east, and north and south as far as the civilized limits extend.

While a few of the male inhabitants of the province of Punta Arenas, dedicate a small portion of their time to agriculture, the majority of them frequent the port, (of the same name) where they gain a pecarious livelihood by discharging the ships that frequent the bay, by fishing, by engaging in the coast trade, or by selling shells and curiosities to the passengers, of the steamers that at regular intervals touch at the port.

The few agriculturalists raise small crops of corn, beans and some vegetables. Indian corn, made into an indigestable kind of bread, which is known as the *tortilla*, throughout the entire extent of Latin America, is the staple food of the masses, while the numerous spontaneously produced fruits of the tropics supplement this humble fare. Notwithstanding the forests teem with deer and other kinds of game, and the branches of the trees that adorn the primeval forests shelter a hundred different kinds of game birds, meat food is but seldom seen on the boards of the poorer class of people.

The little seaport of Punta Arenas is situated on a narrow neck of land that is washed by the waters of the Pacific. It contains but few pretentious buildings; the majority of the houses being built of wood. They are necessarily well ventilated, for during the dry season the weather is unusally hot and sultry, while sand flies and musquitos are a perfect scourge at night. The town contains, about 2,000 inhabitants and is the capital of the province.

The principal traffic centred at this port until the Caribbean coast railroad was constructed as far as Sucio or Carillo. Since that date no small portion of the import trade passes over the latter route. As the coffee plantations are mostly on the Pacific slope the greater bulk of the harvest is shipped from Punta Arenas, on the Pacific Mail coast steamers, which connect the port with Panama on the south, and Central American, Mexican, and American ports to the north.

Besides the Pacific Mail steamers which touch at regular intervals at this port, sail vessels, freighted with English dry-goods and other merchandise, also frequent the place. These ships generally return to Europe, via Cape Horn, laden with cargoes of precious woods, hides, sarsaparilla, rubber and even coffee. Punta Arenas is the principal seaport of the republic, and will continue so to be until the eastern railroad is completed to San Jose, the capital of the republic.

GUANACASTE AND LIBERIA.

These two districts, until lately formed but one, which was known as the province, or department of Guanacaste. This territory is noted for its salubrious climate, rich mines and admirable pasture lands. The greater portion of the province is still claimed by Nicaragua, which republic refuses to satisfy the boundry treaty that gave Guanacaste and Nicoya to Costa Rica. The topography of the district is broken by numerous spurs, of the central mountain range which divides the republic into almost two equal portions. Hidden away among the tall mountains are numerous beautiful little valleys, whose fertile soil, well irrigated by the streams that issue from the hillsides, can produce all the varied flora of the tropics. The foothill slopes, which are utilized by the hardy Indians for their *milpas*, or corn patches, return remarkably bounteous harvests, while the little tablelands that, here and there, break the mountain ranges, produce fine crops of wheat, rye, oats and other cereals of the temperate zone.

Anterior to the conquest Guanacaste and Liberia contained within their limits a dense aboriginal population, while in certain localities are found the ruins of cities that rival in antiquity the remains of the temples and palaces of Milta and Papantla, of Copan and Quirigua. When Cordoba and Gil Gonzales first penetrated into these regions they were welcomed by a hardy race of people who, with awe, pointed out these ruins and told them that many cycles of ages ago, when their fathers first occupied the country, the same ruins, the same relics of past grandeur, met their wondering eyes. But little did the Indian hosts of the conquerors think, that in the nineteenth century, a race of men differing in religion, in language in characteristics from their guests would wander over *their* once thickly populated country and wonder what had become of *their* race. For the aborigines of Guanacaste, of Liberia, of Nicoya and the land of Nicarao, have almost passed away, and but a miserable remnant of the 600,000 red people who sheltered Gil and Cordoba, numbering not more than two or three thousand souls, roam listlessly over the broad savanas, or hunt amid the tropic jungle whose soil, four hundred years ago was cultivated by their industrious and contented ancestors. For the records of the early conquerers teem with comments regarding the prosperous condition of the aborigines anterior to the conquest. The red men of Costa Rica have passed away. The race that succeeded them is also slowly dying out, and in another century will be entirely extinct, unless its mixture with a newer and hardier stock, the infusion of a fresher and a healthier blood shall bring about the creation of a new race which, imbued with liberal sentiments, and energetic and industrous habits, shall restore Costa Rica to a prosperous and happy condition similar to that presented anterior to the Spanish conquest.

It is immigration and a fusion of the races only that can accomplish this great end. The people of Costa Rica, of all

Latin America, approach the nearer in form, characteristics and complexion to the Europeans. The children born of marriages between the intrusive and the native races, are fine specimens of humanity, for the males are stalwart, vigorous and brave, and the females are beautiful, high-minded and pure.

The ladino inhabitants of Guanacaste possess the same physical characteristics of their brethern of San José and Cartago. While some few engage in mining pursuits, and the cultivation of the soil, the majority are stock raisers and are noted horsemen and partisians. The capital of the department is a little town called Liberia, which contains but 2500 inhabitants.

ALAJUELA.

This province is situated in the central portion of the republic and is limited by Heredia on the east and Punta Arenas on the west. While portions of the country are rugged and broken, no small part of its territory is level land, admirably adapted to cultivation. The fertile soil produces all the varied fruits of the tropics, while the higher lands are being laid out into coffee plantations. During the Spanish regime this district was famous for its production of indigo, sugar and cochineal. While the two former are still produced, the latter no longer excites the interest it formerly did. The discovery of numerous substitutes for the dye tint extracted from the cochineal insect, has so reduced its price in European markets, that nopal plantations are no longer cultivated, nor are the insects that thrive on the remaining plants always harvested.

The production of indigo, which once proved such an important industry has been in a measure abandoned, for coffee planting has usurped its place.

Beyond doubt the tropic plains of Alajuela are destined in the very near future to supply no insignificant portion of the crude sugar demand of the markets of the world. The soil is admirably adapted to the cultivation of the precious cane, which attains the highest degree of development, and returns from 4000 to 6500 pounds of crude sugar, or melado, to the acre. When the railroad that purposes to connect the cities of Alaguila and Heredia with the western division of Esparza is finished, the sugar planting industry will assume larger proportions and become of greater importance, year by year.

The city of Alajuela, which is the capital of the province, contains about 8000 inhabitants, the most of whom are Ladinos. The people are mostly supported by agriculture while a few are engaged in the manufacture of hats, pottery, or follow the occupation of mule drivers, carpenters, masons, etc. The city boasts but few large or imposing edifices, and but one really fine church. Alajuela is the western terminus of the railroad and is distant twenty-seven miles from San José, the capital of the republic, and forty-two miles from Cartajo.

HEREDIA.

This department, or province, is limited by Alajuela on the west and San José on the east. Its boundaries to the north and south, being ill defined, cannot be stated with correctness. It ranks third among the provinces in importance, wealth and populousness. The greater portion of its inhabitants are clustered around the city of the same name, while far to the north and south stretch vast regions inhabited only by savage Indians, and wild beasts that roam free and unmolested, the only denizens of the primeval forests and tangled tropic jungles.

The capital of the province, Heredia, has 12,000 inhabitants and ranks as the third city, in size and importance, in the country. It is in daily rail communication with Alajuela on the west and San José and Cartago on the east. It is the centre of a flourishing agricultural region whose products are principally of a tropical nature.

SAN JOSÉ.

This province is the most important and the densest settled of the political divisions into which the country is divided. It is the centre of the traffic of the eastern and western slopes while the greater portion of its cultivated lands is divided into numerous flourishing coffee plantations. The bulk of its import and export traffic is carried on through the Pacific port of Punta Arenas. The coffee harvest is principally shipped from that point on the steamers of the Pacific Mail line. The other products are tropic fruits, sugar and indigo.

The capital city, San José, is situated in the central portion of the province, in a beautiful valley surrounded by fertile foot hills that are cultivated almost up to their very summits. It contains 25,000 inhabitants and is adorned by numerous fine churches, public edifices and private residences. As the the site of the city is 3880 feet above the level of the sea the climate is remarkably healthy. No fevers of any kind are prevalent, even during the rainy season, while pulmonary diseases of any description or nature whatever are practically unknown.

The native inhabitants of San José, as far as physical and intellectual qualities are concerned, rank equal to any people in the world. Numerous of the males possess ruddy complexions and light hair, while a still greater number of their fair sisters are positive blondes. The men are a fine-looking, stalwart race, while the women, with their large, dark, lustrous, deep blue or black eyes, their long flowing tresses, small but perfectly shaped hands and feet, and lithe, graceful, exquisitely formed figures are second to none, in personal attraction, to any of their foreign sisters.

The capital carries on a flourishing traffic with the neighboring cities and towns. The wealthy planters who own the coffee plantations in the vicinity reside within its limits and form a separate social caste, very exclusive and also very proud. The streets are well lighted and well paved, and it will not be long before the entire municipal limits will be lighted with electricity. A line of street cars, that will pass through the principal thoroughfares, will soon be in operation. The workshop of the railroad company is well provided with different kinds of machinery, while the depot is a spacious and commodious building. The locality is well provided with cabs, while all the wealthy residents own at least one family carriage. Three good hotels afford ample accommodations for travelers and native guests.

San José is connected with the town of Carillo, or Sucio, which is the present terminus of the Costa Rican Central Railroad, by a cart road over the mountains, twenty-six miles long. During the rainy season this road is almost impassable in some places, and both freight and passengers are transported on mule-back to the foot of the mountains, but when the dry season comes on it is quickly repaired and becomes one of the most frequented thoroughfares in the country.

CARTAGO.

This department is inferior to San José alone in wealth and commercial importance. It lies between the province of San José and the Comarca—zone or district—of Limon, and is noted for its numerous coffee plantations and stock farms.

The capital city of the same name is connected with San José by a branch railroad fifteen miles long, while a projected line, that will strike the Central route, where the latter crosses the river Reventazon, fifty miles long, will soon connect it with the Caribbean seaport. This city contains 15,000 inhabitants and is the centre of a flourishing agricultural district. It draws its foreign supplies from the ports on either slope, but the greater portion of its coffee crop goes to Port Limon for shipment.

COMARCA, OR ZONE, OF LIMON.

The boundary limits of this vast region have never been correctly defined. Some native geographers consider that it extends along the entire stretch of coast washed by the blue waves of the Caribbean sea, and as far back as the town of Carillo, or Sucio, seventy-two miles inland.

With the exception of a narrow strip of land extending along either side of the Central Railroad, from the town of Carillo to the coast, the rest of this extensive district is a mere wilderness, inhabited only by wild beasts and still wilder Indians. The coast is low and is indented by lagoons, little bays and the mouths of numerous rivers, streams and creeks. This region is covered with a grand forest growth that has seldom been disturbed since the era of the conquest. Several nations of savage Indians still rove the undisturbed masters of this wilderness. The tribes which once held the Spaniards at bay in the territory watered by the Reventazon and Pacuar rivers have been exterminated by their ferocious neighbors.

The Pranzos nation occupies the lands along the banks of the Frio river; the Bizeita tribe the territory drained by the turbulent Sixaula river; while the warriors of the Terrbis tribe still maintain their hold on the vast forests and wild

plains that border the Chiriqui country. These savages are
perfectly independent of the Costa Rican government and
wage relentless war against each other. They trade with
coasting vessels from Nicaragua and the isthmus, and barter
hides, rubber, skins, sarsaparilla and turtle shells for arms,
powder, tobacco and rum. They are exceedingly licentious
and intemperate. The men occupy themselves with fishing,
hunting and fighting. The women cultivate corn, beans and
pumpkins, and are the submissive slaves and drudges of their
lords and masters.

Until within a few months since this entire district was a
free zone. The customhouse and revenue officials were sta-
tioned at Carillo. Complaints having been made to the government that a vast amount of smuggling was carried on, or,
in other words, that goods imported into the district were
smuggled into San José and Cartago, the free zone privilege
was rescinded and the custom and revenue offices were again
established at the port. While some mahogany and cedar
logs are cut at different points along the coast, the most important industry is tropical fruit planting.

Port Limon is situated at the head of a little bay that carries deep water up to the very wharf. It contains a few
wooden buildings mostly owned by foreigners. The greater
number of the inhabitants are civilized Caribs and Jamaica
negroes. The white residents are mostly Americans, who are
either employes of the railroad or are engaged in commerce.
The principal business firm is Keith & Co., who control the
greater part of the traffic that passes through the port, while
the enterprising head of the firm owns numerous fruit and
sugar plantations along the line of the railroad.

Port Limon presents all the characteristics of a Jamaican
village. The streets are crowded with untidy but good-hu-
mored negro women and lazy, intemperate black men, who
work only when compelled by actual necessity. The women,
as a general case, support both their husband and children;
while the latter are a worthless, frolicsome, good-natured set
of little vagabonds, who are in very early life corrupted by the
immoral atmosphere that surrounds them.

The central portion of the republic is famous for several very tall mountain peaks, or volcanoes, as they are called by the natives. Poas attains an elevation of 8895 feet above the level of the sea. Barba peak is 8700 feet high ; Irazu 11,300, and Turrialba 11,350 feet. The great mountain Dota range, which extends from the Pacific almost to the Caribbean ceast, is from 7000 to 9000 feet high, while the tall Nemú, or Pico Blanco, reaches an altitude of 12,000 feet above the level of the Caribbean.

Costa Rica is watered by numerous perennial, but unnavigable, rivers. On the Pacific slope the Tempisque and Las Piedras rivers flow into the gulf of Nicoya, while the rivers Pirris, Guanacaste, El Barranco, Rio Grande, Narango and their numerous affluents, drain the fertile lands that lie between the ocean and the central mountain range.

On the Caribbean coast the Rio Frio, San Carlos, Saripique and Colorado flow into the great San Juan river, while the Reventazon, Pacuar, Chiripo, Sixaula, Changuenola and Chiriqui empty into the lagoons that break the low coast line.

19

CHAPTER III.

The railroad system of Costa Rica would probably have been further developed had not two unfortunate circumstances intervened. About three years ago, General Guadia, one of the most interesting characters depicted in the history of Central America, suddenly died. He had ruled Costa Rica for an eventful period of ten years. For a time he was absolutely dictator, but when he had reformed the most glaring abuses which had, through years of anarchy and confusion, crept into government methods, and re-established the affairs of the republic upon a firm basis, he returned to the constitutional regime, and governed the republic for some years as Constitutional President.

His chief ambition was to complete the construction of the inter-oceanic railroad, before his death or retirement from office. He was pushing the work rapidly from both extremities of the proposed line, when the government engineers informed him that the proposed route, from Carillo to San José, a distance of twenty-six miles over the mountain range that separates the plateau of San José from the low lands on the Caribbean, was impracticable. He asked what they meant by their report. They answered that to construct the twenty-six remaining miles of the road, over the rugged mountain chain, would, if it were actually possible, necessitate an outlay of at least $100,000 per mile. The chief engineer supple-.

mented this assertion with another, to the effect that a single locomotive could scarcely mount the steep incline even if the road were built, unless it was supplied with wings. "Construct locomotives with wings then," was the chieftain's answer. New surveys of the route were made by other engineers, but as no practicable pass could be found the President was obliged to give up the point, and ordered his engineers to search for a route around the mountains either to the north or south.

At length, a practicable route was discovered to Cartago, from a point on the Port Limon and Carillo line, where it crosses the Reventazon river, a distance of fifty miles. Had this route been chosen in the first place it would have saved the republic the cost of the Port Limon—or Central—line from the Reventazon river to Sucio. Or, in other words, would have proved an economy of twenty-five miles of construction work.

General Guadia gave orders to grade the road-bed, over the new route, and some progress was made, when the sudden fall of the price of coffee put an end to further work. With the decline in the price of the staple product of the country came a corresponding financial crisis, thus the new division of the road has not yet been completed.

In 1871 the government obtained a loan of £1,000,000, in London, and work on the present incomplete railroad system was begun. In 1872 another loan of £2,400,000 was obtained. This latter debt was contracted for the express purpose of constructing the inter-oceanic railroad. Of this sum £1,200,000 were actually expended on the enterprise by the end of 1873, when work was suddenly suspended. Up to the present date nothing further has been done to complete the proposed railroad system as far as actual construction work is concerned.

Although two large gaps in the inter-oceanic line remain to be filled before direct rail communication between the two coasts is assured, the little republic boasts the possession of more miles of railroad than any of her sister Central American nations. The complete railroad divisions are as follows:

Port Limon to Carillo........................	72	miles.
Cartago to San José..........................	15	"
San José to Alajuela.........................	27	"
Esparza to Punta Arenas.....................	18	"
Total....................................	132	"

The two large gaps, or breaks, in the purposed route, are:

From the Reventazon river where it crosses the Port Limon and Carillo road to Carillo.......	50	miles.
From Alajuela to Esparza.....................	66	"
Total....................................	116	"

Thus the entire Interoceanic line, when completed from sea to sea, by the only practicable route, that can be found around the mountains to Cartago, and from Alajuela to Esparza, which divisions also present difficult engineering problems, will be 248 miles long.

The financial trouble that followed the fall in the price of coffee can not be said to have as yet terminated, thus the government has not been able to procure the necessary funds to complete the proposed railroad system. A few months ago, Minor C. Keith, Esq., of the well known house of Keith & Co., of Port Limon and San José went to London, to arrange for the bonding of the old debt and, at the same time to procure a new loan of at least £500,000. Mr. Keith has returned to San José but the true history of his mission, and its results, have not yet been made public. The newspapers of the republic hint that he was successful on all points, and assert that work will soon be commenced on the gaps between the Reventazon river and Cartago, and that within two years this division will be completed.

With cheap transportation, from the centres of production to the Caribbean coast, the traffic of the country would soon reach its former prosperous status. Since the year 1875, the value of the imports of foreign wares and the export of domestic produce has shown a gradual and alarming decline. The import traffic for 1883, amounted to £650,000. The exports to about $3,000,000. The value of exports to the United States, for the same period, was $800,000. The imports from the United States amounted to $700,000. Of this $1,500,000 traffic, New Orleans, and the Mississippi valley, notwithstanding the close proximity of the Crescent City to Port Limon, got only $124,000. This includes the fruit trade also, which, sorrowful to say, amounted to 4,162 bunches of bananas only. The domestic traffic of the republic will aggregate to about $14,000,000 annually.

The manufacturing industry of Costa Rica is confined to a few unimportant branches. Certain articles, whose use or value are neither known nor appreciated outside the republic, are manufactured for the domestic demand only. Sugar and rum are produced to some extent, but are seldom exported. Indigo, of a superior class, is made on the plantations and exported from Punta Arenas to Europe and San Francisco, Cal. Quantities of palm leaf hats are made and sold in the country, while excellent tiles and burnt brick are manufactured at different localities to fill the house demand.

As far as the learned professions are concerned, in ratio to its population, Costa Rica can certainly boast that as many of her sons are doctors, lawyers, mining and civil engineers, theologians, philosophers, and scientists of different kinds, as can be found in any of her greater and more fortunate sister nations. Indeed one of the common sayings of the people is: "Costa Rica would be a greater and wealthier country if more of her citizens were miners and planters, and fewer of them lawyers and theologians."

Each of the five republics has produced noted writers. Some of the latter have acquired local reputations as historical essayists and political writers, others as novelists, while the number who are famed for their political talents is legion.

Costa Rica possesses her fair share of all these classes of writers, while not a few of her younger citizens have already displayed no small amount of artistic talent. Portait painters abound. In fact, each educated Costa Rican may be considered as a fair writer and an amateur artist and musician.

The capital city possesses several well appointed colleges and academies. Schools for primary instruction are found in every village, while education is compulsory.

The mining industry never, even during the Spanish regime, excited as much interest as in other portions of Central America. Shortly after the conquest the richest placer gold diggings were exhausted. The deposits of precious metals known to exist in the uncivilized regions have never been disturbed, on account of the irreconcilable hostility of the aborigines. Yet traditions hath it that anterior to the advent of the Spaniards the native caciques drew large supplies of gold dust from that almost *terra incognita*.

Costa Rica is undoubtedly rich in precious and useful minerals. Gold, silver, lead, copper, iron, nickle, zinc and tin mines and valuable quarries of marble have been discovered from time to time, but only gold, silver and copper deposits are worked to any extent.

About eleven miles from Punta Arenas, near the old road to Esparza, is situated the famous gold mine of Trinidad. During the Spanish rule it furnished no small portion of Central America's annual quota of bullion to the Spanish court. The ore is extracted from the side of a mountain. The principal tunnel is 1200 feet above the level of the Pacific ocean. This mine is at present worked on a small scale by a native company.

The Corro del Aguacate contains several well defined gold ledges. One mine in particular, called El Aguacate, has been worked for more than two hundred years; while another, the Sacra Familia, has been in operation for nearly as long a period. It has two separate ledges. One composed of galena and zinc blend, with silver and grey copper ores, which latter also yield a few ounces of silver to the ton. The other lode is gold quartz, very similar, in nature and quality, to that of Trinidad.

The vast quantity of gold dust and golden idols, ornaments and thin plates of the same precious metal given by the native caciques to the first explorers, and the numerous placer diggings that were afterwards found close to the ocean and worked by the avaricious Spaniards, induced the latter, in their delight at having at length hit upon such an "Eldorado," to bestow upon the Pacific slope the name since given to the whole province, or modern republic, viz., Costa Rica, or the rich coast.

But long before the era of independence the creoles and Spaniards discovered that the true source of Costa Rica's prosperity lay not in its mines, but in its unrivaled agricultural possibilities. Before the star of Spanish domination sunk in a sea of slaughter never again to appear above the political horizon, this fact was known and recognized by the masters of the soil. It is true the unjust colonial policy pursued by Spain inflicted a lasting injury upon the agricultural industry of the province, yet its provisions were sometimes evaded or openly disregarded in the most remote localities, and many of the prohibited products were grown on Costa Rican soil.

The declaration of independence and the subsequent separation of the colony from the mother country, give a new and vigorous impulse to agriculture. Capital that had long lain buried or hidden away was restored to circulation or invested in new indigo, cochineal, sugar and tobacco plantations and thousands of acres of extremely fertile land, which had not been employed since the first days of the conquest, again bloomed with valuable and prolific harvests. For a long time cochineal production and indigo planting were the chief agricultural industries, and eventually sugar cane, tobacco and coffee plantations were established, and the new branches of agriculture proved remarkably profitable.

While to-day somewhat more than one-twentieth of the entire republic is under cultivation, but a comparatively small portion of this area is devoted to sugar culture. This industry, strange to say, has attracted but little attention. Only a common kind of sugar is manufactured, while the greater portion of the crude article is turned into rum.

Indigo planting is a much more important branch of agriculture. The plant is produced and the article manufactured on the spot. It is then despatched to Punta Arenas for shipment. It is very doubtful, however, if Costa Rica produces as much indigo as San Salvador. At one time, the little republic shipped more of this article than her diminutive northern neighbor.

The discovery of chemical extracts that eventually supplanted cochineal as a valuable dye stuff, almost destroyed the production of this hitherto precious insect. Numerous plantations were abandoned and the nopal plants, no longer receiving proper care and attention, soon deteriorated and became as worthless as their sister species. Some few plantations are yet operated but it is very doubtful if this industry will ever be revived on a large scale.

Tobacco is produced in all the different provinces. That of Alajuela enjoys the highest reputation for both quality and flavor. The sale of the leaf, and cigars and cigarettes, is yet monopolized by the government, but exportation of both the leaf and the manufactured article is free.

Indian corn, being the staple food stuff of the natives, is cultivated more than any other production. It is very probable that more than a half of the area of land under cultivation is devoted to the production of this invaluable cereal.

The foot hill sides and mountain slopes are cleared, and, just as the rainy season commences, the Indian ranchero plants his *milpa* or corn patch. Small quantities of wheat are produced in the temperate regions of the higher altitude, as well as barley and oats for horse provender.

But the principal agricultural resource of the country is coffee. The provinces of San José and Cartago are the chief centres of this industry. The grand plateau of San José, in particular, is divided into hundreds of flourishing plantations which tax the labor supply of the neighborhood to its full capacity to care for and harvest the yield of the trees.

Mention has been made of the late gradual decline of this profitable industry which has been brought about by the continued low price of the berry in foreign markets. This situation cannot continue much longer. The price of coffee must go up, for the supply cannot fill the increasing demand. The reason for this assertion is based upon a true knowledge of the situation. The continued low price of the article, has had the effect, if not decreasing, at least of not increasing the area of production in all the coffee growing regions of the globe, while in Brazil, slavery agitation has already had a most perverse effect upon this industry. If, then, the area of coffee cultivation is, to say the least, at a stand still, while the amount of consumption is constantly increasing, the increased demand will cause an increase in the price, and the coffee planting in dustry will continue profitable until future over production will again glut the markets of the world.

Even at the present low price of coffee that now rules, its production in Costa Rica would be very profitable if it were not for the scarcity of labor and the comparatively high tariff of wages that obtains. Costa Rican planters assert that if they can sell their produce, on the spot, at 6½ cents American money they will still realize a handsome profit. But the high rate of wages, and the maximum cost of transportation to the coast, renders it impossible for the Costa Rica coffee planters to compete with the slave produced coffee of Brazil. When the Interoceanic railroad is completed and direct and cheap transportation to the coast is afforded, the coffee planting industry of Costa Rica will again flourish even at the low price of the article that now obtains

Within the past three years tropic fruit planting has become a most important industry in the Limon district. In 1884, 120,000 commerciable bunches were exported to New York by the Atlas and Harrison line of steamers. The greater portion of the land along the line of the railroad, for a distance of fifty miles from Port Limon, for several hundred yards on either side of the track, is devoted to banana cultivation. The fruit attains a size and excellence equal to the famous bananas of the Isthmus of Panama, of the Island of Jamaica and even of the Bluefields river in Nicaragua.

One New York house has hitherto almost monopolized the fruit traffic of Limon for the past two years. Recent events have destroyed this monopoly, so in the future the steamers of the Fish and Miller lines will be allowed to freight with bananas at Limon for New Orleans. In this case the steamers on the route will not be able to handle the trade, so larger vessels will soon be required. If the tropic fruit traffic of Limon should once be directed to the Crescent City, it will never again seek another channel, for experience has taught the banana producers that the great seaport of the south, the gateway of the Mississippi valley, is destined in the very near future to become the principal tropic fruit emporium in the world.

But the American friends of Costa Rica have lately begun to conceive doubts of the future of the fruit planting industry in the Limon district. About a year and a half ago government decreed the entire stretch of country between Limon and Carillo a free zone. This wise measure soon produced beneficial effects. A most vigorous impulse was given to the fruit planting industry, and many natives invested money in establishing banana walks at different points along the railroad line. In the month of August, however, the government under the pretence that no apparent increase in the size of the village of Limon, or augmentation of its traffic, was visible, rescinded the decree which had made the district a free zone, the Customhouse was removed again to Limon and all the former vexations and onerous custom restrictions have been re-established.

Parties residing in the Limon district have written to friends in the Crescent City, declaring that the abolition of the free zone privileges will work incalcuable injury to the fruit planting interests. While this recent government action will certainly not prove in any way beneficial to this nascent industry, it cannot be more injurious than the former monopoly of the entire fruit traffic by one single house. The vessels engaged in the trade could not possibly meet its requirements, thus thousands of marketable bunches of bananas rotted on the trees monthly, while the New Orleans steamers, the Heredia and the Lucy P. Miller, were compelled to stop at Bluefields and Corn Islands to pick up scanty cargoes of fruit.

As far as the banana traffic is concerned, as long as a market for the fruit is obtained a sufficient quantity will always be produced to fill the demand, but if the planters are compelled to sell their produce to one particular firm and are not allowed to encourage competing purchasers, but little reasonable hopes can be entertained of the future development of the Costa Rican tropic fruit planting industry. All Messrs. C. A. Fish & Co., can ask or should desire is to be allowed to compete with New York houses for this valuable trade. If this privilege is accorded this New Orleans firm the greater part of the traffic will be diverted to the Crescent City.

The rubber trade, during the past two decades has gradually assumed increased importance. The vast forests of the eastern slope contain innumerable rubber trees whose sap, when congealed, furnishes the crude substance which is converted into so many manufactured articles, in this and other civilized countries. If the same vandalic system of exhausting the trees and killing them at one operation that is persued in other portions of Central America, is also followed by the native rubber collectors of Costa Rica, the supply in the latter country far exceeds that remaining in the northern republics, while the savage Indians jealously guard their trees and furnish but enough rubber to serve as a medium of barter for the few foreign articles they covet or require.

Quite a traffic in hides and skins is carried on by the merchants of either coast with the interior, who ship them to Europe, San Francisco and New York.

The Costa Rican forests contain a great number of valuable timber trees and dye woods, such as mahogany, cedar, rosewood, sandal wood, ebony, vera, zapote, amarillo, fustic, Brazil and oak. The wood-cutting industry languishes on the western slope but since the cessation of British protection, agression, or interference, or whatever it may be styled, on the Mosquito coast, it has almost died out in that locality. But the increased demand for dye woods and furniture timber in the markets of this country and Europe, will certainly bring about its speedy revival. If the forests of British Honduras, Guatemala and Spanish Honduras, are partially denuded of accessible trees, the Mosquito coast, from Cape Gracias south and east to Boca del Toro, is almost virgin territory, has scarcely re-echoed the sound of the woodman's axe.

Along the Caribbean coast of Costa Rica, in particular, this situation obtains. The uncivilized Indians lurk in the forests or hide in the cane jungles that fringe the river banks, and sturdily battle with all intruders. But their numbers are gradually decreasing. Their interminable tribal quarrels and their ferocious system of warfare is gradually bringing about

their extinction. It will not be long before the Costa Rican
Government will be compelled to either subdue or exterminate
them, for, cruel as it may seem to make such an assertion,
their territory is too valuable, and the vast forest and mineral
resources it contains are so necessary to the growing requirements of commerce that they cannot much longer be permitted
to retain possession of it. As they live like beasts of prey
and are as fierce and untameable, they will be compelled to
bow to inevitable destiny and make way for a more civilized
race of people. Their fate will furnish but yet another instance of that terrible and inexorable law of nature: "the
unproducers must give way to the producers."

It is impossible to estimate the advantages that will accrue
to the little republic when this great tract of fertile and valuable territory is opened to immigration and settlement. The
few travelers who have penetrated any distance into this
wilderness, and have had the fortune to return, have told the
most marvelous tales of its fertility and productiveness They
tell of the remains of great aboriginal capitals, whose ruins
strew many square miles of land and, above all, they report
the existence of valuable placer deposits, as rich as those found
and worked by the Spaniards, during the era of the conquest.

But serious obstacles seems to militate against the further
development of the resources of Costa Rica; the scarcity of
the labor supply, the increasing demand for it and the consequently high tariff of wages that obtain throughout the republic. Before the Panama canal drained the neighboring
countries, and even Jamaica, Santo Domingo and Island of
Trinidad, of their surplus labor, those localities furnished a
constant supply of hands who willingly worked for the wages
that were then usual. But the blacks of the West Indian
islands will not labor on Central American coffee, indigo or
fruit plantations for from $18 to $25 per month, when they
can procure steady work, for a long period, at from $1 20 to
$2 00 per day. As the isthmus not only occupies a vast num-
ber of laborers, but also *consumes* many hundreds of them
annually, the supply will never equal the demand in Costa
Rica, until the canal enterprise is finished. Thus, until that

happy period arrives, the labor question will continue to be the most serious problem presented to the statesmen and agriculturists of the little republic.

The actual President of Costa Rica, General Prospero Fernandez, is a most liberal minded and enlightened statesman. He is connected, by marriage, with the family of the late President Guadia, and upon the latter's demise succeeded to his office. General Fernandez is active and industrious. He is also remarkably well disposed towards foreigners. His immigration laws are extremely liberal, while he is most anxious to attract American and European settlers to Costa Rica. He is popular with the masses and is easy of access to all who wish to see him on business. Under his vigorous rule his country has made rapid strides forward in the path of prosperity, and could he but satisfactorily solve the vexed labor problem that so materially interferes with the development of the natural resources of Costa Rica, it would not be long before he would realize his greatest ambition, his dearest aspiration, which is the speedy elevation of his beloved little republic to the highest pitch of internal prosperity and political consideration abroad.

NEW ORLEANS AND CENTRAL AMERICAN

STEAMSHIP LINE.

——):o:(——

C. A. FISH & CO.

AGENTS,

No. 32 South Peters Street,

NEW ORLEANS.

THE STEAMSHIP

Lucy P. Miller,

GALT, Master,

Sails about the 5th of each month for Bluefields, Greytown, Limon and Colon; calling at Corn Island on return trip.

THE STEAMSHIP

HEREDIA,

DOANE, Master,

Sails every twenty days for Bluefields and Limon.

First-class Passenger Accommodations at Low Rates

Consignments of Tropical Products Solicited .

CHAS. SMITH.   THOS. SMITH.   J. B. SINNOTT.

SMITH BROTHERS & CO.,

Almacenistas y Abarroteros por Mayor

—Y—

IMPORTADORES DE CAFE,

NOS. 102, 104 y 106 CALLE DE POYDRAS,

Nueva Orleans, La., E. U. de A.

———o———

SMITH HERMANOS Y CIA.,

Córdoba, México.   Yzabal, Guatemala.

·

———————

CHAS. SMITH.   THOS. SMITH.   J. B. SINNOTT.

SMITH BROTHERS & CO.,

Wholesale Grocers,

—AND—

COFFEE IMPORTERS,

Nos. 102, 104 and 106 Poydras Street,

NEW ORLEANS, LA.

———o———

Smith Hermanos y Cia.,

Cordoba, Mexico.   Yzabal, Guatemala.

El Times-Democrat,

—DE—

NUEVA ORLEANS, LA.

Tiene la circulacion mas grande en el Sud y Sud Oeste de los
Estados Unidos y es el unico de ese pais que
circula en grande escala en la

REPUBLICA MEXICANA,

LA AMERICA CENTRAL,

COLOMBIA,

VENEZUELA,

Y LAS ANTILLAS.

Tiene 400 Corresponsales, y recibe diariamente 24,000 palabras de Noticias Telegraficas.

El "Times-Democrat,"

SUSCRICION ANUAL.

El Diario......................................$12 00
El Semanario.................................. 1 50

————o————

SE PUBLICAN MENSUALMENTE

EDICIONES ESPECIALES

QUE TRATAN DE

MEXICO y DE LA AMERICA CENTRAL.

JOHN P. RICHARDSON,

Almacenista por Mayor de Géneros y Efectos de Novedades,

Nos. 79, 81, 83, 85, 87 y 89 CALLE DE COMMON,

y Nos. 11 y 13 CALLE DE MAGAZINE,

NUEVA ORLEANS, E. U. de A.

Tiene un grande y selecto surtido de especialidades adap·
tadas á los pedidos del comercio de Centro-America, consisti-
endo en breves palabras, de :

GÉNEROS.

Estampados, Cuadros de varios Colores, Rayados de Colores,
Sobrecamas, Algodones, Hilados, Mantas Blancas
y Oscuras, Tejidos para Corset, Silecias, Algodones Oscuros "Lona," y Franellas.

VARIEDAD DE NOVEDADES.

Papeleria, Perfumeria, Jabones de Toilet, Péines, Boquillas,
Cuchilleria, Botones, Alfileres, Agujas, Joyeria, Cepillos,
Efectos para la Pesca, Anzuelos, Ligas, Dedales,
Agujas para Crochet, Portamonedas para Señoras,
Carteras, Espejos, Collares, Lazos para
Zapatos, Ciutas ó Cintillas, de
Alpaca y de Hiladillo.

ROPA INTERIOR PARA SEÑORAS Y CABALLEROS.

Camisas, Camisetas, Chamarras, Calcetines, Calzoncillos
de Algodon, Ropones, Corbatas, Cuellos, Puños, Lázos para
Señoras, y Cuellos de Lino, Tirantes, Medias, Guantes, Cor-
sets, Pañuelos, Sombrillas y Paragüas, Abanicos, Lazos Bor-
dados y Efectos para Vestidos de Señoras, Cencillos para Ve-
rano, de Seda, Satin y Terciopelo.

Ademas, una variedad de Lino de Casa, todos los cuales
serán vendidos á los precios mas bájos.

Los Comerciantes que visiten á Nueva Orleans, son cordial-
mente invitados á que visiten ó inspecten ésta grande y
variada coleccion. Se solicita correspondencia.

JOHN P. RICHARDSON.

NEW ORLEANS AND CENTRAL AMERICAN

STEAMSHIP LINE.

——):o:(——

C. A. FISH & CO.

AGENTS,

No. 32 South Peters Street,

NEW ORLEANS.

THE STEAMSHIP

Lucy P. Miller,

GALT, Master,

Sails about the 5th of each month for Bluefields,
Greytown, Limon and Colon; calling at
Corn Island on return trip.

THE STEAMSHIP

HEREDIA,

DOANE, Master,

Sails every twenty days for Bluefields and Limon.

First-class Passenger Accommodations at Low Rates

Consignments of Tropical Products Solicited.

ROBT. H. CHAFFE.   JOHN C. CHAFFE.

R. H. CHAFFE & BRO.,

ESPECIEROS POR MAYOR

Y COMERCIANTES EN

Vinos, Licores, Tabaco y Cigarros,

Nos. 7 y 9 Calle de Peters y 36 á 44 Calle de Common,

NUEVA ORLEANS.

Apartado No. 329

ROBT. H. CHAFFE.   JOHN C. CHAFFE.

R. H. CHAFFE & BRO.,

WHOLESALE GROCERS,

AND DEALERS IN

Wines, Liquors, Tobacco and Cigars,

Nos. 7 and 9 Peters and 36 to 44 Common Sts.,

NEW ORLEANS, LA.

P. O. Box 329.

FERROCARRIL ILLINOIS CENTRAL

Grand Ruta Jackson.

Grand Ruta Jackson.

ILLINOIS CENTRAL FERROCARRIL

El gran camino continuo para Pasajeros y Flete desde Nueva Orleans hasta todos los puntos Norte, Este y Oeste.

El *gran Ferrocarril Jackson* es construido con *Rielas de Acero! Medida Corriente! Equipos Mejorados!* Camino solidamente construido, y *Rapidez Aumentada!* La mas *igual*, la mas *segura* y la mas *agradable* linea de Nueva Orleans á Boston, Nueva York, Filadelfia, Baltimore, Washington, Buffalo, Chicago, San Luis, Cincinnati, y todas las ciudades del Norte y del Este.

Los carros salones, palaciales, para dormir, de Pullman salen diariamente de *Nueva Orleans* para *Cairo, Chicago, Cincinnati, San Luis, Memphis, Kansas City y Louisville,* sin cambio; y cambian solamente una vez para las ciudades del Este.

Frenos Atmosfericos! Plataformas de Miller! y todas las ultimas mejoras para la seguridad y la conveniencia de los pasajeros.

Llega á Chicago 12 horas, y á San Luis 8 horas mas pronto que cualquiera otra línea, y con gran rapidez á las otras principales ciudades.

Precios de pasaje siempre tan bajos como los de otras líneas que son inferiores.

Oficina para Boletas de Pasaje: PICKWICK CLUB BUILDING, cor. Canal and Carondelet, Nueva Orleans, La.

Comprando sus boletas de pasaje por via de la GRAN RUTA JACKSON, los viajeros estan seguros de ganar tiempo y distancia.

A. H. HANSON,
Agente General de Pasajeros,
A Chicago.

E. T. JEFFERY,
General Superintendent,
A Chicago.

J. W. COLEMAN,
Ass't Agente General de Pasajeros,
A Nueva Orleans.

SCHMIDT & ZIEGLER,

Established 1845.

IMPORTERS,

Nos. 49, 51, 53 and 55 South Peters Street,

NEW ORLEANS, LA.,

Wholesale Grocers,

AND RECEIVERS OF

Coffee, Sugar, Molasses and Rice.

——o——

Also agents for Otard Dupuy & Co., Seignouret Freres, G. H. Mumm & Co., Marie Brizard, and Roger.

And importers of E. & J. Burke, Bass & Allsopps' Ale and Guiness' Stout, Old Irish and Scotch Whisky, Edouard Pernod Absinthe and Kirsch.

Our stock of Canned Goods and Fancy Groceries, being the most complete in the South, we are prepared to sell at low figures. Send us a trial order and judge for yourself.

SCHMIDT & ZIEGLER.

Establecido en 1845.

IMPORTADORES,

Nos. 49, 51, 53 y 55 Calle de South Peters,

NUEVA ORLEANS.

ESPECIEROS POR MAYOR,

Y RECIBIDORES DE

CAFE, AZUGAR, MELASE y AROZ.

——o——

AGENTES Y IMPORTADORES TAMBIEN DE

Otard, Dupuy & Co., Seignouret Freres, G. H. Mumm & Co., Marie Brizard, y Rogers.

E. & J. Burke, Bass & Allsopps' Ale and Guiness Stout, Old Irish and Scotch Whisky, Edouard Pernod Absinthe and Kirsch.

——o——

NUESTRO SURTIDO DE

Conservas Alimenticias y Abarrotes Finos.

es el mas completo del Sur. Estamos preparados á vender á los precios mas bájos. Mándesenos órdenes de prueba y sirvanse juzgar por Vdes mismos.

CHAS. SMITH.   THOS. SMITH.   J. B. SINNOTT.

SMITH BROTHERS & CO.,

Almacenistas y Abarroteros por Mayor

—Y—

IMPORTADORES DE CAFE,

NOS. 102, 104 y 106 CALLE DE POYDRAS,

Nueva Orleans, La., E. U. de A.

——o——

SMITH HERMANOS Y CIA.,

Córdoba, México.   Yzabal, Guatemala.

CHAS. SMITH.   THOS. SMITH.   J. B. SINNOTT.

SMITH BROTHERS & CO.,

Wholesale Grocers,

—AND—

COFFEE IMPORTERS,

Nos. 102, 104 and 106 Poydras Street,

NEW ORLEANS, LA.

——o——

Smith Hermanos y Cia.,

Cordoba, Mexico.   Yzabal, Guatemala

H. DUDLEY COLEMAN,

MAQUINARIA,

Esquina de las Calles de Magnolia y Erato, y No. 9 Calle Perdido:

——o——

Máquinas de Vapor,   Máquinas para acerrar Maderas,
    Calderas,   Molinos para Maiz,
       Despepitadores de Algodon,
          Horuillas ó Ceniceros para Máquinas,
Poleas,   Prensas para Algodon.

Bombas "Jet,"
Cañerias para gas,
Junturas para tubos,
Bándas,
Empatadores,

Gobernantes,
Sembradores,
Elevadores,
y Bombas
para Regar.

Fachadas de hierro para Edificios,   Columnas de hierro,
  Forjaduras para Prisones,   y Sércas de hierro.

———

Pidánsenos Circulares Ilustradas y Precios.

La casa de Maquinarias y Calderas que tiene el mas grande
surtido en el Sur!

Trabajos de Calderas y Obras de hierro colano de todas
descripciones.

Hágase una prueba de nuestros éfectos.

H. DUDLEY COLEMAN,

Fundicion, Esquina de las Calles de Magnolia y Erato.
    Almacen y Oficina, No. 9, Calle Perdido,
Nueva Orleans, La., E. U. de A.

E. REMINGTON & SONS,

MANUFACTURERS OF

MILITARY, SPORTING, HUNTING and TARGET

BREECH-LOADING RIFLES,

SHOT GUNS AND PISTOLS,

ALSO,

Cartridges, Primers, Bullets, Shot, Shells,

LOADING IMPLEMENTS, RIFLE CANES,

AND

SEWING MACHINES.

——o——

REMINGTON

AGRICULTURAL COMPANY,

MANUFACTURERS OF

Agricultural Implements, Patent Clipper Steel and
Carbon Plows, Cultivators, Cast Steel
Shovels, Forks, Hoes, Garden
Rakes, Planters' Handled
Hoes, Mowers.

Wheel Horse Rakes and Hay Tedders, Iron Bridges,
The Remington Fire Engine, operated by
hand or horse power, Hose Carts,
Ladder Trucks, etc., etc.

The Universal Fibre Decorticator

To supersede hand labor on Jute, Ramie, Sisal, Hemp, and
all fibrous plants.

Manufactory and Offices:

ILION, HERKIMER COUNTY, NEW YORK, U. S. A.

RICE, BORN Y CIA.,

77, 79 y 81 Calle de Camp, Nueva Orleans, E. U. A.,

Ferreteria y Quincalleria,

SIN IGUAL EN EL SUR!

SIN SUPERIOR en los ESTADOS UNIDOS!

HERRAMIENTAS SUPERIORES DE

Agricultura, Carpinteria, Herreria, Albanileria, Hojalateria, Toneleria, etc.

Pistolas, Carabinas, Cartuchos de Metal y Municiones, Hornillas y Estufas de Cocina. Alambres, lisos y con pugas, para Cercados, Romanas, Pinturas, etc.

Cuidado especial al Empaque para Exportacion. Correspondencia en Español.

T. J. WOODWARD.   PEARL WIGHT.   CHAS. W. MACKIE.

Woodward, Wight & Co.,

Ship Chandlers and Grocers,

COMMISSION AND FORWARDING MERCHANTS,

40 and 42 Canal Street, New Orleans, La.

Also Agents in New Orleans for

Boston Marine Insurance Co.; Mexican Central Railway Co. (limited), Boston, Mass.;
The "E. D. Albro Co." Cincinnati, O.; Averill's Celebrated Mixed Paints; Bridgewater
Yellow Metal Sheathing and Nails; Portland Cotton Sail Duck; American Ship Windlass Company's Steam Power Capstans; Empire Chain Works Coil, Cable and Mill Chain;
The Jno. A. Robeling's Sons Co.'s Steel wire Hoisting Rope and Standing Wire Rigging;
Stone's Ship's Pumps and Steerers; Carrollton (Mich.) Oar Factory; Bagnall & Loud's
Blocks, all kinds and sizes; Leonard & Ellis' Valvoline Cylinder and Machine Oils;
Downer's 300° Fire Test Mineral Sperm and other Oils; Revere Rubber Co.; Newburyport Iron Foundry and Machine Works; Belden & Reinhard, Oil Manufacturers; Simpson's Diamond Creamery Butter, in 5 and 10 lb. cans; Cushing Process Whisky.

J. FRIEDLANDER & CO.,

COMMISSION MERCHANTS,

192 COMMON STREET,

P. O. Box 2616.   NEW ORLEANS, LA.

E. A. BRANDAO.   J. H. GINTZ.

E. A. BRANDAO & CO.,

STATIONERS,

BOOK AND JOB PRINTERS,

Blank Book Manufacturers,

34 Magazine Street,   New Orleans, La.

Southern Agents for Ullman & Philpott Printing Inks.

I. M. WESTON,   J. D. LACEY,   A. G. HODENPYLE,
President.   Vice President.   Sec'y and Treas.

HONDURAS

TIMBER CO.,

CUTTERS AND IMPORTERS OF

Mahogany, Spanish Cedar,

AND OTHER

TROPIC WOODS

No. 2 MONROE STREET,

Grand Rapids, Mich.

36 Carondelet St., New Orleans, La.

I. M. WESTON,   J. D. LACEY,   A. G. HODENPYLE,
Presidente.   Vice Presidente.   Secretario y Teso.

HONDURAS

TIMBER COMPANY,

CORTADORES E IMPORTADORES DE

CAOBA, CEDRO ESPAÑOL, Y OTRAS MADERAS DE
LOS TROPICOS,

NO. 2 CALLE MONROE,

GRAND RAPIDS, MICH.

No. 36 Calle Carondelet, New Orleans. La., E. U. de A.

—THE—
New Orleans and Belize
ROYAL MAIL
STEAMSHIP LINE.

—

Steamship "*CITY OF DALLAS*,"
(914 Tons.)   C. W. READ, Master.

Steamship "*WANDERER*,"
(531 Tons.)   C. W. CLARK, Master.

Steamship "*Blanche Henderson*,"
(578 Tons.)   L. PETERSON, Master.

Calling at Belize in British Honduras, Livingston in Guatemala, and Puerto Cortez in Spanish Honduras. Under contract to carry the Royal English Mails; also carrying the United States, Guatemala and Spanish Honduras Mails; and having fine accommodations for passengers to Central America and Jamaica.

For freight or passage apply at the office of

MACHECA BROTHERS, Managers,
No. 129 Decatur St., New Orleans.

—

AGENTS OF THE LINE:

JOHN HUNTER,   ANDERSON & OWEN,   W. C. MIRRIELEES,
Belize.   Livingston.   Puerto Cortes.

—

CONNECTING LINES:

In New York—Office of Morgan Steamship Line, Pier 36, North River, and office of Cromwell Steamship Line, 86 West Street.

In Livingston, Guatemala—Steamer Georgia Muncy, for Isabal, Panzos and Gulf of Dulce.

In Puerto Cortes, Spanish Honduras—Interoceanic Railway, for San Pedro Sula and Interior.

I. L. LYONS & CO.,

Almacenistas y Droguistas por Mayor ó Importadores,

Manufactureros Químicos y

Negociantes en Instrumentos de Cirugia,

Nos. 42 y 44 Calle de Camp y 109, 111, 113, 115 y 117 Calle de Gravier esquina á Camp,

NEW ORLEANS, LA., E. U. DE A.

Propietarios de: las Píldoras de "Brodies" para el Hígado. Cordial Astringente de "Brodies" para la Diarrea. Elixir "Lococks" para la Tos. Linimento Arnica de "Abrams." Ungüento "Abrams" para el Sarpullido y Enfermedades Cutaneas. Esencia "Lyons" de Gengibre de Jamaica. Tónico de "Abrams" para Calenturas y los Frios. Amargos Corroborantes de "Garry Owen."

I. L. LYONS & CO.,

Wholesale Druggists, Importers and Manufacturing Chemists

AND DEALERS IN SURGICAL INSTRUMENTS,

42 and 44 Camp, and 109, 111, 113, 115 and 117 Gravier St.,

(CORNER OF CAMP STREET,)

NEW ORLEANS. LA.

Proprietors—Brodie's Liver Pills. Brodie's Astringent Cordial for Diarrhœa, etc. Locock's Cough Elixir. Abram's Arnica Liniment. Abram's Tetter and Ringworm Ointment. Lyon's Essence Jamaica Ginger. "Abram's" Chill and Fever Tonic. "Garry Owen" Strengthening Bitters.

THE DAILY PICAYUNE.

The leading paper of New Orleans and of the South. equal to any in circulation and second to none in merit, is THE NEW ORLEANS DAILY PICAYUNE, published by NICHOLSON & Co. This great daily newspaper, established nearly fifty years ago, by practical enterprising men, as a step forward in American journalism at the South, has grown with the growth of the city and is a power in the land.

THE WEEKLY PICAYUNE.

THE WEEKLY PICAYUNE, made up of the most important matter that appears in the daily, with an original synopsis of the news of the week, is intended for country circulation. Its condensed news, literature features, correspondence, devotion to agricultural interests, makes it the most desirable home paper to be found—certainly in the South—for the low price of one dollar and fifty cents per year. The Weekly Picayune, fifty-two papers in a year, is a library of information and pleasant reading, and a history of the events of each week. It should be found in every Southern home.

THE SUNDAY PICAYUNE.

Although included in the daily subscription, THE NEW ORLEANS SUNDAY PICAYUNE has special features, and may be received separately by subscribers when desired. It is usually a mammoth paper of sixteen papers, and in addition to the full telegraphic, home, foreign and local news reports, The Sunday Picayune contains regular Paris and New York correspondence, with the best information on fashions, household matters, science, the drama, society news and gossip in New Orleans and out of town, and choice selections of poetry, stories and miscellaneous matter, and original contributions from "Catherine Cole," Jenny June, Mollie E. Moore, J. H. Haynie, "Vidette," and many others. The Sunday Picayune is deservedly a popular favorite with all classes.

TERMS OF SUBSCRIPTION:

DAILY. (8 to 14 pp, 7 papers a week)	WEEKLY. (16 pp.)	SUNDAY PICAYUNE. (By mail, 16 pp.)
Twelve months.......$12 00	Twelve months....... $1 50	
Six months.......... 6 00	Six months........... 75	Twelve months.......$2 00
Three months 3 00	Three months......... 50	Six months........... 1 00

ROBT. H. CHAFFE.   JOHN C. CHAFFE.

R. H. Chaffe & Bro.,

ESPECIEROS POR MAYOR

Y COMERCIANTES EN

Vinos, Licores, Tabaco y Cigarros,

Nos. 7 y 9 Calle de Peters y 36 á 44 Calle de Common,

NUEVA ORLEANS.

Apartado No. 329.

ROBT. H. CHAFFE.   JOHN C. CHAFFE.

R. H. CHAFFE & BRO.,

WHOLESALE GROCERS,

AND DEALERS IN

Wines, Liquors, Tobacco and Cigars,

Nos. 7 and 9 Peters and 36 to 44 Common Sts.,

NEW ORLEANS, LA.

P. O. Box 329.

MILLER & HENDERSON'S

—LINE OF—

OCEAN STEAMSHIPS,

COMPRISING STEAMERS

ALABAMA,

Capt. MILLER,

LUCY P. MILLER,

LIZZIE HENDERSON,

S. J. COCHRAN,

Blanche Henderson,

RUNNING FROM

NEW ORLEANS

—TO—

BAY ISLANDS,   HONDURAS,   TAMPA,

KEY WEST,   JAMAICA,

—AND—

CENTRAL AMERICAN PORTS.

Also ports contiguous to the Gulf of Mexico.

——o——

Steamers for sale or charter.

R. B. POST & SON, ⎫
                  ⎬ Agents,
C. A. FISH & CO., ⎭

NEW ORLEANS, LA.

FERROCARRIL ILLINOIS CENTRAL

Grand Ruta Jackson.

Grand Ruta Jackson.

ILLINOIS CENTRAL FERROCARRIL

El gran camino continuo para Pasajeros y Flete desde Nueva Orleans hasta todos los puntos Norte, Este y Oeste.

El *gran Ferrocarril Jackson* es construido con *Rielas de Acero! Medida Corriente! Equipos Mejorados!* Camino solidamente construido, y *Rapidez Aumentada!* La mas *igual*, la mas *segura* y la mas *agradable* linea de Nueva Orleans á Boston, Nueva York, Filadelfia, Baltimore, Washington, Buffalo, Chicago. San Luis, Cincinnati, y todas las ciudades del Norte y del Este.

Los carros salones, palaciales, para dormir, de Pullman salen diariamente de *Nueva Orleans* para *Cairo, Chicago, Cincinnati, San Luis, Memphis, Kansas City y Louisville*, sin cambio; y cambian solamente una vez para las ciudades del Este.

Frenos Atmosfericos! Plataformas de Miller! y todas las ultimas mejoras para la seguridad y la conveniencia de los pasajeros.

Llega á Chicago 12 horas, y á San Luis 8 horas mas pronto que cualquiera otra línea, y con gran rapidez á las otras principales ciudades.

Precios de pasaje siempre tan bajos como los de otras líneas que son inferiores.

Oficina para Boletas de Pasaje: PICKWICK CLUB BUILDING, cor. Canal and Carondelet, Nueva Orleans, La.

Comprando sus boletas de pasaje por via de la GRAN RUTA JACKSON, los viajeros estan seguros de ganar tiempo y distancia.

A. H. HANSON,	E. T. JEFFERY,	J. W. COLEMAN,
Agente General de Pasajeros,	General Superintendent,	Ass't Agente General de Pasajeros,
A Chicago.	A Chicago.	A Nueva Orleans.

www.ingramcontent.com/pod-product-compliance
Lightning Source LLC
Chambersburg PA
CBHW060535030726

47498CB00004B/1198